THE SAINT

THE ASSASSINS GUILD, BOOK #3

C.J. ARCHER

"Money can't buy love, but it improves your bargaining position."
— Christopher Marlowe

CHAPTER 1

Hampshire, July 1599

"He comes! He comes!" Jeffrey, Baron Lynden, tore his equine nose away from the parlor window where it had been pressed for the better part of an hour. He wiped off the smudge it left behind with the lace cuff of his sleeve then arranged himself by the fireplace, propping one padded shoulder against the mantel and crossing his ankles. The pose showed off his legs in all their slender perfection, not to mention the new yellow velvet shoes made by London's finest shoemaker. They'd cost him a sum that could have fed a family from the village for an entire week.

His cousin Elizabeth Buckley suspected that was the reason he wore them now. To Jeffrey's mind, having an earl come to dine was certainly an occasion worthy of yellow velvet shoes and a matching yellow and brown striped silk doublet. He'd even donned a pearl earring and matching broach. Not that Jeffrey needed a special reason to don extravagant attire. Elizabeth had seen him parade to the garderobe in Windsor Castle in a hat adorned with peacock feathers.

"Sit up straight, Arrabella," he said to Elizabeth's older sister.

Arrabella dutifully squared her shoulders, thrusting out her magnificent cleavage. It brought a smile to Jeffrey's face. Not that Jeffrey was interested in Arrabella's cleavage or any of her other virtues, of which there were many—one only had to ask her to be given a list. No, Arrabella's cleavage was important to Jeffrey in the same way a mousetrap is of interest to a cat.

"Lift your chin," he said, lifting his own chin. "Good girl. Now pout those pretty lips of yours. No, not like that, like this." He puckered his lips and nodded as Arrabella did the same. "Place your hands in your lap like an obedient lady."

He didn't so much as flicker an eyelash in Elizabeth's direction upon the word 'obedient', but she was in no doubt that it was meant as a slight on her character. Jeffrey had learned in the last few weeks spent in the Buckley girls' company that they'd grown up since he last saw them. Grown and changed, and not just in looks. Elizabeth might appear the less troublesome of the two sisters with her unremarkable face and figure, but her tongue was sharper than Arrabella's, and her mind too quick for her plodding cousin.

Except when Arrabella was alone with Elizabeth. On those occasions Arrabella's tongue could be as cutting as a knife, and her sweetness vanished like a mist in the sunshine.

"Good girl," Jeffrey cooed to Arrabella in the same tone a master uses with his pet dog. "Lord Oxley cannot fail to notice you now."

"She deserves an extra sweetmeat, don't you think, Cousin?" Elizabeth passed the trencher to her sister.

Arrabella narrowed her eyes. "I don't know what you're doing, but stop it."

Elizabeth returned the trencher to the table. Her mother, Janet Buckley, picked off an orange succade and popped it in her mouth. "Jeffrey, this is of no use," she said around her sweet. "Arrabella is almost betrothed."

"Almost is not always enough, Aunt," he said. "She is not secure until the wedding night. Anyway, Lord Oxley is an earl and a wealthy one at that. If he shows an interest in her, she would be wise to disregard her affection for Lord Greville. In fact, I would insist upon it."

Arrabella gasped. "You wouldn't!"

Elizabeth blinked at her sister's unexpected outburst. It would seem Arrabella's true nature wasn't completely buried beneath the mask of obedience and amiability. It also proved that she had feelings for Greville. The revelation was a surprise indeed.

"I *am* the head of this family," Jeffrey reminded her with a preening stretch of his neck. "I'm sure your father, God rest his soul, would have wanted to see you rise to become a countess as much as I do."

Elizabeth snorted, earning herself a glare from the other three. She shrugged off their rebuke. She doubted their father would have cared whom Arrabella married, as long as his eldest daughter was off his hands. Before Jeffrey's unexpected inheritance of the Lynden title a mere year and a half ago, Arrabella had refused no less than three marriage proposals, and there'd been another three since. According to Arrabella, none of the suitors had been good enough. They were either too ugly, too short, too fat, too dull or too poor. The girls' father had once promised both his daughters he wouldn't force them to wed where their hearts weren't engaged, but Elizabeth began to suspect he regretted making that promise as Arrabella grew more and more prickly.

Thank goodness for Lord Greville. He met each of Arrabella's requirements, and at six and twenty, time was running out for her.

"Elizabeth." The word dropped heavily from Jeffrey's soft lips, perhaps because he'd not wanted to engage the troublesome sister at all. God knew it was probably easier for him to ignore her than talk to her. It was how she preferred it too. "Elizabeth, please *try* to be…" He waggled his fingers as he searched for the right word.

"Demure?" she offered.

He pointed at her. "Yes! Demure women are an asset to any social gathering."

"Dutiful?"

"That too. Most certainly."

"Diligent?"

"Um, I'm not sure…"

"Dull?"

"Do be quiet, Lizzie," Arrabella bit off. She touched the pale golden hair at her temple, which Elizabeth had helped pin in place that morning. She looked beautiful, as usual.

"Hands in your lap, Sis," Elizabeth reminded her. "You wouldn't want Lord Oxley to think you anything other than a demure, dutiful, dull-witted girl."

"I am already betrothed," Arrabella said through clenched teeth. Her temper was rising. A few more pushes, and she might even reveal her true nature in front of their cousin.

"But not to an earl," Elizabeth pointed out.

Arrabella clicked her tongue. "How you *vex* me, Lizzie."

Jeffrey sighed and sagged against the mantel. "He'll be here any moment," he muttered, defeated.

"Coy," Janet suddenly said. She rolled her ample body forward in the chair and picked another sweetmeat off the trencher. Her eyes closed in ecstasy as the sugary sweetness hit her tongue. She sucked a moment then opened them again. "You should be coy, Elizabeth, like your sister." She licked her stubby fingers. "A gentleman likes ladies who flirt and use their wit to amuse him rather than berate him."

"I've never berated—"

"Shrews do not make happy wives."

"Or husbands," Jeffrey added.

Elizabeth appealed to her sister for help, but received only a self-satisfied smirk in response. She should have known better than to try and find an ally in that quarter. Arrabella's greatest talent was in knowing who to side with, and in this argument, Elizabeth would most certainly be defeated.

"You think me a shrew, Mother?"

"I think you far too clever for a girl of twenty who's yet to learn that the world can be cruel to her sex. You haven't the prettiness of your sister, or her sweet nature." She cleared her throat and did not meet anyone's gaze.

Sweet? Good lord. Elizabeth thought about protesting at her mother's outright lie, but remembered that Jeffrey—and the world at large—didn't know Arrabella could be as brittle and cold as an icicle. Nor was she in the mood to educate him. No doubt her sister would falter at some stage during their summer stay at Sutton Hall, and he would eventually see the ice maiden underneath the smiles.

"As such," Janet went on, "you must learn to at least be obedient. If you can't do that, then simply bite your tongue. Otherwise you will be a spinster forever and tasked with looking after your dear old mother for the rest of her days." She smiled triumphantly and Elizabeth had to admit, if only to herself, that her mother had won the battle with those final words.

It was wise not to disagree with Janet Buckley. She was always slow to rouse, but once she got started, she was difficult to stop. She resembled a large boulder in that respect. Difficult to leverage into position and push into the first roll, but after several more rolls, only an impenetrable barrier could stop her.

That impenetrable barrier entered the parlor in the form of a gentleman dressed in a crimson and black doublet, matching trunk hose that swelled at his hips and a hat festooned with glossy black feathers. He was tall with shapely legs and long fingers. It was difficult to tell how broad he was in the shoulders because of the ridiculous padding in his sleeves. Elizabeth dismissed him as a potential husband for Arrabella. Her sister preferred gentlemen who weren't dandies. Elizabeth too had seen enough of them in London in the previous weeks to know that she hadn't the patience for men who preened more than the ladies at court. He was, however, just the sort Jeffrey liked to dine with.

"My lord!" Jeffrey said, sweeping into a low bow.

Arrabella and Elizabeth both stood and curtsied to the earl, although Arrabella's was considerably lower. Their mother struggled to haul herself out of her chair.

"Please, stay seated, dear lady," Oxley said, striding into the room. He took Janet's hand and kissed it.

She giggled like a girl, and her ruddy cheeks darkened with her blush. "Thank you for gracing us with your illustrious presence, my lord," she said. "What a treat it is for me and my girls to dine with you today."

Elizabeth was surprised her mother didn't gag with so much sugary sweetness dripping from her lips.

"This is my aunt, Mistress Janet Buckley," Jeffrey said. "And these are her daughters, my cousins. Arrabella is the elder, and Elizabeth the younger."

Lord Oxley bowed to each in turn with an elaborate flourish of his hand. "Charming. Utterly charming. Tell me, Mistress Buckley, are you also related to Mistress Susanna Holt from Stoneleigh? She was married to a Lynden, was she not?"

"No relation, my lord. Her late husband was Jeffrey's cousin on his father's side. My sister was Jeffrey's mother. An entirely separate branch of his family."

"Families are so complicated!" Oxley declared with a toss of his head that made the feather plumes shimmer. "My own ancestral tree is so knotted and twisted that I must be re-introduced to my cousins every time I go to court. One or two branches were also prematurely lopped off." He winked at Elizabeth's mother and bent down to her level. "Found themselves supporting the Lancasters. Or was it the Yorks? I can never recall. Anyway, the removal of their heads from their bodies soon followed." He slashed his finger across his throat and stuck his tongue out of the corner of his mouth.

Elizabeth cringed. She'd hoped to find an interesting and less sycophantic gentleman than she'd met during her brief London stay before returning to Hampshire, but alas, he was the dandiest of them all, and more ridiculous than even Jeffrey, which was both an amazing feat and a waste considering he was very handsome.

His looks wouldn't be enough to tempt Arrabella to swap her equally handsome and considerably smarter Lord Greville for this fop, even if he were an earl. It would seem Oxley was off the menu this dinnertime.

"Wasn't there another gentleman with you?" Jeffrey asked, peering past Oxley. "I saw you riding in together just now. He seemed too well dressed to be a mere servant."

"Ah, yes, my man Monk. I believe you—"

"Monk!" cried numerous voices, one of which was Elizabeth's. Surely Oxley couldn't mean *Edward* Monk. But it had to be him. The name was an unusual one and the coincidence too great for it to be otherwise.

It was a name she'd not heard in five years. Five long years in which she'd wondered if she'd ever see him again. Wondered whether he'd changed or forgotten them. Wondered what he'd think of her now that she was older. Wondered if he'd recovered from Arrabella's rejection, or whether he'd gone on to make something of himself as he'd declared he would. There were other things too that she hoped the years had wiped from his memory.

She sat. She had to. Her legs were too weak to hold her. Her heart hammered in her chest, its rhythm erratic. He was here. *Here*.

So, unfortunately, was Arrabella.

Elizabeth's sister sat too, slowly, her hard gaze fixed on the wall ahead, her chin tilted up. Always defiantly priggish when it came to Edward Monk, ever since that day. That single, awful day that had damaged the sisters' relationship forever.

And now he was here.

Elizabeth wasn't sure their sisterly bond could survive meeting him again. She wasn't sure *she* could survive it.

"Well," said Oxley, standing with his hands on his hips. "That produced quite a reaction. I see Lynden is not the only one who knows Monk."

Elizabeth's mother cleared her throat and smiled. Elizabeth knew it to be false. "Mr. Monk lived in our village years ago."

"You were neighbors?"

7

Her gaze slid to the left, not meeting his. "No."

"Friends then."

Nobody answered.

Oxley cleared his throat. A tactful man would not pursue the matter, but Oxley apparently lacked tact as well as sense. "Ah. Say no more. Feuds between gentlemen in small villages are not unusual."

Arrabella shot to her feet. "Mr. Monk is *not* a gentleman."

Elizabeth gripped the arms of her chair, digging her fingernails into the wood. If she let go, she feared she'd not be able to stop herself scratching her sister's eyes out. It had been five years since she'd felt such burning anger toward Arrabella, but it would seem it hadn't dissolved completely with time. Not where Edward was concerned.

"Forgive her, my lord," Janet said, quickly. "She's…tired after our long journey."

Oxley held up his hands. "It's quite all right. The journey from London is indeed arduous, even now in the summer when the roads are good. I can understand how it would tire your daughters and make them prone to outbursts. Of course my man Monk is a gentleman. I wouldn't retain him otherwise."

Arrabella opened her mouth, but Jeffrey got in first. "Arrabella!" He took her hand, and Elizabeth saw her sister's fingers whiten. He must have been squeezing hard. "Whatever is the matter with you, Cousin? This is not like you at all." To Oxley he said, "She's usually very meek. A most pleasant female companion, not in the least prone to outbursts. Perhaps she's not feeling well."

Arrabella must have remembered herself. She pressed her hand to her temple and allowed Jeffrey to guide her to sit again. "Yes, I am tired. However, I am very much looking forward to dining with Lord Oxley. I've longed to meet him ever since you said he was joining us, Cousin."

Elizabeth rolled her eyes and caught Lord Oxley looking at her beneath lowered lashes. How odd that he should be watching her and not the scene being played out for his benefit by her sister and cousin. A small crease connected his eyebrows, but it was the only indication that he was trying to read her. Perhaps he'd realized that of all of them, she was likely to give him the most honest reaction to the surprising presence of Edward Monk. Perhaps he wasn't such a fool after all.

She blushed, although she wasn't sure why, and his gaze flicked away.

"I didn't know you retained Mr. Monk," Jeffrey said to Oxley.

"I snapped him up when he left your employ last autumn," the earl said.

"You employed him?" Elizabeth's mother said to Jeffrey. "Why didn't you tell us?"

"I didn't think I needed to list all my past servants for you, Aunt," he snipped. "Nor did I think you'd care. Why would you? The man was nobody when he lived in Upper Wayworth."

Which begged the question, was he somebody now? If he dressed like a gentleman and was retained by a man of Oxley's standing, then perhaps he had indeed risen as he'd once declared he would.

Good for him. Elizabeth always knew he could do whatever he wanted if he set his mind to it.

"Monk proved to be useful to me and extremely capable at… things." Jeffrey cleared his throat. "I'm sure he's proving the same to you, Oxley."

"He is most capable. I'm fortunate to have him since my other retainers have left me. Snatched from me by the most insidious of diseases."

Janet gasped and pressed a hand to her bosom. "The plague?"

"Love."

Elizabeth's bark of laughter escaped despite her attempt to smother it by pressing her lips together. She received a glare from her mother and cousin as a result. Arrabella merely shook her head in disappointment.

Oxley either didn't notice or pretended not to. "One of them wed a London girl, another married your very own Susanna from

Stoneleigh, and just this week I lost a fellow who'd worked for me in the past."

"To the Cowdrey girl?" Jeffrey asked. "I'd heard something of the matter. There was some trouble, wasn't there?"

"All ended now, thankfully. I'll tell you about it over dinner."

"Will Mr. Monk be dining with us?" Janet asked.

Elizabeth couldn't tell from her mother's expression whether she wanted to hear a yay or nay to her question. She strongly suspected the latter.

"Of course," Oxley said at the same time Jeffrey said, "No."

They looked at one another, but it was Jeffrey who quickly backed down under the earl's unblinking stare. "That is to say, er, yes, he is."

Arrabella gasped. "But he's only a—!"

"Arrabella!" Janet snapped. The warning shake of her head made her eldest daughter swallow her protest.

Elizabeth tried not to smile at the small victory. Her sister would not be allowed to stomp on Edward while the earl was present, and she couldn't be happier about it. She tried to catch Oxley's gaze, but failed. He was idly flicking dust off his doublet, apparently oblivious to the stir he'd created.

"He'll be up after he sees to the horses," Oxley said.

"Does Mr. Monk know we're here?" Elizabeth asked.

"I believe he was informed that Lord Lynden returned from his travels accompanied by his favorite female cousins."

He knew, and yet he still wanted to dine with them? Either his heart was healed, or he thought he was more Arrabella's equal now and worthy of her consideration. If the latter, he was in for a shock when he learned of her betrothal. Elizabeth couldn't let him find out at the dinner table when Arrabella coolly mentioned that her future husband was a baron far, far above Edward. A thousand cracks of a whip across his back would hurt less—if he were indeed still enamored with her.

"Why don't I fetch him?" Elizabeth said. "Will I find him in the stables, my lord?"

"Perhaps you ought to remain here," Oxley said quickly. "I'm sure the steward will show him in to us when he's seen to the horses."

"Nonsense."

The earl arched one lazy eyebrow. "Nonsense?" he echoed, his tone strained. It would seem he wasn't used to being gainsaid. Not many gentlemen were, especially by women.

Well, he wasn't Elizabeth's master or a potential suitor. He mattered not a whit. She didn't care in the least if she offended him. She only cared about warning Edward.

"I won't be a moment." She sailed off, glancing over her shoulder as she left. Both Jeffrey and her mother stared after her, mouths ajar.

Jeffrey's snapped shut again, and his face darkened. He wouldn't berate her in front of their guest, but he would later. Elizabeth had to remember to avoid him.

The last thing she heard before she was out of earshot was Janet apologizing to Lord Oxley. "She's a very headstrong girl. I despair of her sometimes. I really do."

"It'll be difficult to find her a husband," Jeffrey said.

"Indeed," the earl said. "No man likes a viper for a wife, eh, Lynden?"

Elizabeth couldn't get away fast enough. She wished she'd seen her sister's response to the conversation, but then again, perhaps it was best that she didn't. No doubt Arrabella sat there with her head bowed and her hands in her lap like a good girl. If Oxley was looking for a wife, she might very well catch the fop's attention if she wasn't careful. If Jeffrey saw even the flicker of interest in the earl's gaze, he'd order her to discard Lord Greville as if he were last week's rancid meat and focus on Oxley instead.

Elizabeth hurried out of the house and across the cobbled courtyard where pink-cheeked maids rushed back and forth with armfuls of linen or pails balanced in each hand. She passed by the extensive outbuildings and even more staff, sweating from the heat and their work. The stable block stood ahead, but Elizabeth paused to soak in the pretty view of the orchards, fields and valley beyond, and to gather her nerves. She wasn't usually so anxious about meeting people, but this wasn't just any person. This was the man she'd been in love with half her life. The man who'd hardly noticed her because her sister's shadow was long, and he'd been unable to see past it.

Elizabeth might have appeared strong of mind, but she knew her heart was fragile where Edward Monk was concerned. She doubted it could withstand the blow if he proved to still be in love with Arrabella.

"Hail, madam!" someone called. Someone with a deep, commanding and wonderfully familiar voice. "Do you know where I can find Lord Lynden and his guests?"

She turned in the direction of the stables and saw Edward striding toward her. Her stomach flipped. Her heart danced. He was taller than she remembered and more powerfully built across the shoulders than he had been five years ago. The combination was quite simply magnificent. He wore a black hat and doublet, the buttons of which glinted in the sunlight. As he drew closer, she saw that they were silver and the clothes superbly tailored to fit his impressive form.

So he had some wealth now. He'd achieved what he'd set out to become all those years ago. *I will better myself.* He'd tossed the words at Arrabella in angry defiance after her rejection of his suit, and they'd never heard from him again. Yet here he was, his promise made good.

Elizabeth felt a stirring of pride in her chest.

He was still handsome too, with his perfect teeth, square jaw and gray eyes. The years had hardened the lines of his face some-what, and his eyes weren't quite as soft. They were cooler, clearer and focused entirely on her.

His gaze quickly swept over her from head to toe. If he recognized her, he gave no indication. She had changed in the last five years, so it wasn't unexpected, particularly at a distance. He strode up to her, his hands loosely at his sides, his manner comfortable, assured. That was new too. There was none of the insecure suitor of the last time he'd been in their house. The youth of five and twenty had been replaced by a man of thirty. And he exuded power.

"Madam, are you all right?" He frowned. "You look a little pale. Would you like to sit down?"

"Hello, Edward." To her surprise, her voice worked, although a small warble betrayed her nervousness.

His frown deepened. "Do I know you? Are you from the village?"

"It's me. Elizabeth."

He shrugged. "Elizabeth who?"

Just like that her stomach plunged. Her heart smashed into her ribs. She *had* changed in five years, but not so much that she was unrecognizable to someone who'd known her for the first fifteen of it. It would seem she really had made absolutely no impression on him. It was almost too much to take in, let alone bear.

She swallowed hard, determined to forge on, because that's what she'd always done. She was not the timid fifteen year old anymore, and she must let him see that. "I'm Elizabeth Buckley from—

Shock rippled across his face. "Arrabella's sister!"

Arrabella's sister. His words sliced through her, cleaving her heart in two. She'd steeled herself for this reaction, yet it hurt far more than she'd ever thought it could. She'd spent five years attempting to distance herself from her sister's side by making her own friends, having her own interests, and it all meant nothing.

She was still 'Arrabella's sister' to the only person who mattered.

CHAPTER 2

"*W*here is she?" Edward scanned the length of the big house as if he would spy Arrabella peering down at him from one of the windows. Of course he couldn't see her since the formal parlor where she and the others sat was at the front of the house, and they were at the back.

"Inside," Elizabeth said quietly. She bit her lip and searched as hard for words as he did for a pretty face in the window. She failed and remained silent. That irritated her more than his disregard of her. She was supposed to be better than this now, yet he made her feel fifteen again, a mere child and an ordinary one at that. She sighed.

The sound drew his attention and he looked at her again. He bowed perfunctorily. "Forgive me, Mistress Buckley. I truly didn't recognize you." He straightened and studied her anew. "You've changed remarkably."

She thought that overstating it a little too much. Her chest was larger, her waist more defined, and her face had lost the softness of childhood, but she was still the same brown-haired, plain little sister of Arrabella The Beauty. Ask anyone, not just Arrabella or their mother.

"Call me Elizabeth. You used to." On the few occasions he'd actually spoken to her directly.

"I heard Lynden had returned with some cousins, and I expected to see you and your sister." His lips stretched into a flat smile. "I'm glad I was right."

"Cousin Jeffrey thought we needed educating in the finer art of living among nobles such as himself. He seems to have forgotten that he's only been noble for less than two years." It came out peevish, but so be it. Jeffrey had stretched her patience to the limit in the time they'd been in his company, and Edward wasn't listening anyway. He was staring at the house again.

He turned back to her. "Giving a man a title he wasn't born to tends to shorten his memory." So he *had* heard her. Well then.

She would have laughed at his joke, but he wasn't smiling. Indeed, his mouth was set in a grim line. At least he had been listening after all and not intent on racing off to find her sister.

"And make him more unbearable," she added in a mutter.

He laughed, and just like that, the tension seemed to leave his shoulders. "You noticed that?"

"How could I not notice him when he dresses like a peacock? The colors of his clothing are enough to hurt the eyes. And then there are his attempts at poetry. I spent a good part of our journey from London pretending to be asleep. Unfortunately, that didn't stop him." For a moment, she worried she'd gone too far in disparaging her cousin. Edward was, after all, almost a stranger to her now, and she would never speak of Jeffrey, or indeed anyone, like that to someone outside the family.

But Edward made her feel comfortable. He always had. A pity he didn't remember.

He laughed again, easing her conscience. "I know what he's like. I worked for him briefly before Hughe took me on."

"Hughe?"

He colored a little and looked away. "Lord Oxley. Sometimes I call him Hughe."

How intriguing. He'd indeed risen high if he was on first name terms with an earl. "You seem to have gone from one fop to another. How ever do you cope?"

"Oxley's a good man once you get to know him."

"He's certainly a brightly colored one. My cousin spotted him when you were both still a distance away. Poor Jeffrey. He'll feel rather drab beside the earl at dinner."

He grinned again and offered her his arm. "You have certainly changed, Elizabeth. I don't recall you being so witty. Indeed, I don't recall you speaking much at all."

She took his arm. The muscle flexed beneath her hand—a powerfully large muscle. "I, uh, didn't. Speak much that is." It was all she could manage. Being with Edward like this, laughing with him and touching him, was the stuff of her girlhood dreams. She didn't want to spoil it by saying the wrong thing.

He led her back to the house, shortening his stride so she could keep up. "Tell me, has your sister changed much too?"

Elizabeth's step faltered, but he held her steady. She wanted to remove her hand from his arm but didn't want to draw attention to her sinking disappointment.

"You'll find out soon enough." They were already crossing the courtyard when she remembered why she'd gone to fetch Edward in the first place. "There's something I need to tell you before you go in."

"Is it something to do with Arrabella?" The hint of hope in his voice clawed at her heart. He was in for a terrible shock all over again. It had been awful to watch him fall apart five years ago. It would be so much worse now that he was a man of fortitude.

"I know you once harbored an affection for her." She waited for him to assure her he no longer did. He remained silent. "So I wanted to warn you that she's engaged to be married."

He stopped. She stopped too. Silence wrapped around them, closing in. She found it hard to breathe. So did he, if the deep rise and fall of his chest was an indication. The muscles in his arm tensed beneath her hand and he stared at her, unblinking.

"Edward, are you all right?"

He inclined his head in a nod. "It has come as a shock, that's all," he murmured, looking to the house. "It shouldn't, considering her age and the rise of her kinsman, but..."

But he'd hoped. Elizabeth had seen it in his eyes and now watched as it faded from them like a fire slowly dying.

"She'd been so selective that I thought...I thought she'd never find a man who met all her standards. I waited too long. I should have returned before now." His quiet voice rambled, and Elizabeth suspected he wasn't entirely aware that he'd spoken aloud.

She squeezed his arm, drawing his attention back to her. His haunted eyes were full of shadows. "You *will* recover, Edward. Indeed, this will give you the opportunity to move on."

"Who is he?" The question came out as blunt and brutal as a hammer blow.

Elizabeth swallowed the rest of her sympathy. He wasn't ready for it. "A baron named Greville. They met in London at the beginning of our stay in the city."

A vein throbbed above the small ruff at his throat, yet the shadows cleared from his eyes. He squared his shoulders and looked stoically determined, as if this was merely one more hurdle to overcome in his quest to win Arrabella.

"When is the marriage to take place?"

"This summer, here at Sutton Hall."

He flinched. "So soon." The arm she'd been holding dropped to his side like a stone. She let it go entirely. "Is he here too?"

"He arrives tomorrow."

He strode ahead, and she had to run to keep up. At the door, he seemed to collect himself and waited for her to pass through before he followed. They walked in silence to the dining room. All faces turned to stare at them upon their entry. Only Lord Oxley rose.

"Ah, Monk, there you are," he said, beaming. "I believe you know Lord Lynden's family already."

Elizabeth stole a glance at Edward. His cheeks were pink, and his gaze focused on one person. Arrabella. To Elizabeth's horror and shame, her sister presented him with her shoulder and studied the array of dishes on the table. She did not acknowledge him. Elizabeth felt sick to her stomach for Edward.

"Do you not remember Edward Monk, Sister?" she snapped. "Surely you must. We were just discussing him in the parlor."

Arrabella stiffened, and for one gut-churning moment, Elizabeth thought she'd show her true colors and announce that Edward wasn't worthy of discussion or some such cruelty. Perhaps if their mother hadn't loudly cleared her throat, Arrabella may have done so. Instead, she turned on a gentle smile. It was false of course, but hopefully Edward didn't realize it. As much as Elizabeth wanted him to wake up and see Arrabella for the viper she was, she didn't want his eyes opened in front of everybody. His love for her was almost as old as Elizabeth herself and could not be shaken off as easily as snow from a branch. Its removal would take much digging to get at its root and would undoubtedly leave deep scars.

"My apologies," Arrabella said. "I had something in my eye." She touched the corner of her eye with her fingertip and blinked rapidly. "There. It's gone. Ah, yes, Mr. Monk! What a lovely surprise. You haven't changed a bit!"

She smiled at him, and he bowed low. When he straightened, his cheeks were redder and his gaze soft as he drank in Arrabella's appearance.

"Come and sit. Please, tell me all about your adventures since we last met. What was it, two years ago?"

"Five," he corrected, "and three months."

Her eyes widened. "That long! Well, Mr. Monk, I'm sure you've seen and done much in that time."

"You used to call me Edward," he said as he sat beside her. "I would ask you to call me that again."

"It's my privilege. And you may call me Arrabella."

Privilege? What game was she playing? She was engaged to Lord Greville. She couldn't abide Edward's lowly standing five years ago. Yet here she was flirting with him! Elizabeth didn't want her to be rude to him, but she didn't want this either.

It must have something to do with Lord Oxley's presence. Edward was his man, after all, and the earl seemed quite eager for him to be considered a gentleman worthy of joining them at the dinner table.

Or perhaps it was Arrabella's way of rubbing salt into Edward's wounds. Let him think she liked him, then cut him to the quick later when nobody was looking. It was how she liked to operate.

"It's very nice to see you again, Mr. Monk," Janet said as she heaped oysters onto her plate. "Have you heard our news? Arrabella is to be wed. To a baron no less."

Elizabeth thanked God she'd had the foresight to warn him first. He answered with a smooth nod. "So Elizabeth told me. Congratulations, Arrabella."

"A wedding!" Oxley burst out. He wiped his lips with the back of his hand. "Marvelous! Wonderful! We should drink to the happy couple." He lifted his wine glass, and everybody followed suit. His eyes twinkled as he watched Edward over the rim.

Edward seemed not to notice as he drank.

"The wedding will take place here," Jeffrey said, puffing out his chest.

"Not at Greville's own estate?" Edward asked, frowning.

"I do like weddings and wedding feasts," Oxley cut in before anyone could answer.

No doubt the first thing Jeffrey would do after his visitors retired was add Oxley to the guest list.

"That makes two weddings in Sutton Grange," Edward said. "Our friend Cole—Nicholas Coleclough—is marrying the Cowdrey girl soon."

"How delightful," Elizabeth said. "I'm eager to meet her as well as Mistress H—"

"We are not *in* Sutton Grange," Jeffrey said, nostrils flaring. "And the Cowdreys are a rustic, rabble-rousing lot."

"Not the new Cowdreys," Oxley declared with a wave of his

glass that had Jeffrey's eyes widening with concern for his expensive drinking vessel. "And the Colecloughs certainly aren't."

"Certainly aren't what?" Jeffrey asked.

"Oh? Didn't I tell you, Lynden? Lucy Cowdrey's betrothed is a nobleman's son."

Jeffrey began to choke. "But...he's a...!"

"He's a gentleman who protects the deserving innocent. He has also worked for me in the past and is my friend, just as Monk is." The earl sounded far more serious than Elizabeth had heard him be so far. He spoiled the effect by stuffing boiled capon into his mouth and draining his glass of wine before he'd swallowed.

Jeffrey nodded quickly. Whatever he'd been going to reveal about Nicholas Coleclough was to remain a secret.

Jeffrey and Oxley fell into gossiping about London, leaving Elizabeth and her mother to watch Arrabella and Edward chatting. She did most of the talking, much of it also about London, who she met there, and the wonders of court and queen. The name of Lord Greville was invoked frequently. If Edward grew despondent about it, he didn't let on. He seemed to be listening attentively, smiling at the right moments and asking questions.

"Good," Janet whispered. She leaned into Elizabeth, almost shoving her completely off the chair with her bulk.

"Pardon?" Elizabeth whispered back.

"Arrabella has mentioned Lord Greville countless times already. That ought to put him off."

"Edward?"

"Yes. Of course Edward." She clicked her tongue. "Who else? Did you see his eyes when he first saw her? He was positively enraptured with her beauty all over again, but now that he sees how Greville has engaged her affections, he won't do anything foolish."

"Let's hope not," Elizabeth muttered, for once in total agreement with her mother.

"Now, if only she'd captured the earl's attention in the same way."

"I thought you were happy that Greville has 'engaged her affections,'" Elizabeth repeated.

"I am. But Oxley is an *earl*." She said it as if he were a wizard who had just performed a magical feat.

"Arrabella is in love with Greville. Even if she weren't, she'd not give a man like Oxley a second thought. He's not the sort she likes."

"She could learn to like him. He's an *earl*."

"Perhaps *I* ought to consider him," Elizabeth joked. "Indeed, marrying him would have two critical benefits. I'd outrank Arrabella *and* not have to be nursemaid to my mother."

Janet savagely tore apart a hunk of bread. "Don't be ridiculous. An earl isn't going to be interested in you when your sister is in the room."

Elizabeth sighed. Dinner was going to be an interminable affair.

* * *

EDWARD MONK FIXED his gaze on the back of Arrabella's elegant neck as she left the dining room with her sister and mother. He willed her to turn around and bestow a smile upon him, but she did not. The sister did. Elizabeth. He remembered her, but not well. She'd been a shy little thing back in the days he'd tried to court Arrabella, keeping to the shadows and speaking rarely. She'd certainly changed in the last five years. Her confidence had grown and her beauty with it. She was also surprisingly witty.

She wasn't as pretty as her sister, but no woman was. Seeing Arrabella again had stolen Edward's breath from his chest and sent his heart pumping like a bellows. Her skin was as creamy as ever, her eyes like clear lakes and her figure luscious. He'd lain awake many nights thinking of her mouth—its shape and softness, the myriad ways in which she smiled or frowned, and how her lips tasted.

He'd kissed her once. She was fourteen and just becoming aware of the effect she had men. She'd tested her new flirting skills out on him because he'd been safe. As a scrawny, stuttering eighteen-year-old son of a mere carpenter, she'd known him well enough to trust him. After an afternoon of feasting and revelry at the Shrove Tuesday festival, she'd taken his hand, dragged him behind the acting troupe's stage and kissed him on the lips. Ever since then, he'd been in love with her.

And she him. She'd told him so. She'd said she adored him, desired him, thought him the most handsome boy in the village. She told him she'd give herself to him, but he must wait for her, save himself for her. He had waited, biding his time as he watched other men try to court her, only to fail. Years went by and he'd had enough of waiting. He asked her to marry him. She'd stared at him, that delicious mouth forming a perfect O, and said the words that had been permanently burned into his memory.

I cannot be a carpenter's wife.

Of course her father wouldn't have allowed their union. Fool that he'd been, Edward had hoped their love would be enough. It wasn't, Arrabella told him. Then she ordered him to forget her.

He couldn't. Now, five years later, it was almost too late to prove that he'd changed for her. Almost. There was still time before she wed. Indeed, there was an entire day before her betrothed arrived at Sutton Hall. Enough time to convince her that he was a wealthy man now and would be a gentleman soon with his own coat of arms.

He could also ask Hughe to speak to her mother and Lynden, subtly dropping hints that Edward could keep Arrabella in considerable comfort now. They would tell Greville that the betrothal was broken and send him away. She didn't love that fellow. Her display over dinner proved it. The same old signs of her affection were still there. Her easy chatter, the quick smile, the blushing as he complimented her on her beauty. She'd flirted with him just as much as she used to.

He was utterly sure her affection for him hadn't waned in the intervening years. His feelings for her certainly hadn't.

"Monk, are you listening?" Hughe's voice sliced through his pleasant thoughts like a blade.

He tore his gaze away from the door through which the ladies had exited. "I am now."

Hughe's jaw hardened, and for a moment, he allowed the mask to drop to show Edward his disappointment. Not in Edward's lack of interest in the conversation, but in his attention to Arrabella. Edward had told him on the ride to Sutton Hall that he was in love with her, and that he planned on leaving Hughe's employ as soon as she accepted his hand. Hughe hadn't been happy with the announcement. He didn't like it when his assassins fell in love. It was bad for business, he claimed, and not easy to find replacements. Edward used to believe that, but recently he'd begun to wonder if Hughe simply felt that his friends were deserting *him*. He was a difficult man to understand, and Edward couldn't be entirely sure what was in Hughe's thoughts.

"Lynden was asking if you could remain here until the wedding either goes ahead or is called off," Hughe said.

"It'll be called off," Edward said. "But why—"

"Uh, actually, Oxley, I was hoping *you* would investigate him," Lynden said, waving off a servant who appeared at the door to clear away the dishes. Lynden didn't know that Hughe was the leader of a band of assassins and Edward his only remaining employee, so why was he asking *him* to investigate? And what did he want him to investigate? Greville?

"Monk is capable," Hughe said.

"Yes, yes, of course. I've employed him myself and found him discreet and efficient."

Hughe filled his glass with more wine from the jug. "Then what's the problem?"

"I, uh, think a more...refined touch is required with this matter."

Refined? Ah, there it was. That word, the one that excluded Edward. *He* wasn't a gentleman yet. Hughe was. Greville too.

Hughe's gaze slid to Edward's. "Lynden thinks Greville is

hiding something. Something that might stop the marriage from proceeding."

Lynden coughed, and his cheeks pinked, as if he were embarrassed to be airing his dirty linen. He should have remembered that Edward had seen some of that dirty linen already.

"I'll happily investigate Greville on your behalf," Edward said, trying not to sound smug.

Apparently he didn't try hard enough because Hughe shot him a pointed glare. "I'm sure you will," he muttered.

"The Buckleys are my old friends. If there are suspicions over this man—"

Lynden snorted. "Acquaintances, not friends." He reached for his glass. "Not even that really."

While he wasn't looking, Hughe rolled his eyes at Edward to soften the blow, but it didn't amuse Edward like it usually would. The blow came down as hard as ever. Perhaps harder. It was going to be difficult to convince Lynden that Edward had risen far enough to be worthy of Arrabella.

"Things are different now, my lord," he began, leaning forward.

Hughe stopped him with a shake of his head. Perhaps he was right. It wasn't the right time. Edward needed to speak to Arrabella alone first.

"Please, Oxley," Lynden said, suddenly covering Hughe's hand with his own. His eyelids lowered as if they were too heavy to keep open. "As a favor to me."

Edward watched in amusement as Hughe calmly extracted his hand.

"I don't do favors, or accept them in return," Hughe said stiffly. "Anyway, I have affairs to settle elsewhere."

What affairs? As far as Edward knew, they had no targets to investigate or assassinate.

Lynden sat back heavily in his chair and sighed. "Very well. Monk it shall be."

"Is there any particular reason you think Greville may not be a suitable marriage prospect for Arrabella?" Edward asked. "Aside from the obvious, that is."

"The obvious?"

He shrugged one shoulder. "She's not in love with him."

"Oh, she is. Very much so. That's the problem. Love should be left for dalliances, not marriage. Everyone is happier that way, don't you agree, Oxley?"

"Quite agree," Hughe said with a deep sigh. "Marriage is a business to be avoided for as long as possible. Unfortunately my mother, the Dowager Countess, disagrees. Duty and all that."

Lynden studied his glass and nodded. "It makes me glad my mother is dead."

Edward cleared his throat. "The reasons, my lord?"

"Ah yes." Lynden straightened. "They met at court. You know what it's like there lately, Oxley. Tell your man how the queen ages, and everybody worries. No heir has been announced, and nobody knows who to throw their support behind. One thing about the next monarch is almost certain; however, it will not be a Catholic. When Arrabella came to me and told me that Greville was going to ask for her hand, I questioned some courtiers. It seems there are suspicions that the younger brother is a secret papist."

"That's a serious accusation," Edward said. Catholic dissidents were not only heavily fined for their non-attendance at a Church of England mass, but many Catholic nobles were suspected of plotting against the Protestant queen. It was a dangerous thing to be a papist.

Hughe slumped in his chair. The position, as well as the padding he'd strapped around his stomach, made him appear dissolute. In many ways, it wasn't far from the truth, although Hughe's body was as lean and muscular as Edward's. "A man cannot be held accountable for his brother's sin," he said.

Lynden held up his hands. "I agree, most vehemently. But my fear is that Greville is a papist too. You must discover whether he is or not, Monk."

"Why did you initially ask Lord Oxley to investigate?" Edward asked.

Again Lynden's cheeks reddened. He twisted the stem of his wine glass between his fingers. The fine Venetian glass sparkled in the sunlight streaming through the window. "His company brightens this place up immeasurably!"

"I do try to make up for my man's lack of color," Hughe said with a sour look at Edward's black garb.

Edward narrowed his gaze at his friend, but Hughe ignored him. He rose and bowed to Lord Lynden. "We must leave you, I'm afraid."

Lynden's face fell. "So soon? I had hoped you'd walk with me through the garden. Er, or with my cousin."

"Which one?"

"Arrabella of course."

"Thank you, but no. We must be away. I leave early tomorrow morning and have some matters to attend to first."

"You wish to walk with the other one?"

"Elizabeth," Edward told him. "Her name's Elizabeth."

"If you prefer her, Oxley, she's available. Perhaps more so than her sister since there is no prior betrothal. And she's a very…interesting girl. Some would say amusing."

"But others would not?" Hughe snorted. "No, thank you. I don't wish to walk with any girl who may want to trap me into matrimony. Now, I must leave you altogether, but Monk will return to the house later. I expect him to be kept in the style befitting my friend and not a servant."

"Of course." Lynden clasped Hughe's arm with both his hands. "Safe journey, Oxley. Be sure to keep yourself in good health so you can hurry back to me—er, us—in time for the wedding."

Hughe extricated himself and signaled for Edward to follow him. They left the dining room and passed through a series of rooms decorated in rich colors. The ladies were in none of them. Edward wondered if that had been intentional on Mistress Buckley's part to stop him seeing Arrabella again. No matter. He would be back before nightfall.

Outside, the gravel crunched underfoot as they made their way to the stables. Before he'd gotten far, an odd sensation swamped him. Someone watched.

Arrabella.

However, it wasn't her face that peered down at him from a high window, but her sister's. She lifted a hand and waved. He waved back then hurried to catch up to Hughe who'd stopped a little ahead to wait for him.

"I thought it was the other one who loved you," he said.

"It is. Elizabeth is just being friendly."

Hughe merely grunted.

CHAPTER 3

*E*lizabeth rejoined her sister and mother in the less formal parlor just as Jeffrey strode in from the direction of the dining room.

Janet held out her hand to Elizabeth. "Well?"

Damnation. She'd forgotten her mother's fan. She'd promised to fetch it from her apartments, but had gotten distracted by Edward leaving with Oxley. It had surprised her when he'd turned to look at her. Her first instinct had been to pull back, but she was glad she didn't. That was the sort of thing she used to do when she was younger, but not anymore.

"I couldn't find it," she said.

Janet clicked her tongue. "It's in the trunk near the bed. Did you look in there?"

"I think so."

"Good lord, Lizzie, must I look for it myself?" She did not get up, however, but flapped her hand in front of her face. "It is so hot. Do you not have a cooler room, Jeffrey? Jeffrey? Are you listening?"

Jeffrey moved away from the window with a deep sigh. Elizabeth took up the position in the embrasure and watched as

Edward and Lord Oxley rode away from the house. "You spoke, Aunt?" he said.

"It is too hot in here," she moaned. "Look at my ankles." She lifted her skirt to reveal her ankles. "They're the size of tree trunks!"

"Shall I have wine brought to you straight from the cellar?"

"I suppose that will have to do. Fetch more of Mrs. Holt's succades too. They're terribly soothing."

Jeffrey bowed. To Elizabeth, he said, "Be a good girl and see to your mother's needs."

"And don't forget my fan this time," Janet said.

"Bella, will you come with me?" Elizabeth asked.

Arrabella looked up from her sewing. "Why?"

"For company."

"Since when did you need company to run errands?"

"I thought we could discuss how you'd like me to arrange your hair for the wedding."

"Oh yes, let's." Arrabella carelessly threw her sewing into the basket at her feet as if she couldn't be rid of it quickly enough.

"I already know how her hair will be arranged," Janet protested.

"I know you do, Mother," Arrabella said with a placating smile. "But since Lizzie will be the one arranging it, I need to tell her your ideas. Shall we walk in the orchard, Sis? It's so pretty out there today."

Their mother clicked her tongue again. "It's too hot. Stay indoors and out of the sun. You don't want freckles on your wedding day."

"Yes, Mother."

"Don't forget the succades, Elizabeth!"

"Before you go," Jeffrey said. "I ought to tell you that Mr. Monk will be staying with us for a while."

Elizabeth went very still. Edward. Here. Under the same roof. She turned her face away so nobody could see her blush.

"What!" Janet exploded. "Whatever for?"

"Lord Oxley asked me to accommodate him, and I agreed."

"Good lord," Arrabella muttered. "That's all I need."

Elizabeth whipped round to face her sister. "What's that supposed to mean?"

"It means he stretches my nerves to breaking point when he behaves like a lovesick puppy."

"You ought to be flattered that such a man takes notice of a spoiled cat like you."

Arrabella spluttered, sending spittle onto the rush matting. "You jealous little mouse. Is it my fault I have men begging me to marry them, and you have none? Hmmm? And what do you mean 'such a man'? He's nothing but a carpenter, Lizzie. He may be handsome and strong, but so are dozens of other men and most of them with prospects better than Edward's."

"He is also kind, clever—"

"Girls!" Jeffrey snapped, holding up his hands for peace. "Go on your mother's errands and take your petty squabbles with you." He shook his head. "Honestly," he added in a mutter. "This house was so much quieter before *women* invaded it."

Elizabeth stormed out, her sister at her heels. "Slow down," Arrabella called out.

Elizabeth walked faster.

"Lizzie, wait. I thought you wanted to talk about my hair."

"I don't particularly care how you look for your wedding, Bella."

Arrabella gasped. "You don't care! Elizabeth, I am your sister. How can you not care about me?"

In the same way you don't care about me, Elizabeth wanted to tell her. "It was a ruse to get you away from Mother, so we could talk privately."

Arrabella came up beside her, puffing hard. "Are you going to lecture me about Edward Monk again?"

"Wait until we're outside."

"I am not at your service, Lizzie. I cannot be beckoned to follow you like a dog." Nevertheless, she followed anyway.

Elizabeth asked a maid they encountered on the stairs to fetch wine and succades for her mother and the fan from her bedchamber too, then headed outside with her sister. She didn't stop to speak until they were in the shade of the apple trees. The air smelled sweet, and the sunshine soothed her anger a little. It was an afternoon made for lazing on the grass and daydreaming, but unfortunately she had to contend with her sister.

"You shouldn't call him that," she said.

"You do want to talk about Edward again," Arrabella said on a groan.

"Calling him a lovesick puppy demeans him. It's cruel."

Arrabella plopped down on a grassy patch beneath a large tree with dense foliage. "I can't believe you're beating that old drum again. Let's talk about my hair instead."

Elizabeth sat beside her and drew her skirt up to her knees to cool her legs. "I wanted to ask you what it was you said to Edward at dinner."

Arrabella drew her skirt up too, to her mid-thigh. She kicked off her shoes and waggled her stockinged toes. "Nothing that I can recall now. Just idle chatter. Why?"

"You didn't tell him that you weren't in love with him perchance?"

"Of course not."

"Why?"

Arrabella looked at Elizabeth as if she were a simpleton. "He didn't ask anything of me, and the subject never came up. I told you, it was just idle chatter."

"But you could see that he is still in love with you. Everyone could. It was obvious," she added quietly.

Arrabella gave a predatory smile. It sent a chill down Elizabeth's spine. "Oh yes. As much as ever."

"Why let him think that he has a chance with you? It's too cruel, Bella." Too cruel to him and too cruel to her. Unless he was free of her sister, he could never be Elizabeth's.

Arrabella leaned against the tree trunk and drew her skirt up even further, almost at the junction of her thighs. Elizabeth looked around to ensure no gardeners were in sight. "It's not what he wanted to hear," Arrabella said.

"Why do you always have to do exactly what everybody wants and expects? It's infuriating."

"Only to you. Besides, I didn't want to create a scene in front of Lord Oxley."

Elizabeth blinked at her. Her sister actually made a good point. It was surprising that she'd considered Edward's feelings at all. Still, she shouldn't have encouraged him either. "So why flirt with him?"

"I wasn't flirting."

"You were."

"I was simply being me. If men take it the wrong way, that's their fault."

Elizabeth lay down on her back with a groan and flopped a hand over her eyes. "Poor Edward. It's going to be a shock when he sees you for what you really are. And one day, he *will* see."

Arrabella said nothing.

"He's too good for you," Elizabeth went on. "Much too good. When you're old and ugly, you'll be sorry you didn't realize that earlier."

She expected Arrabella to tell her she'd never be ugly, but her sister remained quiet. Surely she hadn't fallen asleep already. Elizabeth opened her eyes and was surprised to see her sister staring at her, her lips a little apart.

"You…you're in love with him," Arrabella whispered.

Elizabeth felt a hot flush spread over her face and ripple across her scalp. She closed her eyes and put her hand over them again to hide her embarrassment.

Arrabella burst out laughing. "My God! You *are*."

Elizabeth clamped her mouth shut. Anything she said would make matters worse, so she remained quiet.

"Oh, darling Sis," Arrabella said, her voice serious. "I fear for your heart. I truly do. Poor Edward is still in love with *me*, and I'm sure he always will be."

Elizabeth tried not to let her words touch her, but it was so hard. She wanted to shout at her sister, claw her eyes out. She wanted to cry too, until there were no tears left.

"I can do something about that, Lizzie. Next time I'm alone with Edward, I'll tell him you love him—"

"No!" Elizabeth sat up. "Don't you dare!"

Arrabella pouted. "I'm trying to help you."

"I don't want your help. If you care about me at all, you will tell Edward nothing. Understand?"

Arrabella clicked her tongue in the exact manner of their mother. Elizabeth knew it was all the response she'd get, but she was sure her sister would obey her wishes. Reasonably sure.

A gardener approached them between the rows of apple trees, whistling as he checked the unripened fruit. Elizabeth pushed the hem of her skirt down to her ankles. Her sister did not. She closed her eyes, pretending to be asleep. Elizabeth went to flick Arrabella's skirt down anyway, but the gardener spotted them at that moment. He stopped whistling and nodded a greeting without taking his eyes off Arrabella's legs.

Elizabeth cleared her throat and he continued on his way. "You never learn," she hissed at her sister.

Arrabella opened her eyes. "What are you talking about?"

"You court the attentions of men you have no interest in. It's unfair."

Arrabella stood. Her skirt swished around her legs and settled into place. "You are such a prig, Lizzie. You're going to die a dried up old maid with that attitude."

"At least my conscience will be clear."

"At least *I* won't be stuck living with Mother for the rest of my life." Arrabella slipped on her shoes and strode off in the direction of the house.

Elizabeth sighed and watched her go. Perhaps her sister was right. Perhaps she would die not knowing the feel of a man's hand on her bare thigh, or his kiss on her lips. It wasn't that she didn't *want* to feel those things, and more. She most certainly did.

The problem was, the only man she did want to entice into her bed hardly even noticed she existed.

* * *

HUGHE'S MANSERVANT met Edward and Hughe at the door to one of the guest parlors at the Plough Inn with a sealed letter. Hughe scanned the script and threw it onto a table with a grunt of irritation. It slid off and landed on the rushes. The servant picked it up and placed it on the table and waited for instructions from his master.

"Leave us," Hughe told him. "Send up ales then take the rest of the afternoon off. We leave early in the morning."

The servant departed, and Hughe sat in a chair with a heavy sigh. He rubbed his thigh. The old injury he sported must have been aching. He removed his hat and set it with more care on the table than he did the letter. The parlor linked two bedchambers, one each for Hughe and Edward. It wasn't large, but suited their needs. Indeed, the Plough Inn's rooms were better than many that Edward had slept in since joining Hughe's band of assassins eight months before. His mattress was free of lice, and fresh water was brought to his room every morning. When he was in disguise, and not known as the Earl of Oxley's man, he'd stayed in some hovels that weren't fit for rats. When he did travel with Hughe—and Hughe was being himself—he lived like a king. Quite a change from being crammed into a three-room house with his entire family of seven.

Arrabella couldn't fail to notice how far he'd risen since they last met.

Arrabella. God's blood, she'd looked as beautiful as ever. She'd not changed in the least. She could still melt a thousand hearts with that smile. Still tempt him with a mere lowering of her lashes and one coy glance in his direction. Thank God he'd saved himself for her. The night he finally held her in his arms and claimed her would be pure pleasure.

All he had to do was convince her that he was a better man than Greville. By her smiles and keen interest in him over dinner, it was clear that she was still in love with Edward. Greville didn't stand a chance.

"Aren't you going to read that?" Edward asked, nodding at the letter. "It could be important."

"It's from Cybil."

Cybil was Lady Fitzwilliam, the wife of the elderly Lord Fitzwilliam, and Hughe's current mistress. At least, Edward thought she was his current one. Perhaps she was the previous one. He couldn't keep up. The man had a different mistress every week it seemed. Most of them were like Lady Fitzwilliam, young and beautiful and married to elderly men. Others were women too far beneath his status to be more than bedding partners. All were willing. None were eligible. Hughe fled from women in search of a husband like the nobility fled the city during the plague.

Edward picked up the letter. "Read it. You at least owe her that."

"She'll only berate me."

"Then it's less than you deserve."

Hughe arched an imperial eyebrow. "Would you like to polish your halo now, or shall I order one of the servants to do it?"

Hughe was mostly an amiable fellow, and Edward liked him, but there were some aspects of his friend's behavior he loathed. The way he treated his mistresses chief among them. The earl thought nothing of discarding them in favor of another, but only after the woman in question had fallen in love with him.

"She's a good woman," Edward said, shaking the letter in Hughe's face. "Read it."

"She was fun, until she grew serious and began talking of love."

"That's your own fault. You charmed her into your bed and made her fall in love with you." He shoved the letter right under Hughe's nose.

Hughe snatched it and removed a knife from his belt. "I warned her that I don't believe in love."

"How can you not believe in love after everything you've seen?"

Hughe sliced through the seal with more force than necessary. "Your heart is too soft for your own good, Monk. You'd better be careful or that girl will crush it."

"*Your* problem is that your heart is too cold."

Hughe flicked the letter with his finger. "Did you and Cybil write this together? That's exactly what she states here. 'There's ice inside your heart.' Ah, listen to this, it's almost poetic. 'You are no gentleman, but a cur not fit to lick my boots let alone my—' Perhaps I should end it there. It goes on in a rather repetitive tone." He folded the letter and returned it to the table beside his preposterous hat. "Cybil has quite the vulgar tongue. It was one reason I liked her in the beginning. She was vulgar in bed too."

"Stop it, Hughe. I don't want to hear it."

"Of course you don't. Too much talk of vulgar women will make you want to break your vow, *Monk*."

Edward looked away, his face heating. He'd not discussed his inexperience with anyone, yet he knew Hughe had investigated him thoroughly, including that aspect. He'd never mentioned it before, however, which meant Edward must have riled him to snapping point. Whatever was it about Cybil and her letter that had pushed him to the limit?

Hughe kicked off his boots and stretched out his long legs. A knock at the door announced the arrival of their ales. A bouncy breasted maid bobbed an awkward curtsy at Hughe. He smiled at her as if she were a bright spot on a dark day. She blushed fiercely and almost spilled ale from the jug before Edward rescued the tray. She stammered out her thanks and blushed harder than ever. Hughe dismissed her with a slight bow and another smile.

"Flirting with the maids now, are we?" Edward said, pouring ale from the jug into the tankards.

"Merely reminding myself of my masculinity. Being the dandy can shake its foundations on occasion."

"Dinner with Lynden being one of those occasions?"

Hughe accepted the tankard with a grunt. "Next time he makes eyes at me, I'll thank you not to laugh."

Edward felt the tension slip from his shoulders like water. His friend was back to being simply Hughe again and not the prick of an earl he played at times. "But it was hilarious."

"Not from where I was sitting."

"Hughe, if you wish to dress like a dandy, you have to expect advances from others with tendencies that bend in that direction."

"The man needs to be careful if he doesn't want to be arrested. Anyway, I ought to be able to dress how I like and not suffer unwanted attentions from either male or female. It's most tiring."

"It was rather diverting for me. Just wait until I tell Cole and Orlando."

"Do that and I'll run you through with my sword."

Edward grinned. "A little murderous conduct will put to bed any rumors of feminine proclivities. Perhaps you ought to start a fight or two in the taproom later. Better yet, bed all the women in the village *then* start a fight."

Hughe gave him a withering glare. "Have you quite finished?"

"I could go on."

"And I may just do as you say and sleep with all the women in the village." He leaned forward. "And the ones up at Sutton Hall. That Arrabella Buckley is a peach just waiting to be—"

Edward shot out of his chair and grabbed Hughe by his over-sized lace collar. He pulled it tight at his throat, but the flimsy material unpinned and came away in his hands.

"Don't speak about her like that again," Edward growled, returning to his seat.

Hughe watched him through lowered lashes. He looked lazy enough, innocent almost, like the dandy he portrayed in public. Yet, if one knew the real Hughe, it was easy to see the strength in his hands, the force of will lurking at the corners of his eyes and the determined set of his jaw. Hughe wasn't a man to be teased or tested. Not if one wanted to remain alive and unharmed.

"You love her." Hughe's voice was flat, apparently disinterested. Edward knew he was not.

"I do."

"And you think she reciprocates, despite being betrothed?"

"You and I both know betrothals are not always between lovers. Besides, you saw how she was with me at dinner."

"All I saw was a woman who likes the attentions of men flirting with you."

Edward's blood heated in his veins. His grip tightened on the tankard. "That wasn't flirting."

"Looked like it to me."

"You're no expert on matters of the heart, Hughe." He nodded at the letter.

"Flirting has nothing to do with the heart. You should remember that, Monk, if you wish your heart to remain whole."

Edward fell silent. He stared at the liquid in his tankard, imagining Arrabella's pretty face. The face that came to mind wasn't Arrabella's, but her sister's. It must have been because hers was the last he saw of the two.

"Tell me about her." Hughe spoke quietly, seriously, the goading tone having vanished as rapidly as it had risen.

So Edward did. He'd kept his feelings to himself for so long that they wanted to be aired. It would be safe to do so with Hughe. Whatever his faults, he would never betray a confidence. What Edward told him would go no further than this room.

He told Hughe about growing up as a carpenter's son and falling in love with the local gentleman's daughter. Her cousin Jeffrey Lynden hadn't inherited his title then, but she'd still been far above Edward's lowly reach. She'd rejected his suit, knowing her father wouldn't approve.

"Still, I persisted. I declared my love so many times that I lost count." He smiled, remembering the way she used to blush when he got down on one knee, or when he handed her a bunch of wildflowers. Her soft kisses on his cheek had encouraged him to try again, and again. "When my parents were still alive, they begged me to set my feelings aside and look to more suitable girls in the village, but I refused. I loved her, and she loved me."

"She told you that?"

He shook his head. "She wasn't so forward."

Hughe frowned and fell into silence. He sipped his ale thoughtfully.

"The one barrier to a union between us was our different stations. She was the daughter of a wealthy gentleman, and I a carpenter's son and apprentice. Once that barrier was removed, I knew we could be wed. So I set about removing it. When my parents died suddenly I closed my father's shop. I left the village and traveled the country, seeking a patron." He shrugged. "I wasn't really sure what I was going to do, but I knew I couldn't become a better man stuck in Upper Wayworth my entire life. Luckily, I found Lord Whipple."

"The Catholic."

"A good gentleman. He was kind to me. He educated me and allowed me to live in his gatehouse in return for my labor on the estate."

"So his patronage came at a price."

"Doesn't everything?"

Hughe gave a nod. "Go on. What else happened during your time with Whipple? I've discovered very little about you from those days."

"Whipple taught me how to speak like a gentleman, and how to read and write. He taught me how to interact with my betters, and how to command respect from other men. I stopped working as a laborer and took on various roles for his lordship, including assisting the land steward and even representing Whipple in business matters during his illness. I grew up under Whipple's tutelage," he said softly. "He was like a father to me, and I regretted moving on. But I had to. Whipple didn't pay overmuch, and I needed money. Without it, I couldn't buy myself a coat of arms."

"Lynden hired you upon Whipple's recommendation."

"For a grand sum, yes. It was more money than I'd ever seen in my life, until I worked for you." Edward hadn't been sure about assassinating people at first, but Hughe and his men assured him they only assassinated the deserving who evaded justice. Besides, Hughe paid exceedingly well.

"Yet you never forgot Arrabella Buckley," Hughe said.

"Never."

"Now what? You plan to convince her to forget Greville and marry you instead."

"I do."

Hughe lowered his head, shaking it. "Fool."

Edward didn't resent Hughe's bitterness. Losing Rafe, Orlando and Cole in quick succession to women had been a blow to him. Now he was faced with losing another. His last assassin. "If you don't want to lose me to Arrabella, why did you suggest to Lynden that I stay and investigate Greville?"

"Because unlike you, I'm convinced that the more time you spend with her, the more you'll come to realize you don't love her after all."

Edward eyed his friend. What was he playing at? "That's absurd."

"Believe me, you'll soon be cured."

"How can you know?"

"I know women."

"And?"

"And that woman…she's not for you."

Edward stood and grabbed Hughe by his doublet. "What is that supposed to mean?"

Hughe held up his hands in surrender. Edward let him go. The fine silk was now a creased mess over the earl's heart. "Just an observation. I could be wrong."

"You are." Edward strode out of the parlor into the adjoining bedchamber. He undressed and threw his belt and doublet onto the bed.

Damn Hughe to hell. He knew nothing about women's minds or hearts. How could he when he treated his mistresses so poorly? Arrabella might not be Edward's yet, but she would be as soon as he told her that his quest to become a gentleman was almost complete. On his last visit to London, he'd paid the College of Heralds an excessive sum to overlook his base-born status and grant him a coat of arms. It was only a matter of time before it came to be.

All Edward had to do was make sure Arrabella didn't marry in the meantime.

CHAPTER 4

*C*ole and his betrothed, Lucy Cowdrey, hailed Edward from their cart as it approached the entrance to the inn yard. He eased his horse to a stop and relaxed his grip on the reins.

"I thought you weren't leaving until tomorrow," Cole said.

"Hughe leaves tomorrow." Edward glanced back into the yard where the earl still stood after seeing Edward off. "I've got a matter to attend to up at Sutton Hall."

Lucy gasped. Her face paled. Edward had forgotten that she knew what line of work her betrothed had been in before he'd met her. The work that Edward and Hughe still performed.

"It's nothing of that nature, Mistress Cowdrey," he assured her.

"Oh," she said, expelling a breath. "Thank goodness."

"Aye," Cole muttered. "We don't want any more trouble."

Lucy touched his knee, and he closed his hand over hers and gave her a soft smile.

Cole had been embroiled in a nasty incident with the nearby villagers, almost losing his life. No wonder he wanted only peace now.

"Good morrow, my friend," Hughe said, coming up beside Edward's horse. He bowed to Lucy, although not with the elaborate flourish he would use if he were pretending to be a dandy.

42

Lucy, as well as Susanna Holt, knew Hughe was more ruthless killer than fop. "Good afternoon, dear lady. I hope we find you well this beautiful day."

"Yes, thank you, my lord."

"Hughe will do. Or Oxley. My friends never use formalities."

Cole gave a derisive snort. "Sometimes we refer to him as Tyrant or Prick."

"But only behind his back," Edward added.

"And they call themselves my friends," Hughe said with mock horror. "There's simply no respect for men of rank these days."

Lucy giggled. "You're leaving us tomorrow, my…Hughe?"

"Alas, I am called home to Oxley House. I wish I could stay in this pretty village. The people are much friendlier."

"Oh? They're not friendly at your home?"

"The Dowager Countess lives there. If you knew my mother, you'd understand why I travel so much."

She suppressed another giggle. "You'll be welcome at Sutton Grange whenever you wish to return, and especially at Coleclough Farm."

"You've changed the name already?" Edward asked.

"Not officially. We're still waiting on the papers from Father. He'll bring them when they come for the wedding. You will be back for that, won't you, Hughe?"

He bowed. "I wouldn't miss it for the world. As much as I'm sorry to lose my good friend, I'm glad he's found someone who can put up with his obstinate nature."

"You're not losing a friend, Hughe," Cole said quietly. He placed his arm around Lucy's shoulders. "You're gaining another."

"Absolutely right," Hughe quipped. It was difficult to tell from his smile whether he agreed with Cole's sentiment or not. Although he did indeed like Lucy, Edward knew he was sorry not to have Cole as his companion anymore. They'd been close friends for some years, and been through much together. "Anyway, I still have Monk here." He slapped Edward on the back. "I'm quite sure he won't be marrying soon."

Edward scowled, but that only made Hughe grin harder. Damn him. He still seemed to think Arrabella would reject him again.

Just wait. You'll see.

"This matter up at the Hall," Cole said, leaning forward and resting his elbow on his knee. "Is it something that should concern us?"

Edward shook his head. "It's a family matter that Lynden wants us to investigate."

"He has concerns over his cousin's betrothed," Hughe chimed in. "He's worried he may be a Catholic. Monk will find out what he can."

"You've met him?"

"Once, at court. His name's Greville. Seemed like a good fellow to me."

"Good men can be rotten beneath the surface," Edward said.

"Or not," Hughe countered.

"Of all people, *you* should know that the face a man presents to the world is sometimes a mask."

"But not always. We could argue about it all day, Monk. Or you could return to Sutton Hall and see the Buckley girl again."

Edward wondered if he could get a punch in before Hughe saw it coming and dodged it. He deserved a hiding.

"Are the Buckleys Lynden's cousins?" Cole asked.

Edward nodded. "Arrabella and Elizabeth are their names."

"You're enamored of one of them?" Lucy said to Edward. She had that wistful look on her face that women sometimes get when they sense love in the air. "Which one?"

"The eldest, Arrabella." He felt the color rising to his cheeks. "I've known her all her life. She's a great beauty."

Lucy smiled at his embarrassment. "I'm sure she is. And what else is she?"

"What do you mean?"

"Is she sweet-natured? Clever?"

"Both. You'll like her."

"I'm sure I will. Please tell her to expect an invitation from me. Perhaps you can escort the ladies to Coleclough Farm."

He bowed his head. "Happily."

Four riders on horseback slowed to a trot as they approached the inn. Cole moved his horse and cart forward to unblock the passageway into the yard, and Edward shifted his horse to the side. The riders' cloaks were covered in dust, and the horses' flanks glistened with sweat. Travelers on horseback were usually gentlemen, and gentlemen weren't common in Sutton Grange. Edward had been in the village often enough to know they were strangers to the area.

"Interesting," Hughe muttered. He stood beside Edward's horse, his hand rubbing its neck. He looked to be engrossed in the task, but Edward knew he was watching the newcomers, as he was too. Cole also eyed them from beneath the low brim of his hat. It seemed instincts could not be cast off as easily as one's method of employment.

The riders approached. The two men in front appeared to be deep in conversation. Their words traveled to Edward on the breeze.

"...to go tonight," the one on the left said.

"Tomorrow, as planned," said the other. His voice had a note of command that brooked no argument.

Yet the other rider did not give in. "I see no reason why we must stay here," he said with a sneer at the inn's facade. "The big house will be more comfortable."

"Shut it, Greville."

Greville! So this was Arrabella's betrothed? Edward's gut twisted. He recognized it as jealousy. Greville was handsome, his clothes well-tailored. He sat straight and tall in the saddle. But if he were the baron, why was he taking orders from the other man?

"It's easier to exchange it here," the man said. "Now be quiet and ride through to the stables. I'm hot and tired and in need of a quenching ale."

He nodded at Hughe and Edward as he passed them and

entered the inn yard. Greville also nodded. The other two riders followed behind.

"Good afternoon, gentlemen," Hughe called after them. "A fine day for traveling. Have you come far, sirs?"

"We left London three days ago," said Greville, dismounting. "I am the baron of Greville. You look familiar, sir. Who do I have the pleasure of greeting?"

Hughe bowed. "The earl of Oxley, at your service."

"Oxley!" Greville seemed startled to see a nobleman in the Hampshire backwater. "I remember you now. We met at court once."

"Aye. This is my man, Monk."

Edward nodded a greeting. He waited for Greville to introduce his men, but he didn't. Not even the one who'd been ordering him about. So did the other man outrank him or not? Who *was* he? He looked older than Greville by a good ten years. Greville looked to be in his early twenties. He had fair hair, and the only blemish on his face was a small white scar on his chin. The other man had a scar stretching from the corner of his mouth to his cheek. It made him look like he was bestowing a gruesome half smile. His coal black eyes locked with Greville's colorless ones until Greville looked away.

"Excuse me," he said, slapping the dust off his doublet sleeve. "I'm parched. Is the taproom through there?"

"Aye," Hughe said. "Perhaps we can sup together in the dining room later. The innkeeper's hospitality rivals that of any great house. You won't be disappointed."

"Glad to hear it."

He went to walk off, but Hughe called after him. "Are you staying in Sutton Grange long?"

Greville stopped, his smile tight. "We're resting here today before going up to Sutton Hall in the morning."

"Ah yes, Lord Lynden's home. I've just come from there, and my man leaves for it now. A most pleasant individual is Lynden. How do you know him?"

"I met him in London some weeks ago." Greville went to walk off, but Hughe once again called after him, and he paused. One of his men groaned, and the one who'd been speaking to Greville as they arrived muttered something under his breath.

"I'm sure you'll be welcome up at the Hall if you'd like to travel on there today," Hughe said. "Lynden wouldn't mind."

Greville's glance flicked to his companion. The man glared back and folded his arms. "We'll keep to the arrangement," Greville said. "Thank you, Oxley. I'll look forward to seeing you again later."

Hughe let him go, much to everyone's relief. Once the men were inside, he took Edward's bridle and led the horse out to where Cole had taken his cart a short distance away. He'd stopped outside a cobbler's shop, and Lucy was speaking to a friend out of hearing distance. She cast a quick glance in Cole's direction, then moved even further away, allowing the men to talk alone.

"Odd conversation," Hughe said. "The other man seemed like a retainer, nothing more."

"So why was he giving Greville orders?" Cole asked.

None of them had an answer for that.

"Do you want me to stay the night at the Plough and watch them?" Edward asked.

"No, you go on to the Hall as planned," Hughe said. "I'll watch Greville tonight."

Edward's relief was a palpable thing in his chest. He *needed* the time to talk to Arrabella before Greville got to her. Tonight, she was all his.

"Meet me on the northern road out of the village after breaking your fast, and I'll report what I learned." Hughe took Edward's arm in farewell. "I'll return to the valley in a week or so."

"Come to me if you need help," Cole told Edward. "Not Orlando. He's too worried about Susanna now that her baby's time is close."

"Aye," Edward said. He would only go to Cole if he was desperate, but he didn't tell him that. Cole had a new life now, a peaceful one. He wasn't going to disturb it unless the situation became dire.

Investigating Greville would be a harmless enough matter, one that would allow him to pursue Arrabella in earnest.

* * *

TRUE TO HIS WORD, Edward was given one of the best bedchambers in Sutton Hall. The bedchamber and adjoining study and wardrobe were located high in the eastern wing, not far from Lynden's own apartments. The ladies had been assigned bedchambers in another part of the house. Edward hadn't spoken to them since his late afternoon return, although he'd seen Elizabeth strolling through the garden from his window. She didn't seem to care that her face would freckle in the sun, unlike most ladies he knew.

Not that Edward knew many. He avoided them as much as possible. His vow to save himself for Arrabella made being around the fairer sex somewhat awkward and occasionally even painful. But it would be worth it. Their lovemaking would be the sweeter for waiting.

He'd found out from one of the maids that Greville and his men would be sharing three bedchambers between them. He spent the remainder of the afternoon inspecting them.

Supper was announced as the sun went down. Lynden, Arrabella and Elizabeth joined him in the dining room, but their mother had a headache and kept to her rooms.

"It's the heat," Arrabella explained with a sympathetic frown. "Poor Mother suffers greatly from it."

Edward managed to seat himself beside her, with Elizabeth and Lynden opposite. Unfortunately, he didn't get the chance to speak to Arrabella alone. The smaller party meant conversation was shared among all four, rather than just the two. Besides, Elizabeth did not seem keen to speak to her cousin at all. Edward wasn't surprised. The man was a fool, and she had a sharp wit. She wouldn't suffer men like him easily.

"You must tell us where you've been these last few years,

Edward," Elizabeth said, leaning forward eagerly. "I've longed to hear of your travels."

Her earnestness took him by surprise. No one had ever shown interest in his journeys before. "You have?"

"Oh yes. Cousin Jeffrey said you worked for him here, but what about before that? Where did you go after leaving Upper Wayworth?"

"I was retained by Lord Whipple."

"Retained? As what?"

"I undertook some building work for him in the beginning." Edward felt his face heat. He wasn't usually ashamed to admit he'd done menial work for Whipple, but sitting beside Arrabella made him aware of how grubby it was. Everything about her was elegant, perfect. Everything about him was humble, low. "Later, he entrusted me with matters of business for his estate."

"But you can't read or write," Arrabella said.

Opposite him, Elizabeth stiffened. Her eyes widened as her piercing gaze drilled into her sister. He didn't look at Arrabella to see her reaction. He had to get his news out before he dared do that.

"I can now," he assured her, finally peeking at her from the corner of his eye. He smiled. He couldn't contain his satisfaction or his happiness at simply being near her again. She arched her brows in surprise at him. "Indeed, there's quite a few things about me that have changed."

She said nothing, but returned to pushing her food around her trencher. She ate none of it, even though it was hearty and delicious.

"Indeed you have," Elizabeth said quickly, filling the awkward silence. "Thankfully none of the things we always liked about you are different."

Arrabella suddenly jumped and let out a yelp. "Uh, yes. Yes, we still like your...friendliness." She reached under the table and appeared to rub her leg.

Edward sat back in his chair, his gaze focused on Elizabeth. She was concentrating on her food, not looking at him. If she'd just kicked her sister, she showed no sign of it. Something was going on between them, and he hadn't a clue what. It served him right for avoiding females for the better part of his life. Now he didn't know how to read them.

"Tell us about Lord Oxley," Lynden said, breaking the thick silence.

Edward shrugged. "There's little to tell."

"Nonsense. I've never encountered such an interesting gentleman. Who are his friends? What does he like to do?"

Arrabella suddenly stood. "May I be excused? I'm not hungry."

Lynden chuckled. "Anxious about your betrothed's arrival? Go on, be off with you."

Edward stood too. His chance was about to slip away from him if he didn't go after her. "Good night," he said to both Lynden and Elizabeth.

She half rose from her chair as if she would try to stop him, but sat heavily down again and shoved her trencher away. She rubbed her temple as if a headache bloomed.

"Is everything all right, Monk?" Lynden asked.

Edward left without answering and raced through the chambers until he spotted Arrabella. He called after her, but she kept walking. "Arrabella, may I speak with you?"

She mustn't have heard him. He caught up to her and took her by the elbow.

"What is it *now*?" she snapped, jerking free.

He stepped back, stung by her vehemence. "I-I'm sorry. I know you're tired, but I hoped we could spend some time alone together."

She threw her arms out wide. "We're alone now."

He cleared his throat. This wasn't going at all as he expected. "Perhaps later when you're not feeling so tired."

"We'll talk now and get it over with."

"Arrabella…is something wrong? This isn't like you."

That seemed to calm her a little. Her stance relaxed, but her gaze shifted from his face to peer out the window. She sighed deeply. Something troubled her. There was only one thing it could be.

"Does Greville's pending arrival upset you?"

She focused on him once more, a frown scoring her pretty forehead. He wanted to smooth it away with his thumb. It didn't belong there. "Of course not. Why should it?"

"We can get you out of it."

"Out of what?"

"The betrothal. Have you told Lynden how unhappy it makes you? Perhaps he's not fully aware of the depths of your feelings."

"What are you talking about?"

"You don't deserve an unhappy marriage, Arrabella."

She opened her mouth to speak, but he put a finger to her lips.

"Arrabella, my sweet, I can make you happy."

She pulled back and fisted her hands on her hips. Her frown deepened. "Edward, it's time to stop this nonsense."

"I agree. Tell Lynden and your mother that you want to marry me instead. I have the means to—"

"What?" She covered her mouth with her hands, but it didn't smother the high-pitched giggle. "Oh, Edward, you poor puppy."

His stomach dipped and rolled. He didn't like the sound of this. "Arrabella?"

"I can't marry you," she said, eyes bright.

"You didn't let me finish. I have the means to keep you in comfort now. I'm a wealthy man."

"Oh, Edward." The brightness dimmed. Her mouth flattened into a sad smile. "It's not enough."

Panic made his throat tight, his chest ache. "I'm going to be a gentleman. I've paid the herald. It's only a matter of time before my coat of arms is registered."

"You *paid* to become a gentleman?"

"It's entirely possible these days. With Lord Oxley's backing, it is easily done. I'll be granted my coat of arms soon." It wasn't as easy as he made out, and quite a lot of money had exchanged hands, but she didn't need to know the details. He grasped her shoulders. "So you see, I'm your equal now. We can wed and you will come live with me on Hughe's estate until I purchase a house. It can be near your family if you—"

"Stop it, Edward." She pulled away. "Stop talking like this."

Numbness crept slowly across his heart like ice. Why was she being so stubborn? "But Arrabella...I love you. I want to be with you. I always have."

He moved to her, but she put up her hands, warding him off. "I didn't want to say this to you," she said. "But Elizabeth told me it's the fair thing to do. So this is me being fair."

What did her sister have to do with any of this?

"Edward, I don't love you. I never have. Well, once perhaps, when I was a child and didn't know my own heart. But not now."

He stood there like a tree rooted to the ground. He couldn't move. Couldn't think. He tried to tell her that he didn't understand, but when he opened his mouth, no words came out.

"Did you hear me?" she said, peering up at him. "I don't love you. I love Greville, and I'm going to marry him."

Still he couldn't speak.

She clicked her tongue and turned away. She was going to leave him. If he let her go then she might never be his. He grabbed her elbow and pulled her round to face him.

"What are you doing?" she cried. "Let me go!"

He gripped harder. "I don't understand. We've always loved each other. You told me so."

"I may have once. I don't recall. If I did, it was a child playing an adult game. Now let me go, or I'll scream."

He let her go and caught the back of the nearest chair to steady himself. The room was tilting. His head felt light and his mind not altogether there. "I-I don't understand."

"For goodness sake. It's not complicated. You must give up your foolish notion of marrying me."

Why was she saying these things? How could he make her see that he was worthy of her now? "I'll be a gentleman soon."

"Then I'm pleased for you. But it changes nothing. I am marrying Greville."

"Is it because he's a baron and I'm merely a gentleman?"

"You're not a gentleman *yet*."

His heart ground to a halt. A lump the size of a pear formed in his throat. He couldn't swallow past it.

"I don't love you, Edward, that is the crux of it." She patted his arm as if comforting an acquaintance who'd been given bad news. It was bad news indeed. The worst. But he was no mere acquaintance. "Now, don't despair. There is someone who does love you. All is not lost."

He hardly heard her through the pounding of the blood between his ears. Not lost? "What?" he muttered.

"My sister Elizabeth."

Someone gasped behind him. He did not turn around. He knew his face was a picture of shock and sorrow, and he didn't want anyone else to see him. He simply stared at Arrabella, trying to take in everything she'd said.

"She loves you, Edward." Arrabella looked past him. "Isn't that right, Lizzie? Come here and tell him."

Slowly her words infiltrated the fog in his brain. He turned to see Elizabeth standing in the doorway. She was pale, her lips pinched tight. She did not come in as Arrabella requested. Instead, she made a small choking sound in her throat, then turned and fled.

Edward stared at the empty doorway. His heart kicked inside his chest, smashing into his ribs. He dared not look at Arrabella. Couldn't. It was awful enough knowing Elizabeth had witnessed his humiliation, but to see the pity in Arrabella's eyes would be too much.

She touched his arm. "You should go after her."

"I don't love her," he said, somewhat stupidly. At least, it sounded like a stupid thing to say to his ears.

"You might come to."

"Is she...is she the reason you cannot love me?"

She blinked slowly. "I haven't loved you for a long time, Edward. Who's to say what the reason is. It simply is." She gave him a sad smile then walked off, out of the room.

Edward watched her go. Her skirts swished from side to side with the sway of her hips. Hips he'd dreamed of caressing only last night.

But she wasn't his. She was Greville's. When had he lost her? Before he left Upper Wayworth or after?

Who's to say what the reason is.

He turned to look at the other door where Elizabeth had stood. *She* was the reason. Arrabella hadn't wanted to upset her sister by claiming the man Elizabeth wanted.

CHAPTER 5

"*H*ow dare you." Elizabeth did not raise her voice. She didn't want their mother in the next bedchamber to hear her shouting at Arrabella. She didn't want more humiliation piled upon the heap already threatening to suffocate her.

How could she ever face Edward again? How could she sit across the table at dinner and pretend nothing had changed?

"Calm yourself, Lizzie," Arrabella said with a roll of her eyes. "Leave the dramatics to the players."

"I am not being dramatic. I am—" *Humiliated*. "How could you betray me like that? I asked you not to tell him."

Arrabella lifted her shift over her head and threw it on the bed. She stood naked in front of Elizabeth, her hands on her hips. No doubt it was a pose struck to show the younger sister how magnificent her figure was in comparison to Elizabeth's less shapely one.

"I've done you a favor by telling him," she said, pouring water from the ewer into the basin. "Now that he knows you love him and I do not, he can give *you* his attentions instead. I don't understand why you're so upset. It was quite nicely done, I thought."

"No, Bella, it was not *nicely* done. It was spiteful, vicious."

Arrabella almost dropped the ewer as she spun around to look at Elizabeth. "Whatever do you mean? I'm only trying to help."

"Then stop it. I don't want your help. All you've succeeded in doing is embarrassing me. Perhaps that was your intention all along."

"God's wounds, Lizzie. You sound like a madwoman. You ought to be thanking me, not railing against me. One word of advice." She bared her teeth in a sneering smile. "Be sure he is the man you truly want. He's annoyingly dogged."

"He won't pursue me now. Do you know why? Because he's still in love with you. His heart is not a lever. He cannot switch it back and forth at will."

"Stop being a little girl, and think like a woman. Go out and find your man. It's not too late."

No, but it was too early. Too soon. Her foolish sister either didn't know the depths of Edward's feelings or how long a broken heart took to heal. Perhaps both.

There would be no reasoning with her, no way to make her see that she had just utterly humiliated Elizabeth in front of Edward. It was all too much, too horrible. She got into bed, curled into a ball and pulled the covers over her head.

* * *

EDWARD ROSE EARLY to meet Hughe on the road out of Sutton Grange. It was not yet warm, but the sky was clear and promised another blisteringly hot day. Hopefully, it would keep the ladies indoors where he could easily avoid them. Or one of them at least —Elizabeth. He didn't want to see her or talk to her.

He didn't want to avoid Arrabella, however. Perhaps if she spent more time with him, she'd see that he was good enough now, and that Elizabeth was no rival for his affections. She never had been. Damnation. If Elizabeth hadn't fallen in love with him, perhaps Arrabella's affections would have remained steady. It was a slim hope, but he clung to it. He needed to. The alternative made him feel hollow.

He spotted Hughe's dust before he heard the horse's hooves on the road. He rounded the bend a little ahead of the cart driven by the single manservant who'd accompanied him. The back of the cart was filled with trunks stuffed with Hughe's clothes. He rarely traveled light.

"Monk," Hughe said in greeting. "All's well with you this morning?"

"I've had better days."

Hughe signaled for his man to drive on. "Lynden prattle all night, eh?"

"He did want to know all about you."

Hughe pulled a face. "I don't see how talking about me can make you so ill-tempered. You look like you were up all night, and I don't think you find me *that* interesting that you'd be lying awake thinking of me."

"The Buckley women are proving to be more of a challenge than I thought, that's all."

Edward expected Hughe to be triumphant since he'd predicted Arrabella's reluctance, but he leaned heavily on the pommel. "You have my sympathies, Monk. I may never have suffered the fate of a broken heart, but I have it on good authority that it does heal in time."

Edward didn't bother to correct him. He didn't want to hear more on Hughe's theory that Arrabella wasn't right for him.

"What did you discover about Greville?" he asked. If the man proved to be a Catholic like his brother, there might be reason to end the betrothal.

"Nothing." Hughe's horse Charger shifted beneath him, eager to get away. He brought it under control with a few soothing words. "Greville and his party stayed up until the watch called midnight. They were definitely waiting for someone, but whoever it was never arrived. This morning I overheard Greville and the other fellow arguing over whether to remain longer at the Plough or go to the Hall as planned. I learned his name is Paxton, although we weren't formally introduced. Greville seemed to treat him like a servant when he thought someone was watching, but in their private conversations, Paxton treated *him* with disdain."

"Odd."

"Greville held his own in the argument, despite Paxton's conviction. He said he was eager to get away and see his betrothed."

Edward ground his back teeth together.

Hughe gave him a sympathetic look. "If it makes you feel any happier, there is definitely something amiss. Find out what it is. It may or may not be enough to break their betrothal."

"I will. You can count on it."

"I know I can. But Monk, be warned. Whatever you learn may not be enough to change her affections for him. Be prepared to still lose."

A quip died on Edward's lips. Hughe spoke with sincerity and none of the biting wit he usually employed.

"Who won the argument?" he asked instead.

"Greville. He said it would look suspicious if they remained in the village when they were supposed to be up at the Hall."

"It would. As it is, there will be questions as to why he didn't go straight there."

Charger shifted again and it took Hughe longer to settle him. "He wants a run before the day heats up," he said, patting the horse's neck. "I'll return in a week or so. In the meantime, be careful, Monk."

"Always."

"Give my regards to Cole, Orlando and their ladies." He gave Charger the signal and the big white horse leaped forward.

"I'll give your affections to Lynden too," Edward called after him.

Hughe's rude hand gesture was barely visible in the dust kicked up by Charger's hooves.

Edward rode quickly back to Sutton Hall, hoping to arrive before Greville so he could speak to Arrabella. He was too late. The baron and his retinue were already at the stables, untying their packs. Stable lads took the horses and led them to stalls and water.

Greville nodded a greeting as Edward rode up. "It's Monk, isn't it? Oxley's man?"

Edward dismounted and handed the reins to one of the lads. "Aye. And you're Lord Greville." His gaze shifted to the others. Two of them collected their belongings while Paxton stood a little apart. He stared at Edward, his black eyes fathomless. "Are they your servants?" he asked Greville.

"Retainers." Greville's glance flicked to Paxton then away to the house. "Do you know the family well?"

"Well enough."

"Is Arrabella in good health? And the rest of her family?"

"They're in good spirits."

He flashed a sheepish smile. "Arrabella and I are betrothed."

Edward was beginning to think he was younger than he'd first thought. He couldn't be more than twenty or so. No man blushed so readily when he spoke of his woman. He looked like a lovesick—

Bloody hell. Is that how Edward behaved around Arrabella? He knew he blushed, and occasionally stammered. God's wounds, no wonder Hughe teased him.

"I must go to her," Greville said, heading for the stable door.

He was half way to the house when Arrabella emerged at a run from the arched entrance to the courtyard. She let out a squeal upon seeing Greville. He broke into a run too and caught her as she propelled herself into his arms. He swung her around, and they kissed passionately, not caring who saw.

Edward couldn't watch anymore. It made him feel sick. He was about to turn away when a movement behind them caught his attention. Elizabeth stood in the archway, her hands clasped in front of her. She was too far away for Edward to see her face clearly, but he had a strange feeling that she was watching *him*, not the lovers.

A fist closed around his heart and he looked away. The fist

squeezed, making breathing hard. He tried to block out the image of Arrabella and Greville kissing, but it was impossible. The sight was burned into his memory like a scar.

"Sickening, isn't it?" Paxton said.

Edward didn't know when the other man had come up to him. He didn't look at Edward, but at his master. The scar distorted his smile so that it was difficult to tell if it was sincere or a sneer.

Edward fought for control. He focused on Paxton and the mystery surrounding him rather than Arrabella. Slowly, his breathing return to normal and his thoughts sharpened. He watched the other man closely for any clues as to his role.

The other two servants wore simple gray woolen tunics, but Paxton's clothes were that of a traveling gentleman. If one stood Paxton and Greville side by side, it would be impossible to tell from their clothing which was the baron and which the retainer. Indeed, with Paxton being the elder, he would have been Edward's first choice.

"They haven't seen each other for all of four days," Paxton said. "Just wait until they're our age, eh? Won't be so keen then."

Our age. Edward was thirty, the other man likely more. Not so old compared to Arrabella. "She's twenty-six."

Paxton seemed surprised. "Late to be marrying for the first time."

"She's been waiting for the right man."

"Know a lot about what's in her heart, do you?"

Not enough. Edward pushed off and dared a look at the lovers. Arrabella had stopped kissing Greville, but still clung to his arm. Elizabeth was with them, listening to Greville. He must have said something amusing because she smiled. Arrabella's tinkling laughter drifted on the breeze to Edward.

He drew a deep breath and joined them. Fortunately, he was saved from speaking to Greville with the arrival of Lynden. He dominated the conversation, urging Greville inside out of the heat.

"Aunt Janet will be happy to see you again," he said.

"And I her." Greville was saying all the right things and smiling like he'd struck a seam in a gold mine.

The party headed back to the house. Just before they disappeared into the courtyard, Greville glanced over his shoulder to the stables. Edward looked back too and saw Paxton watching them, his arms crossed over his thick-set chest. It would be left to one of Lynden's servants to show him to his room.

* * *

THE DAY PASSED INTERMINABLY SLOWLY. It was made worse by three things: listening to Janet's sycophantic gushing over Greville, watching Arrabella and Greville touch each other whenever they thought no one near and having Lynden ask him every hour if he'd learned anything yet.

Edward was so heart sore and desperate to avoid them all that by suppertime he forgot his resolve to not speak to Elizabeth. When he stumbled upon her in the garden parlor, he did not turn around and leave.

She poured him a cup of wine from the jug on the table. "Drink up. I believe it's the strongest wine in the house."

He took the cup. "Tested it, have you?"

"Frequently."

He saluted her with the cup before taking a sip. It was indeed strong and burned his throat as it went down. "It may be the strongest, but it's also the foulest I've ever tasted."

"You'll become used to it."

He sat on a chair, close to her. "After three or four cups?"

"More like ten."

He laughed. It was good to laugh again. It felt like an age since he'd done so. The wine was certainly effective, if somewhat earthy. "I can't believe Lynden drinks this stuff. I thought him a gentleman of quality."

She snorted softly. "You have seen the way he dresses, haven't you? I'm not sure quality is a word I'd use to describe that green doublet."

"It did resemble the color of pond slime."

"My cousin is not a man of half measures." She peered into her cup and wrinkled her nose. "Perhaps that explains this wine. It's certainly not halfway good."

He laughed again. Twice in the matter of a few moments. The wine may taste disgusting, but it worked faster than any he'd drunk before. "I should introduce him to Hughe's cellar."

"You'd better not. He may never want to leave."

"Because he likes wine so much?"

"Because he likes your Lord Oxley." Her teeth nibbled her lip and despite the darkening room, he saw her cheeks blush. "I should not, uh, I mean—"

"It's all right. Hughe is cut from a different cloth than your cousin." Vastly different. "The broken *female* hearts all over England can attest to that."

Her eyes widened. "Really? But he showed no inclination toward Arrabella or myself."

"He prefers his women to be less available."

She worried at her lip again, biting the bottom one with her teeth.

"Don't do that." He leaned forward, but suddenly sat back again. He'd been about to cup her cheek to make her aware of her habit. Why in God's name would he do that? Why did it bother him whether she bit her lip at all?

He gripped his cup harder with both hands in the hope that would suppress any future urges to touch her. He drained the cup and poured himself another. He needed fortifying.

She set her cup down and stood. He thought she was going to leave and opened his mouth to ask her to stay, but shut it again. He'd come into the garden parlor to avoid everyone and think of his next plan to conquer Arrabella's heart, yet he'd not thought of her since seeing Elizabeth. Odd.

She didn't leave. The room had quickly grown darker as the

sun sank below the horizon. She struck a flint and lit the candles on the mantelpiece. The flames flickered in the gentle breeze coming in through the open windows, throwing their dancing light over Elizabeth's face as she returned to her chair so near his own.

She was a beauty. How had he not noticed before? She wasn't as obviously pretty as her sister, but more subtly so. Her hair was a shade darker, her lips not as red, and her cheeks still held the roundness of youth. Indeed, none of her features were remarkable on their own, but together they made her face extraordinarily pretty. Her skin was smooth and clear, her throat white. He wondered what it would be like to caress it. She wore an open ruff that joined her collar, exposing the hollow at the base of her throat, the dip at her shoulder and the delicious swell of her breasts.

He wanted to kiss her there, lick her. What did smooth, white skin taste like? Would she let him? Would she sigh and push herself against his mouth?

His cock hardened painfully at the thought. God's blood. After long years of practice, he'd learned to control his urges. Or so he thought. Not this night. Not with this woman.

The wrong woman.

Damned wine. The stuff was dangerous. He'd somehow drunk two cups without noticing.

He should get up and walk out, not for his sake, but hers. Yet he couldn't. Not if he didn't want her to see his cock jutting out like an obscene codpiece. He crossed his legs and swallowed hard.

She watched him with a puzzled expression. "Are you all right?" she asked. "You look like you're in some kind of pain."

She had no idea *how* painful. "Must be the wine. It's potent."

"Does it not agree with you?"

"I think it agrees with me a little too much." He didn't know what he was saying, but at least his cock was subsiding.

Don't look at her breasts. He concentrated on her face, but that

63

was a mistake too because it set his heart hammering. Must be because she was a beauty. *Talk about something else. The wine.*

"Why is a girl like you drinking this filth?"

She blinked at him over the rim of her cup. "I'm hardly a girl anymore, Edward. I'm twenty." She spoke quietly, as if she were almost too embarrassed to talk to him in such an easy, friendly manner.

"Still a girl to an old man like me," he said, remembering Paxton's words.

"Can you not…" Her voice warbled and she cleared her throat. "Will you ever see me as a woman?"

That was the problem. He *was* seeing her as a woman for the first time. He shouldn't be looking at her at all when it was Arrabella he loved. It felt like a betrayal, even though that was nonsense.

Hell. He needed to speak to Arrabella. Get her away from Greville. He had to get away from Elizabeth, or Arrabella would think he did love her and would continue to push him away for her sister's sake.

Fuck! Everything was a mess. *He* was a mess.

He pressed his finger and thumb into his eye sockets to suppress the headache blooming there. He stood. The floor swayed and he almost sat back down again.

"Edward?" Elizabeth was in front of him, peering up into his eyes. She was small, reaching only to his chest. He liked that. Liked the way her soft eyes never left his. Worry filled them, and he liked that too.

Bloody hell, what had come over him?

"Edward, are you all right?" She bit her lip again. She had to stop doing that. It was a pretty little lip, softly pouting in the middle and curving wickedly at the edges. Innocence and seduction. That was Elizabeth in a nutshell.

He wondered whether the rest of her was innocent, seductive or both. Her thighs for instance, and breasts.

She frowned, biting her lip harder. It didn't deserve such

cruelty. He touched his hand to her cheek, resting his thumb at the corner of her mouth.

She expelled a tiny breath and released the poor, pouty flesh. He smiled. Better. But not enough. The lip needed some gentler attention. He bent his head and kissed it.

She tasted of wine, but something sweeter too. Her breath warmed him, and her lips fluttered against his, much like his heart inside his chest. He could tell that she'd never kissed anyone before. He'd kissed enough girls over the years to recognize the fact, although he'd never taken those kisses further. He'd always pulled back before his frustration mounted to the point where he couldn't stop.

He didn't want to pull back this time. His frustration was already at breaking point.

She reached up and circled her arms around his neck. It sent him over the edge. He deepened the kiss, explored her with his tongue. She responded by digging her fingers through his hair and moaning softly. She leaned into him. Her breasts pillowed between them, soft and full. He wanted to touch them. Needed to palm one, feel its heaviness.

He touched the exposed flesh above her gown, tentatively, not wanting to take more than she was prepared to give. He worried that he might not be able to stop once he had all that soft flesh in his hand.

She took his hand and directed it under her breast. He cupped it. It was full and indeed heavy, but there was too much fabric in the way. He dipped his thumb inside the top of her bodice and shift and pulled them gently down. Down. Exposing her breasts.

He broke the kiss and pulled away to look at her. She was a goddess. Perfection. The stiff fabric of the bodice pushed her breasts up toward him like an offering. The nipples bloomed fat and soft.

He sighed in wonder. He'd seen breasts before, but never touched them. He ached to touch. Everything from his heart to his cock felt tight with the need to feel them, taste them.

But it wasn't until she guided his hand to one that he finally did. It was more than he could hold, and it was impossibly smooth beneath his callused palm. He stared in wonder, not wanting to drag his eyes away from all that delicious creaminess.

"So soft," he whispered.

She cupped her other breast and offered it to him. The nipple was too plump and succulent to ignore. He licked it. Delicious.

She gasped and arched her back, pushing her breast into his mouth. He took more of it, sucked. Her body jerked. She clutched at his head as if to steady herself and held him at her breast. The nipple hardened in his mouth. He gently nipped it with his teeth and massaged the other breast, teasing the nipple to a point.

Dear lord, it was like nothing he'd ever expected. How had he denied himself this pleasure? How had he ever kept control for so long?

Because she wasn't there, a small voice in the back of his head told him.

Her hands stilled in his hair. "I heard something," she whispered.

Hell, damnation and fuck.

"Lock the door," she said. "Someone might enter."

"Me. I'm going to enter you."

Her giggle made him look up. He gasped.

Elizabeth.

He pulled away and pressed the heel of his hand to his temple. He stared at her, and she stared back. Her face slowly darkened with her blush. Her lower lip wobbled and she bit it. He did not rescue it.

God's wounds, how old was she again?

Her naked breasts rose and fell with her deep breaths. He forced himself to look elsewhere and closed his hands into fists. He dug the fingernails into his palms. It took all his strength, but he managed to not touch her again.

His head hurt. While kissing her, holding her, he'd forgotten his headache, but now it returned with a vengeance. Probably to punish him.

"I don't want you to stop." Her voice was small. It sounded far away. Too far.

"I want…" He wanted to take her. Ravish her in the garden parlor. Feel those breasts against his bare chest. Feel himself inside her.

But she wasn't Arrabella. His love.

Bloody hell, his aching head!

"I must go." Yet he didn't leave. Should he apologize? Help her with her clothing? Explain about his feelings for Arrabella?

Damnation, he was a cur. A low dog not fit for anyone, let alone a woman like Elizabeth. No, *Arrabella*!

Fuck.

He had to get away. He spun on his heel, but a woman's laughter made him stop dead. Had someone seen? The laughter came from the balcony that joined both the parlor and the music room next door.

He and Elizabeth exchanged alarmed glances, then both swung into action. She hurriedly stuffed her breasts back into her gown, and he blew out the candles.

The laughter continued, but was soon lost in a deep sigh. Arrabella. She was on the balcony with someone. Bloody Greville.

In the moonlight coming through the windows, he could just make out Elizabeth's pale face beside him. Her gaze shifted from him to the balcony. Then her mouth fell open.

He turned to see what she'd seen. Arrabella was indeed on the balcony with Greville. They were standing in profile, her head thrown back as he kissed her throat. But what had shocked Elizabeth wasn't the kiss, but the state of their clothing. Greville had removed his doublet and shirt, and Arrabella's gown and shift were unlaced. They slipped to her waist, exposing her breasts. Greville pawed at them, drawing gasps of desire from her.

She pushed him gently away and cupped her breasts, offering

them up to him. It was the same thing Elizabeth had done for Edward moments before.

Greville took one in his mouth, freeing his hands to push Arrabella's gown all the way down. The skirts and shift billowed at her feet so that she appeared to be standing on a cloud. She sighed again as his hands snaked down her breast, over her waist and hip, around to her inner thigh.

She gave a small gasp as she tipped her head back. Edward could hear her panting from where he stood several feet away.

"Ravish me, my lord," she said between her breaths. "I want you."

Beside him, Elizabeth moved. She covered her mouth with her hands, her eyes transfixed on the scene. It broke the spell that had come over Edward.

This was Arrabella. *His* woman.

No. Not his. Greville's. She had kissed him and allowed him to touch her. She'd *begged* him. They were going to be wed because she loved *him*.

Edward was the biggest fool in all England.

His stomach heaved. Bile rose to his throat. He wanted to throw up. Wanted to get away from the sounds of their lovemaking, mocking him.

He strode out of the room, not caring who saw him. But neither Arrabella nor Greville looked up from each other. They were too absorbed by their own desire to see anyone else.

At the last moment, he remembered Elizabeth. He hesitated, not wanting to go back and have his nose rubbed in his blind stupidity, but not wanting to leave Elizabeth alone after what he'd done to her. He may not be a gentleman as Arrabella had pointed out, but he liked to think himself better than a dog.

But Elizabeth emerged from the room too, and, without looking at him, ran past. He didn't go after her. There was nothing he could say to make the situation better.

He stalked ahead, not knowing where he was going until he was outside. The night air was warm and dark, the stars and moon hidden behind clouds. He headed to the stables and made it before throwing up in a nearby shrub.

He squatted, steadying himself with a hand on the ground. He blinked rapidly, angry at himself for feeling so emotional over a woman. A woman who didn't love him and probably never had. He sucked in deep breaths, determined not to let those emotions come to the fore.

It didn't work. He got up and slammed his fist into the stable wall. It was wooden, not brick thank God, but his knuckles hurt like the devil. The pain felt good. He welcomed it.

He headed into the stables and saddled his horse. What he needed was a good long ride, maybe a few drinks, and definitely a woman.

When Elizabeth's face came to mind, he paused. His cock hardened at the memory of her soft breast in his hand, the way she'd gasped when he kissed her.

Not that woman. Too young, and too much like her sister.

Not Arrabella either. It would never be her. He'd saved himself, but now the weight of his abstinence was crushing him. It was a burden he'd carried for so long. What in God's name for? What had been the point?

He needed to shove it off and be free again. There was only one way to do that. He took the road into the village and made straight for the White Hart, not the Plough. The Plough was too respectable, and the innkeeper's daughter was a good girl. The serving wenches at the White Hart, however, had told him to come looking for them if he ever wanted to break his vow of chastity.

And God's blood he wanted to break it.

CHAPTER 6

*E*lizabeth slept little and rose at dawn when the maid delivered fresh water and a clean shift to her bedchamber. Usually, she slept while the girl did her chores, but this morning every sound seemed as loud as a peeling bell. She rose and washed, rubbing the damp cloth over her body, lingering at her breasts. The nipples still tingled with the memory of Edward's kisses and still ached for his touch. Being with him had been the stuff of her dreams, a long-held desire finally become real.

Then dashed on the rocks like a ship in a storm. Her heart had ached all night as she tossed in the bed, reliving every moment of their time together in the garden parlor. The way he'd kissed her, cupped her breast, exposed her nipples and taken them in his mouth. The way her body had responded, arching toward him, aching and throbbing, wantonly giving herself to him.

Only to be rejected as Arrabella came into view.

Elizabeth should not have been surprised that he'd been too drunk to know who he'd been kissing, but she'd thought—hoped— that it had been *her* he'd wanted and not her sister. From the look on his face as he watched Greville make love to Arrabella, there was no doubt which he loved. Elizabeth was second choice, the available one, the one who would willingly relieve his itch while he pursued the other.

She should have hated him. She should have been cursing his name, wishing all manner of ills to befall him. But she did not. Her heart was too bruised to feel anything but sorrow. Besides, she was worried about him. She'd seen him foolishly ride off in the night. What if his horse stepped in a hole in the darkness? What if vagabonds pursued him?

After dressing, she headed to the stables. It may have been early, but the outbuildings were busy as maids collected fresh eggs from the henhouse and bread from the bakehouse. Farm hands checked equipment before heading out to the fields, while the stable boys prepared the horses.

She spoke to the first groom she found, a reed-thin lad with stringy hair and pocked skin. He looked up from the horse's hoof he was checking as she approached and gave a friendly nod of greeting.

"Has Mr. Monk returned from his ride?" she asked.

"No, mistress. He must've gone out a'fore we woke. His horse ain't here, and the tack's missin'."

"I saw him leave late last night." She gazed out to the drive where she'd last seen him. Where had he gone? Why wasn't he back?

"Foolish to go ridin' in the night," the lad said, setting the horse's hoof down.

"What's your name?"

"Warren, mistress."

"Do you have any saddles for a lady to ride aside, Warren?"

"Aye."

"Then saddle a horse for me. I'm going into the village."

"You can ride?"

"Of course. I'll need an escort."

The lad puffed out his chest. "It'd be an honor."

He would do. It was only a short ride into the village. She didn't plan on going beyond. "Very good. I'll return soon."

She hurried back to the house to change her boots and put on riding gloves, a light cloak and hat. She left a message with one of the maids to deliver to her mother when she awoke. With any luck, Elizabeth would be back by the time her family rose. Arrabella and Janet usually slept late. Arrabella would probably be particularly late if she'd stayed up into the night with Greville. Going by the way they were pawing each other on the balcony, the night would have been a long one for both. Elizabeth should have been shocked at her sister's behavior, but considering she would have willingly done the same thing with Edward, she could not judge her too harshly.

Less than an hour later, she and Warren rode into Sutton Grange. She'd been into the village only once. Despite begging her sister and mother to go again, they'd refused, preferring to remain in the house, out of the sun and dust. Elizabeth should have gone without them, then she would have become more familiar with the place.

Sutton Grange was a pretty if somewhat faded jewel. The main road ran the length of the village like a river with smaller tributaries feeding into it. Wooden shops and houses huddled together, the crooked structures propping each other up. An extensive green provided a safe area for the children to play as their mothers went about their errands. Warren informed her that a market was held there weekly in the harvest months.

"Tell me about the inns here," Elizabeth asked him. "Specifically ones that have accommodation."

"There's two, The Plough and The White Hart. Milner's the innkeep at The Plough. If you want to know what goes on in the village, he's your man. The Plough is a clean place, and the food's hearty. It's where Lord Oxley and Mr. Monk stay when they're here."

"Would he open up in the middle of the night for Mr. Monk?"

"Mayhap."

"What about women?" She hoped Warren would understand

her meaning without her having to explain. "Does The Plough have…willing girls?"

"The White Hart's the place for that," he mumbled into his chest. "So I heard."

Edward had been drunk and angry, and most likely frustrated. He would probably seek out a woman. She'd go to The White Hart.

She may not know much about lying with men, but she'd asked her maid for details when her mother wouldn't answer her questions. Janet might prefer to keep her daughters innocent on the subject, but Elizabeth preferred knowledge to naivety. If she couldn't get that knowledge through practical experience, secondhand from the maids would have to do. According to her maid, if a man were desperate, he wasn't too particular about where he dallied.

"I'll see if he's here," Warren said when she dismounted in The White Hart's yard.

"No. Stay here." She handed him the reins.

She found Lowe in the dining room, talking to one of his guests who ate a sausage off the end of his knife. She introduced herself and asked if Edward was there.

The innkeeper looked like he'd slept in his clothes. They were rumpled and stained down the front. His face was in similar condition. The man was as wrinkled as a prune and from the look of the food stuck in his shaggy beard, he'd had boiled egg for breakfast.

"You from the Hall?" he asked her.

"My name's Elizabeth Buckley. Mr. Monk said he might be coming here last night and asked me to fetch him in the morning if he hadn't returned." She gave him a smile. She could play the sweet young lady quite believably when she had to. She just preferred not to unless absolutely necessary. Not like Arrabella who employed the guise regularly.

Lowe bared crooked teeth in what was either a genuine smile or a sneer. It was difficult to tell. "He's upstairs, first room on the left." He laughed, making his belly shake beneath his doublet, and slapped the other man on the shoulder.

The guest jerked away, as if he didn't want Lowe touching him. He was of middle age and wore his black hair long, tied back with a strip of leather. He was dressed well, but if one looked closely, the patches were evident. Perhaps he was an impoverished gentleman, or a merchant fallen on hard times. His dark eyes watched her intently. She couldn't fathom why he found her so interesting, but it made her uncomfortable.

Elizabeth hurried out and up the stairs. She knocked on the first door on the left. It was answered by a woman carrying a pair of worn leather shoes. Her unbound hair fell around her shoulders in a tangled mess, and her bodice wasn't laced all the way up. Her breasts were in danger of spilling out altogether. Behind her, Edward lay under a sheet on the bed.

Elizabeth's stomach rolled, even though she saw nothing she hadn't expected. Of course he could do as he pleased with a willing woman, but it felt like she'd been slapped across the face nevertheless. He'd taken a serving girl to bed, not *her*, despite what had happened between them the night before. Indeed, he'd gone straight from touching Elizabeth's breasts to this woman's. She'd been replaceable, as insignificant to him as a shirt he'd exchanged for another.

Their time together had meant nothing to him.

Her eyes clouded, but she fought for composure. She'd come to retrieve him and take him back to the house. She wasn't leaving without him. At least he wasn't injured.

"I'm here to collect Mr. Monk," she said.

The woman smiled toothily and glanced over her shoulder at the sleeping form. "You're a lucky lass," she said with a wink. "If you grow tired of him again, send him my way. I'll see to it he don't want for nothin'. For him, it's free." She slipped past Elizabeth and scurried down the long gallery to another door through which she disappeared.

Elizabeth stared unblinking at Edward. Perhaps she ought to get Warren after all. She'd not thought through this part of the plan. Was Edward naked under that sheet?

She left the door open and entered. The bedchamber reeked of wine, and empty jugs and cups littered the floor. The only furniture was the bed, a chamber pot and a chair. A basin of dirty water sat upon the chair and a grubby cloth hung over the back. Edward's clothes formed a trail to the bed, as if he'd removed them as he walked toward it.

She approached the bed and peered down at his face. His beautiful, handsome face with its strong jaw, roughened from stubble. She caressed his cheek with the back of her hand, unable to resist touching him.

His eyes fluttered open and she pulled back. He sat up, then groaned and clutched his head. "God's blood," he muttered in a low rasp.

She was too busy gazing at his bare chest to respond. The sheet had fallen to his hips, exposing his upper body. She swallowed hard and tried to look away, but it was useless. She was compelled to look *at* him. How could any woman ignore all that glorious muscle? His shoulders were broad and strong, his chest too. It was covered with a light smattering of hair that tapered off at his waist. Ridges of muscle rippled over his stomach, all the way down to where the sheet hid the rest of him. She'd felt what he had down there last night. It had been hard and long as it pressed into her, wanting her.

No, not *her*. Any woman. Clearly it hadn't mattered who.

"Edward, are you all right?"

He didn't answer.

"Edward, I've come to take you back to Sutton Hall."

He grunted. "I know the way."

She bit her lip. She hadn't expected rudeness. Embarrassment, yes, but not this. "I saw you ride off in the night and grew worried."

"I don't need a nursemaid."

She crossed her arms and tore her gaze away from his chest to look at his face. His eyes were closed and his hand buried in his hair. He'd not looked at her directly since he'd first opened his eyes.

"You were drunk," she snapped, her ire rising. "Riding off in the middle of the night was foolish. You may not have saddled your horse properly, or it could have injured itself."

"Did you come here to lecture me?"

"Get up."

"Go away."

"Not until you come back with me."

"What does it matter to you what I do?"

It mattered so much that it hurt seeing him in such a state. "Because I don't think you want to be here, not like this," she said gently. "I also think you need help getting home. Your face is quite gray. Are you still drunk?"

"God, I hope so," he muttered.

Why was he being so obstinate? "I don't know how you found your way here in that state, but I'm not convinced you can find it home again."

"Sutton Hall isn't my home."

"Get up, Edward."

"No."

She sighed. There was only one thing for it. She grabbed the sheet and stripped it off the bed. He did not cover himself as she expected him to. Instead, he looked at her and grinned wolfishly.

"Like what you see?" he growled.

"Um…" 'Like' was such an insipid word to describe the effect his nakedness had on her. She couldn't tear her gaze away from his powerful thighs and the thick member resting there.

He cleared his throat. "Let me know when you're finished."

The heat in her face rose, but she would not let him embarrass her. It ought to be the other way round! "It's quite fascinating. I've never seen one before. Thank you for the education."

"Bloody hell." He snatched at the sheet, but she held it out of his reach. "Give me that back."

She took it off the bed completely. "Get up."

He cocked his head to the side and narrowed his gaze. "If you insist." He stood.

How was it that he seemed so much more magnificent *without* clothing? Surely it should be the opposite. He ought to be vulnerable and perhaps even appear smaller in his nakedness. But no. Edward Monk was a man who did not need padded shoulders in his doublet. He was a wonderful specimen of manhood.

"Close your mouth," he said with a lopsided grin.

"Ha. Very amusing."

He went to wash himself but took one look at the water and swore. "Putrid."

Elizabeth angled herself to get a better view of his rear. It was as nicely muscled as the rest of him. The skin looked impossibly smooth, more than any other part of him, including *that* part. She ached to touch the dip in his buttock cheeks.

She sighed. There would be no touching Edward Monk today. He was in a foul mood, possibly still drunk and definitely angry.

"You shouldn't have come here," he said. "This is none of your business."

"I'm making it my business."

He swung round. His gray eyes flashed, his mouth twisted into an ugly sneer. "I don't want you here!"

Eyes up, Lizzie. Don't look down at...that. "I know Arrabella's actions last night hurt you. I know you hoped for a different outcome. But getting drunk and throwing yourself at the White Hart doxies is not going to help you recover."

"Isn't it? How do you know? I actually feel better this morning. Better than I have in *years*. I should have done this a long time ago."

He should have slept with whores? Good lord, had Jeffrey's wine turned him mad?

He came toward her, one slow step at a time, a predatory grin on his face. "Would you rather I threw myself at *you*?"

She swallowed and stepped back. Her thighs hit the bed. She sat on the mattress and stared up at him.

"You would, wouldn't you? Arrabella said you wanted me."

Arrabella said Elizabeth was in love with him. She wanted to point out the difference, but her throat was too tight, and her head woolen. It was quite impossible to talk with Edward standing before her, his arms spread wide, his magnificent body taking up her entire field of vision. Besides, she suspected it would only make her more embarrassed and the situation worse.

"Well, here I am," he said. "Take me."

She wanted to cry, or perhaps slap him across the face to shake him out of this odd mood. She didn't like him like this. He didn't frighten her, but she wanted the gentlemanly man back again. This was not the Edward she knew. He'd changed in a few short hours. What would it take to change him back? What could she say to fix him?

He placed his fists on the bed on either side of her and leaned down. His mouth was inches from hers, their noses almost touching. His grin broadened.

He was going to kiss her. She could see it in his eyes and the tilt of his mouth. She wanted him to kiss her, ached for it.

But not like this. She didn't want to kiss this angry, hurt man. A man who was not hers, but still in love with Arrabella. It would take time for him to recover from the shock of seeing her with Greville, and Elizabeth needed to remember that. Needed to remind herself that he *would* recover. In the meantime, she could be his friend. Nothing more.

She was about to shift away when he kissed her. It wasn't like the sweet kiss they'd shared the night before. It was a battle. He ravaged her mouth, bit her lip—twice—and pushed her back on the bed.

She slapped him. He paused, his face a picture of shock. She rolled off the bed, grabbed the basin of water from the chair and threw it over him.

He coughed and spluttered. "That water was filthy!"

"Good."

He shook out his hair, spraying droplets around the room, over her and his clothes. "I take it you don't want me to kiss you."

She thought about telling him that she wanted his kisses very much, but only if they were sincere and given with love. She didn't think he was ready to hear it.

She picked up his shirt and tossed it to him. "Get dressed. I'll wait for you in the innyard."

Elizabeth left, not expecting him to follow. It didn't matter if she went home without him. The main thing was that she'd found him, and he was safe.

* * *

EDWARD DRIED himself with the bed sheet. It looked cleaner than the cloth draped over the chair back, although considering what had occurred in the bed, perhaps it wasn't. He threw the sheet away and massaged his head, trying to ease the pounding in his skull. It didn't work. A forge had set up residence and wasn't going anywhere for the rest of the day.

Christ. Going by the number of empty wine jugs on the floor, he'd drunk enough to sink a ship. Pity it hadn't obliterated his memory too. He remembered it all, from kissing Elizabeth to seeing Arrabella with Greville, to sleeping with the whores. Three to be exact, although only one had remained the entire night.

So much for his vow to save himself for Arrabella. It was well shattered, along with a few other illusions, chief among them the notion that intimacy between a man and woman was supposed to be sacred. His first proper time—because he couldn't count those early fumbles with girls in his father's barn—hadn't been the event he'd expected it to be. Although it had definitely relieved his frustrations, the relief hadn't lasted. He still felt as tight as a whip, with a deep, unsatisfied ache in his belly.

Why the hell had he waited so long for *that*?

Arrabella, that's why.

He'd been blind. How could he have mistaken her flirtations for love? Women had flirted with him before. He knew it meant nothing. So why did he think she was in love with him?

Because he'd wanted her to, desperately. He'd spent years thinking of her, saving himself for her, bettering himself *for her*. The mere thought that it was for nothing shattered him to the bone.

It was all ruined now. His efforts were wasted, pointless. To make matters worse, he'd treated her sister terribly, both the previous night and in the morning. Last night, he'd wanted Elizabeth in his arms and would have broken his vow readily if they hadn't been interrupted. What sort of man did that? Certainly no *gentleman* would have.

Then this morning, he'd been too embarrassed to look her in the eyes. He couldn't face seeing the disappointment reflected there, or the hurt. She was in love with him, and he had taken advantage of her. Thankfully, she'd shown neither sorrow nor pity when she'd found him in bed with the whore. Her anger was a welcome relief. He deserved it. Perhaps it meant she was cured and no longer in love with him. Who could blame her after what he'd done?

Adding more fuel might keep her anger burning. With the mood he was in, he had fuel in abundance.

He pulled on his shirt, not bothering to lace it, and finished dressing. He buttoned up his jerkin, picked up his belt and strapped it on. No sword. Christ, he must have been drunk when he left the house. He never traveled anywhere without it. Riding at night, alone and unarmed except for a single dagger was indeed foolish. Hughe would be furious if he found out.

Edward headed downstairs and found Lowe in the cellar, inspecting a wine barrel. "What do I owe you?" he asked, opening his pouch.

"Two shillings on account of the girls." Lowe accepted the coins with a lick of his lips. "Good night?"

Edward made to leave.

"Monk in name, not in nature, eh?"

Edward swung round and grabbed Lowe's jerkin at his chest. "What happened in that room last night is my business. If I hear it spread about the village, I'll come looking for you."

Lowe's bushy beard shook as he swallowed heavily. He held up his hands in surrender. "Aye! Aye! It won't come from me or my girls. I know what you did to those Larkham lads when they came for your friend. I want none of that trouble here."

Edward let him go. Whether the slippery eel kept to his word or not would remain to be seen.

He left the cellar and ventured out into the innyard. The bright sunlight stung his eyes. He shielded them and peered toward the stables. Warren the groom from the Hall was there, holding the reins of his and Edward's horses. Elizabeth stood by another horse, stroking its neck. She looked small beside the beast, but not insignificant. There was a presence about her that couldn't be ignored, something powerful and compelling.

She lifted her gaze to his. Her mouth set in a determined line, her eyes willed him to approach and leave with her. He could not look away, even if he wanted to. He did not want to.

A pit opened up in his stomach. Somehow, facing her now was harder than facing her in the chamber. He kept his gaze on her and crossed the yard.

"Good mornin', sir," Warren said, smiling.

He nodded at the lad and took the reins. He was about to mount when Lowe came out of the inn at a limping run. "Wait, wait!" He came up to Edward, his chest heaving with the effort of his sprint.

"What is it?" Edward asked. Bloody hell, did he owe the man more?

"I forgot to ask something when you…" He flattened his jerkin where Edward had grabbed it. "There was a man staying here last night. This morning he asked after a gentleman named Greville. I'd not heard of him, but one of my girls had. Said he stayed the

81

previous night at The Plough." He hawked a glob of spit on the cobbles.

"That's right," Elizabeth said. "Lord Greville is a guest of my cousin's at the Hall. He arrived late in Sutton Grange and stayed the night at The Plough because he didn't want to disturb us at such a late hour."

Lowe frowned. "No, miss, he arrived mid-afternoon, so my girl said."

"Your girl is wrong."

"My girl is never wrong. She knows all that goes on in the Grange."

"Not this time."

Edward held up his hand for silence. He wasn't going to be the one to tell Elizabeth she was wrong. The mood she was in, she'd probably tear his head off. Interesting that Greville had lied about his time of arrival to Lynden and the Buckleys.

"You stopped me from leaving to tell me that?" he asked Lowe.

"No, sir. My girl told the fellow that Greville went up to the Hall yesterday morning. He asked for directions, but since you were returning, I thought you could escort him."

An extra member in their party meant less opportunity to talk to Elizabeth alone. On the other hand, it would be an opportunity to find out more about Greville if the man knew him well. "Fetch him. We'll wait a moment or two."

Lowe limped off.

"Your assistance please, Warren," Elizabeth said, her hand on the sidesaddle pommel. "There are no platforms suitable for a lady to mount here."

Warren handed his horse's reins to Edward. Edward crossed his arms and watched as the skinny lad placed his hands around Elizabeth's waist and hoisted her up. Or tried to. Her feet didn't leave the ground. She didn't appear to weigh much, but the lad hadn't grown into his gangly limbs yet. He was all bone and no muscle.

Warren tried again, turning bright red with the effort. He

managed to lift her off the ground this time, but only an inch. "God's balls!" he exploded as he let her down again.

Elizabeth scowled at him.

"Apologies, miss, but you're heavy."

Elizabeth sighed. "Is there a particular girl you favor by any chance, Warren?"

He appealed to Edward for help in answering the question, but Edward was too intrigued to interrupt. "Er, one of the scullery maids up at the Hall smiles at me sometimes. Betty's her name."

"Then whatever you do, don't ever tell Betty she's heavy, even if she weighs as much as this horse."

Edward bit back a grin. "Would you like me to try, Miss Buckley?"

"For goodness sake, call me Elizabeth. You did yesterday."

His grin vanished. Yesterday their relationship had been on an entirely different footing. Today he wasn't sure how he should act around her. She'd seen—and experienced—far too much of him for everything to remain the same.

She glanced at him sharply. "Let's see if you have better luck. All those muscles should be good for something other than decoration."

"Decoration? Does that mean you like the way my muscles look?" He had the great satisfaction of seeing her blush to the tips of her ears.

"I'm sure some women do," she countered, angling her chin at him. "Shall we ask one of Lowe's girls?"

Bloody hell she had a sharp tongue. Edward wouldn't put it past her to fetch one of the girls and insure his humiliation was complete.

He shoved the reins into Warren's chest. The lad took them and looked away. The pock scars on his face were white against his reddened cheeks.

Edward grabbed Elizabeth hard around the waist and pulled her closer. She let out a little gasp and tensed. He liked the way his hands fit into the dip above the swell of her hips. If he moved them a little higher, he'd be touching her breasts. He could still feel the weight of them in his palm from the previous night, and the taste of her nipples on his tongue.

He stared into her eyes, unable to tear himself away from the bright blue orbs that peered back at him with curiosity and something else. Desire? It hadn't been there moments before when she was spitting words at him. He could feel the tension leave her body. She relaxed into him, drawing closer still so that there was a mere breath of air between them.

He wanted to touch her again the way he'd touched her last night. See more of her bare skin, feel its silkiness sliding against him. Have her hands wrapped around his cock and her gasps of ecstasy in his ear.

And for a brief moment, he thought she wanted it too.

Then something changed. He wasn't sure what. She broke the gaze, and the spell broke too. She did not pull away, nor did she admonish him. Instead, she wrapped her fingers around his upper arms and squeezed his muscles.

"Well," she said, giving him a wicked smile. "It seems they're useful after all. I'm sure all your women will be quite pleased to discover that if they haven't already."

He flinched. Her words stung. For some reason he didn't want her thinking he was a womanizer. He wasn't sure why it bothered him so much.

"I have no women," he said.

Her gaze flicked past him to the covered gallery leading to the guest rooms on the second level. "If you say so. Lift me, please."

He picked her up. Warren must have been even weaker than he appeared, because she was light. He settled her on the saddle, and she rearranged her skirts, but not before he saw her ankles and calves. They were slender, shapely. He wanted to kiss the skin there and work his way up.

He gently took her foot and placed it in the stirrup instead. If his fingers lingered longer than necessary, it was only because he was entranced by the fine bones and the small dips between them.

"Mr. Monk!" Lowe called from the inn door. "He's already gone."

Edward sighed and let her ankle go. He thought he heard Elizabeth sigh too, but he must have been mistaken because she was already talking. *She* seemed to have her wits about her. He was still trying to gather his up from where they'd scattered.

"We didn't see him come out here," she said to Lowe.

"He had no horse," the innkeeper said. "Must have walked or gotten himself a ride on a passing cart."

Edward took back the reins from Warren and mounted. "Do you know what he wanted with Lord Greville?"

Lowe shrugged. "No, sir."

"I'm not sure that's your business," Elizabeth told Edward.

He shot her a scowl. She could be bold when she wanted to be. "Greville and his men are four in number. If they want to cause trouble, they could."

"Why would you think he'd bring problems to the doorstep of his betrothed?"

"I don't. I just like to know everything about the people I'm in close quarters with."

"Are you always this suspicious?"

"Yes."

She turned her horse round and headed out of the innyard. "So your suspiciousness isn't because Greville is going to marry my sister?"

He gripped the reins tighter and followed her. "I can assure you I treat all new gentlemen of my acquaintance with equal suspicion." Hughe had taught him that. The number of gentlemen, and noblemen in particular, who proved to be other than they first seemed was astounding.

"I can assure you, Greville is a good man," she said as he drew up alongside her on road. "We met with him on numerous occasions in London."

"Yet you hardly knew him very long. Mere weeks?"

"Long enough."

"I disagree." He would have liked to tell her his reason for investigating Greville. She was clever and observant. She may have noticed some oddities in his behavior, or some other clues.

She sighed. "Edward, I know she hurt you, but—"

"Don't," he snapped. "Don't speak of her, or them, or what you saw at the White Hart. What's done is done."

"So you won't try to stop them marrying?"

Yesterday, he'd hoped Greville would turn out to be a Catholic, so Lynden would stop the wedding. Today, he didn't care. It would make no difference to him. He'd already lost Arrabella. Her actions on the balcony had proved that beyond doubt. Whether Greville was still around or not wouldn't change the fact. It wouldn't bring her back to Edward. She'd never been his to gain back anyway. She'd known Elizabeth loved him and had not wanted to upset her. She was a good sister with a kind heart. That heart didn't belong to him and never would.

God, it still hurt just as much as it had when he'd watched them together on the balcony. It was a different pain now. Not piercing as it had been then, but more of a constant ache in his chest. He'd lived a lie for *years*. Worse than that, he'd defied a father whose only wish was to have his eldest son work alongside him. Edward had always wondered if that defiance had led to his parents' early deaths. Once they were gone, he'd left Upper Wayworth, determined not to return until he'd made himself into someone worthy of Arrabella. It had been his determination that had kept him strong, kept him believing in himself, kept him hopeful for the future.

Until now. Arrabella wouldn't be his. All that striving, believing and hoping, dashed like a ship on the rocks. What a waste.

He watched Elizabeth's straight back as she rode a little ahead of him out of the village. She held herself well in the saddle. Her spine was straight, her head high. She was in full control of the horse and herself.

He would like to see her lose some of that control. He wanted to make her arch her back to meet him and tilt her head so he could kiss her throat. He wanted her in his arms and his bed. Wanted to hear her beg.

Then after he seduced her, he was going to leave her. She should feel what he now felt. She needed to see that her selfishness had cost him everything.

CHAPTER 7

$\mathcal{T}$he invitation to dine at Stoneleigh arrived while
Elizabeth was in the village. Fortunately, her mother
and sister had kept to their rooms through the morning and not
noticed her absence. She didn't want to tell them about Edward,
and she didn't like to lie either.

Elizabeth wasn't surprised when her mother didn't join the
party headed for Stoneleigh, claiming the heat was too much for
her. It was hot, although not excessively so, and she hated to walk
even in cooler months. The invitation had included Jeffrey,
Greville and Edward too, and all five set off for a stroll across the
fields. Jeffrey had wanted to ride, but Arrabella hated riding. She'd
declared that walking would assist in balancing their humors. Elizabeth suspected she just wanted to fall back with Greville where
they could have a more private conversation.

Unfortunately, Edward didn't let them.

"Did the fellow find you?" he asked Greville. He looked remarkably better than he had when Elizabeth found him that morning in
the whore's bed. He wasn't quite so gray around the jaw, and his
eyes weren't streaked with red lines anymore. She did her best to
ignore him, but it was impossible. For one thing, she simply found
him too handsome *not* to look at, and secondly, she was interested

in Greville's answer. She did wonder if Edward's question was merely a way of disturbing the lovers, but if it was, he made no sign of it. Indeed, he walked alongside Greville, not Arrabella, and did not meet her gaze.

"What fellow?" Arrabella asked.

"I was in the village this morning and heard of a gentleman who wished to see Greville. He left before I could bring him to the house myself."

"No gentleman came this morning," Arrabella said.

"Greville?" he prompted.

"I *said* no gentleman came," Arrabella bit off. "Is my word not good enough for you anymore, Edward?"

Edward slowed and stared at her, then had to extend his stride to catch up. "Perhaps Greville had a visitor while you were still abed. I didn't mean to imply—"

"He would have told me if someone came to see him." She hooked her arm through her betrothed's. "Isn't that right, Greville?"

"Aye, quite right, my angel."

They forged ahead, leaving Edward behind, staring slack-jawed at their backs. Elizabeth walked alongside him.

"You're looking a little pale again," she told him. "The effects of last night coming back to haunt you?"

He shook his head as if flicking off droplets of water, or a bad memory. Still, his gaze did not leave Arrabella and Greville, now several steps in front of Jeffrey who slashed at the long grass with his sword.

"Edward? Are you awake or are you sleep walking?"

He turned to her and she swallowed further taunts. His eyes did indeed look haunted. Perhaps it had something to do with Arrabella's harsh words. He had probably never experienced her cutting remarks.

"Go away," he said and strode off.

She watched him with an ache in her heart. He *would* recover. He just needed time.

* * *

STONELEIGH WAS A PRETTY manor house nestled in the valley. Jeffrey had told Elizabeth that its lands had been more extensive once, but the elderly Mr. Farley had sold much of it off during lean years. His daughter had a passion for growing orange trees in the walled garden, and her new husband had set himself the task of returning the estate to its former glory.

Farley was abed when they arrived, but Orlando Holt met them at the door. He was exceedingly handsome, if one liked boyish dimples and eager smiles. He greeted Jeffrey somewhat coolly, but beamed at Arrabella, Elizabeth and Greville.

When it came to Edward, he slapped him on the shoulder. "I heard you were still here, Monk," he said.

"You can't be rid of me that easily," Edward said.

"Seems we can't be rid of you at all."

Edward grunted out a laugh.

Orlando showed them into the large parlor where his pregnant wife sat with her feet propped up on a low stool. Elizabeth smiled broadly when she saw her. Finally a woman to outshine Arrabella! Even with a swollen belly, Susanna Holt was an extraordinary beauty. However would Arrabella cope not being the brightest star in the sky?

"I'm so very pleased to meet you all," Susanna Holt said with genuine affection. "I only wish I could have paid you a call at the Hall earlier, but…" She rubbed her belly and smiled.

Jeffrey made the introductions, then had to make them all over again as another couple arrived. Lucy Cowdrey and Nicholas Coleclough were the Holts' other neighbors, and good friends. The two women clasped one another's hands, and the men nodded at each other as if proper greetings weren't necessary.

The women sat while the men stood and discussed the latest news from London. Jeffrey swelled with importance. Having just come from the city, he had much to tell. Although Greville had been in London only days before, he remained quiet, stealing glances at Arrabella. He did not seem interested in talking with the men.

"Isn't it wonderful to have more female company in the valley?" Susanna said to Lucy.

"Indeed. Will you be staying long with your cousin?" Lucy asked the sisters.

"Only until my wedding," Arrabella said. "Then Greville and I will return to his home."

"The wedding will be held here?" Susanna asked. "Not at Lord Greville's residence?"

"He said he wants me to be near my family. He's very considerate, and Mother doesn't like to travel."

"Will his family have to come far for the happy event?"

"He has only one younger brother. I've not met him, and I don't think he's coming."

Lucy clapped her hands. "Another wedding! How wonderful. I'm marrying soon too. Perhaps we can compare plans." She cast a wistful glance at the rather large and stern figure of her betrothed. They were such a starkly different couple that Elizabeth was surprised they were a match.

Nicholas Coleclough turned then, as if he could sense Lucy watching him. He smiled at her and his eyes softened. Elizabeth changed her mind. It was obvious that he was completely in love with Lucy, and she him. They were perfect for one another.

"My gown is made from the finest silk," Arrabella said, smoothing down her skirts and giving Lucy a tight smile. Elizabeth knew that smile and hated her sister for what it meant. "And yours?"

"Nothing quite so grand," Lucy said with a laugh. "Fine cloths rarely make their way to Sutton Grange, and I haven't time to order any from London. We want to marry as soon as the banns are read."

"Greville bought me pearls from Goldsmith's Row to wear."

Lucy's gentle eyes twinkled. "How romantic! Pearls will look beautiful against your skin."

Arrabella leaned a little forward as if waiting for a further response. When she didn't get it, she prompted, "And your wedding jewels?"

"I think Nick's father is bringing something for me to wear. He mentioned it when he was here. He returned to Coleclough Hall to fetch them and Nick's other belongings."

"Your betrothed is the *younger* son? He won't inherit the title?"

"That's right. We'll live here on the farm."

Arrabella settled back in her chair and looked down her nose at Lucy. "Greville is the eldest. He inherited last year. It's a great responsibility, but it does give him occasion to attend court. Have you been to court?"

"Good lord, no, and thank goodness for that. I don't think a farmer's daughter would fit in amidst all the other ladies such as yourself and your sister."

"Rest assured, my sister doesn't really fit in either." Arrabella's laugh sounded like a cackle to Elizabeth's ears.

The smiles on Lucy's and Susanna's faces slipped. They both looked away, discomfort etched into the furrows on their brows.

Elizabeth forced out a laugh for the sake of her hostess. What she really wanted to do was cut her sister down to size, but she wouldn't do it in front of such nice people. Ordinarily Arrabella would be as sweet as strawberries. Indeed, she would usually go out of her way to ingratiate herself to them. What had gotten into her? Elizabeth could only think that she felt somehow insignificant in the same room as the pretty Lucy Cowdrey and the beautiful Susanna Holt. If there was one thing Arrabella loathed, it was to be unnoticeable.

"When is your babe due?" Elizabeth asked Susanna, eager to change the subject.

"In another week or two," Susanna said, rubbing her belly again. "Hopefully no more."

"You look radiant with happiness."

Therein followed a discussion about babies, nurseries and

more wedding chatter, but only between the three. Arrabella did not join in.

Their conversation ended abruptly when Lucy suddenly said, "Is something wrong with Monk?" She leaned inward and did not glance in the direction of the men. "He looks very sour indeed. That's not like him."

"You know him well?" Elizabeth asked.

"Well enough that I know this moodiness isn't natural. He's always been a quiet, serious man with deep convictions."

"What sort of convictions?"

"A strong sense of justice for one thing. There some trouble here recently involving Nick, and Monk was a rock to us. He and Hughe were unshakable in their support. I'll always be indebted to him." Her eyes briefly welled with tears before she swallowed and went on. "Yet even through those difficulties, he was agreeable. Nothing like this. What's happened to change him?"

"He's in love with me," Arrabella declared too loudly.

Out of the corner of her eye, Elizabeth saw Edward flinch and Greville stare down at his feet. The other two men shifted their gazes to Edward before looking away.

Susanna laughed. "Surely not."

Arrabella shot her a glare, and Susanna's laughter died. "Oh," Susanna said. "That must be, er, awkward."

"I've tried to tell him that I'm betrothed to a wonderful gentleman, but he hasn't given up hope. I expect he never will. So you see, he's received quite a blow."

Elizabeth couldn't stand to hear any more of her sister's self-indulgent prattle. Arrabella was right, but there was no need to tell his friends. How many more twists of the knife would she give?

Elizabeth rose and went to the window. The garden was pretty, but she hardly saw it. She was too heavy of heart. A moment later, she felt the hair on the back of her neck rise. She turned, and her gaze connected with Edward's. He quickly looked away again and appeared to concentrate on something Orlando Holt said.

93

* * *

"So what have you learned about him?" Cole asked, crossing his arms and leaning his shoulder against the brick wall surrounding the garden. He, Orlando and Edward had separated from the others, claiming an inspection of the orange trees was in order. Realizing that the three men wanted to talk alone, Susanna and Lucy had kept the other guests occupied.

"Aren't you retired?" Edward asked. "Why all the questions?"

"Old habit."

"Not easy leaving the Guild behind, is it?" Orlando said with a lopsided grin in his friend's direction.

Edward, a relative newcomer to the Guild, watched as the two retired members exchanged knowing glances. Then both broke into grins. Edward didn't understand them at all.

"What's so funny?" he said.

"You are," Orlando said. "And Hughe. We had some interesting times with him. I'll miss it."

"Not enough to give up this," Cole said quietly. Of the two of them, his transformation from single-minded assassin to contented lover was the most dramatic. His deep affection for Lucy sometimes made Edward feel like an intruder when he was in their presence. He'd never seen a love like theirs or like Orlando and Susanna's.

"So tell us about Greville," Orlando said. "We'd like to help if we can."

"There's little to tell. One of his men, a fellow named Paxton, prefers giving orders to taking them. There was also a stranger in the village looking for Greville. Greville claims he never saw him, but two of the grooms mentioned a stranger arrived on foot and spoke to Paxton."

"Is it the same man?"

"I don't know. I never saw him."

"Then go into the village and ask around," Orlando said, inspecting a leaf on the nearest orange tree.

"I haven't had the opportunity," Edward ground out. "I had to dine here and play nice."

"You could have asked this morning," Cole said, his grin widening. "He was there early," he told Orlando. "Very early."

Orlando stopped inspecting the leaf and arched a brow. "Doing what?"

"Something you wouldn't expect our *monkish* friend to be doing."

Orlando crossed his arms and his mouth curved into a lopsided smile. "This sounds interesting. Who's taken your fancy?"

"Shut it," Edward snapped.

Cole chuckled. "It wasn't any *one* girl in particular. No less than three of The White Hart doxies at once."

Orlando's mouth fell open. "God's blood, Monk! Lowe's whores? Are you that desperate?"

"Fuck you."

"Clearly *you're* the one who was fucked."

"I can do as I please. I don't answer to either of you, or to Hughe."

"Hughe will probably argue the point," Cole said. "Anyway, I thought you were in love with the Buckley girl?"

"Which one?" Orlando asked.

"The elder. Didn't you hear her announce it?"

"I heard. I just wanted to hear it from his lips. Surely he couldn't be in love with her. The other one's much more his type."

"Considering his type is apparently a whore who can be bought—"

Edward took advantage of Cole's distracted state and punched him in the stomach. Cole expelled a breath but recovered quickly. He swung his fist. Edward ducked, but only just in time.

"Enough!" Orlando stepped between them. "I'll have no fighting here."

Cole apologized and resumed his position of leaning lazily against the garden wall. It was a deceptive stance, Edward knew. There was nothing lazy about Cole. He nodded at Edward. "I didn't think you were so sensitive. It's nothing to be ashamed about."

Orlando agreed. "I'm relieved you went to Lowe's girls. There are several eligible widows in the village who are our friends. Any one of them probably would have accepted you into their beds, but I'm glad you didn't seek them out. If you left behind a collection of broken hearts, it would make our lives uncomfortable."

Christ, this conversation wasn't happening. Edward wished the world would swallow him up and take him away from these two.

Orlando slapped him on the shoulder. "I'm glad you discarded your vow of chastity. It's not natural for a man to go that long without a woman."

Edward glared at Orlando, then switched to Cole. He'd never spoken of his vow to either man.

Cole shrugged. "Hughe and I worked it out after you'd been in the Guild for about a month. You had women flirting with you, yet you paid none of them any attention. It was he who suggested you were saving yourself for one woman in particular."

"So, are you?" Orlando asked.

"Am I what?"

"In love with Arrabella Buckley as she claims?"

"That's none of your affair."

"Don't get too attached. She'll be wed soon."

"Unless Lynden finds something to condemn her betrothed," Cole said. "There's still hope."

Orlando shook his head. "Be careful there, Monk. Be sure she's the one you want. If she is, and she finds out you had something to do with uncovering Greville's unsuitability, she may hate you forever."

"Thank you for the lecture," Edward said on a sneer.

Cole laughed. Edward turned on him. "And you... I preferred you when you were foul tempered and silent. Falling in love has turned you both soft."

Cole straightened to his full height. He was a big brute, with a spine of iron. The man wasn't soft in the least. "It seems to have turned you sour, Monk," he said.

"I'm not in love." Not anymore.

"The Buckley girl would disagree."

Edward bit the inside of his cheek and tasted blood. He'd heard Arrabella's declaration in the parlor. He'd heard a lot of things, including the way she'd tried to make Lucy feel inferior by comparing wedding details. It was a testament to Lucy's happiness that she hadn't noticed.

Elizabeth had. She'd tried to detract her sister from her course and quickly changed the subject at the first opportunity.

Arrabella's behavior had shocked him. He'd never seen her like that, and not known she could be so cruel to someone she'd just met. She'd changed so much in the last five years. The old Arrabella would never have done that.

"What about the other one?" Orlando asked.

"What other one?" Edward said.

"Elizabeth Buckley, Dim-wit. Did her sister get it wrong, and you're actually in love with her?"

"No! Christ. What makes you say that?"

"You couldn't stop looking at her."

Edward blinked at him. Orlando arched his brows, waiting. "I... don't know why I was looking at her." Surely he hadn't been. Perhaps once or twice, but not excessively.

"Does it have anything to do with the fact she collected you from The White Hart this morning?" Cole asked.

"How do you know any of this?"

Cole looked amused, damn him. "I was in the village this morning and saw Milner. He told me all about it. My guess is he saw you leave and asked Lowe."

"That man has a big mouth."

"I think he was more jealous that you went to The White Hart and not The Plough."

"Maybe he needs to get whores," Orlando quipped.

Edward narrowed his eyes at him. "I would hit you if I didn't think Cole would hit me twice as hard."

Cole slapped him on the back. "You'd better be more careful if you don't want your business becoming village gossip."

Orlando nodded. "Go to Larkham if your urges become too much."

"My urges are under control," Edward snarled. And if they were not, there'd be Elizabeth Buckley to relieve them. She seemed willing enough if the previous night was anything to go by, and he was determined to have her. Have her and leave her.

"So what did the Buckley girl think when she had to collect you from The White Hart?" Orlando asked.

"She didn't have to *collect* me, and I told her so."

"Nicely?"

"What do you think?"

Orlando winced. "Did she say anything?"

Edward shook his head and stalked off toward the arched exit. "I'm not discussing this with either of you."

"Moody prick," Cole said.

Despite the dark cloud hanging over his head, Edward smiled. It wasn't that long ago that he was saying the same thing about Cole.

* * *

"Did you see the size of her belly?" Arrabella said. "She's enormous!"

"She's about to give birth!" Elizabeth said. Good lord, could her sister find any more faults with Susanna Holt? So far most had been imaginary, and this one was the most spiteful of the lot.

They walked a little behind the men, out of earshot. Their progress back to the Hall was much slower than before they'd eaten the grand feast. Elizabeth felt a little sleepy from the wine and could have happily napped in one of the fields for a few minutes. The sun was still warm, the soft grass inviting. She yawned and stretched.

Instead, she had to listen to her sister. "Don't disparage Susanna," Elizabeth said. "I liked her and Lucy."

Arrabella sniffed. "I'm not disparaging either of them. I'm merely pointing out a fact. Susanna will never get her shapeliness back after the child is out."

"I'm not sure she cares. She told me she just wants a healthy baby."

"Her husband will care."

Elizabeth had heard enough. She detached herself from her sister and strode ahead to join the men. Greville seemed to take that as his cue to slow down and walk behind with his betrothed. He was welcome to her. Elizabeth wondered if he knew what sort of woman he was taking on. Probably not since she rarely showed that side of herself to anyone. If he'd overheard Arrabella mocking Lucy in the parlor, he would probably put it down to tiredness or some such lapse.

She was surprised when Edward fell into step alongside her. They were alone, Jeffrey having fallen back to admire his meadow.

Edward didn't speak to her at first, although she got the feeling he wanted to say something. They walked several more minutes together in strained silence, before he finally spoke.

"You're tired," he said.

What an odd way to begin a conversation. "A little. Why?"

"I saw you yawn. It wasn't a great leap from there."

"I got little sleep last night."

He stared straight ahead, neither acknowledging the reason why she'd slept so poorly, nor reminding her that he'd had less. It would seem talking about what had happened between them, and afterward, was off the list of potential conversations. She struggled to think of something else to say since he didn't make any further attempts.

"I don't think we should take Arrabella's word that the fellow didn't come to the Hall," she said.

"I don't."

"I don't mean to infer that she's lying, but Greville may not tell her everything. Indeed, did you notice how he let her do all the answering? Very odd, although it's typical of Bella to take over like that. Perhaps he saw no reason to gainsay her."

"Perhaps."

"It might be a good idea to speak to the servants and find out if someone came to the house."

"I already have."

"Oh? Then why did you need to ask Greville at all?"

He said nothing, just continued to walk, keeping apace with her shorter strides.

"Did any of the servants see him?"

"A man did come this morning to speak to Greville."

"And did he?"

"Did he what?"

"Speak to Greville?"

Again, he remained silent.

She sighed. "Full of lively chatter today, aren't you?"

He stopped and rounded on her. She stopped too and squared up to him. His gray eyes flashed and if she didn't know him so well, she would have been a little worried about his temper. "I don't see that it's any of your business."

"I don't see that it's yours either." She fisted her hands on her hips. "Greville is at least almost a member of my family."

"What do you want to prove, Elizabeth? That he's a potential danger? That he's somehow going to cause trouble?"

Her hands dropped to her sides. "I wasn't thinking of trouble, merely finding out who his friends were. What do you know, Edward? Is there a problem with Greville?"

He swore under his breath and strode off. She had to run to catch up. She grabbed his arm and forced him to stop again.

"Edward, tell me what you mean. Why these suspicions? Who do you think the man is, and why won't you tell me what he wants with Greville?"

His eyelashes flickered ever so slightly, but it was enough to know he was about to lie. "You're mistaken. I have no suspicions. Natural curiosity, that's all."

She shook her head. "You know more. I know you do, I can read you."

"You cannot."

She wanted to tell him that she'd had a lot of practice, but didn't think reminding either of them of her love for him was productive to the conversation. She had another thought. "Why are you even here, Edward?"

His shoulders slumped a little. "You want me to go?"

"No! I, uh, it's just that you gave no real reason for staying behind at Sutton Hall when Lord Oxley left."

"I'm keeping an eye on things for my friend, Cole. He was in trouble recently with the Larkham villagers. He might need me."

She had believed it at the time, but not now that she'd seen Nicholas Coleclough in the flesh. "I think your friend is capable of taking care of himself. Not only that, but he has friends of influence, including Orlando Holt, Jeffrey and even Lord Oxley."

He shrugged one shoulder.

"I think you're here for another reason. Something to do with Greville."

He turned and strode off. "Now who's the suspicious one?"

She had nothing to say to that, so kept walking. The more she thought it through, the more suspicious she got, and the more worried. The reason Edward was at the Hall had something to do with Greville and the other man from the village. Edward must have wanted to discover what their connection was and use it to drive a wedge between Greville and Arrabella.

It would seem he was still in love with her and still held hopes of winning by removing Greville from the picture. Arrabella would never be far from his thoughts, ever. She would play a role in everything he did, every decision he made.

Her lower lip wobbled. She bit it and tasted blood.

"Elizabeth?" His voice was so soft she almost didn't hear him. He stared at her sore lip, a small crease joining his brows.

"Yes?"

He cleared his throat and looked straight ahead. "I wanted to ask you if I could come to your rooms later. After supper. Before bed. That is, before you retired for the night. That's if you're not tired or—"

She tripped over something, perhaps her own feet. Edward caught her before she fell and steadied her. For one brief moment his intense gaze settled on her, pinning her to the spot. She saw desire in it, but something else too. He was uncertain. But of what? Her answer?

"Yes," she murmured quickly before her nerves fled, and she changed her mind. "Come to me tonight."

CHAPTER 8

The maids knew nothing about a stranger coming to see Greville, so Elizabeth went in search of Warren. She found the groom sitting on a stool near one of the stall doors, oiling a saddle. The scents of oil, leather and horse filled the warm, dense air of the stable block.

"Mistress Buckley, ma'am. Are you requesting a horse for tomorrow?"

"No, Warren, I've come to ask you a question, although I'm not sure you can help."

He beamed. "Sure I can, ma'am."

"Do you recall this morning when Mr. Lowe informed us that one of his guests wanted to see Lord Greville?"

The horse in the stall shifted, rustling the straw strewn across the floor. Elizabeth glanced around, but no one was nearby. She wasn't sure if she should be concerned about being overheard, but she'd prefer to be safe, just in case Greville was hiding something he didn't want Arrabella's family to discover. Yet merely thinking it seemed absurd. He was such a nice gentleman. What could he be hiding? Surely the stranger's reason for speaking to him was something quite innocent.

"Aye," Warren said. "I r'member."

"Do you know if he made it up to the Hall?"

His eyes brightened. "I can answer that!"

"Go on then."

"He arrived on foot after we got back. Not sure why we didn't see him on the road." He shrugged. "Maybe he hadn't left the Grange before us like we thought. Anyways, he asked to see Lord Greville."

"And did he speak to his lordship?"

"No, ma'am, he spoke to his lordship's man, Mr. Paxton."

Paxton? "Do you know what they discussed?"

"Not 'spifically. The traveler looked to be arguing with Paxton and pointing at the house. I think he wanted to talk to Greville only and Mr. Paxton refused to fetch him."

"Do you know if Lord Greville ever did speak to him?"

"I don't think so. He got scared, see."

"What do you mean?"

"Mr. Paxton pushed the fellow in the chest then tried to snatch his pack. It was like he was tryin' to get somethin' that the other man had in there. Paxton would have punched him I reckon if Mr. Umberley, the land steward, hadn't stepped in. The traveler ran off. Mr. Paxton called after him to stop, but he just kept runnin'."

"The poor man. Do you know where he went?"

"No, ma'am. Just ran back down the drive, he did."

"Thank you, Warren, you've been most helpful. Just one more question. What did he look like?"

"Longish dark hair tied back, eyes as black as night and dressed like a gen'leman in need of new clothes."

She'd seen someone matching that description in Lowe's dining room, eating breakfast. She had to tell Edward. He would already have learned the same things she had from Warren, but he'd not seen the fellow at The White Hart. He couldn't identify him. She could.

She hurried back to the house, but paused before racing up the stairs. It was suppertime, and Edward was coming to her rooms soon. In her eagerness, she'd forgotten how confused he'd left her after their walk back from Stoneleigh. She was sure he desired her, yet he also wanted Greville out of the picture so he could pursue Arrabella. Perhaps she shouldn't give him more ammunition against the man.

On the other hand, if there was something about Greville that the family ought to know, it would be better to work with Edward than separately.

She made up her mind to discuss the situation with him when he came to her. Should that be before or after he seduced her?

* * *

EDWARD DIDN'T NEED a candle to find Elizabeth's rooms. He knew his way around Sutton Hall, and there was just enough moonlight coming through the windows to illuminate furniture. He entered her small parlor and tapped on the adjoining bedchamber door. She opened it immediately.

He wasn't sure what he'd been expecting her to wear. Perhaps only her nightshift, or a housecoat to cover her nakedness. Not the same clothes she'd worn during the day. Weren't ladies' outfits held together with pins? What if he missed one as he helped her undress, and she got pricked?

"Good evening," she said, stepping aside.

He checked behind him, but there was nobody about. It was late and the entire household had already retired for the evening. He slipped into her room and she shut the door behind him.

They stood some distance apart and didn't speak. He tried to think of something appropriate to say, but everything sounded trite in his head. He wasn't good at flirting. He wasn't good at speaking to women he was about to seduce at all. The sum total of his experience was zero. Last night didn't count. He'd not had to do any talking let alone seducing.

"Would you like some wine?" she finally asked, resting her hand on the jug handle.

"Is it the same stuff as last night?"

Her eyes brightened with amusement. "No."

"Then yes, I would." He needed some fortifying, but not to the extent of their previous encounter. His drunkenness of that evening was better left forgotten, as well as the events afterward.

If he thought about where he'd gone, what he'd done and the look on Elizabeth's face when she saw him in the morning, he wouldn't be able to proceed with the seduction. Recalling his humiliation would only dampen his desire, and he didn't want to do that.

If he was to go through with this, he needed that desire to over-come his reservations. That and the wine. Perhaps he should have fetched a jug of the stronger stuff after all.

He accepted the cup and drained it in one gulp.

She took a sip of hers and watched him over the rim. "You don't drink in half-measures."

He set the cup down but refused her offer of a refill. "That should be enough," he said.

"Enough for what?"

"To, uh, quench my thirst."

"Oh. For a moment there I thought you needed it to settle your nerves." She gave him a fleeting, uncertain smile.

Something tugged at his insides. This confident, accomplished woman was as nervous about the encounter as he was. What a relief! His humiliation would have been unbearable if she were more experienced.

He took hold of her cup to take it out of her hands, but she clutched it tighter. "You have to let it go if you are to undress," he said.

"Um...Edward, we need to talk first."

"I prefer not to." He didn't want to risk changing her mind. He didn't want to risk changing *his* mind. He wanted her. He wanted to be with her, touch her, and feel what it was like to claim a woman who wasn't paid.

Yet…

Christ. He shouldn't be doing it. It was all so very wrong. He wasn't the type of man who ruined the reputations of young ladies.

Fuck.

He poured himself another cup of wine and drank it all. "Elizabeth—"

"No, me first. I need to tell you about the man from the village."

She wanted to discuss his work? So much for thinking she wanted him. First he'd gotten Arrabella wrong, and now Elizabeth. He didn't know how to read women *at all*.

"Are you all right?" she asked. "You look a little ill. Do you need to sit down?"

"No."

She inspected the jug. "Perhaps you shouldn't have any more wine."

"It's not the wine."

"But there *is* something?"

He sighed. "What did you wish to tell me about the fellow?"

"I asked Warren if he'd seen him here."

"You did *what*?"

"Shhh. Mother's rooms are next to mine."

He dragged his hands through his hair. "Elizabeth, why did you speak to him?"

She shrugged. "Why not? I was as curious as you to learn if the fellow ever reached the Hall."

"You shouldn't have asked."

Her gaze narrowed. "Why not?"

He said nothing. Sometimes remaining silent was the only way a man could stay out of trouble where women were concerned. Particularly this woman. She was much too observant. She would easily catch him out in a lie.

"What are you not telling me, Edward? Who is the man?"

"I don't know."

"But you do have suspicions. Tell me. I need to know if my family will be affected."

He strode to the fireplace and leaned a hand on the mantel. He stared down into the clean grate. There was no fire tonight. The evening was warm. A gentle breeze drifted through the open window, cooling his heated face.

Behind him, Elizabeth sighed. "Very well. Since I'm not quite so stubborn as you, I'll tell you what I learned. The man from the village has something that he wanted to deliver to Greville, but he never did. Paxton wanted it, but the stranger wouldn't give it up and they almost came to blows."

He knew all of that. "And?"

"And I think we need to find out what he wanted to deliver."

"We?" He laughed and turned around. She stood closer than he'd realized, her arms crossed over her chest. Her bust swelled delectably above the bodice. He swallowed hard. What were they talking about again?

She cocked her head to the side. A smile played on her lips and the candlelight danced in her eyes. She was enjoying herself. "We need to find the man and search his belongings."

"And how do you propose *I* do that?"

"*We* could ask at the inns in Sutton Grange."

He crossed his arms too and took a step toward her. "That sounds like man's work."

"Nonsense. Women are quite capable of talking."

"A truer word was never spoken."

Her smile finally broke out. "Do you agree to let me come along?"

"No. Absolutely not. Why should I?"

"Because I can identify him."

He straightened to his full height. He hadn't been aware he'd bent down to her level. "You can?"

"I saw him in The White Hart when I came for you." Her gaze slid away from his, thankfully. He didn't want her to see his heating face at the reminder of that morning.

"What does he look like?" he asked.

"Dark hair tied back, dark eyes."

"That describes any number of men. Did he have other distinguishing features?"

"He dressed like a gentleman, although his clothes looked well worn. I think he may have fallen on hard times. We already know he doesn't have a horse."

A good observation indeed. He nodded, impressed.

"What do you think he wanted to give to Greville?" she asked.

He lifted one shoulder. "I don't know."

"Come now, Edward, tell me. You must have some idea. I know you're already suspicious about Greville."

"I swear to you that I don't know what it is." At least he didn't have to lie about that.

"Very well. I believe you." She sighed. "So we're agreed that we'll go into the village tomorrow and ask if anyone has seen him."

"I've agreed to no such thing."

She took a step closer. "There can be no harm in it."

She had no idea. But he didn't want to warn her away. That would only pique her curiosity more. He suspected that a curious Elizabeth Buckley was a dogged one. His only hope was to leave without her knowledge.

Speaking of leaving… "I must go," he said, moving to pass her.

She blocked his exit. "Already? But…" She bit her lip.

"I changed my mind about…that." He sighed without meaning to, then lifted his gaze to see if she'd heard it.

She gave him a small smile. "You can't leave until you agree to let me go with you."

"Is that a joke?"

"No."

He moved left to go around her. She moved left too, blocking him. He shifted right. She shifted right. "Elizabeth! Don't make me pick you up and bodily remove you."

She crossed her arms. "Promise me."

"No."

She widened her stance and arched a brow. Bloody-minded woman. He placed his hands on her waist and stepped closer to get better leverage. Familiar sensations shot through him, arrowing to his groin. He'd had a similar reaction when he'd assisted her to mount her horse in the innyard.

He did not move her aside. What man would want to let go of a soft, beautiful woman? Not he.

There was something intoxicating in her smoky eyes as she tipped her head back to look up at him. Her eyelashes lowered. Her lips parted. Her deliciously plump chest rose and fell above her bodice in time with her erratic breathing.

He wanted to touch her skin, feel its warmth. Feel her. But what if she didn't want him to?

It didn't matter, because he was *compelled* to touch her. He had to. He lowered his head and pressed his mouth to the swollen flesh. Her breath hitched.

She did not move away.

She touched his head, gently holding him to her breast. He took that as a sign and kissed the deep valley between the two mounds.

She groaned and arched her back, pushing herself into him. He couldn't get enough of all that creamy skin. He wanted to feel her against him. He wanted to lick every part of her, nip the rosy tips of her nipples, hear her sigh his name.

Last night, drunk to his eyeballs, he'd freed her breasts from the confines of her bodice. But now he wasn't sure if he should repeat the move. Had she enjoyed being on display like that? Being touched by him there?

He was too damned sober. Being sober meant thinking, and he definitely didn't want to think. For years, all he'd done was think. Think about Arrabella. Think about what it would be like to bed her. Think about *not* taking other women.

Now, he just wanted to feel.

"Oh, Edward," she murmured.

He paused. He'd never heard his name said in quite that way.

Breathy. Eager. It filled his chest, his head, made his own breath come quicker. Made his cock hard.

She wanted him.

He wanted her. Every piece of him ached for her touch.

"Kiss me," she whispered.

He knew how to kiss. This part he could do. He brought his mouth down on hers. Her lips were soft and plump, like her breasts. They trembled against his, uncertain. He touched his tongue to her mouth and she opened for him instinctively.

She tasted of sweet wine and roses, and something more delicious that was all Elizabeth. Something that broke him into little pieces and clouded his mind. Something subtle in flavor that threatened to overwhelm him, swallow him whole.

His body hummed, and his skin felt like it was on fire. He was hot all over. Hard. So hard for her.

She removed his hand from her cheek and cupped her breast with it. His fingers clawed at her bodice, desperate to free her from the tight confines. Desperate to lick her nipple.

"Take me," she urged him.

He pulled back and studied her face. Her cheeks were flushed. Her skin shone. Her eyes were closed, but she reopened them. Her gaze connected with his, and he could swear she looked into his soul. Did she see his desire? His need?

His fears?

"I want you to take me," she murmured.

He swallowed heavily. Did she mean on the bed, or here, standing up? That might be awkward.

Stop thinking!

She tugged at the laces of her bodice, never taking her eyes off his. She removed the two pieces of her outer clothing and set them on the table. Her perfect round breasts pushed against the fabric of her shift. The dark circles of her nipples were clearly visible beneath the thin linen. If he touched one, would it harden? He wanted to tease it to find out. Lick it, suckle it and nip it with his teeth.

His groin ached. His cock throbbed. Being so close to her was sheer torture on his body. His mind wasn't holding up too well against the onslaught either.

"I need help." Her voice was small, hesitant. She blinked up at him and he stared dumbly back.

"Help?" he echoed.

"There are pins at the back of my skirt. Would you—"

He stepped away and put up his hands. Her eyes widened as she registered what he was doing. Or rather, what he *wasn't* doing. He wasn't undressing her.

"We must stop." His voice cracked. He cleared his throat. "This is wrong."

Then why did it feel right?

She crossed her arms over her chest. Despite the poor light, he could see her face blush. She blinked rapidly. "Oh. I thought you wanted this."

Hell and damnation *yes*.

"I…that is…you're an innocent."

She tilted her chin ever so slightly, defiant in the face of her confusion. He liked that. He'd like to take that chin in hand and force her lips to part in a kiss for him too, but that wasn't going to happen. Not now that he'd come to his senses.

"Since when does that stop a man?" she asked.

Since that man didn't know what he was doing.

"Is it because of Arrabella?" she said.

"Arrabella?"

"My sister. You still love her."

He sat heavily in the chair. "No." It felt like a weight left his shoulders. A weight he didn't even know he'd been carrying around. *He didn't love Arrabella anymore.* Seeing her behavior at Stoneleigh had opened his eyes to her true nature. She was narcissistic, petty and vain. He didn't want to spend five minutes alone in her company now, let alone a lifetime.

Elizabeth grunted and turned away. She didn't believe him.

"I admit that my intentions in coming here tonight weren't honorable," he said. "I wanted to seduce you as a way of punishment. I was angry and upset. It stopped me thinking rationally. I'm sorry."

"You're talking in riddles. Why did you want to punish me?"

"For your role in keeping Arrabella and I apart."

She swung round to face him. He liked the way the movement made her breasts jiggle beneath the thin fabric of her shift. Liked it so much he couldn't stop staring at them.

"Kindly look me in the eye and not at my bosom when you tell me something like that."

He shifted his gaze to her face, even though his own cheeks burned. Her eyes flashed darkly.

"What do you mean I kept you apart?" she pressed.

"Arrabella never considered me as a suitor because of you. She knew you were in love with me—"

"Wait. She knew no such thing until two days ago."

"Two days!"

"She wasn't in love with you *before* she learned of my feelings, Edward. Do not place the blame for her rejection at my feet."

He cocked his head to the side and regarded her. She seemed in earnest. There was no mocking smile, no hint that she lied to save herself from humiliation. It seemed Arrabella had never loved him because, well, she just hadn't.

Elizabeth picked up the two pieces of her bodice. "As to me being in love with you, that was a childish infatuation. It's over now."

He eyed the bodice. "Then this…"

"This is a seduction, nothing more. I want you to seduce me."

He swallowed heavily. "Why?"

She threw her arms wide, making her breasts wobble again. "Because I want you to! You're a man. Do you need a reason?"

"Yes."

"Then here's one." She set the pieces of the bodice down on the table and approached him slowly, like a cat slinking up to its prey.

She placed her hands on the arms of the chair, trapping him. "I will never marry."

"You may one day."

"Don't," she snapped. "Don't say that I might, or that I couldn't know that, because I do. I will die a shriveled-up maid. Before I do, I want to experience everything life has to offer, including what it feels like to have a man. I choose you."

Edward couldn't tear his gaze away from her. Her face was set like stone, her mouth flat and hard. Even with anger sizzling just below the surface, she was not only beautiful, she was intriguing. The way her lips curved in a Cupid's bow and kicked up at the edges. The way her eyebrows didn't quite meet in the middle when she frowned. The way her nose wrinkled when she was thinking.

"Seduce me, Edward." Her breath whispered across his skin like a warm summer breeze. "Help me feel like a woman. Teach me the pleasures of the flesh."

"Teach." He slurred the word like a drunkard. "Me. Teach you?" He wanted to laugh, but no sound came out. He sat there, frozen to the chair, and stared at her earnest, innocent face.

Then it fell into place. She didn't know his first proper time had been last night. It hardly counted either because the women had taken charge, not him. He couldn't even remember all of it.

Hell.

"Edward?" She blinked at him and straightened.

"Your reputation…" he tried.

A shadow of relief passed over her face. "I don't care about it. We'll be careful, if that's what you're worried about. You must know some tricks that will stop me producing a child."

"Tricks?"

She shrugged, and her shift slipped, revealing one delectable shoulder. He stared at it, wanting to kiss her there.

"Don't men know things like that? You must, otherwise you'd all have bastards running around the country, and— Edward? You've gone quite pale. What is it?"

"Nothing," he muttered, standing. Nothing but utter humiliation when she learned his knowledge was as limited as her own.

"I'm offering myself to you. Why won't you—?"

"I can't." He forced himself to look away. It was easier to walk out when he couldn't see her. "I must go. Good night."

He strode past her and did not look back. He didn't want to see the hurt in her eyes when she thought she was the only woman he'd ever rejected. But how could he explain it to her without sounding like a fool? Better to be a cur than that.

CHAPTER 9

" *L* izzie! What are you still doing abed?" Arrabella's shrill voice pierced Elizabeth's skull.

Elizabeth pulled the covers over her head.

Arrabella wrenched the covers down and clicked her tongue. "Get up, Lazy Lizzie."

"Leave me alone." *I want to wallow.*

"I need you."

"Do you need me to fetch something, or mend something? Or perhaps your hair doesn't sit perfectly, and only I can fix it."

"Well, aren't we feeling superior today? My maid is perfectly able to do my hair."

Elizabeth groaned and tried to grab the covers again, but her sister held them back. "What do you want, Bella?"

"I want you to help me look for Greville. I can't find him."

"Did you lose him playing hide and seek?"

Arrabella crossed her arms and gave Elizabeth a cold glare. "Very amusing. Now get up, or I'll throw water over you."

Elizabeth had no choice but to give in. When her sister got in this mood, there was no avoiding her. "Can I at least break my fast first?"

"Bring some bread with you."

"Where are we going?"

"To look for Greville of course! Honestly, you are acting particularly thick this morning. What's gotten into you?"

The question should have been *'who'd* gotten into her?' The answer was nobody. That was the problem. Everything Elizabeth had ever learned about men's needs pointed to the fact that a willing woman was never turned away. It would seem she was unique in that regard. What was wrong with her? She washed regularly. She had good teeth, and while her figure wasn't as luscious as her sister's, she was neither too fat nor too thin.

She eyed Arrabella. *She* was the reason Edward hadn't taken the opportunity presented to him last night. He was still in love with her.

Elizabeth wanted to bury her face in the pillow and stay in bed all day, but her sister was having none of it.

"Stop being selfish, Lizzie. I need you."

"Why can't you look for Greville yourself? Why does it have to be me?"

"Because you can ride, I can't."

"You can, you just don't like to because you look awkward on a horse. The only reason you look awkward is because you never bothered to practice."

Arrabella grabbed Elizabeth's ankles and dragged her toward the end of the bed. Elizabeth shrieked and kicked. She had the great satisfaction of connecting with Arrabella's elbow.

Arrabella let go to rub it. "It's mid-morning, Lizzie. Would you like to be known as the sister who was too lazy to get out of bed? That's the way you're headed, my girl. The maids are already gossiping."

Elizabeth knew it was a trick to get her up, but it worked. The thought of being considered as lazy as her sister filled her with horror. She sighed and climbed out of bed. Arrabella shot her a smirk of triumph.

"There's no need for the self-righteous satisfaction," Elizabeth said. "I'm only getting up because I'm hungry." And because she knew that lying in bed would only give her the time and peace to think about Edward's rejection. Looking for Greville would help take her mind off her humiliation. She wanted to speak to him anyway. If she could find out before Edward what the traveler had wanted with him, it would give her some satisfaction.

"Why do you wish me to find Greville?" she asked as she pulled on a clean shift. "Why not wait until he returns?"

Arrabella plopped down on the bed, all the fight having left her. Something inside Elizabeth twisted at the sight of her sister's troubled frown. "Something's wrong. I don't know what, but a woman can see when her man is troubled."

"Have you tried asking him what it is?"

"He told me it's not woman's business."

Elizabeth sighed. If she ever did marry, it would not be to a man who thought her unable to cope with financial or other masculine matters. Of course, finding a man like that would be rarer than stumbling across treasure.

If Greville had given Arrabella that response, then he probably hadn't told her about the traveler coming to the Hall. Elizabeth wouldn't tell her either. Arrabella would only worry more.

Elizabeth fetched a blue bodice and the gray sleeves from her trunk. They went well together, particularly when matched with the gray overskirt. The outfit was a simple arrangement with few of the embellishments of the one she'd worn the day before to the Holts'. This day seemed like it would be quite a different sort of day, and she needed something more appropriate for riding. She put on a single underskirt then the overskirt that required no forepart or other pieces.

"Help pin me, will you?" she said, turning her back to her sister.

Last night she'd asked the exact opposite of Edward. He'd refused. Her face heated at the memory. She closed her eyes and shut it out. Shut *him* out. "Ouch! You stuck me!"

"Stop moving," Arrabella scolded, grabbing Elizabeth's hip and pulling her closer.

"I didn't move. You did that on purpose."

"There." Arrabella spun Elizabeth around. "Hand me the bodice."

Elizabeth passed her the two pieces and lifted her arms. Arrabella seemed to enjoy lacing her up extra tight, but Elizabeth hated the way it pushed her breasts up. "If you'd like me to breathe, then loosen it a little."

"It looks better when it's tighter."

"But it feels more comfortable when it's looser."

Arrabella clicked her tongue and loosened the laces. "You'll never get a husband if you don't display those beauties."

"I'd like a man to like me for me, not for my breasts."

Arrabella snorted. "And I'd like to be a princess. Neither of us will get our wish."

"Men *are* capable of looking beyond the obvious to the woman underneath."

"Name one such man."

Elizabeth chewed her lip, but eventually gave up with a shrug. "Are you implying that Greville likes you for your figure and not your soul?"

"Greville loves me. I don't care how he fell into that state, but I suspect it wasn't my sparkling wit or my soft heart that trapped him."

Elizabeth laughed. "True words."

Arrabella pulled a lock of her sister's hair. "There's no call for your superiority, thank you."

"I'm not being superior."

"You are. You think because you're smarter than me that you're better. Well, Little Sister, I have news for you. Gentlemen don't like clever girls. They like pretty ones. And while you may be pretty, you're also too clever for most. You show up their own lack of wit, and no man likes that. So take my advice, play up your prettiness and close your mouth unless it's to kiss. Every man likes a girl who kisses him willingly, and is prepared to do more, even before they're wed."

"Not all of them." Edward for example. At least, only where

119

Elizabeth was concerned. She was quite sure if Arrabella had offered herself to him last night he'd have grasped the opportunity.

Arrabella gave her a sharp look. "What do you mean?"

Elizabeth ignored her. "Help me with my hair."

"Forget your hair. We've wasted enough time. It looks lovelier loose anyway." She fetched Elizabeth's riding boots from the hearth. "Put your boots on and be off. It grows late."

"You really are worried about him, aren't you?"

Arrabella sighed. "He's been acting odd since yesterday morning, and every time I ask him why, he closes up. I haven't even seen him today, and that itself is unusual. He likes to eat breakfast with me in the mornings and…" She cleared her throat as a blush crept across her cheeks. "He wouldn't normally leave without speaking to me. But he left no note, no word, nothing."

Elizabeth sat on a chair and pulled on her boots. "Is Mr. Paxton with him?"

"Yes. The grooms said they rode out with their other two men earlier today."

"Then I'm sure nothing is wrong."

"Nevertheless, I'd like you to find out. I would have asked Jeffrey, but he's useless, and Edward can't be found either."

Elizabeth's head jerked up. "He's not here?"

"The grooms said he rode out some time after Greville and his men left."

"Did he go in search of them perhaps?"

Arrabella gave her a curious look. "Why would he do that?"

"Uh, no reason." Elizabeth stood and strapped her girdle around her waist. Her sister left, and she went to follow, but remembered something. "Just a moment." She found the sketch she'd done the night before while lying awake after Edward left. She rolled it up and tucked it into the pouch attached to her girdle.

The sisters parted on the landing, and Elizabeth headed down to the kitchens where she grabbed a hunk of bread. She'd finished it by the time she reached the stables.

"Warren, prepare a horse for me, please," she directed the lad.

"Going for a ride alone, ma'am?"

"I think so. Do you know in which direction Lord Greville's party headed?"

He blinked slowly. "You too, eh?"

"Me too what?"

"You're the third one to ask me that question."

"Who else has asked?"

His mouth twisted and he screwed up his nose. "Not sure I should say. One of 'em said not to tell you."

She regarded him levelly. "Said not to tell *me* specifically?"

"Aye."

How odd. "Let me guess. One of the people who asked after Greville was my sister."

"Aye."

"And the other doesn't want me to know he's looking for Lord Greville?"

He shuffled his feet, kicking up straw.

"I think it must be Mr. Monk." There could be no one else who didn't want her to follow him. He'd already ordered her to stop asking about Greville's visitor. Going by the way Warren wouldn't meet her gaze, she'd guessed correctly.

"You don't have to answer," she told him. "I wouldn't want you to break a confidence. Can you tell me in which direction he rode?"

He shook his head.

"Can you tell me in which direction Lord Greville rode then?"

"Aye. His party took the village road."

"Thank you. I'm heading into the village to do some shopping today too as it happens. I'll need some assistance with my packages. Will you come?"

He beamed. "Yes, ma'am!" He raced off into the stables and returned some minutes later with a horse equipped with a side saddle and another for himself.

They arrived in Sutton Grange a short time later. The village hummed like a busy hive as servants and housewives tried to finish their transactions before the heat of the day became too intense. Elizabeth received more attention than her last visit. Being a little later in the morning, there were more people about. Some nodded greetings or smiled, while others openly gawped. Children patted the horses or shyly touched the fabric of her skirt before being called away by their mothers.

"The chandler here's the place to go if you want candles or lamps, miss," Warren said, pointing at a shop with clean windows and swept stoop. "Mr. Lane and his wife are good people. Then there's the apothecary next door, but mind he don't overcharge you. If it's haberdashery you want, then Jolimont is your man."

She tuned him out and surveyed the immediate vicinity. If she were Greville and in search of the traveler, she would head to one of the inns. Since he'd been last seen in The White Hart, she urged her horse in that direction.

"Ma'am?" Warren called after her. "Where are you going? The shops are here."

"I wish to quench my thirst in the Hart."

"Er, try The Plough. It's closer and cleaner."

"Perhaps afterward."

"Afterward?" he choked out. "But—"

"Thank you, Warren. There's no need for protests. I know what I'm doing."

That shut him up, but his poor head looked like it would explode with the effort of not arguing. He glowed as red as a furnace.

The Hart was further down the street, and they had to pass The Plough to get to it. She looked through the larger inn's arched entranceway and was surprised to recognize Edward's horse in the yard beyond, tethered to a post.

"On second thoughts, we will go to The Plough." She steered her horse through the archway and dismounted in the yard. "Stay here." She handed the reins to Warren. "I won't be long."

"Are you sure you don't want me to come, ma'am?" he called after her.

"Quite sure, thank you."

The ostler tipped his cap in greeting. "Good morning, ma'am."

"Good morning. I'm looking for Mr. Monk. Is he inside?" If Edward had already found Greville or the traveler, then she would kick herself for not riding faster. She wasn't sure why she wanted to beat him, she just knew that she did. Perhaps it was pride, or even petulance. It didn't matter. All that mattered was showing Edward up at *something*.

Oh, and finding out what it was the traveler wanted with Greville too of course. Elizabeth really did believe that the only people who had her family's best interests at heart were family, and Edward was not.

"In the taproom, ma'am. Take that door there. It leads right in."

"Is he with anyone?"

"Just Milner, ma'am, the keep."

She let out a breath. So it would seem he hadn't found Greville or the traveler yet. She thanked the ostler and headed through the door to the taproom. It was too early for most drinkers, and the room was quiet. It was a cozy space with dozens of tables and stools, low ceiling beams, and a long bar. A serving girl scattered herbs on the floor rushes, and two aged men sat snoring in different corners.

Edward stood at one end of the bench, talking to an older man. He had to be Milner, the innkeeper. Edward's back was to the bar, something that struck Elizabeth as strange. Most would face one way or the other, their elbow resting on the surface, but Edward stood looking into the room. Then she realized why. From that position he could see who came through the front door leading to the street, as well as the door she'd just used. The only place he couldn't see was behind the bar itself.

He turned to her fully, and the look of surprise on his face was worth a thousand pounds. "What are you doing here?" he asked.

"Good morning, Edward," she chirped. "What a pleasant circumstance to meet you here."

"Aye, of course, but…" He coughed. "Are you looking for me?"

"Good lord, no. Why would I want to do that?"

Milner laughed then pressed his lips together to smother it. He eyed Edward carefully as if he were a little afraid of offending him, then scampered away, but only so far as the other side of the bar and still within hearing distance. He set about drying a jug.

Edward paid him no mind. He crossed his arms and smirked at her. "What are you doing here, Elizabeth?"

"If you ask Warren, I'm shopping."

"I'll be talking to Warren. I told him not to tell you where I went."

"There you go again, assuming that I'm here looking for you. You should never assume anything, Edward."

He arched a brow. "Clearly not. So what are you doing here? And do *not* tell me you wanted a drink."

"I'm looking for Greville and the other man, of course."

He took several moments to answer, and when he spoke, his voice was a low hum. "Elizabeth, we discussed this. Leave that business to me."

"What business, Edward?" She matched his quiet voice with her own. She suspected he didn't want the eavesdropping Milner to overhear. That only intrigued her more. "What do you know about Greville that you're not telling me? Why is the mysterious visitor looking for him?"

He expelled a measured breath and searched the ceiling.

"I doubt you'll find the answers up there," she said.

"No, but perhaps Milner has some patience hidden in the beams. You, Elizabeth Buckley, are a very trying woman."

"So I've been told."

She waited, but Edward merely watched her from beneath half-lowered lashes. She waited some more and was finally rewarded with cracks in his steely facade. He swore softly and rubbed his hand over his jaw.

"If last night had ended differently, would you be torturing me today?" he asked.

A tiny stab at her heart proved that she wasn't yet recovered from his rejection. "We shall never know, shall we?" She would not let him see how he'd hurt her. Whatever pride she had left had to be fiercely protected.

"Elizabeth," he murmured. "I am sorry for—"

"Don't. I don't wish to discuss it. It's over, forgotten and buried. Let's leave it there."

He nodded once then pushed off from the bar. "I cannot stay here any longer. Are you all right to make it back to the house on your own?"

"Stop treating me like a child, Edward."

He sighed.

"I have Warren with me," she said. "I'll be quite all right, thank you. Good day."

"Good day, Elizabeth." He eyed her curiously when she didn't move. "You're not leaving yet?"

"No. I haven't even begun my business."

"So…you really didn't come here looking for me?"

"No!" She opened her pouch and removed her sketch of the stranger. "I'm going to ask the innkeeper if he recognizes this man."

Edward studied the parchment. "You did a drawing of him?"

"I thought it would make my enquiries easier if I could show a picture instead of simply describing him."

"Then why didn't you give it to me? It would have been helpful."

"If you hadn't left in such a hurry last night perhaps I could have done it for you then."

"I thought we agreed not to speak of last night."

He was so exasperating! "Excuse me. I need to show this to the innkeeper."

"Allow me." He held out his hand for the parchment.

She put it behind her back and tilted her chin. "It's mine."

"Aye, but I'm a friend of Milner's, and this is not something you should involve yourself in."

"It would seem we're faced with the same issues as yesterday. This is my family's business, not yours, Edward. You never did answer me satisfactorily when I asked you *why* you are concerning yourself with this matter."

"The stranger and Paxton almost came to blows yesterday, and that isn't good for the harmony of the household. I want to get to the bottom of their association before anybody gets hurt. Besides, your family, and I have always been close. I want to protect you."

She snorted. Prevent Arrabella from marrying Greville more likely.

"Haven't you already asked the innkeeper about the stranger anyway?" she pressed.

"Aye, and he didn't know of whom I spoke. Perhaps the sketch will help. Few travelers come to Sutton Grange without Milner noticing them, even if they never make it to The Plough."

"Mr. Milner!" She beckoned the innkeeper, and he pretended to be surprised, although she knew he'd been listening in.

"Aye, ma'am? Can I get you something?"

She showed him the sketch. "Do you recognize this man?"

"He's the fellow I mentioned," Edward added, looking over her shoulder.

Milner took the parchment and nodded. "Aye, I do. I saw him leaving the village yesterday morning, not long after you two."

Elizabeth felt Edward shift his weight beside her. "Do you know his name?"

"No."

"What about his business here?"

Milner shrugged. "He stayed at The White Hart. You should ask that fool Lowe these questions."

"I have," Edward said. "He didn't know either."

That would save Elizabeth a trip to the Hart. "Thank you, Mr. Milner." She rolled up the parchment and tucked it back into the pouch on her girdle. "Are you sure the man hasn't returned to the village since yesterday morning?"

"If he has, I haven't seen him nor heard of his return," the innkeeper said. "And I hear most things."

"That you do, Milner." Edward nodded his thanks.

"What about Lord Greville?" Elizabeth asked. "I was told that he headed toward the village this morning. Have you seen him or any of his men?"

"Aye, ma'am," Milner said. "As I told Mr. Monk here just now, Lord Greville and his men came looking for the same stranger as you. I'd not seen this picture, so I couldn't help them."

"Do you know where they went after they left here?"

"They headed out of town, that's all I know."

Wherever they were, they must still be searching for the traveler too. If he were on foot, perhaps they'd caught up to him already if they'd chosen the right direction.

"There was one curious thing," he went on. "Lord Greville wanted to return to the Hall immediately, but his man urged him to continue the search. His lordship gave in after much whining."

That certainly was curious, and yet more evidence that Paxton had considerable sway over Greville, not the other way around.

"I'll be off," Edward said. He strode past Elizabeth, and was gone before she could give her thanks to the innkeeper.

She ran out of the taproom and caught up to him in the innyard. "Where are you going now?"

He signaled for the ostler to fetch his horse. "Nowhere that concerns you."

"That is hardly fair."

He stopped suddenly and faced her. "Fair? What has fairness got to do with any of this? We did not come together, so we're not leaving together."

"But I allowed you to use my sketch!"

"You didn't *allow* me."

"And not a single word of thanks either."

He sucked air between his teeth. "Ostler, my horse!"

The ostler brought his horse around and Elizabeth gathered up the reins for her own from Warren. The lad stood quietly by, a small smile on his lips. At least somebody was amused. She most certainly wasn't. Edward was going to continue to look for Greville without her. She could either follow him, or go her own

127

way. Since he hadn't any more of an idea where Greville might be than her, she saw no reason to spend any longer with him than necessary. Last night's rejection had cured her of her affections.

Well, perhaps not quite. She still desired him. Still wanted to kiss him, although rather more aggressively than before. Instead of kissing him tenderly, she liked the idea of grabbing him by his shirt and pulling him on top of her. Or pinning him to the bed. Perhaps even tying him up so he couldn't—

God's blood! Where had that idea come from? And how could she even look at Edward now without thinking of him tied to her bed, naked.

Best not to look at him at all. That, and avoid him as much as possible.

She hid her burning face in her horse's neck as she steered it toward the mounting block. Unlike The White Hart, The Plough had one for ladies to use. She settled herself in the saddle and urged her horse out of the innyard. Warren followed her, and behind him rode Edward.

Once they were out on the main road, Edward peeled away from them. He tipped his hat to her. "See you at dinner, Elizabeth."

She lifted a hand in a half-hearted wave without directly looking at him. It wasn't until he presented her with his back that she openly watched him ride off through the village. He headed in the opposite direction of the Sutton Hall road. She suspected he was going to Stoneleigh to ask his friends the Holts if the stranger had come their way.

She would see him again at dinner. What an interminable affair that would be if she had to avoid looking at him the entire time. Even more interminable if Greville hadn't returned and Arrabella moped about with a sad face.

"Which shop do you wish to go to first, ma'am?" Warren asked.

"We're not shopping. We're going back to the Hall." If Greville had returned, she could speak to him before Edward.

CHAPTER 10

*G*reville had not returned by dinnertime at midday.

Jeffrey frowned at the feast his servants had carried in and set on his table. He'd invited not only Greville's man Paxton to dine, but the other two in their party as well as his own land and house stewards. It was a generous gesture coming from a man not known for it.

"It's most rude of them not to be here," he muttered, hands on hips as he stood at the head of the table. "Most rude."

Arrabella drew in an impatient breath through her nose. Elizabeth, sitting beside her, glanced at Edward from beneath her lashes. He toyed with the empty cup in front of him and stared at Arrabella.

"He must have been waylaid," their mother said. "It happens. Now, pass me the beans, Lizzie. The butter too. Beans always taste better with butter."

"He should have more care," Jeffrey said, striding to the window. He looked out, sighed, and ambled back to the table. "I cannot abide tardiness, particularly when an invitation has been extended to his men."

"What if he's lost?" Arrabella said, her voice wobbly. She was near to tears.

"Bah! The man cannot get lost around here. There are so few roads, and they all lead to Sutton Hall."

"Rather like Rome," Elizabeth quipped.

Out of the corner of her eye, she saw Edward trying not to smile.

"Stop it, Lizzie," Arrabella spat.

"Bella," their mother scolded.

Arrabella pouted. "Jokes are not necessary."

"I agree. Lizzie, kindly keep your mouth shut unless you have something useful to contribute to the conversation."

Elizabeth helped herself to the beans before passing them to her mother. She might as well enjoy the food if she was forbidden to speak. Besides, she suspected Jeffrey hadn't finished being offended about his guests' absence, and it would be rather amusing to watch Arrabella try to be ladylike and keep her mouth shut.

"Does the man do this a lot, Aunt?" Jeffrey asked Janet. He didn't wait for a reply before continuing on. "I admit to scarcely knowing him. If this is his way of thanking his host, then I don't think much of him."

Arrabella suddenly stood, forcing her chair to scrape on the floor. "I cannot believe you would be this cruel! He could be lost or hurt! What if he and his men were set upon by vagabonds?" Her voice rose with each word so that by the end of her sentence, the pitch was shrill.

Janet took Arrabella's hand and tried to pull her back down to her seat. "Be calm, dear. Remember, you're always calm."

Arrabella was forced to sit but sprang immediately back up again. "You ought to be out looking for him, Jeffrey."

"What has come over you, Cousin?" he said. "This is most unlike you. Far more like your sister."

Elizabeth knew she'd somehow make it into the conversation in a negative light. She always seemed to. There was no point arguing with him. It never did any good. Indeed, it would only serve to reinforce his opinion.

Edward snorted a laugh. The sound drew Arrabella's attention.

She turned on him, fists clenched at her sides, teeth bared like an animal about to attack.

"I would duck if I were you," Elizabeth told him. "She's at the point where she throws things. Not the parsnips, please, Bella. I quite like the look of them."

"You heartless cow!" Arrabella screamed. Her face had gone beyond red to mottled.

Elizabeth wondered if perhaps she had gone too far in her teasing. But it was so rare for her sister to show her temper in public that she didn't feel as awful about it as she should. Indeed, this was the first time either Jeffrey or Edward had seen Arrabella on the edge of exploding. Both men stared at her. Jeffrey's mouth had flopped open, but Edward's face was closed, unreadable. It was impossible to tell what he thought of his beloved's tantrum.

Janet took her eldest daughter's arm again and tried to force her to sit, but Arrabella pulled away. She was still focused on Elizabeth. "I told you to go looking for him, and what did you do? You went to the village and returned with nothing! You're hopeless, Lizzie! Hopeless and useless, and it's no wonder nobody likes you!" She spun around and stormed out of the dining room, past the servants pretending not to watch.

Jeffrey was the first to speak, although he couldn't manage entire sentences. "Well, I…I've never seen such…"

"Forgive her, Cousin," Janet said, simpering and smiling as if her life depended upon his forgiveness. "She's overwrought with all the wedding plans. And of course, she's worried. Girls tend to get flighty when they're worried."

"Flighty?" Jeffrey echoed. "That wasn't flighty, that was a gale!"

"You must forgive her."

"Must I?"

"Elizabeth?" Edward's voice cut through their conversation despite being softer. He spoke her name with such concern that Elizabeth forgot she wasn't going to look at him directly and looked at him directly.

"Yes?"

"Are you all right?"

She blinked. He was asking *her* if she was all right? "Yes, perfectly."

"You're not upset by what she said?"

Elizabeth laughed. "No. I'm used to it."

He frowned. "She says that sort of thing often?"

"From time to time. Not usually so loudly or so publicly, however."

He turned his attention to the door through which Arrabella had just stormed. He still looked a little rattled by her tantrum, as if he wasn't sure how to react.

"Monk!" Jeffrey bellowed. "You need to go in search of Greville."

Janet gave a little gasp. Her hand fluttered at her chest. "Do you think something has happened to him?"

"Unlikely, but a search will appease Arrabella."

She looked happy with that explanation and stopped fluttering. "In that case, I see no reason to disturb my dinner further. Lizzie, pass the pork crackling."

* * *

ELIZABETH FOLLOWED Edward to the stables after dinner. She was the very last person he wanted to talk to. Even Arrabella with her petulant rages would be better. At least she wasn't demanding to go with him, nor was she the sort of shrew whose very presence reminded him of his inadequacies in the bedchamber. All he could think about when he looked at Elizabeth was how his panic had him running from her room.

On the other hand, Arrabella *was* a shrew. If he'd not noticed it at the Holts', he certainly noticed it at dinner today. It was testament to Elizabeth's good nature that it didn't trouble her. Indeed, Elizabeth had a remarkable fortitude. She was determined to find Greville, for one thing, and get to the bottom of the stranger's reason for speaking to him. Edward had an inkling that she wouldn't give up easily.

"Two searchers are better than one," she told him, trotting to keep up.

"It won't be one," he said, refusing to slow down. Perhaps if he got a head start and got away, she'd give up and return to the house. "I'll ask some of the grooms to join me in the search. You'll stay here."

"And listen to my sister for the rest of the day? No thank you."

He was fooling himself. She wasn't going to give up. If he got away without her, then she would simply go on her own. She was *that* determined. He slowed and allowed her to catch up. They were almost at the stables. The sun beat down on his back, heating his black jerkin. He would remove it as soon as he was out of sight of Elizabeth. If she ever left him alone that is.

"I see your point, but it changes nothing," he said. "I don't want you coming. In all seriousness, there could be something wrong. Having you join in will only mean an extra person I need to watch out for."

"I don't need anyone to watch out for me."

"That's debatable."

She put one hand on her out-thrust hip. "Have I proven to need constant chaperoning? Or rescuing? I'm quite capable of riding around searching for someone. Four someones. They can't be too difficult to find."

It might not be as easy as that, but he couldn't tell her everything he knew about Greville. Indeed, he didn't know much more himself, but instinct told him something was wrong. Thanks to working with Hughe, he'd learned to trust instincts.

Elizabeth's hand dropped to her side and her face grew long. She swallowed heavily. "Do you think that man has harmed Greville?" she asked on a whisper.

He stopped and looked down at his boots because it was easier than looking into her worried face. It wasn't natural to see anxiety in her eyes. She was a confident woman—too confident for him— and seeing her afraid for her sister's betrothed worried Edward more than Greville's actual disappearance.

"It's not worth worrying about what may or may not have happened until we find Greville and his men," he told her. "Stay with your sister for now. She needs you."

She opened her mouth, no doubt to protest yet again, but Arrabella's shout stopped her. They both turned to the house to see the elder Buckley sister running toward them, her skirts gathered up to keep them out of the dirt. She wasn't looking at either of them, but off to the west.

"He's back!" she cried. "I saw him from my window."

Edward squinted at the horizon. A cloud of dust became visible before the group of riders themselves. He counted four men on horseback in no particular hurry.

"It is them," Elizabeth said.

"I told you so." Arrabella came to a stop beside them. She gasped for breath and flapped both her hands at her red face. "God's blood, I'm so hot. Lizzie, help me cool down before Greville gets here. I'll die of humiliation if he sees me looking like a beacon."

"Plunge your head into the horses' trough," Elizabeth said. "That'll cool you in an instant. I'll hold your hair back."

Edward thought she was serious until she winked at him. He tried not to smile, but it broke out anyway. She had a wicked sense of humor.

Either Arrabella didn't hear or chose to ignore her. She kept her gaze on the advancing riders. "He seems unharmed," she said. "Thank goodness for that. They must have simply been lost."

"Or deliberately avoiding dining with us."

"Stop it, Lizzie. Don't say it even in jest. I have a suspicion that Jeffrey already dislikes Greville, although I don't know why. Saying things like that will only make it worse for him. Nothing must get in the way of our wedding."

Finally, the riders arrived at the stables and dismounted. Greville slapped the dust off his clothes, and one of the other men plunged his entire head into the trough. He shook his hair, sending droplets of water over the party, including Arrabella who'd run up to Greville. She clicked her tongue at the man, then ignored him to take Greville in her arms.

"You're filthy!" she cried, holding him at arms' length. She wrinkled her nose. "And you smell."

"We've been riding all day," Greville said. "I'm parched. I'd kill for an ale."

"Come inside out of this heat." Arrabella took his elbow and began tugging him in the direction of the house.

"Where did you go?" Elizabeth asked. "You missed dinner. Our cousin was most disappointed."

Greville winced. "Then I'll apologize to him. I'll explain that we were...waylaid. Hopefully he'll understand." He shot a glance at Paxton. The other man said nothing. He was looking at Edward.

"You didn't answer her question," Edward said. "Where did you go?"

"I fail to see how that's your business," Paxton said. The older man had the sort of narrow-eyed glare that would have most people apologizing and scurrying away. It only served to make Edward more suspicious. If he had nothing to hide, then he wouldn't have a problem telling them where they went.

"Did you go in search of that traveler?"

Greville's gaze slid to Paxton. He swallowed heavily. "Uh, we went for a ride, that's all."

"Did you get lost?" Arrabella asked.

"Yes! We had no idea where we were. Isn't that right, Paxton?"

Paxton removed his gloves without taking his gaze off Edward. Edward arched a brow, waiting for an answer, but all Paxton did was nod. It was hardly convincing.

"So you didn't see that man who came looking for you yesterday?" Elizabeth asked.

"I said, it's not your business, miss," Paxton growled. The scar on his face whitened. "Now, if you don't mind, I'd like to eat my dinner." He strode off, but stopped a few paces away. "Greville!" he called over his shoulder.

"Coming." Greville gave Arrabella a flat-lipped smile and followed his man like a dog.

Arrabella blinked after him. She seemed baffled by the men's behavior, but she too followed them into the house.

Edward and Elizabeth watched them go. "How odd," she murmured. "Paxton is acting like he is the master."

"And Greville is letting him." Edward had never met a nobleman who allowed ordinary men to treat him as inferior. They all acted as if they were entitled to be master of their underlings. It was something drilled into them from the day they were born. Being in charge was as natural to a nobleman as breathing. Even Cole, who had wanted to distance himself from his upbringing, had an innate air of superiority about him. It wasn't something he could walk away from as easily as he'd walked away from his family home.

Yet here was Greville proving the natural order of things wrong. It made for an odd situation and got Edward thinking. It was time to talk to Lynden about how well he knew the baron of Greville. But first, a little investigating.

"Most odd," Elizabeth repeated before he could leave. "Don't you think, Edward?"

"I wouldn't know."

"Of course you do. You're a keen observer of people."

He frowned. "What makes you say that? You hardly know me."

It was her turn to frown. "Of course I know you. I've known you my entire life. Just because you barely knew I existed doesn't mean I didn't notice *you*."

His stomach twisted. Had he really been that much of a prick to her all those years ago? He supposed he'd had eyes for Arrabella only, but still…surely he hadn't completely ignored Elizabeth.

And yet he could hardly remember her. She'd been small and insignificant, and terribly shy around him. Not this confident beauty who stood before him now. If her wit had been as sharp then, he would certainly have noticed. As a twenty year-old, Elizabeth was quite the force. He couldn't ignore her even if she wore sackcloth. There was just something so compelling about her that demanded he *see* her.

It made walking away from her difficult. He still wasn't sure how he'd managed it last night when she'd all but offered herself to him. Embarrassment could make a man do strange things.

He could feel that embarrassment creeping up his neck again. He turned around and walked off toward the stables to hide his reddening face. Bloody hell, what had gotten into him?

"Where are you going?" she called after him.

"To see to my horse."

"Isn't that what the grooms are for?"

He didn't answer. Everything he could think of sounded foolish in his head. Best to shut up and let her assume what she wanted. Thankfully she didn't follow.

Warren was brushing sweat and dust from Greville's horse when Edward reached the stables. The animal's head hung low as it fed from a bag. Its muscles quivered. It had been ridden hard, the other horses too.

"Where's Greville's other two men?" he asked Warren.

"Gone to find something to eat. Turds." He spat on the straw.

"Is that your general observation?"

"Look at this horse, and the others. Poor creatures. Been ridden hard all day, and in this heat too. It ain't good for 'em, sir. Ain't good at all."

"Did the men happen to mention where they went today?"

"No, sir, and I didn't ask."

Edward could try and force it out of one of them, but he didn't want them going to Paxton. At the moment Greville and his man didn't suspect Edward was watching them, and it was better if that's how the situation remained. He could do more if he went about his work unnoticed.

"I'm going for a ride," he said.

"Want me to saddle your horse?"

"I'll manage."

He rode for the rest of the afternoon, but not hard. He checked as many fields and barns as he could before nightfall, but found no evidence of the traveler. Perhaps he'd left the area altogether, although Edward doubted it. He'd walked to Sutton Hall looking for Greville. He wouldn't want to come all that way then leave without speaking to him. Confronting Paxton might have been off-putting, but surely not enough to detract the man from his errand.

If Edward was in the traveler's boots and wanted to speak to Greville yet avoid Paxton, he would wait until nightfall and approach the baron when he was alone. That meant he'd have to remain close to the house so he could slip in and out easily. He wouldn't be hiding in a field or barn somewhere, he would be nearby.

Edward returned his horse to the stables and brushed him down.

"Want me to do that, sir?" Warren asked.

"I'll do it. Tell me, have you noticed anything unusual lately? Any strange people, strange noises or goings on?"

Warren pushed out his lower lip as he thought. "Not partic'larly. What sort of things?"

"Missing food, perhaps, or disturbances in the night."

"You should ask in the kitchens about the food, but I can tell you one odd thing. I spotted one of the maids sneaking into the brewery after dark. I would have thought she was fetching more ale, but she took something *in* with her, not out."

"What was it?"

He shrugged. "I don't know. It was too dark to see." He sidled closer to Edward. "I fink it was a lover's tryst or some such thing."

"Did a man go in before her, or after?"

Warren shrugged again. "I didn't bother to keep watching."

"Thank you, Warren. Good lad. Mind you don't tell anyone about the maid. She might get into trouble with his lordship."

"Aye."

Edward finished seeing to his horse, and instead of returning to the house, he went straight to the brewery. The late afternoon sun hung heavily in the west but provided enough light into the brewery's high louvered windows for Edward to see. It was warm inside although no fire burned in the central furnace and the bricks were cool to touch.

He eyed the ladder leading to the loft space. If he were hiding out in a brewery, he'd have to situate himself in a far corner away from where the brewer would carry out her day-to-day tasks. Up there.

He climbed slowly, alert to any sounds. Something scurried in the straw. It could have been a rat, or a man. Edward paused, his hand one rung from the top. There it was again, and this time the scurrying was accompanied by the faint whine of steel.

He ducked just in time. The blade whipped past his head, knocking off his hat. It struck the beam and lodged there. The man wielding it swore and pulled hard on the weapon. Edward had but a moment in which to act. He grabbed the man's sword arm at the wrist and forced him to let go. The man cried out in pain as he came close to the edge of the loft above Edward's head.

"I don't want to harm you," Edward told him. "But I will if you fight me."

The dark-haired man stared at him. He lay on his chest just above where his sword was still stuck in the beam. He nodded quickly.

Edward let him go.

The man pulled back out of sight. God's blood, why did he do that?

Edward got his answer in the form of a knife blade coming straight for his face. He ducked again and weaved to the side. The blade missed, but only just. The ladder slipped a little.

"Bloody hell!" Edward cried. "I told you I wouldn't harm you."

"State your business."

"You state yours. *You're* the interloper."

"I'm the one with the blade, and I have the upper hand. I'll ask the questions."

Edward drew his sword. "My blade is longer." He slashed, but the man jumped backward. "And I disagree that your position gives you the upper hand." He continued to climb the ladder, wielding his sword ahead of him. The man could charge, forcing Edward off the ladder, but it would be difficult to stop himself falling off too. He would probably wait until Edward was almost past the loft floor before he struck again.

He was right. The attacker came at him again with his dagger. Edward was prepared and easily parried the blow. The man came again and again, and each time Edward forced the advancing blade away until he was completely off the ladder and standing on the loft floor. He squared up to the traveler.

Elizabeth's skill at rendering his likeness was remarkable. She'd captured the man's stringy black hair and small eyes perfectly, and she'd done it all from memory. It was a pity he couldn't commend her on the drawing. He'd have to keep this meeting private. Now, if only he could convince the fellow of that.

"I won't tell Greville or Paxton you're here," he told him.

The man's eyes darted around as if he couldn't focus on any one thing. He wasn't a good swordsman then. Being able to focus on the enemy was an important aspect in a one-on-one battle. Having a longer weapon than the enemy was another.

What Edward hadn't bargained on was the man throwing his dagger.

CHAPTER 11

*E*dward dove to his right, but the blade nicked his face. He touched his cheek and his hand came away bloody.

"Now what did you go and do that for?" He wiped his hand on his sleeve. "It'll be difficult to explain this without telling them I was attacked."

"You'll think of something."

"Or I could tell them the truth."

The man's eyes widened. "Don't."

"Give me one good reason not to."

The man withdrew another dagger from up his sleeve.

"That's quite a compelling one," Edward said. "But not compelling enough." He indicated his sword. "So why not put your weapon down and talk to me?"

The man widened his stance, preparing to do battle. He was no coward, Edward would give him that. "I'm not an unreasonable man," Edward told him. "I don't want to harm you."

"Cocky, aren't you?"

"No, just good. I've been trained by one of the best swordsmen in England."

"Who?"

"Lord Oxley."

The man snorted. "The man's a dandy and a fool."

Interesting that the fellow knew of Hughe. That meant he was either a nobleman himself or associated with one.

"Is he?" Edward asked lazily. "Well then, if you're so confident in his lack of ability, attack me."

The fellow charged low and dodged Edward's parrying blow at the last moment. He then launched himself bodily at Edward. Edward stepped to the side and watched the man fall to the loft floor. He landed with a thud and an "Oomph."

Edward pointed his blade at the fellow's neck and pressed his boot to his back, pinning him. "That looked like it may have hurt."

The man spat out a piece of straw but didn't answer.

"Now, let's start this conversation again, shall we? My name is Monk. I don't want to harm you. I only want to talk."

"Then talk."

"Tell me your name."

"It's none of your business."

Edward pressed his foot down harder. The man grunted. "Christ, I'm tired of hearing those words. If you won't answer, then *I'll* tell *you* a little about your business. You wish to speak to Lord Greville alone, not with his men around him. You have something to give him, and he alone."

The man didn't speak, but he did seem very surprised that Edward knew so much. Unfortunately, it was all he knew.

"If I let you stand, will you try to kill me again?"

"I wasn't trying to kill you, just maim you or scare you."

Edward laughed. "Listen. I'm no friend to Greville or his men. I'm simply a guest of Lord Lynden's with a desire to keep trouble from his door. I won't harm you."

He nodded. "Then I won't harm you."

Edward sheathed his sword and removed his foot from the fellow's back.

He stood. "So what do you want from me?"

"Answers."

"Then I fear you'll be disappointed. I don't want to give any."

"You haven't heard my questions yet."

The fellow wiped the back of his hand across his sweaty forehead. "Go away."

"No. I am Lynden's man, and you are on his property without invitation. Unless you can give me satisfactory answers, I'll turn you over to him. And don't think you can fight me, because I'm clearly better at this than you."

The man grunted. "What makes you say that? That display proved nothing."

"Perhaps not, but I think you have revealed, and lost, your only two daggers. Perhaps if you had more, then you would be in with a chance, but I doubt you do. You would have retrieved it already. I, on the other hand, have more than two secreted about my person." He shot the man a smile. "And I'm very good at using all of them. So, sir, we could fight first and then I ask you questions at sword point after I turn you over to Lord Lynden, or we talk without all the messy fighting."

"Will you turn me over to Lynden or...one of the others?"

"That depends on what you tell me. So, what is it to be?"

The man hesitated for a long time, longer than Edward liked. Fortunately for Edward's patience, he eventually nodded. "Go on. Ask."

Edward glanced around at the loft space. A blanket was laid out between two wine barrels and the man's pack was just visible behind another. A trencher with nothing but crumbs sat near the blanket and an empty tankard beside that. It would have been an uncomfortable place to stay, not to mention hot with the constant smells of brewed ale thickening the already warm air.

"You would be more comfortable in the house," Edward told him.

"I don't hear a question."

Edward tried again. "Your name, sir?"

"Best. James Best, from Sussex."

"Did one of the maids bring you food, Mr. Best?"

Clearly he hadn't expected that question. Best blinked and

lifted one shoulder. "Aye, but I'll give no names. I don't want to cause trouble to anyone else."

Commendable. He'd not expected it. "Never mind, keep her name to yourself. It's not important. Who is your master, Mr. Best?"

"What makes you think I have a master? I wear no livery."

"Everybody has a master, except the queen herself."

"My master is a man named John Ayleward from Sussex."

"And are you here on Ayleward's business?"

"Aye."

Edward perched on the edge of a barrel, being sure to keep his sword arm casually across his knee so that he could quickly draw if Best came at him. "This questioning could take all night at this rate. Why not just tell me everything. Start with who this Ayleward is."

"He's Lord Greville's brother."

Edward's heart skipped in his chest. He'd not known the family name was different from the title. Most barons were the same. So John Ayleward was the younger sibling and a known Catholic, and here was his man trying to give Greville something. Lynden's suspicions of Greville's involvement in a Catholic plot had seemed farfetched to Edward when he'd first heard it. Yet Lynden may have been right. Ayleward's man had certainly behaved oddly so far. Why do that if he had nothing to hide?

"Then why doesn't Lord Greville's brother's man approach Lord Greville in the light of day? Indeed, why not enquire after him at the Hall door? Lord Lynden would be happy to accommodate you while you conduct your business with Greville."

"Lord Greville doesn't want me here. Indeed, he's been avoiding speaking to me alone."

"Doesn't Lord Greville like his brother?"

"Not particularly."

"Why?"

Best's gaze shifted away. "That's something you'll have to ask him."

"So what is it you're doing here if Lord Greville wants nothing to do with his brother?"

"Mr. Ayleward would like his brother to return to the family home with his betrothed. He sent me to tell Lord Greville."

The younger brother was making a request of the older, the baron? Even odder. Best's answer was also a little too smooth, and Best still did not look Edward directly in the eyes. Besides, it didn't quite add up—Greville had stayed at The Plough on his first night in the area because he'd *known* Best was coming to meet him. That much had been clear from the overheard snippet of conversation between him and Paxton. He may have waited reluctantly, but it proved that Best's arrival wasn't impromptu.

"Is that so?" Edward said. "Then what is it you tried to give him? A letter?"

Best's gaze flicked to Edward's then away. "I don't know what you're talking about."

Edward sighed. "You were seen attempting to deliver something to Greville. Paxton intervened. You wouldn't give it to him."

"You're mistaken. There's nothing but my spoken plea from Mr. Ayleward to his brother."

The man was a poor actor. Edward was an expert, like all the members of the Guild. He knew to look a man in the eyes when he lied to him, and to keep his stance relaxed. Best was as rigid as a maypole.

Edward picked up Best's satchel and emptied its contents on top of the blanket. Best didn't protest. He stood by and watched as Edward picked through his belongings. There was no letter, no seal, or anything except the things a traveler would need for his journey.

"Put out your arms," Edward told him.

Best complied and didn't move as Edward patted his clothing, taking particular care with seams in case Best had sewn the item into one of them. Nothing.

Edward stepped back. The item may be hidden somewhere within the brewery or other outbuildings for safekeeping until

Best was able to slip it to Greville. Edward would do a thorough search later when it was completely dark.

"Tell me, Mr. Best," he said. "Why isn't Greville's marriage taking place at his family estate? Is it this feud?"

"There is no feud, as such, no bad blood. Just...they're not as close as some brothers, even though Mr. Ayleward hasn't moved away. He's still only a young man, not yet married. I've known the boys their entire lives. I helped raise them, but I became more Ayleward's man than Greville's after their father died. As to why the wedding will be held here, you would have to ask Lord Greville that. It was his decision. I imagine he wanted the lady to be near her family."

Everybody was saying that, yet Arrabella's family was perfectly capable of traveling to Sussex. Indeed, why couldn't the wedding be held in their own village of Upper Wayworth? She had friends there as well as family. Yet Greville had agreed to have it at Sutton Hall. Had it been Lynden's request, Arrabella's, or Greville's himself?

"It's an unusual situation," Edward said.

Best merely shrugged one shoulder. Edward didn't believe the man didn't know the reason. There was something he wasn't telling Edward about the brothers. Could it be related to their being Catholic? He could certainly understand why Best would want to keep that information private.

"You walked here all the way from Sussex?" Edward asked.

"Aye."

"Why didn't your master give you a horse?"

"You would have to ask him that."

"He's not here. I'm asking you."

Another shrug of his shoulder. "I cannot answer you."

"Can't or won't?" Edward sighed. He was getting nowhere. He could try and beat the answer out of him, or he could use a less bloody method. "I'd like to help you with your errand, Mr. Best. I'll speak to Lord Greville while Paxton isn't around and urge him to visit you here."

"Urge? Do you mean force him?"

"Would you like me to?"

"It may be the only way. He doesn't wipe his own arse without Paxton watching, and that seems to be the way Greville likes it."

"Paxton is a mystery," Edward said. "What do you know of him?"

"Nothing. I'd met met him until I arrived here."

So he hadn't been Greville's man for long. That was a curiosity in itself. Usually retainers were friends from childhood, or like Best himself, men who'd been trusted by the father. They were rarely newcomers.

"Do you want me to speak to Greville on your behalf then?" Edward asked.

"Aye. If you could, sir, I would be obliged."

"Then be obliging and tell me why you don't have a horse."

Best hesitated, then squared his shoulders. "My master couldn't spare one."

"Not even for such a long journey for his trusted man?"

"I told him there was no need. I don't mind walking."

"He's impoverished, isn't he?"

Best thrust out his chin. He didn't need to answer for Edward to guess that he was right. No good master would allow his long-time retainer to walk to another county if he had his own horse. A rider could flee most dangerous situations, a traveler on foot could not. Hughe would never send his men without a mount unless it was necessary for their disguise. Then again, Hughe was as rich as the queen herself.

So if Ayleward was poor, was Greville? Surely not, or Lynden wouldn't have agreed to his marrying Arrabella. If there was one thing a fool like Lynden could do well, it was sniff out persons of money and influence. So perhaps Greville kept his younger brother on a tight leash by curbing his finances. Perhaps that was why Best had been sent—to plea for funds, and it had nothing to do with embroiling Greville in a Catholic plot after all. If so, why the secrecy?

Pride.

Of all people, Edward knew how poverty could drive a man to extreme measures. He'd left his family and traveled on foot all over England to better his own circumstances. He'd become good at avoiding questions about his past and his purpose, just like Best. His master and Edward were not so different.

He slapped Best on the shoulder. "I'll do my best to bring Greville to you."

"My gratitude to you, Mr. Monk."

"Is there anything you need? Food?"

"The maid has been helpful. I want for nothing."

"Then I'll leave you in peace. Next time I visit, kindly don't point your sword in my face." He touched his cheek. The cut had stopped bleeding and didn't sting as much.

"Hopefully, the next time you visit you'll have Greville with you, and I'll have no need of weapons."

Edward doubted Greville would come no matter how many times he asked. He'd avoided Best up until now, and Edward saw no reason why he'd suddenly change his mind.

* * *

ELIZABETH WATCHED the maid leave the main house through the kitchen door. She carried something, but it was too dark to see what. Elizabeth left her hiding spot behind the potted topiary in the outer courtyard and followed at a safe distance. The girl headed to the outbuildings at the rear of the house. She bypassed the bakehouse and granary, and entered the brewery.

Elizabeth did not follow. That would be foolish indeed. She was only glad that her suspicion had proven correct. She'd realized that if the traveler wanted to speak to Greville alone, he would remain close to the house. He would also need to eat. A willing maid could be easily encouraged to provide for a handsome stranger. It had only been a matter of waiting in the dark and watching for one of the girls leaving the kitchens with a parcel.

The maid exited the brewery much sooner than Elizabeth expected. She had to stand very still in the shadows as there was no time to hide. Thank goodness for the darkness and her black cloak. She watched the girl walk back to the house, but did not follow.

Elizabeth eyed the brewery and contemplated her next move. She shouldn't go in. The man might be dangerous. It galled her, but there was only one person she could trust with the information —Edward.

She was about to leave and return to the house when a sound coming from inside the bakehouse gave her pause. It was the lightest of sounds, barely noticeable. A mouse or cat knocking a crate perhaps? A sack of flour being moved? But who would be inside at this hour? It must be approaching midnight.

She stared at the darkened window, thinking through her options, when a candle flame came into view before disappearing again. It had lit up the handsome features of Edward Monk.

She blew out a breath, glad beyond words that it was only him. But what was he doing? She would find out, and tell him she'd found the traveler too.

She pushed open the door and was about to softly call out Edward's name when a shadow of his size and shape slammed into her. The breath left her body, and she was propelled backward. She hit the wall with such force that something fell off the shelf on her left and splattered over the floor. Her chest constricted. Her throat closed. She couldn't breathe, couldn't get air into her lungs no matter how hard she tried to suck it in.

Edward pulled away. There was no light anymore, the candle having gone out, but she knew for certain it was him. It even smelled like him.

He grabbed her shoulders and held her up. If he hadn't, she would have slid to the floor. Her legs could barely hold her.

"Elizabeth?"

She managed a wheeze in response. Air! She needed air.

"Christ! I'm sorry."

Help me, Edward.

"Bend forward and stay calm," he said.

Calm! How could she be calm when she couldn't breathe?

He pressed his big hand to the back of her neck and gently pushed her head down. "You're only winded," he said in that wonderfully smooth voice of his. "Try to breathe normally, and you'll be fine in a moment or two."

She did as instructed and slowly her chest filled with delicious air.

"There," he said, letting go. "Better?"

"Yes. Thank you. Oh, wait." She slapped him across the cheek. "There, now I'm better."

He hissed. "I suppose I deserved that, but in my defense, I didn't know it was you."

"You didn't think of finding out who I was before you hit me? I could have been one of the maids."

"The maids have no reason to be out this late, especially without carrying a light. Nor, I might add, do you."

Even so, attacking someone for entering the bakehouse in the dark was an extreme response. "You thought I was someone specific, didn't you? Who were you expecting?"

"First things first. Are you hurt?" He bent down until his face was very close to hers, but she could make out very little of his features in the darkness. "Damnation, I can't see a thing. Wait here."

He disappeared and a moment later a flint was struck and the candle lit again. He held it up between them and peered at her with a deep frown scoring his forehead.

Yet it was she who gasped. A gash stretched across his cheek and blood trickled from the corner. "I hurt you!" She gently took his face in her hands and caressed her thumb just beneath the cut. There wasn't a lot of blood, but it should be seen to anyway. "My poor Edward," she murmured. "I'm so sorry."

She had a ridiculous urge to kiss it better. She plucked the candle out of his hand and set it on the shelf nearby. Then she leaned into him. He did not pull away. Indeed, he seemed to be leaning closer to her too. His skin was hot beneath her hands, the stubble on his chin rough, but his cheeks were smooth. She stroked him, careful not to touch the wound, and kissed the corner of his mouth.

Her heart quickened. She heard his breath catch in his throat. He swallowed hard, and for a moment, she thought he would pull away, that he didn't want this.

Then he turned his head slightly to kiss her properly, mouth against mouth, lips to lips. He caught her round the waist and held her tightly. Body against body. Once more she was rendered short of breath, but this time she didn't care. He was kissing her. Holding her. Finally!

His other hand dug through her hair, sending the pins scattering onto the bare flagstone floor. He held her head in place, but she didn't want to move, didn't want to be anywhere else except in his arms. She opened her mouth, and his tongue gently explored, hesitant at first, as if testing if it was what she really wanted. Then he deepened the kiss, and she was lost. Utterly lost. All that existed was Edward, his demanding mouth, his strong body, and the hard member pressing into her.

He wanted her. There was no doubt this time. She knew what happened when a man desired a woman, knew what happened to him *down there*. If his urgent, hungry kisses weren't enough of a sign, then his hard length certainly was. There could be no doubt.

She wanted him too. Desperately. With every tingling nerve and each thud of her heart, she wanted to have all of him. Wanted to know him intimately, in the way only a lover could. It was as if the act would be a way to see inside his head and his heart, to learn everything that made Edward Monk the man he was. There was nothing she desired more in the world.

Whatever had happened the previous night to send him from her room, she would not let happen again. It would shatter her. His hot kisses wound her up so tightly that another disappointment on that scale would undo her completely.

Yet she couldn't remember what had triggered his departure. Couldn't remember much of anything. Her mind felt like it was stuffed full of cotton—stuffed full of Edward. She couldn't think, could only feel, and what she felt was a powerful welling of emotions. Almost too powerful to be contained within her trembling, aching body.

Body. She wanted to touch his, trace the contours, learn every inch of him. She clutched at his jerkin and managed to undo some buttons without really trying. He did the rest and threw the jerkin away. Next, his shirt. That too was easy and disappeared in the same direction as the jerkin.

He stood before her, naked from the waist up. Gloriously, beautifully naked. She pressed both palms against his chest, and slowly felt her way down, following the path of hair. His nipples hardened beneath her touch, and he sucked air between his teeth. It came out ragged, like he was barely in control. His half-closed eyes watched her as she ventured over his stomach, dipping her fingers into each hollow between the ridges of muscle.

Then, he bent to kiss her again, and she let him. The kiss was more frenzied, something she'd not thought possible a moment ago. It sent heat swirling through her, beginning at the juncture of her thighs and shooting along her limbs. She was hot and her body felt loose, not quite under her control.

Edward let go of her to concentrate on her clothing. She wore a neat little jerkin over her bodice which he removed easily enough. He tugged at the laces of her bodice, but she'd double knotted them and he couldn't undo it. He grunted with frustration and broke the kiss.

She giggled. "I'll do it," she said between her unsteady breaths. "You get yourself undressed."

But he did not. He stumbled backward until he was up against a stack of crates. His wide eyes stared at her. His Adam's apple bobbed furiously.

It was happening again.

"Edward, no." She wasn't sure how she found her voice, but she did. It was calmer than she felt. Inside, she was screaming at him. Her body was in turmoil, her heart hammering out a protest at his abandonment. "Don't go," she whispered. "Please, don't. I want you. I want—"

"No." He shook his head over and over. "Don't. We can't… I can't…"

"Why not?"

More head shaking. He looked stricken, horrified. What was it about her that repulsed him? He dragged his hands through his hair and turned away, presenting her with his brawny shoulder.

"Talk to me, Edward." Good lord, she sounded pathetic. She *felt* pathetic, and hated it. She was supposed to be the strong sister, yet here she was pleading with a man. She doubted Arrabella had ever had to do that.

The candlelight cast long shadows over his profile so that he looked spectral, otherworldly. "Talking will only make it worse," he muttered.

"It already is as worse as it can get!" She wanted to shout, but her voice would not go above a whisper. Tears welled, close to the brim. She could not force them away, no matter how many breaths she took or how hard she tried to steady her rapidly beating pulse.

"I…I'll leave the candle with you," he said. He spoke quickly, like he needed to get out of the bakehouse without delay. Like he needed to get away from her. "Are you all right to get back—"

"Stop it, Edward!" She closed the gap between them and grabbed his arms. He went rigid as if he were readying himself for another slap. "Stop it," she said again. The tears clogging her throat distorted her voice. She swallowed, but they did not abate. "You cannot kiss me as if your life depended upon it, then toss me aside."

"I'm not tossing you. I…I simply cannot take this further. It would be wrong of me."

"I don't care, Edward. I *want* you to take me."

"Nevertheless, I won't do it."

"But you want to." She let go of him and folded her arms against

153

a sudden chill. She dug her fingernails into her palms as a stinging reminder to keep her hands to herself. He'd made it clear that he didn't want them on him. "I know desire, and I felt it in your kisses, Edward."

He said nothing, nor did he meet her gaze. The moment stretched unbearably thin.

"Do you still hate me?" she finally asked.

His head jerked up. Finally he met her gaze with his own. "Hate you?"

"You blamed me for preventing Arrabella from falling in love with you."

"Did I really say that?" He sighed and rubbed his hand over his face. When he pulled it away, he looked at her with tenderness that brought the tears close again. "I apologize for saying that. I don't believe it anymore. Arrabella was never going to be in love with me." He shrugged. "Besides, I've learned some things about her in these last two days that make me glad she didn't reciprocate."

Elizabeth's heart ground to a halt. Her body went numb. She could hardly believe what she was hearing. "You're no longer in love with her?"

"I'm not even sure if it was love. It felt like it at the time, but now…now I think I was more in love with the ideal of Arrabella, and not the real person."

"To be fair, she never let anyone see the real person. These recent days have been an exception."

"I know she's your sister," he said, somewhat hesitant, "but I don't particularly like the real Arrabella."

She giggled. She couldn't help it. It just burst out of her. She was so happy to hear him say it, and mean it, that she felt quite giddy. "Oh, Edward. If you're not in love with Bella anymore, why…why not make love to me?"

He shook his head but did not speak.

"If I want you and you want me, where is the harm?"

He made a sound in his throat as if he were choking.

"Are you worried about the possible consequences?" she asked.

When his only answer was to blink at her, she supposed she'd guessed correctly. "That's why I suggested you employ a preventative method," she went on. "You must know what to do."

He stepped away and picked up the candle. "I have to go."

"Are you worried that you'll be forced to marry me when Jeffrey finds out?" The question came out before she thought it through. As soon as she'd said it, she wished she could take it back. She might as well open her chest and tell him to rip her heart out with his bare hands. Of course he didn't want to marry her. He couldn't even bring himself to ravish her. To hear him admit it would be torture.

He held the candle up between them. His eyes were very round, the dark centers huge. His lips parted, yet he still didn't speak.

She had to say something. The weight of her question pressed down on her, suffocating. She had to clear the air. "I know it's not what you would want. It's all right. I understand. I know you're your own man and having such a momentous decision taken from your hands would be tantamount to trapping you. Is that it?" *Please say yes. Please allow me the dignity of thinking it's not because you don't want me.*

"Elizabeth, I'm...I'm not sure what to say."

The tears that had been hovering on the brink for some time finally broke their banks and spilled down her cheeks. She swiped at one, but they fell in a torrent, too fast to stop them all. Inside her ribcage, her heart cracked. He didn't want her, didn't desire her, and probably didn't even like her.

"Yes," he said quickly. "Yes, that's it. I'm not ready for marriage."

He was almost thirty, and he would have married Arrabella if she was available, but Elizabeth didn't remind him of those things. She wanted to believe him so much, even if he didn't speak the truth. She may be fooling herself, but then she was a silly fool when it came to him.

She gathered up the frayed ends of her nerves. "Well then, I won't trouble you again."

"Elizabeth—"

"Don't. We've both said our piece. Let's not suffer any more humiliation, so we can depart as friends."

He picked her jerkin off the floor. "Take the candle. I can make my way out by moonlight."

She took the candle and jerkin and left the bakehouse while he dressed. A fresh batch of tears accompanied her walk to the house. She was almost at the inner courtyard when she realized she hadn't told him about the man in the brewery, nor did she know why he'd been sneaking about the bakehouse after dark. That would have to wait for another time. Her heart was too sore to see him again tonight.

The sound of running footsteps on the cobbled courtyard caught her attention. Who was out at this time of night? A servant? She held the candle up high as a man's face came out of the shadows. Two men. Greville's retainers, but not Paxton. She wiped away her tears and was about to ask them what they were doing when one grabbed her arm. She dropped the candle in fright, and the flame went out.

"There you are," he said. "We been lookin' for you."

"Let me go, or I'll scream."

The man sneered and tightened his grip. The other man shoved his face in hers. His breath stank of onion. "Why were you askin' all them questions in the stables, miss?"

"Wh…what?"

"We heard you speak to the groom, askin' about the traveler at The White Hart."

He must mean the time she'd questioned Warren after returning from the Holts'. The men must have been nearby, perhaps in the stall with the restless horse.

"I don't see how it's your concern." Her heart pounded in her chest, and she willed it to be calm. Surely these men wouldn't hurt her. "I was curious, that's all."

The man holding her twisted her arm. She gasped as burning pain ripped up to her shoulder and down to her hand. These men weren't going to back down. They weren't gentlemen. They were brutes and angry ones at that. They would have no qualms about hurting her.

"What do you want?" she begged.

"Mr. Paxton wants to know why you're meddlin' in our affairs. We been watchin' you, and we know you've been lookin' for that fellow. Mr. Paxton don't like that."

"Then tell Mr. Paxton to speak to me himself. Now, let me go."

"You tell us what you're doing, and we might consider it."

IF SHE JUST TOLD THEM something to satisfy them, then surely they would let her go. She would go straight to Jeffrey and have them thrown out of Sutton Hall. "There's nothing to tell. I'm curious by nature and simply wanted to find out who that man was and—"

She didn't see Onion Breath's hand until it was too late. He grabbed a bunch of her hair and pulled hard, forcing her neck back. Searing pain ripped across her scalp.

She screamed.

Onion Breath covered her mouth with his other hand, smothering her. She struggled against him, using her elbows and feet to try to free herself. Her foot connected with his knee, eliciting a grunt from her attacker.

"Bloody wench!" He let her go, but only long enough to pull back his arm and ball his hand into a fist. "You'll pay for that."

CHAPTER 12

*E*lizabeth ducked. She expected one of the men to haul her up by her hair, but he did not. The sounds of scuffles broke through the throb of pain. She glanced up.

Edward had engaged both men in a fight. She opened her mouth to cry out, perhaps distract one to give him a chance at beating the other, but she quickly realized he didn't need her help. One man lay on the ground on his side, holding his stomach, while Onion Breath swung his fist at Edward. He dodged it easily and threw a punch. It landed on Onion's chin. He reeled backwards, tripped over his friend and landed heavily on the cobbles.

Edward drew a dagger from the inside of his boot. He beckoned them. "Come get me." His rasping voice sounded like it was being squeezed out from between his clenched teeth. "Give me a reason to gut you, because right now I want to hurt both of you very badly."

Elizabeth blinked at the man she thought she knew so well. He didn't sound or act like his usual controlled, calm self, but like a fierce, bloodthirsty warrior. He'd easily dispensed with two brutes as if they were mere bumbling children. And he kept a knife inside his boot. The sweet, awkward youth she remembered from Upper Wayworth was nothing like this man. This version was thrilling. His total command over the situation and the two assailants sent a flood of delicious heat through her body.

Onion Breath got up and ran off, disappearing into the darkness. Edward kicked the other man's foot. He groaned and got to his knees with considerable effort. Edward thrust the dagger under his chin.

"Lord Greville will hear of this," he hissed. "Lord Lynden too. Pack your bags tonight because you'll be leaving in the morning. And if you go near Miss Buckley, or any other member of the household or staff tonight, I'll kill you. Understand?"

The attacker nodded quickly. Edward removed his blade, and the man raced after his friend.

Elizabeth, sitting on the cobblestones, wanted to ask Edward if it was wise to let them go, but her body had begun to shake uncontrollably. She doubted her voice would be strong enough for talking. Besides, she was crying again. Damnation, why couldn't she stop? A huge sob wracked her. She lifted her skirt and buried her face in it. It failed to smother her emotions.

Strong arms surrounded her, and she was tucked into an equally strong body. Edward drew her onto his lap and cradled her head against his chest. His heart thudded an erratic rhythm in her ear as if he'd just run a mile. He was not as calm as he appeared.

He gently swept her hair off her hot forehead and planted tiny, chaste kisses there. He didn't speak, but that was good. She didn't want him to soothe her with words, just with his sweet kisses and touches. She felt safe against that solid body, comfortable. Like she belonged there.

The thought only made her heart ache more and her tears flow swifter. Her emotions were still raw after his rejection in the bakehouse. She'd convinced herself that she'd been mistaken, and he didn't desire her, but this tenderness confused everything. It was enough to drive a girl to madness.

"Shhh," he whispered into her hair. "I won't let them hurt you."

She knew it too. Knew it deep down in the pit of her stomach that he would do anything to keep her safe. "I don't know why I'm crying," she managed.

"You're crying because you were scared, and now you're relieved. It's all right. It's a natural reaction to a shock like that."

"You wouldn't cry."

He chuckled. "I'm somewhat less fragile than you."

The contrary woman inside her wanted to tell him she wasn't fragile, but she lost the battle. Elizabeth wasn't going to ruin the moment. She was going to snuggle into Edward for as long as he allowed it and relish his manliness and the feeling of being protected.

It lasted only a few more moments before he pulled away. He touched her chin and peered down at her face, but it was too dark for her to make out more than the reflection of the silver moon in his eyes.

"Are you hurt?" he asked, voice thick.

"I don't think so." Her arm may be bruised, but her scalp no longer rippled with pain.

He cupped her cheek and stroked his thumb along her jaw. "I cannot believe anyone would want to hurt you." He swore softly. "Greville needs a good thrashing for bringing the likes of them here."

"I'm not sure it's Greville's fault."

His hand stilled. "What do you mean?"

"They're Paxton's men, working under Paxton's orders, not Greville's. When they questioned me, it was only Paxton's name they mentioned."

"Questioned you?" His hand stilled. "They weren't trying to... have their way with you?"

"I don't know. Perhaps they may have, but it was answers to Paxton's questions that they wanted."

"What questions?"

"They wanted to know why I was asking after the traveler from The White Hart."

"What did you tell them?"

"That I was curious by nature. I don't know if they believed me. But they were very clear that it was Paxton who was their master, not Greville. Edward, what's going on?"

He touched the back of her neck and massaged the knot between her shoulder blades. Dear lord, it felt so good. She groaned and pressed her forehead against his chest.

His hand stilled. His body tensed. He cleared his throat. "Come inside. I want to inspect you for injuries."

"I'm unharmed."

"Nevertheless, I want to see for myself." He stood, pulling her with him. He wrapped his arm around her waist as if propping her up, although she didn't need it. She didn't tell him to let her go.

"You're the one with the cut on your cheek," she said. "I only have a bruise or two."

"The cut's nothing." He took her hand and walked with her back to the house.

"It's not nothing. What if it festers?"

"I'll get the village wise woman to look at it if that makes you feel any better."

"It doesn't. I feel guilty for causing it."

"I probably should tell you that you didn't hit me quite that hard. The cut was already there."

She stopped. "Then who—?"

"Not now, Elizabeth."

She bit her lip and allowed him to lead her into the house via the kitchen entrance. The large kitchen was empty and dark. He struck a flint and lit a taper from the tinderbox then put the flame to three candles.

"Sit," he ordered, indicating a stool beside the enormous fireplace. A cauldron hung over the glowing coals, spicy smells wafting from it.

He scanned her face, her neck, then pulled up her sleeves to inspect her arms. He paused when he saw the bruising and sucked in a deep breath. "Fuck." He strode to the door then back again.

A shiver trickled down her spine as he came within the circle of light. His jaw was as hard as marble, his gray eyes like frozen lakes. She'd never seen him so furious.

"I'll escort you to your room." He was so formal and cool, as if the heat and light that made up Edward Monk had switched off inside him.

"Where are you going?" she asked.

"To find Paxton."

"And?"

That steely gaze slid to her then away. She shivered again. Did he mean he was going to hurt Paxton? Oh God. Perhaps she ought to go with him and stop him doing something foolish.

He took her hand again and led her to the door. "I'll rouse a maid to assist you," he said.

"No. Please, let them sleep."

"Your sister?"

"God no."

"You shouldn't be alone, and I can't stay with you."

Yes, you can! But she did not say it aloud. She knew it would do no good. He looked utterly determined to confront Paxton, and she knew she had to let him go. If nothing else, it may help expel the fury from his system. Besides, Paxton deserved to experience Edward's wrath after what he'd done. She had no doubt it would be fierce.

EDWARD OPENED the door leading to Elizabeth's private rooms. He checked the shadows of her parlor, the recessed window embrasure, under the desk, then repeated his search in the adjoining bedchamber. Empty. No one was waiting for her. Still, he did not sheath his knife. He clasped it harder as he watched Elizabeth light candles.

Anger still throbbed inside him. It was an effort to remain composed, but he managed it for her sake. He'd never known white-hot fury like this before. The need to make Paxton and his men pay for what they did to Elizabeth drove him almost to madness. He could think of nothing except smashing his fist into their faces. They'd hurt her. They deserved to be hurt in return.

She handed him the candle. Her fingers brushed his, sending warmth washing up his arm. The fog that had clouded his mind ever since seeing her bruises dispersed, taking some of his anger along with it. Unfortunately, it allowed other emotions in, chiefly an echo of the panic from when he'd realized she was being attacked.

He'd felt sluggish as he raced to her after hearing her cries. Desire had done that. Desire for her in the bakehouse. There was no denying it. He'd wanted her. Wanted to lie with her, enter her, and lick her all over. He wanted to know what she tasted like, and hear her whisper his name as she quivered from his kisses. He'd been so close too. There was nothing standing in his way anymore. His feelings for Arrabella had disappeared entirely. Only his worry about taking a woman of Elizabeth's status remained. He would hate himself for ruining her chances of making a good match, or if he got a child on her. Would pulling out at the last moment work? Should she drink a preventative potion afterward?

He'd been worrying about those things when Elizabeth had laughed. His fingers had felt like lumps of clay as he'd tried to undo her bodice, and she'd laughed at his frustration. On top of his worry, it had been enough to dampen his desire. What would a woman like Elizabeth want with an inept dolt? Better to keep her respect than be sniggered at, or worse still, pitied.

"Edward." She touched his face near the cut on his cheek. Her gaze locked with his. "Will you stay with me tonight?"

He shook his head.

"There's a mattress under the bed if you don't want to share—"

"No. I can't. I need to speak to Paxton." And he needed to stay away from Elizabeth. Without his anger to protect him, he was open to desire again. He couldn't withstand her a second time in one night. "Are you sure you don't want me to fetch someone?" he asked.

She sighed and shook her head.

He walked away. His legs felt leaden, his heart bruised. He glanced back at her from the doorway and almost returned to her. She looked so small and vulnerable standing in the middle of the chamber, her hair tumbling around her shoulders, her teeth nibbling her lower lip. She blinked hard at him. He knew her tears were close.

"Lock the door behind me," he said. "Don't let anyone in. Not even the maids." He closed the door and waited until he heard the key in the lock. Then he simply stood there and breathed. Just breathed. He concentrated on the task at hand. He recalled his anger and nurtured it, until all sentimental emotions were once more relegated to the back of his mind. All he could think about now was making Paxton pay.

He headed to his bedchamber to fetch his sword. He'd left it behind because he'd not wanted it to get in the way while he searched the bakehouse. That had almost been a mistake. It was fortunate Paxton's men hadn't carried swords either, or the fight would have been fairer. If they had daggers—and they would have been even bigger fools not to carry them—then neither had a chance to retrieve their weapons. Perhaps they'd expected Elizabeth would be easy prey and not bothered.

The thought of what they might have done to her if he hadn't intervened sent an explosion of fury through him. He went straight to Paxton's room, a small chamber in the upper eastern corner, but he wasn't there. Damnation! His men had alerted him. His things were still in the room, so he hadn't left altogether. Good. Edward needed to get his anger out on somebody.

He went to Greville's chambers a level below. He was about to barge in when he heard voices coming from inside.

"You'll do as I say," Paxton snarled.

"We do this my way." Greville's voice was more a plea than a command. "No one need get hurt."

"It may be too late for that."

"Wh…what have you done?"

Paxton laughed. The sound almost drove Edward over the edge. But he needed to stay where he was, just a moment longer. He needed answers, and he doubted he would get them by asking.

"We'll worry about that tomorrow," Paxton said. "For tonight, I need you to find Best. I know he's here somewhere, but he won't reveal himself to me. He will to you."

"Why can't you just leave him be?" Greville whined. "He's a good man and has nothing to do with our business."

"Wrong, *my lord*. He may be the answer to both our problems."

"No!"

"I know what he is. I know what he wants from you. If you do it—"

"No!" Greville shouted again. "I will not."

"Fool," Paxton spat.

"Why can you not wait until I am wed?"

"Because now that I'm here, and I've seen what Lynden is like, I have doubts about the effectiveness of your plan. He doesn't seem as simple-minded as you think."

"He is. I assure you, all will work out, but you must be patient."

"I've run out of patience. Find Best tonight, otherwise I tell your betrothed everything in the morning."

"No!" Greville croaked. "No, don't—"

"Do not touch me." Paxton's voice was a low growl that Edward had to strain to hear. Greville must have pushed him or grabbed him in his desperation.

"But—"

The sound of a fist connecting with flesh cut Greville off. He cried out and something got knocked over, crashing to the floor. Edward rested his hand on the door handle, but did not enter.

"I told you to let me go, you little prick," Paxton said. "Now." His pause was filled with the sound of another punch and Greville's grunt. "Do as I say." *Punch.* "Or I'll tell the Buckley girl."

Edward gripped the handle harder and almost pushed, but the fighting stopped. He held his breath and listened. How badly had Greville been hurt?

"I will kill you for that!" Greville shouted. "I'll fucking kill you."

Paxton merely laughed.

Edward barged in. Paxton swung round, his fists closed at his sides. Greville lay on the floor, dabbing at his bleeding lip with his shirt cuff.

"What do you want?" Paxton growled.

"I want to kill you too," Edward said. "But I'll settle for hurting you instead." He swung his fist.

Paxton hadn't expected it. He ducked too late, and Edward connected with his jaw. He stumbled backward onto the desk, sending the inkstand tumbling off the other side. It broke into pieces and ink spread through the mat. Edward advanced and grabbed the front of Paxton's jerkin. But Paxton was ready for him this time and shoved at Edward's chest. He was stronger than he looked, and Edward let him go.

"You might scare my men," Paxton sneered, drawing his sword, "but you don't scare me."

He charged, but Edward parried. Paxton careered into a chair, splintering it. Both Paxton and the chair pieces slammed onto the floor. Greville laughed manically as he scrambled into the corner, out of the way.

Paxton got up. He bared his teeth and engaged Edward. His sword skills were middling. He was a little too slow to parry all of Edward's thrusts and was singularly uninventive. Edward was of a mind to have some fun. He dodged Paxton's parry and nicked his chin. Paxton grunted in pain.

"That's for hurting Elizabeth." He landed a punch on the same spot, sending Paxton onto his haunches. "That too."

"Elizabeth?" Greville cried. "What did he do to her? Is she all right?"

Edward ignored him. He quickly side-stepped as Paxton's blade drove toward his face. Paxton stumbled forward, and Edward moved behind and shoved his boot into the other man's arse. Paxton fell onto his knees on the floor.

"Get up," Edward ordered. "Then get out of this house. You're not welcome here anymore."

Paxton got up, but did not straighten. He bent over and breathed hard. "You don't have the right to order me about."

Edward flicked his wrist. The tip of his sword sliced across the back of Paxton's sword hand. He let his weapon go with a cry.

"This blade gives me every right," Edward snapped.

Paxton straightened. "You cannot protect yourself from me *and* my men."

Edward laughed without humor. "Your men are pathetic."

"They were unarmed."

"You think arming them will make a difference?"

"You prick. I don't take orders from you. I am my own man, and if I want to stay here, I will. I'm not leaving until my business is complete." He narrowed his gaze at Greville, still cowering in the corner, but listening intently to the conversation. "Understand, Greville? I will not leave until I get what I want." He snatched up his sword and stalked out of the room.

Greville emerged from the corner and threw his hands in the air. "Why did you let him go?"

"So he can pack his things and gather his men."

"You think that little display will make him leave?" He snorted and dusted himself off. "Paxton is not so easy to remove as that. I hate him." He hawked a glob of spit into the bedpan.

"Then why have him around?"

"You think I have a choice in the matter? Come now, Mr. Monk, you saw what happened here tonight. Paxton is not someone I can control."

"Then learn to do so."

Greville cocked his head to the side and narrowed his eyes. He studied Edward from head to toe. It was as if he was seeing him for the first time. "Who *are* you, Mr. Monk?"

"Nobody of consequence."

"I know that. Arrabella told me of your origins and how you've been in love with her for years." He sighed. "I feel as if I must apologize for winning, but I'm not entirely sure that I have won."

"You're welcome to her. I'm cured of any tender feelings I felt for Arrabella."

Greville sighed again, all the fight having gone out of him. He looked like a defeated man. "Then you are indeed fortunate."

"Tell me why Paxton is acting as your retainer. Clearly he's not in your employ."

"That matter is private."

"Does it have anything to do with Mr. Best hiding out in the brewery?"

Greville tossed his head, flicking his fringe of hair off his forehead. "The brewery? So that's where he's been. Have you spoken to him?"

"Aye. He asked me to fetch you without Paxton finding out."

"I won't go. I want nothing to do with his…errand."

"What errand is that?"

Greville picked up the pieces of the splintered chair, but they were too damaged to put back together. "I don't know."

Edward snatched the chair leg off him. Greville gasped and stepped back. Good. Better if he was afraid of Edward than thought him an ally. "Does it have something to do with Best being your brother's man and your brother being Catholic?"

Shock rippled across Greville's face. Clearly that little family secret was not widely known. "H…he's not."

"Does your betrothed know she's marrying into a Catholic family?"

"Now, wait there! I attend mass at a Church of England. Ask my vicar! Go on, write to him if you don't believe me. It's true that our parents were of the old papist faith, but we have—"

"Spare me." Edward sheathed his sword. He could thump the answer out of him, but he'd had enough violence for one night. He'd beaten the man who was responsible for hurting Elizabeth, and that's all that mattered. It was clear from Greville's earlier reaction that he hadn't known Paxton's men had set upon her.

"I haven't got time for this now," he went on. "We'll continue this conversation later."

"I swear there's nothing to tell!" Greville paced the floor and rubbed his hand down the back of his neck. "Best has come looking for me for a reason known only to he and my brother. I don't wish to learn what it is."

"Yet you waited a night for him in Sutton Grange before coming here."

"That was at Paxton's urging. I wasn't interested. It's true that I knew he was coming to meet me, but I didn't know why. I still don't."

"Then why does Paxton want to meet him so badly?"

Greville shook his head and continued to pace. Sweat beaded on his brow, dampening his hair. With the splattering of blood on his shirt and face, he seemed somewhat manic. "Only Paxton can answer that."

Edward doubted it, but said nothing.

"My brother and I are not close. I doubt he sent his man here because he wants to help me, and I don't wish to help him in whatever he wants."

"How do you know he wants something from you? Perhaps he has news for you."

"Then the fucking turd should send me a message!"

No, Edward really didn't have time for this. He had more questions, but they would have to wait. "We'll speak again in the morning."

He turned for one last look at Greville before he closed the door. The man stood amid the broken furniture, rocking back on his heels, his hands covering his face. Edward could swear he heard him muttering to himself.

ELIZABETH AWOKE hungry and somewhat confused. Why wasn't there clean water in her basin? Then, she remembered she'd locked her bedchamber door. The maids wouldn't have been able to enter. She unlocked the door and opened it to see if a basin of fresh water had been left outside for her.

What she found was Edward sound asleep on a chair, his arms crossed over his chest and his feet propped up on another chair opposite. He wore the same clothes as the night before, but he must have returned to his room at some stage because his sword lay across his lap. Had he slept there all night to watch over her?

Elizabeth's heart lurched. No one had ever been so considerate of her before. She was the one who always took care of everything for the family. She conducted the household affairs after her father died because neither Arrabella nor Janet were capable. She was the one who oversaw the servants and made ends meet when Jeffrey was late paying the annuity. She'd never *needed* anyone to watch over her before, yet that didn't mean she hadn't *wanted* it. Edward's gesture made her feel cherished. In some ways it didn't matter that he'd rejected her, because she would always have this image of him guarding her door. She would hold it in her memory and bring it out again when the loneliness became unbearable.

She crept back into her bedchamber and gently closed the door again so as not to wake him. She dressed in the simplest, easiest to assemble outfit she owned and combed her hair before pinning it. She wondered if one of the maids had discovered her hairpins in the bakehouse this morning. Her heart skipped a beat and she bit her wobbly lip. She would never be able to enter the bakehouse again without her heart aching.

A light knock on her door roused her. "It's me," Edward said.

She opened the door, but he didn't enter. He leaned one shoulder against the doorframe and crossed his ankles. His sword was strapped to his side.

"Good morning," she said. "Sleep well?"

"Well enough. How is your arm?"

"A little bruised, but otherwise fine. Your cheek?"

He touched it as if he'd forgotten the cut was there. Some of the dried blood flaked off. He mustn't have even washed his face. "I need to go. You should remain within sight of people until I return."

A shiver trailed down her spine. "You don't think Paxton's men will try to hurt me again?"

"I doubt it, but I don't trust him. I'm going to check his rooms now and see if he followed my advice and left."

"But you don't hold out much hope."

"If he's still here, I'll need to speak to Lynden. Do you mind if he finds out about..." He nodded at her arm.

"No. Do everything necessary to get those men away from my family."

"I will. Don't worry, Elizabeth, I won't let anything bad happen to you, or your family."

She wanted to kiss him in thanks, but refrained. She wasn't sure how he would react and she didn't want to risk another rejection. "Thank you, Edward," she said simply. "My family has a true friend in you."

She watched him go then slipped on her shoes and headed down to the kitchens. She ate two boiled eggs and chatted to the maids as they worked. They made her laugh with their stories, helping take her mind off the events of the evening. Indeed, she felt calm, as if all her problems had vanished into thin air.

It was quite some time later when Edward found her. It wasn't to her that he spoke first, however, but the staff.

"Did anyone see Paxton and his men this morning?" he asked the kitchen maids.

They shook their heads. "Must've left bright and early," one girl said. "I been up since before the sun, and I ain't seen those men nowhere."

"They've gone?" Elizabeth asked him.

"His room is empty, as is that of his men."

She blew out a breath. "I knew I felt happier this morning. That must be why. They're not here."

"Bad news, they were," said another maid. "I didn't like 'em." Echoes of agreement filled the kitchen.

Edward left and Elizabeth followed him out. "Is this your doing?" she asked. "Did you threaten him last night?"

"I told him to leave. I honestly didn't think he had any intention of going." He shrugged. "He seemed to have a deep interest in keeping an eye on Greville."

"Why?"

"I don't know. Neither would tell me."

"Do you think…" She swallowed. "Do you think I ought to be worried about Greville's suitability for Arrabella?"

He stopped walking and looked at her for a long moment. "Let's go for a walk in the garden."

Where no one could overhear them.

They strolled along the terrace, side-by-side. It was going to be another warm day. The sky was a bright blue empty canvas, and the trees could have been statues for all they didn't move. They ventured down to the rose garden and wound their way between the garden beds. Elizabeth breathed in the scent of the flowers, feeling somewhat lulled by the sunshine and having Edward at her side.

"I don't know why Paxton came with Greville," he said. "I couldn't get to the bottom of that mystery. Now that he's gone, I doubt I ever will."

"His presence did seem very odd," she said, shaking off her contentment. "Do you know if it had something to do with that traveler?"

He hesitated then sighed. "Elizabeth, there's something I need to ask you, but first I must tell you what I know." He stopped walking and indicated she should sit on the stone bench situated in front of a cone-shaped topiary.

"Oh?" She sat and he sat beside her. "This sounds intriguing."

"I found the traveler yesterday."

She gasped. "Where? In the bakehouse?"

"The brewery. I was in the bakehouse looking for the item he wanted to give Greville. The item that Paxton tried to grab off him, but didn't. His name is Best, and he's Greville's brother's man."

She listened as he told her about the brothers' fractured relationship, Ayleward's poverty, Best's need to give Greville something, and his reluctance to say what. It was intriguing, but what she found the most interesting was that Edward told her all of it. No man had ever talked to her as an equal, yet Edward didn't seem to think her incapable of grasping the details or the broader meaning.

"If Ayleward is impoverished, does that mean Greville is too?" she asked. "No, surely not," she said, answering herself. "I saw him splash his wealth about in London. You only have to look at his clothes and the quality of his horse to know he's a rich man. Besides, Jeffrey wouldn't allow Bella to wed a man with no money." Too late she remembered that Edward had wanted to marry Arrabella and came from a family of no fortune.

She stole a glance at him, but if he were put out by her comment, he didn't show it.

"I suspect he's keeping his younger brother on a tight leash, controlling his spending," was all he said.

"Why would he do that?"

Edward said nothing, and it was the first time she thought he was holding back a piece of information from her.

"It doesn't matter now," he said. "Paxton is gone. Best can give Greville the package and then leave."

"And my sister can marry Greville and disappear off to his estate."

"That's the thing I wanted to ask you. Do you know why the wedding is to be held here and not at Greville's ancestral home?"

"It was Greville's suggestion. He wanted Arrabella to be with her family, but didn't think Upper Wayworth was important enough. He wanted a grand gesture and that required a grand estate."

"Then why couldn't you and your mother and cousin travel to *his* estate?"

It was a good question, and not one she'd considered before. "Greville suggested Sutton Hall for the reasons I just gave you, and

Jeffrey eagerly agreed. He wanted to show off his estate to the guests, some of whom will be courtiers. Jeffrey hasn't been master here for long, and the previous Lord Lynden was very charming by all accounts. Poor Jeffrey has high standards to live up to, and he will do quite a lot to try and surpass them."

Edward smiled crookedly. "He doesn't like to be overshadowed, even by a dead man."

She laughed. He knew her cousin well.

The *clip clop* of horse's hooves turned their attention toward the gravel drive. Edward stood and peered over the bushes.

"What's he doing here?"

She looked too and saw Edward's friend Nicholas Coleclough on horseback, another three horses tied up behind. They went to meet him and were intercepted by Warren and another groom.

"Good morning," Coleclough called out.

"A little early for visitors, isn't it?" Edward asked, patting his friend's horse.

Coleclough grinned and dismounted. "Now is that any way to speak to the man who just returned Lord Lynden's valuable property?" He indicated the horses tied to his own.

"They ain't ours," Warren said.

Coleclough frowned. "I passed them on the road into the village just now. Since Sutton Hall is the closest stables to where I found them, I assumed they must be Lynden's. Fine animals like that should be stabled, not allowed to run wild."

"Aye." Edward inspected one of the horses while the grooms inspected the other two.

"I know 'em," Warren said.

"Aye," said the other groom. "They were ridden by Paxton and his men."

Edward and Coleclough exchanged glances. "Is Paxton here?" Coleclough asked.

"No. They left overnight following an incident." Edward's gaze shifted to Elizabeth's. "Nobody saw them leave."

"Monk! Monk!" The high-pitched shout made the horses ears twitch back and forth.

Elizabeth turned to see Jeffrey running toward them from the terrace. It was an odd sight. He had a handkerchief pressed over his mouth, and his face was very pale.

"Is he going to throw up?" Coleclough said.

"Monk, your assistance is required in the far western paddock," Jeffrey called out before he'd reached them.

"What is it?" Edward asked.

"Umberley has just informed me they found Paxton and his men there. Dead."

CHAPTER 13

The three bodies were laid out on the floor in the barn. They were dirty, having been buried in a shallow grave in one of the fields, and covered in dried blood. Their throats had been cut.

"Looks clean," Cole said, inspecting Paxton's wound. "I'd say a—"

"What are you doing?" Lynden cried from the entrance.

So he'd finally decided to join them. Edward had begun to think he wouldn't show at all. Lynden might have been the Justice of the Peace for the valley, but he didn't seem too eager to see dead bodies. Indeed, he looked quite horrified. So much so, he'd forgotten to cover his nose and mouth with his handkerchief.

"We need to determine how he was killed," Edward explained.

"That's a matter for the coroner."

"The coroner won't be here for days, Cousin," Elizabeth said. "There's no harm in having a look in the meantime."

Edward eyed her as she bent over one of Paxton's men. Despite ordering her to remain behind, she'd followed Edward's example and untied one of the roaming horses. She'd ridden *astride* all the way to the barn, easily keeping apace with Edward and Cole. The ferocious pace they'd set hadn't deterred her. From the way she peeled back the bloodied cloth around the dead man's neck, she didn't seem particularly deterred by blood and violent death either. Edward had to admit that he was impressed with her mettle. Most women would recoil at the sight, and some men too. He looked to Lynden.

"No harm!" the baron gasped, incredulous. "Elizabeth, don't touch him! It's disgusting."

"On the contrary. It's interesting," she said. "I've never seen such a deep cut before. There is quite a lot of blood too." She indicated the splattered clothing.

"There'll be even more on the ground where they died," Cole told her. "Wounds in the throat tend to spurt rather than flow."

Lynden gurgled and pressed his handkerchief to his mouth once more.

Edward was about to tell his friend to shut his mouth about the particulars, but Elizabeth wasn't the least bit pale. She seemed intrigued. She asked several questions about the stiffness of the body, the size of the wound and the possible weapon that could have caused it.

Cole's answers had Lynden running from the barn, his face as green as pond slime.

"I'd say a dagger rather than a sword," Edward said, taking another look at Paxton's injury. "The wounds aren't so much gashes as stabs."

"So whoever did it would have blood over their clothing," Elizabeth said. At Edward's raised brow, she came up to him, imaginary dagger raised, and stabbed him in the throat with it. "If a wound in the neck spurts blood, I would be covered too."

Edward tapped the right side of his neck. "The wounds are here, not on the left. You're right handed, as are most people. Standing in front of me would mean you stab my left side, but standing behind me, you'd stab me on the right." He took her shoulders and turned her round. He swept the silky wisps of hair off her neck and placed his palm on her throat over the imaginary wound. Her skin warmed his hand. Her pulse throbbed a steady rhythm. He breathed in her sweet fragrance, filling his chest with it. She smelled like roses and sunshine.

He felt the moment her pulse quickened. It fluttered like a butterfly. His blood rushed through his body in response. He touched his other hand to the curve of her waist. When she didn't move away, he put his arm around her.

Ever so slowly, inch by inch, she tilted her head, giving him a tantalizing view of her lowered lashes, her pink cheeks, her parted lips. He wanted to taste them again.

Cole cleared his throat. Elizabeth stepped away. "I'd better see if Jeffrey is all right," she said. Then she was gone.

Edward turned back to the grim scene, but didn't really look. He caught Cole watching him, a wicked smile on his lips.

"Really, Monk?" he drawled. "In front of me and surrounded by dead bodies?"

Edward's face heated. He lost all sense of time and place when he touched Elizabeth. Cole had disappeared, as had the bodies, and it had been just the two of them. Touching her was proving to be an immense distraction.

"Where is that disciplined, single-minded man I trained?" Cole's eyes twinkled with mischief. "He wouldn't have been distracted by a chit. He wouldn't have been distracted by anything, except maybe a pile of gold."

The brutal assessment of Edward took him by surprise. Is that how Cole saw him? As a greedy, cold-hearted mercenary? He considered Cole a friend now, but perhaps that was overstating their relationship. Cole was a nobleman's son—why would he be friends with Edward?

"Have you bedded her yet?" Cole asked.

"Shut it."

He grunted. "You should. It'll relieve the immediate urge."

"Fuck you, Cole."

Cole laughed and slapped Edward on the shoulder. "Come now, tell me what you think about these murders before someone comes in."

"What I think is that you're retired. Go home to your betrothed and leave this to me."

Cole raised his eyebrows. "I only want to help."

"I don't need your help."

"Everybody needs help sometimes, Monk. Besides, I owe you." The light in his eyes dimmed. Shadows passed over his face. "What you did for me when I was in need went beyond mere duty to the Guild. You took care of Lucy when I couldn't, and I'll never forget that." His nostrils flared, and he drew in a deep breath. When it came to talking of that worrying time and the effect it had on Lucy, Cole turned from brutal killer to kitten in an instant. "So don't think you can escape my help because you're too embarrassed to admit you haven't bedded a woman in an age. Not counting Lowe's girls, of course."

'In an age.' Is that what he thought? Hughe and Orlando too? That was fine with Edward. It was humiliating enough admitting that he'd saved himself for a woman who didn't love him. It was beyond embarrassing admitting that he'd never slept with a woman. Ever. And Lowe's girls definitely didn't count.

"I think whoever did this snuck up behind each man in turn and slit his throat," Edward said, looking once more at the bodies. "They must have been alone, otherwise they would have come to the rescue of the other, and there are no signs of a fight."

"What about the cut on Paxton's hand and chin?" Cole asked.

"I inflicted those last night."

Cole raised a brow but made no comment. "So either a single killer got to each of them without alerting his next victims, or they were attacked all at once."

"That means at least three murderers. Vagabonds?"

"Who left behind valuable horses?" Cole shook his head. "Unlikely."

If it hadn't been a robbery, there must have been another reason. A more personal one. It wasn't a great leap to assume the murderer or murderers was known to the victims.

"Were there any disturbances in the small hours?" Cole asked. "Unusual noises, shouts?"

"None that I heard, but the house is large. Besides, the men could have been killed in their asleep."

"Or simply didn't notice their attacker. I agree with your assessment that the murderer came from behind. Even if he were left handed and approached from the front, the angle is all wrong." He crouched beside Paxton's body and separated the two edges of the cut.

Edward peered past him to get a closer look. "Agreed."

"God's blood, what are you doing?"

They turned to see Greville standing in the doorway, Elizabeth by his side. Beyond them, Lynden sat on the grass, his knees drawn up and head bowed.

"Stop that at once!" Greville snapped. "Don't touch them. It's not Christian."

Cole stood, straightening to his full height. He was a formidable size with an air of menace about him. Greville stopped in his tracks and swallowed.

"We're simply trying to discover what happened," Edward explained.

"I can see from here what happened," Greville said with a look of disgust at the bodies. "Their throats have been cut."

Elizabeth opened her mouth to say something, but Edward shook his head and she closed it.

"Did you hear any noises last night?" Edward asked him. "Any shouts perhaps?"

"I saw them leave."

"Really? When was that?"

"How should I know? It was dark. Some time after you left my bedchamber, but well before dawn. I couldn't sleep and went down to the larder to find something to eat. That's when I heard them. They made very little sound. I doused my candle and hid in the larder as they passed. I didn't want to confront them. You understand why," he added, looking away.

"Did they carry their belongings?"

"Yes."

"And they went to the stables?"

"I don't know. I didn't follow them. They must have. Aren't their horses out there? They must have wandered here after…that happened."

"I found them riderless on the village road," Cole said.

"Well, there you have it. They were set upon by vagabonds after they left the Hall."

"Mayhap," Edward said. Beside him, Cole stood very still, giving nothing away. Elizabeth too remained silent.

"We should send out a party to search for the villains," Greville announced with a toss of his head that flicked his blond hair across his forehead. "I'll organize some men." He cast another glance at the bodies, but quickly looked away again, his face blank. "May their souls find peace in Heaven."

"If that's where they go," Elizabeth muttered.

Greville stared at her, shock slackening his jaw. "You have reason to believe they won't?"

"They attacked me last night."

"Christ," Cole said. He looked at Edward. "You knew?"

Edward nodded. His heart felt like a rock in his chest. Elizabeth needn't have told anyone if she didn't want to. But she had, and bravely too without a hint of distress. He wanted to take her in his arms all over again.

"Monk told me," Greville said. He suddenly took a step away from her, and if his eyes widened any further, they'd pop out of the sockets. "That gives you a reason to want them dead, Mistress Buckley."

Edward crossed the space between them in the time it took to blink. He grabbed Greville's doublet. Fury made his hands twist hard in the blue silk. Greville whimpered. "Don't you dare say another word against her good character, or I'll shove the tongue that utters it down your throat."

Out of the corner of his eye, he saw Elizabeth's hands move to clasp tightly in front of her. So tightly, the knuckles went white.

Edward twisted Greville's doublet again, producing a squeak from the pathetic turd. "If you wish to point the finger at someone who wanted to see these men gone, then point it at yourself."

"Wh…what?" Greville cried.

"I heard you threaten Paxton last night."

"Me threaten him? He had me beneath his boot! I was in no position to do anything to him."

"Nevertheless, I heard you. Now might be a good time to tell me why you were pretending he was your man."

Greville gave a derisive snort. His top lip curled. "I have nothing to say to you, Mr. Monk. Kindly let me go."

Edward did. He wouldn't get answers out of him in this manner. The problem was, he didn't know how to make Greville talk, short of hurting him. What secrets did he possess that made him fear a dead man more than Edward?

"Lynden must write to the coroner," Cole said.

Greville smoothed the front of his doublet. "There's no point having the coroner here if we can't hand him the culprit. By the time he comes and declares the men murdered, the vagabonds will be long gone."

"Nevertheless, due procedure should be taken."

"Agreed," Edward said. "Greville, go tell Lynden what's to be done."

"Why me?" Greville sounded like a petulant child told to run along by his parent.

"You're welcome to stay and inspect the wounds with us."

He pulled a face. "Are you coming, Mistress Buckley?"

"I'll be out soon," she said. "Perhaps you ought to return to the house with my cousin. I'm sure Arrabella will need reassuring by now if she's heard of this. She'll be beside herself with worry if you're out here when violent vagabonds are on the loose."

"Right. Of course. Can't have the ladies worrying."

He tossed his head and marched out. All three watched him speak to Lynden then both of them rode off.

"Let's get to work." Edward knelt beside Paxton's body. "Cole, check the other two for papers, seals, anything that might tell you who they are and what they're doing here."

"You don't believe they're Greville's men?" Cole asked, also kneeling.

"No, and nor would you after what I tell you Best said."

"Who's Best?"

He was about to answer when Elizabeth picked up one of the packs lying beside a broken plow in the corner of the barn. Edward hadn't noticed them before. They bore blood splatters and were as dirty as the bodies.

"What are you doing?" he asked her.

"Checking this pack." She unstrapped the flap and tipped the contents onto the packed earth floor. "It must have belonged to one of them and may contain something that will give us answers."

"Elizabeth," he said on a sigh. "Why not return to the house with Lynden and Greville?"

"Why would I want to do that? I might miss something interesting."

"This isn't a game, Elizabeth."

"No, but it is a riddle, one I'd like to help you solve." She flashed him a smile. "I'm very good at riddles."

"I don't doubt it," he muttered.

"I know you don't think vagabonds did this. The horses weren't taken, nor anything from these packs it would seem." She held up a knife with a bone handle. It would have been worth something to thieves.

She picked up the empty pack. He snatched it off her. She snatched it back.

"Rifling through a dead man's things isn't a task for a lady," he said. "Cole, explain to Elizabeth that she needs to return to the house where she'll be safe."

"Since we don't know who did this, I think Miss Buckley will be safer with both of us." Cole shrugged an apology.

"Precisely!" Elizabeth scooped up the contents and tipped them back in the pack.

Edward could have thumped Cole. So much for their friendship. He doubted he'd want Lucy exposed to such gruesome sights, yet he had no qualms allowing Elizabeth to see it *and* participate.

Edward knew he wasn't going to win the argument. He sighed and picked up the third pack as Elizabeth tipped out the contents of the second.

"Now that you two have ceased squabbling, will somebody tell me what's going on?" Cole said. He'd not found anything on the bodies and joined them to look through the contents of the packs.

Edward told him what he'd learned from Best about Greville, Ayleward and Paxton. "Paxton definitely wasn't Greville's man," he said. "The attack on Elizabeth confirmed it. Greville may be a fool, but he wouldn't employ men who would harm a lady."

"I believe you're right," Elizabeth said with a grim set to her mouth.

"He admonished Paxton about it last night."

"What else did you learn?" Cole asked.

"They fought. Or more precisely Paxton hit Greville."

"That explains the cut on his lip," Elizabeth said.

"I'd wager there's more bruising on his body."

They finished searching through the packs then refilled them.

"Nothing," Elizabeth said with a shake of her head. "Only bits and pieces you would expect."

"It's not so surprising," Edward said. "If someone went to all that trouble to kill them, they would have been sure to remove any documents that may give away his identity."

"You have to confront Best." Cole handed him a wooden cup. "If Greville won't tell you why he's here, then it's the only way."

"I've already asked him. He wouldn't answer."

"You could hit him."

"That might work."

Elizabeth looked at one and then the other. She threw up her hands. "Or you could simply ask him again. Circumstances have changed now." She nodded at the three bodies. "He may not be so reluctant to tell you what he knows."

"It's worth a try. I'll go see him. It's time he came out of the brewery and showed himself anyway."

They left the bodies and packs and rejoined the horses tethered outside. Cole was the first to mount. "Lucy will be wondering where I got to." He reached down and clamped Edward's shoulder. "Be careful. Come to me if you need my help." He nodded at Elizabeth then rode off.

Edward turned his attention to her. He wished he hadn't. She pulled her skirts up to her knees, put one foot in the stirrup and hoisted her leg over the saddle. He saw a lot of underskirt and a flash of the creamy skin of her thigh. No matter how hard he tried, he couldn't banish the sight of the delectable morsel from his mind's eye. Indeed, although she had settled her skirts about her, he still saw more than he had a right to. Sitting astride like that made her skirts ride up, revealing her calves. They were shapely, the curve reminding him of the gentle flare of her hips. He wondered what it felt like to follow the line of that curve with his hands. His tongue.

"It's just a leg, Edward. We all have them."

"I, uh…"

She laughed and urged her horse forward. He had to race to catch up, but decided not to ride alongside her. He remained a little behind where he could admire her at a safe distance and not be subjected to her devastating wit.

There was a great deal to admire. She was an excellent rider, despite the mount not being her usual one. She bent low over the horse's neck to control it and seemed as one with the animal. The two together were a graceful combination. He'd never seen a woman ride so superbly before. He'd never seen a woman ride astride at all.

Then again, he'd never met a woman like Elizabeth Buckley.

Nor was he likely to again.

* * *

ELIZABETH EXPECTED Edward to tell her to run along back to the house, but he did not. After they left their horses at the stables, he waited for her and they walked to the brewery together.

"What are your thoughts on the deaths?" he asked her.

She stopped. Stared at him. Had he really just asked her opinion on a serious matter? Nobody had ever done that. No one.

When he realized she'd fallen behind, he stopped too and arched a brow. "Are you all right?" He came back to her and peered into her face. "You're not having a delayed response to the gruesome scene in the barn, are you?"

"No, of course not. I've seen dead men before."

"Murdered ones?"

"Uh, no. Don't worry, I'm not going to faint on you."

"The thought never crossed my mind. You seem a most unshakeable woman."

"You're forgetting how I cried like a babe last night."

His eyes shuttered as it always did at the mention of the attack. She was beginning to think it bothered him more than it did her.

"I was merely surprised that you're allowing me to come with you to question Best," she said.

"He's not dangerous. If he were, I'd be locking you in your chambers to ensure you didn't come with me."

She snorted. "I'd like to see you try."

They resumed walking. Sutton Hall had dozens of house staff, and it appeared as if they were all bustling between the outbuildings. Maids carried baskets of linen, pails of water from the well, or vegetables from the garden. They greeted Elizabeth with a smile and blushed when Edward acknowledged them.

The brewery was hot and smelled smoky. A stout maid with her sleeves rolled up to reveal forearms as big as hams sat beside the furnace. She blinked sweat from her eyes and gave them a curious look.

"Mornin', sir, ma'am."

"Good morning," Edward said. "Excuse the intrusion. We won't be long. Best!" he shouted. "Show yourself. It's Monk. I wish to talk to you."

No answer. The maid frowned and glanced around. "There ain't no one here but me."

"Best! It's bloody hot in here. Come down, and get some fresh air."

Still no answer.

"Paxton is dead," Edward called out. "His men too."

A face Elizabeth recognized peered over the edge of the loft floor. It was redder than the last time she'd seen it in The White Hart, but unmistakable. She'd know those small, black eyes and long dark hair anywhere.

The maid cried out in surprise and stumbled off her stool. Edward caught her. "How long's he been up there?" she asked.

"A few days."

"I ain't been in much of late. The furnace ain't been burnin' for near a week."

"What trick is this?" Best called down.

"No trick," Edward called back. "Paxton and his men are indeed dead, so there's no reason to hide anymore."

Best's gaze flittered around the brewery, settling on Elizabeth. He frowned. He didn't appear particularly glad to have his hiding spot revealed.

"It's terribly hot in here, Mr. Best," she said. "Please come into the house and receive refreshments. My cousin will welcome you."

His only response was a scowl at Edward. "You promised not to tell anyone."

Edward shrugged. "Paxton is gone. I don't see the point in hiding. Besides, I want to know if you killed him or not."

"I bloody well did not!"

"Prove it."

Best reached behind him then revealed his sword. He shook it at them. Edward sighed and crossed his arms. "We're not going to go through that again, are we? You know you won't win."

"I'm ready for you this time."

"True. But there are witnesses. Besides, I don't care to see any more bloodshed today. There was quite enough of it all over the bodies."

The maid whimpered into her apron.

Elizabeth had heard quite enough. "Mr. Best, if you do not come down and tell us everything you know, your name will be the first one given to the coroner as the possible killer. How would your master like to find out his errand was not completed because his man was hung for murder?"

Best squeezed his eyes shut and lowered his head. Elizabeth felt sorry for speaking so bluntly, but the man needed to know the consequences of his inaction.

"Very well," he said heavily. He sheathed his sword and climbed down the ladder.

The maid shuffled away without taking her gaze off him. Best gave her an apologetic shrug. Elizabeth held her breath. He reeked of sweat. Not surprising considering the brewery was as hot as an oven.

"Come to the house," Edward said. "You can clean up and take refreshments."

"Not the house. Somewhere quiet and cool, but not where Greville can see me."

"I thought you wanted to speak to him."

"I do, but I don't want him seeing me speak to you."

"Then we must remain here," Elizabeth said. "Greville is unlikely to venture to the outbuildings."

"The rear of the brewery is in the shade," Edward said. "We'll go there."

Best slumped his shoulders and trod ahead of them. He looked like a beaten man. Elizabeth took that as a good sign. If he were defiant, she'd expect him to avoid answering their questions, or perhaps give outright lies, but a resigned man was a man going to tell the truth, no matter how much he didn't want to.

Once around the back of the brewery, they couldn't be seen from the house. Best leaned against the brick wall with a heavy sigh. He rubbed his shoulder absently, as if an old injury bothered him.

"Your presence will unlikely remain a secret much longer," Edward warned him. "Not now that the brewery maid has seen you."

"Hopefully Greville won't know that I spoke to you. She's not likely to talk to him, is she?"

Elizabeth touched his hand. He looked terribly forlorn, and she hated to think that it was hers and Edward's fault. Despite the runaround he'd given them, he didn't seem dangerous. Indeed, he simply seemed tired. Traveling for weeks and sleeping in the brewery would exhaust anyone, and Best was no longer a young man.

"He doesn't need to know," she said. "We'll tell him you wouldn't speak once we discovered you. Then you can have a nice rest in one of the chambers."

He smiled gently at her. "Thank you, ma'am. You're too kind. I wish I wasn't about to tell you something that will make your family want to end your sister's betrothal to Greville."

CHAPTER 14

"You recall that I told you my master, Ayleward, lives meagerly," Best said to Edward.

Edward nodded. He leaned closer to Best, as if to convince him to hurry with his story. He seemed even more interested in discovering Best's secrets now that he knew it affected Arrabella's betrothal to Greville. Despite his declaration to Elizabeth that he was cured of all feelings toward her sister, she wondered if he'd spoken the truth. His profound interest in Best's story would prove otherwise.

"Well." Best cleared his throat. "Greville does too."

"He's impoverished?" Edward started to laugh then stopped when Best didn't join in. "But he has a grand estate in Sussex."

"It was once grand, but not anymore. Much of the land was sold after Greville inherited from his father, and the farms that remain are poorly managed. He doesn't make a good landlord, and he let go the only man in his employ who did. He only knows how to spend money, not make it. The house is old and in need of repairs, and there's simply nothing left to spend on it."

Elizabeth couldn't believe what she was hearing. She'd not thought Greville capable of thinking up a ruse on such a grand scale, let alone maintain it for so long without anyone finding out.

In truth, she always thought him lacking in sense with only his handsome face and amiable nature to recommend him. "That's why he didn't want the wedding to be held there. He was too embarrassed."

"Or he didn't want his future bride and her family discovering just how poor he is," Edward said. "She might have second thoughts. I'd wager Lynden wasn't aware of it?"

"No, or he wouldn't have been so keen for the marriage to take place."

"Nor would Arrabella."

"Why not?" she asked. "She loves him."

"She loves him as long as he's got the means with which to keep her." The bitter twist of his words wasn't lost on her. "You know better than anyone what she's like."

She felt compelled to argue the point to protect her sister's reputation, but had to concede that he was right. No one knew it more than he too. The fact that it still rankled him enough to mention it bothered her more. It proved he had not shed all feelings for Arrabella entirely.

A knot tied up her insides. Any hopes she'd had of capturing his heart were dashed for the last time. The very last time. He would never be truly free of Arrabella. If his rejection of Elizabeth didn't prove it, this display certainly did.

The knot tightened. An ache burrowed deep in her heart and lodged there.

"Why can't he raise any loans?" Edward asked, oblivious to Elizabeth's pain.

"He's too ashamed to ask any courtiers within his circle," Best said with a sad shake of his head. "Ashamed and desperate to maintain the image of a wealthy man. If he shows any signs of poverty, he will be shunned and make a poor match."

"But Arrabella is hardly a wealthy heiress," Elizabeth said. "If he wants to wed her for money, he's chosen the wrong woman."

"She isn't the prize. Lynden is."

Elizabeth waited for an explanation. It was Edward who gave

it. "I overheard Paxton and Greville discussing the matter. By marrying Arrabella, they were hoping to dupe Lynden somehow. My guess is that once he discovered how poor his new relation was, he'd feel compelled to help him for Arrabella's sake. I cannot imagine she would want to live in a crumbling ruin with no money to spare for luxuries."

"Indeed not."

"Then either she would press her cousin, or Lynden himself would offer to give Greville money outright, or loan it to him on easy terms."

It was a plan that would have worked too, knowing her cousin and sister. Arrabella was selfish enough to beg for money to improve her new home, and Jeffrey was vain enough to not want to be linked to a poor relation.

"Lynden told me he investigated Greville thoroughly before he agreed to the match, " Edward said. "And yet this is proof that he couldn't have."

"Jeffrey told you that?" Why was her cousin confiding in a guest? Did he see Edward as a stand-in for Lord Oxley since he was the earl's man?

He looked away. A muscle pulsed in his jaw as if he were clenching his teeth. His reaction got her thoughts racing in all directions again. If he'd simply shrugged off her question, she wouldn't have thought anything of it. Now her curiosity was stirred once more. She'd always thought Edward's presence at Sutton Hall strange. Now she was sure there was something more to it than simply being nearby for Coleclough's sake. Whatever it was, Jeffrey knew.

"It's likely that Lord Lynden merely asked some of the other courtiers about Greville," Best said. "Since none have been to Greville's estate for years, they wouldn't know of its situation."

"Greville was generous with gifts too," she told them. "Arrabella's collection of jewels expanded after he took an interest in her. None would expect him of being poor from his behavior, or his clothing. But how could he afford it all? Where did the money come from?"

"Paxton," Edward said.

"Aye." Best nodded. "Mr. Ayleward was in correspondence with his brother before Lord Greville left London. After he engaged Miss Buckley's affections early in his visit, he borrowed heavily from a goldsmith. He told his brother that he'd captured her interest up to that point with nothing but the gifts God gave him."

"I'm sure the fact he was a baron charmed her more," Edward said, gruff.

"Nevertheless, he assured Ayleward that she was in love with him. Once he was certain of her feelings, only then did he seek out a loan. The goldsmith was more than happy to give him what he needed with the promise of gaining it back, with interest, from Lynden after the wedding."

Elizabeth groaned. "What a mess. Did he not think about what would happen if Jeffrey discovered the truth, or if Arrabella's affections waned? She's fickle when it comes to men. She falls in and out of love with the change of season. It's one of the reason's she not yet wed. That and the fact my father wouldn't force her."

"I suspect Greville thought the effect of his charms would last beyond the summer," Best said with a smirk. "He's different in every way to his brother. John Ayleward is studious. He can read and write a dozen languages. He studies the New Sciences as well as astrology. He cares little for chits like Miss Buckley. Pardon, ma'am, no offense meant."

She sighed. "None taken. I've heard it all before and said similar things about her myself. So is Paxton—*was* Paxton—the goldsmith that Greville borrowed from?"

"No, his name was Hicks. I suspect Paxton was *his* man, sent to keep an eye on Greville and ensure he went through with the marriage."

Edward blew out a breath. "And now he's dead. Hicks isn't going to like that."

"Pray he won't find out for some weeks, by which time my

sister is untangled from the mess and free of Greville. She cannot be allowed to marry him now, even if she still wanted to."

Edward frowned at her. "You're that set against her marrying a poor man?"

"No! I am against her marrying a deceptive one who will stoop to trickery and false flattery. We're not even sure if he likes her, let alone loves her."

"Love is not a necessary ingredient in marriage. But I agree on your other points. He has lied to her and your family every step of the way. I'll alert Lynden immediately."

"Oh no, please wait. Let me speak to her first. She needs to be given the chance to end the betrothal."

"And pray wait until I've left the area." Best winced, as if the thought of confronting Greville gave him pain. "He won't be happy when he discovers I told you everything."

"I'll wait until late today to talk to him," Edward said. "Elizabeth, refrain from telling your sister until then. I suspect the walls will come crashing down once she learns of Greville's deception."

"Very well, although I don't like the delay. What if he thinks we suspect him and he decides to leave?"

"He won't suspect anything, nor will he leave. He's got too much invested here in your sister. What of your own affair, Best? Have you delivered your master's message to Greville?"

Best's face closed up. He narrowed his eyes and regarded Edward with steeliness. "I promised to tell you about Paxton. I've done that. Whether I've discharged my business or not is none of your affair."

Edward gave him an assessing look. "I'd wager you haven't, or you would have left already. Am I right?"

Best pushed past him. Edward's hand whipped out and caught the man's elbow. Best was much smaller, but he didn't flinch or cower. He cocked his eyebrow and waited.

Elizabeth expected Edward to say something, but he didn't. He must have an inkling as to why Best was chasing Greville from his conversations with Jeffrey, yet he gave nothing away.

Was that because she was there, and he didn't want her to know too?

"You're right," Best said, shrugging Edward off. "I haven't discharged my task. It'll have to remain that way since I cannot stay near Greville now that I've told you about his affairs. He'll kill me. Besides, there is no way Greville can fulfill his brother's request. Not with the deaths hanging over his head."

Elizabeth gasped. "You think *he* killed them?"

"Of course. So does Mr. Monk."

She stared at Edward. He blew out a breath and nodded. "It's very likely," he said. "He had good reason to want Paxton dead. I also overheard him threaten Paxton last night."

She groaned and passed her hands over her face. Arrabella was going to be utterly devastated. And it was going to be up to Elizabeth to pick up the pieces of her sister's broken heart.

"Elizabeth? Are you all right?" He gently took her by the shoulders. His thumbs rubbed slow circles, sending little rippling sensations through her body.

She gave him a weak smile. "I'm fine. My sister won't be."

"We'll tell her together."

"Thank you, but I'd better do it alone. She might think it was all your doing because…" She swallowed the rest of her sentence and almost choked on it.

"I don't care what she thinks." But he dropped his hands to his sides and avoided her gaze, which didn't give Elizabeth much confidence that he spoke the truth. He had been in love with Arrabella for so long, it was almost impossible to believe he could give her up within a matter of days.

Best cleared this throat. "I need to tell my master how matters fared here before I left. Shall I tell him you hold his brother to await the coroner's arrival?"

Edward rubbed his forehead and nodded.

Best sighed. "A sad event. There's little love between them, but Ayleward wouldn't have wanted this."

"Nobody does," Edward said.

Elizabeth caught him looking at her, a deep line connecting his brows. He opened his mouth to speak, but she walked off before he had a chance. It was time to find out why he was at Sutton Hall at all.

* * *

ELIZABETH FOUND Jeffrey in his study, his head in his hands. The chamber was a masculine one with the wood paneling covering all the walls and not a tapestry in sight to break it up. It was quite unlike Jeffrey. There was none of his flamboyance and color, no embellishment of any kind. She supposed he'd not redecorated after the last Lord Lynden's death. Perhaps he liked the reminder of his cousin, who was by all accounts much admired.

"Jeffrey, are you all right?" She approached carefully, afraid that any sudden movement might produce a wail of sorrow from him. "It has been a rather trying morning for you, hasn't it?"

He dragged his hands over his face and looked up at her through his fingers. "It has, my dear. Most trying. The burdens of being me are heavy today."

She knelt beside him and touched his arm. One thing she'd learned from Arrabella was how to deal with the likes of Jeffrey. Sweet and demure was more effective than demanding and dogged. "Can I get you something? Wine?"

"What have I done to deserve this?"

So much for her offer. It was as if she wasn't even there. She bit back her retort and remained at his side. Patience was another feminine virtue he admired, but one that did not come naturally to her. She mustered it up from deep within.

He suddenly stabbed a leaf of parchment on his desk with his finger. "I'm writing to the coroner. He left Larkham barely a week ago. He must think this valley full of savage barbarians. It does not look good for me to be associated with these folk. Not good at all. What must he think of me? Eh, Elizabeth? Answer me that."

She increased the pressure on his arm, and he looked at her

properly for the first time since she'd entered. His eyes appeared bruised, the lines in his forehead deeper. Poor Jeffrey indeed. He wasn't very good at being baron, or Justice of the Peace. He was more suited to the ornamental life of a courtier rather than the practicalities of running an estate the size of Sutton Hall. She hoped he never lost his land steward, Umberley, or he would be in danger of ruining himself the way Greville had.

"It'll be all right," she soothed. "You'll have to order the bodies be moved to the cellar where it's cooler. If the coroner is some days away, your barn will smell foul before long."

Jeffrey groaned and turned green again.

"Would you like to read your letter to me? Perhaps hearing it aloud will help." She was very careful not to offer to read *to* him or rewrite it. Jeffrey wasn't like Edward. He didn't think her capable of comprehending complex matters. So she listened to his droning voice and subtly offered suggestions without being obvious about it. He made the changes, and by the end, he was pleased with the results of *his* efforts.

"Heat the wax for me," he said, folding the parchment.

She heated the sealing wax and poured it for him. He pressed his ring into it and handed the letter back to her.

"See that it's sent, my dear."

"Certainly. I'm so glad we got to spend some time in each other's company. We've all been terribly busy with the wedding preparations, and now this sorry business with Paxton."

He pulled a face. "Sorry indeed. Poor Greville must be feeling the loss of his men keenly. I left him with your sister, and he seemed quite upset by it all."

Killing three men in cold blood would upset most people. Elizabeth shivered. It wasn't a flippant matter, and she ought not to treat it as such. If Greville were a murderer, then she needed to watch over her sister until Edward was able to confine him.

"Speaking of Greville, I'm very worried about his suitability for Arrabella."

He'd been tidying up his desk, but he paused to look at her. "What are you inferring?"

She leaned closer and lowered her voice. "Edward had to confide in me about your suspicions. Don't blame him," she added quickly when he clicked his tongue. "He needed my help to, uh, spy on Greville."

"He did?" He shook his head. "I wish he'd kept it to himself. I always thought Monk discreet. It's why I wasn't unhappy when Oxley offered his assistance. He proved himself extremely capable the last time I employed him."

She'd almost forgotten that Edward had worked for Jeffrey before. Doing what?

"At least you're family and not a servant," he went on. "You won't tell your sister, will you?"

"About what?" she asked, curling a lock of her hair the way she saw Arrabella do when she was acting the empty-headed waif. "My involvement?"

"No, foolish girl, about Greville's Catholic connection."

Catholic! Greville was a papist? No wonder Jeffrey was worried. Elizabeth didn't think he particularly cared what a man believed, but he did care about doing the right thing. Jeffrey wouldn't do anything that drew negative attention to him from the people who mattered, and the people who mattered were those with influence at court. The queen didn't have Catholics at court. Those that practiced the old faith considered themselves lucky not to be noticed at all. Those that did get noticed usually found themselves under suspicion at best, and headless at worst.

"We must wait until Monk has found out for sure, and only then can you tell Arrabella," he said. "Understand? I know what tattlers women can be, particularly sisters. It's why I cannot believe Monk enlisted your help. Surely a man of his age and experience must know that females cannot be trusted to keep their mouths shut. I should have a word with him."

"No! Please don't. He'll only admonish me for speaking out of turn to you. I promise I'll keep quiet."

He pursed his lips and gave her a scowl. "Very well. Be off with you, and take the coroner's letter with you." She kissed the top of his head and he patted her arm. "You're a good girl when you want to be."

The problem was, she didn't want to be his version of 'good.' It was dull. She much preferred solving the intrigues surrounding Edward and Greville.

She left his study and went in search of the house steward. She found him and gave him instructions to see that the letter reached its destination. She then looked for Edward and finally found him back where she'd started, in Jeffrey's study. Greville was there too, sprawled in a chair, his head propped up by his hand.

Had Edward confronted him already? But no, the shadows under his eyes were a sign of exhaustion and worry, not distress. It would seem Edward had been true to the word he gave Best and not confronted Greville yet.

His gaze drilled into her, as if he could read her mind. She gave him a nod and a wink, which had his brow arching in curiosity.

"What shall be done with the bodies?" Jeffrey asked. Neither he nor Greville acknowledged Elizabeth's arrival. If it hadn't been for Edward, she might as well have been invisible. Never mind. It gave her the opportunity to listen in to their conversation. "They cannot stay in my barn for three days waiting for the coroner. Not in this heat. They'll stink the place out."

"Do you have a dungeon?" Greville asked.

Jeffrey screwed his face up in disgust. "Does this look like a moldy castle to you?"

"Move them to the cellar," Edward suggested. "Have your men do it soon before it gets too hot."

"Good idea. That's settled. The coroner has been sent for, and men are out searching for the vagabonds. Hopefully they won't be gone long. They've work to do."

"Do Mistress Buckley and Arrabella know?" Edward asked.

"Did you not hear my aunt's screech?" Jeffrey pinched the

bridge of his nose. "It filled the house. Elizabeth, you should go to her."

Elizabeth was startled into moving forward. She didn't think Jeffrey had seen her at all. "Isn't my sister with her?"

"Aye," said Greville on a sigh. "But I don't think she's much help. She's as agitated as her mother, crying and pleading with me to be careful with murderers on the loose." His mouth turned down in disgust. "I had to get away and seek out the company of sensible *men*."

"You can correct her of that behavior after you're wed," Jeffrey said. "A beating or two should do it. If she proves to be particularly slow at learning, then it may take more."

Elizabeth stared at her cousin. Any earlier sympathy she felt for him vanished. "Does that advice come from your vast store of knowledge regarding women, Jeffrey?" she asked.

"I, uh...well, yes, I suppose it does." He shifted uncomfortably in his seat.

Greville sniggered. By now he would have learned that the only knowledge Jeffrey had of women was how to dress as flamboyantly as them, smell as pretty and flourish his hand as daintily.

"You should have stayed to comfort Arrabella," Elizabeth told Greville. "She needs you."

"She needs *you*. You're her sister."

"*You're* her betrothed."

Greville pushed himself to his feet and looked Elizabeth up and down. "You may be pretty, but your tongue is much too sharp. I pity the poor man who weds you. That's if you can find one who'll have you." He pulled on the hem of his jerkin to straighten it then stomped peevishly out of the study.

"Elizabeth?" Edward asked softly. He looked concerned, and his raised brow seemed to be asking her if she was all right.

She nodded. He nodded back then followed Greville out to keep an eye on him as agreed. She went in search of her sister to comfort her, but her thoughts kept wandering back to Greville, and his petty display in the study. He was usually so charming, but the polished mask was beginning to peel off. He didn't seem quite as keen to fawn over Arrabella anymore. It was a curious thing considering he'd gone to so much trouble to ensure the family didn't find out about his debts. Yet he no longer looked like a man in love.

She would discuss it later with Edward, before he confronted Greville over the murders. For now, she would be with her sister and mother and try not to go mad listening to their fretting.

* * *

EDWARD FOLLOWED Greville discreetly for the rest of the day. He'd already decided to confront him after supper. That would give Best enough time to be far away. Edward had considered speaking to Greville immediately then locking him in a chamber, but decided against it. He'd promised Best, and Greville didn't seem to want to leave anyway. He did seem agitated, however. He walked around the outside of the house, twice, then sat in the garden for an age, his head in his hands. He returned to the house in the afternoon and retired to his room for the rest of the day and into the early evening.

Edward slipped away to speak to Lynden, something he'd tried to do earlier only to find Greville in the study with him. He informed Lynden of his suspicions regarding the deaths. Lynden accepted his opinion with shocked silence at first, but after hearing the explanations, gave a resigned nod.

"You'd better lock Greville in his rooms. I'll fetch the key."

He retrieved the key from the house steward and gave it to Edward. They parted ways since Lynden refused to join him. He didn't want to muddy his hands with the sordid mess any more than he had to.

Edward made his way through the house to the guest apartments housing Greville. He paused when he saw Elizabeth pounding her fist on the closed door. It was a long time before Greville answered.

"What do you want?" he snapped.

She bristled at his tone. "My sister is asking for you. Even though it's against my better judgment, I think you should go to her."

"My head aches." He shut the door.

She thrust her hands on her hips and glared at it as if she could make him re-open it through force of will. When he didn't, she stamped her foot and muttered, "Pizzle head."

"That sums him up nicely," Edward said, coming up behind her.

She spun round, her hand at her breast. "You startled me. You shouldn't sneak up on people like that."

"I wasn't sneaking."

"You were. It's what you do, isn't it? Sneak about and spy on people."

He cocked his head to the side. It would seem she'd gotten Lynden to reveal more than he should have. He shouldn't be surprised. She could outwit Lynden without even trying.

"Speaking of which, I have some questions," she said.

"Why am I not surprised?" He nodded at the door. "Can they wait? It's time to talk to Greville."

"Of course." She sighed. "I hoped he would do the honorable thing and call off the betrothal before we exposed him. It seems he's not interested in speaking to Arrabella at all." She nibbled her lower lip.

Without thinking, he put his thumb to her chin and drew the lip out. "You shouldn't do that. Your lip doesn't deserve to be savaged."

She blinked owlishly at him. "Oh," she said, breathy. She skimmed her fingertip over her lip. He found he couldn't take his eyes off it. He wanted to touch her there, feel the soft plumpness of her mouth, capture the smiles, the frowns, the wry twists of those delicious lips.

"Can we talk afterward?" she asked.

He nodded numbly.

"Meet me in your chambers." And then she was gone. It wasn't until he'd shaken off his stupor that he wondered why she'd suggested they meet in his rooms.

He wondered why he'd accepted.

He opened the door without knocking. The room was a small study for the guest's sole use. Adjoining it was a small chamber, and then the bedchamber was beyond that. Edward found Greville sitting on the bed, propped up against the pillows, a cup in one hand, a jug in the other. His shirt was open and his feet and legs bare.

"Ever heard of knocking?" Greville growled, filling his cup from the jug. "I might have been fucking my betrothed."

"Your betrothed is in her room with her mother, wondering why you're not coming to her."

"Perhaps if she didn't order me to come, I would. I don't take kindly to being told what to do."

"Therein lies your problem, I'd wager."

"What?" He wiped his mouth with the back of the hand that held the cup. Wine spilled down his chest. He didn't seem to notice. "What are you mumbling about, man? And what the bloody hell do you want anyway? I'm busy."

"I'm here to talk to you, primarily."

"Talk! In that case, you need some wine. This is strong stuff." He looked around for another cup. Finding none, he held out his own. "Take this. I'll use the jug."

Edward took the cup and set it on the table. Greville pouted. "I spoke to Best," Edward said. "He told me about the debts, the goldsmith—"

"The prick!" He pounded the mattress with his fist. "The little traitorous prick!"

"Did he give you the document?" Edward wasn't sure whether Best's package was a document or not, but he suspected it was.

"He tried to. I wanted nothing to do with it. So where's he now? Lapping up Lynden's hospitality too, eh? Bet he likes living like a lord in a fine house like this."

"He's gone."

"Oh? Good." Greville rested the jug on his lap. "So what else did he tell you?"

"That you're only marrying Arrabella to get to Lynden's money."

Greville snorted. "That surprises you?"

"Yes, actually. I thought you two were in love."

Another snort. "So did I. Indeed, I *was* in love in the beginning. She's a fun girl with great big teets. Have you seen 'em?" He laughed. "Course you have. You were in love with her too."

Edward sighed. It was going to be difficult getting sense out of him in his drunken state. "I was mistaken."

Greville sobered. "As was I." He drank from the jug, spilling wine down the sides of his mouth. He belched. "So have you told Lynden?"

Edward nodded.

"I should thrash you for that, but you're bloody handy with a sword. And fists. Besides, I don't think I can stand right now." He saluted Edward with the jug. "Powerful stuff, this. Sure you don't want some?"

"No thanks."

"Ah well. The more for me, eh? So it's over? Does the little trollop know?"

Edward considered thumping him, but decided Greville would probably suffer more if he kept talking. "Not yet. Elizabeth will tell her soon. There's one other thing, Greville."

"Hmmm?"

"Did you kill Paxton?"

"Me? Kill Paxton?" He laughed. "You did see him thrash me last night, didn't you?"

"Did you kill him and his men?"

"No."

"You had the most to gain."

"Did I?"

"Getting rid of Paxton would solve all your problems."

"Temporarily. Hicks would send another man soon enough to

break all the fingers in my hands. That was the threat. Did you know? Paxton described it to me in great detail. He said he would get his men to hold me down then snap each bone in my hand, one by one. Then he'd move onto the other hand." He made a small mewling sound in his throat and stared into the jug. "I'm not sure how that will ensure I pay back my loan. I can hardly get my hands on repayments when those very hands are useless."

"I have to lock you up until the coroner arrives. If he concludes murder, which he undoubtedly will, you'll have to be locked up until the next assizes."

Greville's head jerked up. His glazed eyes managed to focus on Edward after a few moments. "Bloody Lynden. I can't believe he would allow a fellow baron to be treated like a commoner. Soft prick," he added, bitter. "The man likes it up the arse, did you know that? Bet he's got a catamite stashed around here somewhere. It's not you is it, Monk?" He sniggered a laugh. "Monk. What kind of toss-pot name is that?"

Edward was tired of listening to his rambling. The man was definitely drunk and possibly mad as well. "I'll be back in the morning with breakfast." He left, locking the outer door to the study behind him.

A moment later he heard the rattle of the door handle, and Greville's muttered, "Fuck."

He went in search of Elizabeth and found her coming out of her sister's rooms, holding a candle. The lines bracketing her mouth tugged downward, and her eyes were shot with red. She looked exhausted.

"How is she?" he asked.

Just then the door opened and a wild creature with swollen red eyes and a thicket of tangled brown hair threw a shoe at Elizabeth. Edward caught it before it hit her.

"I hate you!" Arrabella screamed at her sister. "I hate you both! You have no idea what you've done to me!"

Janet came up behind her daughter and forcibly grasped her

shoulders. "Come back inside, Child. You can't afford to have Jeffrey hear you ranting like a madwoman. He'll lock you away."

Arrabella turned and sobbed into her mother's bosom. Janet waved Elizabeth and Edward off. He handed her the shoe and shut the door.

Without a word, Edward led Elizabeth upstairs to his chambers. They could talk there without being overheard, or hit by flying shoes. Just talk. Nothing more. After the gruesome events of the day, seduction was the last thing on his mind. He should easily be able to keep it that way. Just as long as he didn't look at any of the enticing parts of Elizabeth's body, like her mouth or eyes. Her hands were beautiful too, and her throat, so they were off limits. It would seem he would have to stare at her ear the entire time. Better that than risk falling for her charms again and suffering the ache in his groin that always came after an intimate encounter with her.

CHAPTER 15

"She's upset and angry," Elizabeth said. They sat in Edward's bedchamber. Not being an important guest like Greville, Oxley or the Buckleys, he'd been given a smaller room that had no adjoining study or closet. At least the chamber was large enough that they could sit away from the bed. Far away. Then again, Edward doubted it could ever be far enough for him not to think of tumbling Elizabeth in it.

"Very angry," he agreed. "The shoe was a clear clue."

She gave him a tired smile. "I told her about Greville's debts, and our suspicions that he murdered Paxton. She didn't believe me at first, and railed at me, telling me I made it up because I was jealous of her. After giving her a catalog of the proof, she calmed down, and I thought it safe to leave. It would seem that calmness didn't last long. What about Greville? How did he take the news of his detainment?"

"He's drunk, which is probably a good thing."

"Did he deny it?"

"Yes, but gave me no convincing argument to support his innocence. In fact, he seemed resigned to his fate."

"Perhaps his Catholic faith will help him get through the ordeal."

He crossed his arms. "And what trickery did you employ to get Lynden to admit that?"

"Feminine wiles," she said lightly.

"Ah yes, those. I'm well aware of their power." Despite his conviction that he wouldn't look at her, he couldn't drag his gaze away from her eyes. Where before they'd been clouded with tears and shadows, now they shone like bright stars. Mischief danced in them, teasing, luring. He braced himself against the onslaught of sudden desire rushing through him. Or tried to.

"Were you ever going to tell me you're working for Jeffrey to uncover the truth about Greville's faith?"

"No."

She made a miffed sound through her nose. "After all we've been through together?"

"What have we been through?"

"I looked at the bodies with you. We spoke to Best together." She leaned forward. "I fetched you from The White Hart."

"I did not *need* fetching."

"That point is debatable."

"Not from where I'm sitting."

She smoothed down her skirts and sat back again. Her face flushed to the roots of her hair. He could feel his own face heating at the memory of the manner in which she'd found him at the Hart.

Thank goodness she returned the subject to less humiliating matters. A pity it was also a return to her interrogation.

"What is that you do for Lord Oxley precisely?" she asked.

"Whatever he requires of me."

"And does he require you to discover facts about others? Spy on them?"

"On occasion."

"How extraordinary. Is he some sort of agent for the crown?"

"If he were, it would be foolish of me to tell you."

She rolled her eyes. "I'm hardly a person of consequence in

national affairs. Tell me, what sort of other things does Lord Oxley have you doing on his behalf?"

He shifted uncomfortably in his chair. He didn't like lying to her, but he couldn't tell her about the Assassins Guild. For one thing, it was against Guild rules to tell anyone who wasn't a spouse. For another, he wasn't sure how she would react to discovering that he got paid for killing people. Granted, those people deserved it after committing brutal crimes and escaping justice, but it was still a confronting thing to tell anyone, let alone a lady.

On the other hand, Elizabeth was no ordinary lady. He doubted she would faint upon hearing what Oxley employed him to do. If anyone understood his occupation, it would be her.

"I see it's a secret," she said when he didn't answer. "I suppose your friends Mr. Coleclough and Mr. Holt were also employed by Lord Oxley?"

"You're full of questions tonight."

She sighed and pushed a hand through her hair, only to be stopped by the pins and combs. She removed her hand, dislodging two pins and getting a lock caught on the ring on her finger. "I'm frustrated beyond measure," she said, trying to untangle the hair, but only succeeding in making it worse. "My mind is racing so fast I can hardly keep up. I'm sorry. I'll stop asking so many questions now." With a click of her tongue, she tried to pull her hand free. The ring wouldn't release the hair. She sucked air between her teeth, and he could see she was about to tear out the lock by the roots.

"Here," he said, coming to her aid. "Allow me."

She sat still as he untwisted the knotted hair. Her face was level with his stomach, her knees bumped his own. He could feel the warmth of her through the layers of his clothing and hear her breath catch in her throat.

"I wish I could tell you more about what I do," he suddenly said. "I know you would be discreet, but Hughe's rules are strict."

"I understand," she said. "It's just that this business has set me on edge. I feel so useless, Edward. I want to do something, but I'm not sure what. I'm not even sure if something is required to be done. It's more a feeling. Does that make any sense?"

He freed her hair and took her hand in his own to draw it away. Her fingers were small and slender against his big ones, the skin smooth and a little brown from the sun. She closed her fingers and his grip tightened in response.

She lifted her gaze to his and he fell into the deep pools of her eyes. He didn't care. Didn't want to climb back out or be rescued. What a fool he was to think he could sit alone with her in his bedchamber and not kiss her.

"Feelings should not be ignored," he murmured. "They tell us things. Important things."

"What sort of things?" Her voice was a breath of air against his lips. He hadn't noticed that he'd bent down to her level.

"For instance, your feelings are telling you to take action." He hardly knew what he said. The words just seemed to fall from his lips.

"Very true." She brought up her other hand to touch his face. Her fingertip traced the line of his cheek down to the corner of his mouth. Her hot gaze followed it.

"And my feelings," he said, "are telling me to kiss you."

Either she closed the gap between them, or he did. It didn't matter. They came together in a crash of lips and hands. He couldn't stop touching her. Her face, her hair, shoulders and waist. And she couldn't stop touching him. Her fingers dug through his hair, trailed down his neck and raked across his shoulders. She dragged his shirt off, tearing the laces asunder. He wore neither doublet nor jerkin, and the shirt was easily shed and discarded.

She broke the kiss and pressed her mouth to his chest. Her tongue teased the nipple and heat arrowed through him, centering on his groin. He groaned and tipped his head back, wanting more of that tongue, that mouth, those hands. She wrapped her arms around his back and held him against her. Her breasts pillowed, and he was given a tantalizing view of their soft swell, the deep, shadowy valley between. He trailed his fingertips over them and watched her flesh quiver as she trembled.

Another night, he had dipped his finger down the front of her bodice and touched her nipple. Lord, but he wanted to do so again. Wanted to pull the gown and shift down and free those beauties.

But he hesitated. He'd been drunk then. He wasn't now.

She gave him no time to take the thought further. She unfastened his breeches and shuffled them down. She clasped his arse and squeezed. The grin she gave him was wicked and filled with promises of what was to come.

His cock, still caught inside his breeches, hardened painfully. His stomach did a little flip of protest. This was going too fast. He needed to rein in his galloping thoughts, take control of the situation. Think before he acted. There was so much to think about. If they were going to go ahead with this—

She pulled his breeches all the way down, and all thoughts were blown from his mind. He tried to regain some semblance of composure, but it was impossible. He kicked the breeches away and stood there, entirely naked…and didn't know what to do next.

She seemed to have no such problem. After staring at his cock for several long moments, she touched it. Heat blasted through him, right to his core. It filled him, made his balls heavy and his cock thick. God's blood, but he wanted her to touch him again.

She giggled. "It moved."

The strange bubble that had enveloped him ever since they'd kissed burst. He felt disoriented and shaken, like he'd woken up from a vivid dream. Part of him wished he could return to it, but his pride had been pricked by her laughter. Yet it wasn't that which had him snatching a cushion off the chair and scrambling to cover himself. It was the sickening sense that he couldn't do this to Elizabeth. She was far too special to be had for a night then discarded.

Then again, he didn't have to discard her. Not now.

"No," she whispered hoarsely. "No, you don't. Not again." She picked up his shirt and breeches and threw them out the window. She stomped back to him and whisked the cushion out of his hands, but instead of throwing it to its doom out the window too, she held it to her chest. The fight suddenly left her, and tears spilled down her cheeks. She buried her face in the cushion and sobbed.

The sight broke his heart. "Elizabeth," he murmured. "Don't, please."

She dropped the cushion back onto the chair and angrily swiped at the tears. "You think I want to cry? You think I want to love a man who doesn't love me back?"

Love? She loved him? But she'd claimed she no longer did.

"Do you think I like kissing you then being set aside?" she shouted. "My nerves can't take it anymore, Edward. You're hot for me then you turn cold. You seem to want me then you push me away. You told me I am a woman of action, so I acted on my feelings. Yet you throw those feelings back at me, claiming you're doing the honorable thing. There is nothing honorable about breaking my heart."

"You're right," he said, throat tight. He felt cold to his bones. Everything she'd said rocked him, knocking him off balance.

Her face suddenly crumpled. "Is it her? Do you...do you still love her?"

"Arrabella? No. Good lord, no."

"Desire her?"

He shook his head and took a step closer. He was acutely aware of his nakedness, but tried not to think about it. All that mattered was showing Elizabeth that he had no feelings for Arrabella anymore. He would do anything to make her see. Say anything. Nothing mattered except making her understand that.

"We need to talk," he said.

"I'm past talking."

She heaved in a shuddery breath and lifted her chin, defiant, strong. Beautiful and seductive. Witty and clever too. Dear God, how had he not noticed? How had he not seen how she made him laugh? Made him happy?

"We have nothing more to say to one another," she said. "Kindly refrain from speaking to me in the future until such time as you leave Sutton Hall."

She turned to go, and panic seized him. She couldn't leave! Not now. She loved him, and he was going to be left with an empty hole the size of her inside him.

He caught her arm. She spun around and slapped him. He did not let her go until she struggled. She stalked off to the door and opened it. She was slipping away from him.

"I was embarrassed," he said quickly. "That's why I stopped."

She paused, turned around. A small frown marred the smooth skin of her forehead. "What do you mean?"

Ah hell. He had to tell her. There was no other way. He swallowed heavily. "I was too embarrassed to…take this any further."

The frown deepened. She seemed to suddenly remember she held the door open and closed it. "Too embarrassed to lie with me?"

He nodded. Swallowed.

"But why?" Her gaze slipped to his groin. "Is there something wrong with it? With you? You look perfect to me."

He wished he had his clothes, but they were outside, probably stuck in the bushes below. It seemed foolish to wrap a sheet around his body. So he crossed his arms and gritted it out.

"I've never…you know…"

She shrugged one shoulder. "No, I don't. Never what?"

He cleared his throat. He'd rather be naked in front of the entire female population of the village than say what needed to be said. But he forged on. "I've never lain with a woman before." There. Done. Now for her laughter.

"Yes, you have, you dolt. I've even seen you with a girl at The White Hart."

"That doesn't count. They were whores, and I was drunk. I don't recall much."

She cocked her head to the side. "'They?' There was more than one girl that night?"

"You're changing the subject."

213

She almost smiled, but he could see she wasn't quite listening. Her mind was racing ahead as usual. "So you're telling me you've never slept with a woman, aside from that night? But you're almost thirty!"

"The first few years of manhood were the hardest. I admit to fumbling my way through some experiences back then, but not, uh, entering a woman. Later, denial became a habit, and habits are easy to maintain."

She drew in her bottom lip again. He did not try to remove it. There would be no touching between them. Not now. Hell, he needed another shirt.

"I'm not sure I follow," she said slowly, as if choosing her words carefully. "Why have you denied yourself all these years? You're a handsome man, strong and kind. I've seen the way the women look at you in the village. It would be easy for you to take one of them and unburden yourself. An experienced widow perhaps if you were nervous about the first time."

He saw the moment she guessed the answer to her own question.

"Arrabella," she said quietly. "You were saving yourself for her."

He nodded. "I've been a fool. Years ago I could blame my misguided love for her on youth, but more recently…"

"It became a habit?"

"Of sorts. It was easier thinking of her waiting for me in Upper Wayworth than the alternative."

"Having no one waiting," she whispered.

His heart plunged. A deep well opened up inside him and something that had been lurking down there rose to the surface. It had been suppressed for a long time. A very long time. Now that he'd given it a voice, or rather, Elizabeth had, it would not stay down. It swelled and surged like a bleak, black tide, threatening to overwhelm him.

His vision blurred. His throat closed. He looked down and watched her shoes as she stepped nearer. He wished he knew what she was going to do, but he didn't. She was a mystery, and he was such a fool when it came to women. All he knew was that his secret, the secret he never really knew he carried, was out.

She placed her hand on his chest, over his wildly beating heart. "You don't have to be alone anymore."

Her words stripped away any last remaining bravado he possessed. It was as if she could see into him and saw the darkness inside. He felt raw, exposed. She might as well be holding his heart in her hand with the all the power she held over him. With a twitch of her fingers and a few words, she could destroy him or save him.

"Edward, did you think I was laughing at you just now?"

He shook his head, but he knew she wasn't convinced by it. She gently cradled his face in her hands. Their gazes locked. The candlelight did a merry dance in her eyes. "My sweet Edward. My beautiful, honorable man. You have no reason to be ashamed. I admire you all the more for your loyalty to her."

He tried to swallow, but the lump in his throat was too large. "The thing is, I don't know what to do." Hell and damnation. This wasn't coming out right. "That is, I know where everything is supposed to go, but as to the finer points…I'm at a loss." It didn't feel so awful saying it out loud, not as humiliating as he thought it would be.

"Well, I have a secret too." She placed a hand behind his head and gently drew him down to whisper in his ear. "I'm also a virgin. We can learn the finer points together."

He chuckled. Just like that his apprehension fled. She hadn't laughed at him. She didn't think less of him. She still wanted him. How had he gotten to be so fortunate?

He pressed his forehead to hers and looped his arms behind her back. He held her close and she sighed into him.

"You can try things with me, and I'll tell you whether I like it or not," she said. "And I'll try things on you, and you tell me if it's nice."

"I suspect I'll like everything."

She smiled. "First, help me out of all these clothes."

"Gladly, but…I wasn't lying when I said I'm worried about the consequences. You're a lady."

"My sister is a lady, and she's been lying with Greville for weeks."

He didn't mention that they were betrothed, or that Greville was a nobleman. It was different.

"It's all right," she went on. "I know how to prevent a baby from being planted in me now."

"Did you ask your sister?"

"Good lord, no. I asked a maid. She said the best way is for you to pull out of me and spurt your seed elsewhere." She unlaced the bodice of her gown, and he unpinned her skirt. She lifted her shift over her head, and he was given his first view of her glorious nakedness. She was all curves and contours and softness. A narrow waist, flared hips, and full, heavy breasts tipped by fat pink nipples. Her legs were longer and leaner than he expected considering she was small compared to him. His gaze was drawn to the thatch of hair at the juncture, hiding her secret place. Then there was her skin, so smooth and milky. His fingers ached to feel how smooth, but he kept his hands to himself. What if she didn't want him to touch her yet?

"You're leaking." She nodded at his groin.

Clear liquid hovered on the end of his cock like a dew drop. He was as hard as a rod for her, and so very aware of her nakedness, only inches away. It took every bit of control he possessed to keep his hands to himself. "Elizabeth?"

She looked up at him, a small expectant smile on her lips. Her cheeks were pink, her eyes sparkling in the dimly lit room. "Yes, Edward?"

"May I…touch you?"

Her smile widened. "Yes."

He still hesitated. Where to start? Elizabeth answered the question for him by taking his hand and placing it on her breast. The flesh was as soft as it looked. More so. She was so white that the blue veins were easy to see, yet the nipple was a dusky shade of pink, unlike any color he'd seen. He teased the nipple with his fingers and marveled at how it peaked.

Elizabeth's breath quickened. He glanced at her and saw that her eyes were closed, her lips parted. He brought his hand up to her other breast and smiled at her gasp. She swayed into him, and her hands caught his arms to steady herself.

She opened her eyes and studied him as he'd studied her. Her gaze followed her hands as they skimmed up and over his shoulders, down his chest to his belly. One hand snaked around to his arse and cupped him, while the other continued down and circled his cock.

He groaned low in his chest and closed his eyes. He'd thought he couldn't grow any more, but he could feel his cock swelling at her touch. She let it go, but only to explore his balls. She cupped them, toyed with them, rubbed them. A tidal wave surged into his groin.

He pulled away. "Unless you want me to end now, you'd best stop."

She gave him that wicked grin again. Vixen. He kissed her mouth, hard, wanting to taste that smile, taste her. She wrapped her arms around him and pressed her soft, pliant body into his. He circled his finger around the small dimples at the base of her back until she moaned against his mouth. Then he picked her up and carried her to the bed. He laid her down gently and rose above her to get a better view. She was a nymph, a sorceress, and he was completely under her spell. He didn't care. *This* was what he wanted. What he'd waited so long for.

Elizabeth.

He kissed her breast, took her nipple into his mouth. She tasted of raspberries, smelled like desire. He settled himself alongside her and kissed a trail from her breast to her stomach, her hip and thigh. Her scent grew stronger. He'd never smelled anything as sweet. He wanted to bury himself in her and taste her. All of her.

She widened her legs and arched her back, beckoning him. He couldn't resist. He kissed her folds. She moaned softly and parted her legs further. He didn't know what he was doing, or why. He just followed gut instinct, and instinct told him to taste her *there*. It may have been a strange thing to do, but he didn't care. She seemed to want it as much as he if the hands gripping his head were any indication.

He licked and found that she moaned louder every time his tongue flicked the small nub. So he kept on licking, and touching too, dipping his finger inside her wetness. Her moans turned to gasps. Her fingers twisted in his hair. Her hips rose up and she ground herself against his mouth. His cock responded with a deep throb.

"Edward!" Her back arched. A violent shudder rippled through her. Had he hurt her? He went to pull away, but she held him in place. "Not yet!"

He smiled against her folds and licked slowly until the shudders lessened. She finally let him go, and he sat back on his haunches.

She smiled at him, not so much wicked anymore, but sated and soft. He loved that languid look on her, loved how her face glowed with pleasure. Her eyes were unfocused as if she'd awoken from a beautiful dream.

"I feel loose," she murmured.

"Are you all right?" Despite her smile, he wasn't entirely sure. Her reaction had been considerable.

"Oh yes. My body is humming."

"Your body is beautiful. You're beautiful."

She reached for him and drew him to her for a kiss. It was slow and soft at first, but the pressure quickly built inside him again. He couldn't get enough of her. She responded by deepening the kiss and taking his cock in her hand.

He sucked air between his teeth and held himself tight. He wanted to explode right there in her hand, but he fought the urge. He wanted to be inside her more than anything, and he knew he couldn't do that if he ended too soon.

She guided him to her opening, and he dipped the head of his cock inside. Her moist warmth enveloped him. He pushed in a little more and met her barrier.

"I don't want to hurt you," he said. God help him if she asked him to stop now.

"It will only hurt for a moment, and just this once." She pushed on his arse as if ordering him to enter her all the way.

He inched himself in, pulled back, then gently thrust again. Her barrier broke, and he caught her gasp with his kiss. He stilled, afraid that she'd regret it, or that it was more painful than she'd expected. He cradled her with one arm, propping himself up on his elbows, and held her against him.

The kiss changed to one of sweetness and he knew she was all right. Her fingers skimmed over his back, teasing and massaging the muscles. She thrust her hips up a little and he took that as a signal to keep going. He gently pushed himself all the way in.

A deep, guttural groan rose up from his chest. Being in her was like nothing he'd expected. It was comforting and thrilling at the same time. He wanted to savor it and be gentle, yet part of him wanted to race to the end because he needed to know what it would be like with her. He tried to be slow. He really did. But fierce, overwhelming desire coursed through his body and he quickened his pace. Power surged through him, hot and maddening. He couldn't control it, could only ride along with it.

"Pull out," she reminded him.

Thank God. He'd forgotten, so much did he want to stay inside her. As the surge broke through his final barrier of restraint, he withdrew and spurted his milky seed over her belly.

She kissed him hard on the lips as his body released itself. He shuddered, and the final spurts painted her. His skin felt hot, his limbs weak. He broke the kiss and collapsed on the bed.

Elizabeth found a cloth and wiped herself clean, then returned to the bed. She flipped onto her side and watched Edward as the last remnants of his lust faded. A sheen of sweat glistened on his brow, and his eyelids closed as he breathed a contented sigh. She smiled and admired this man who'd claimed her. This beautiful, muscular man with the smooth skin, powerful shoulders and handsome face.

He drew in a deep breath and opened his eyes again. He smiled and cupped her cheek. She turned her face and kissed his palm.

"Well?" she asked. "What do you think?"

"I think I am a happy man." He caressed her shoulder with his knuckles. "Are you sore?"

"No." There had been a moment of sharp pain when he broke her barrier, but that's all. Everything else had made up for it, and more. "I liked what you did with your tongue."

His smile widened. "I noticed."

"Perhaps next time I can try something with my tongue. Just as an experiment."

He made a gurgling sound in his throat and his gaze heated. "You can experiment on me whenever you like."

"Good, because I have an insatiable curiosity. I want to learn everything that you like."

His eyes hooded. "Talk like that will rouse me again soon."

She touched his sated member, lying in its nest, and discovered it was not asleep. She kissed him and he drew her down to lie half on top of him.

"Come here, my sweet," he murmured.

She settled in beside him, draping her leg over his, and snuggled in. He kissed the top of her head.

They lay together in silence but didn't sleep. He gently stroked her back and she planted small kisses on his throat. It was nice to lie in bed and not think of anything in particular. She wanted nothing more than to feel the solidness of his body against her, the strong beat of his heart, the heat of his skin.

Eventually his breathing changed, and his hand stilled. He was asleep. The night air had cooled and she gently extricated herself from his arms and got up. She closed the window and peered out at the crescent moon hanging in the sky. How had she got to this point? How had she been so fortunate as to have this wonderful man at her side?

She didn't want to think of her sister at such a moment, but thoughts of her came anyway. For the first time in her life, Elizabeth felt sorry for Arrabella. She could have had Edward if she'd looked at him properly and seen him for who he was. But she'd chosen vanity and greed over happiness, and now she was paying the price.

Elizabeth's sympathy surprised her. It troubled her too, because it revealed something she'd not known existed inside her, a darkness that had festered for five years, perhaps more. That's how long she'd been angry at Arrabella. Angry and bitter. Elizabeth blamed her for blinding Edward, for holding his heart hostage, for not loving him the way he deserved to be loved. If Arrabella had only told him years ago that she didn't care for him, he would never have left the village to better himself. If he hadn't left, he might have come to notice Elizabeth in time. But his love for Arrabella had taken him away from Elizabeth, and she'd been furious with her sister ever since.

Hot tears welled but did not fall. There was still time to mend the bridge that had collapsed between them. Still time to forgive and let go of the past. Elizabeth felt as if she could finally move forward, and be the sister she always should have been. Perhaps Arrabella wouldn't be in such a mess now if Elizabeth had helped her sift through the suitors in London. It didn't matter anymore. All that mattered was that she could help her through her heartbreak. It was ironic that Arrabella's life was falling apart when Elizabeth's was coming together so perfectly.

She padded over to a trunk and removed a blanket. Edward lay on the bedcovers and she didn't want to disturb him. He looked so beautiful in slumber. His face had relaxed, his lips formed a small smile that had her wondering what dreams he dreamt. She slipped in beside him and spread the blanket across them both. She rested her head on his chest near his heart and closed her eyes. Still asleep, he circled his arm around her.

She drifted off, happy and safe in the knowledge that Edward was hers.

* * *

Elizabeth didn't want to part from Edward the following morning. She could have lain with him all day, sleeping and making love until suppertime. Apparently, he had the same idea.

"I wish I could stay longer," he said, kissing her nipple. "But I have to deliver breakfast to Greville. I don't want the servants to do it. I don't trust him."

Talk of Greville reminded her of Arrabella. She should go to her. "Stay a few more moments. We can be quick." She reached down between them. His member was engorged again, despite being spent twice more through the night.

He groaned low in his throat. "If Greville starves, it's your fault." He cupped her sex and gently rubbed her sensitive nub.

She grinned and kissed him. They tugged and teased, nibbled and licked one another until both were panting. They climaxed together.

Edward washed her gently with the water from the basin then cleaned himself. He helped her dress, although he didn't pin her very well. No matter, she would change as soon as she got back to her room.

"I wonder if my breeches and shirt have been discovered yet." He nodded at the window.

She giggled. "I'd forgotten about that. I am sorry, Edward. I was in a foul temper."

"It was hardly a temper." He kissed her nose, her chin. "You had every right to be angry with me. My behavior may have seemed honorable to me, but I know now how it must have seemed to you."

She wouldn't deny that she'd been upset and scared. Scared to lose him. She watched as he dressed, admiring the powerful thighs, the long lines of his body, the broad shoulders. She would never grow tired of the sight.

He winked at her, kissed her again and opened the door. "Come to me when you're free," he said, eyes dancing merrily. "We need to talk."

She nodded eagerly. They had much to discuss. From his happiness, she guessed that he already knew she didn't care about his status. She'd always been perfectly content to marry a carpenter.

They parted. He headed down to the kitchens to fetch Greville some breakfast, and she made her way to her own rooms to change. She got as far as her sister's chambers. Either her mother had excellent hearing, or she just happened to open the door as Elizabeth passed.

"There you are! Where have you been?" She didn't wait for Elizabeth to answer, but grabbed her arm and pulled her inside.

Janet sagged as if the world were dragging her down. Her jowls, the sacks under her eyes, her shoulders, all drooped. Elizabeth felt a twang of guilt that she'd had such a wonderful night when her mother and sister had suffered.

"Is she asleep?" Elizabeth asked, peering past her mother into the bedchamber beyond.

Janet heaved a sigh. "No. She slept fitfully during the night and is awake now. She's lying on the bed, staring into space. What are we to do, Lizzie?"

"We can be here for her as long as she needs us. She needs to grieve as if he were already dead. She will move on, in time."

"Oh no. You don't understand." Janet blinked back tears. "I forgot you weren't here when she told me. It's worse than you realize, Lizzie. Much worse."

"How can it be any worse than having her betrothed hung for murder? What has she told you?"

A movement in the bedchamber doorway caught her attention. Arrabella stood there looking ghostly in her white shift, her tousled hair framing her pale face. The only part of her with any color was her eyes. They were two red orbs inside black circles.

She came forward, one hand splayed across her belly. "I'm with child, Lizzie."

CHAPTER 16

*E*lizabeth's gasp filled the room. "How far along?"

"I've missed two courses," Arrabella said.

"Two!"

Arrabella rubbed her flat belly as if she could already feel the babe growing inside. There was no happiness on her face, none of the joy that should accompany such an announcement. Grim resignation clung to her like a shroud. She looked like a girl again, lost, scared, alone. Elizabeth went to her and folded her into her arms. Arrabella sobbed into her shoulder.

Elizabeth glanced at her mother. Janet shook her head. Her own tears started anew, and she dabbed at her eyes with a handkerchief. She had very good reason to be distressed. Arrabella could not keep the baby if she didn't marry. If she did keep it, Jeffrey would cut her off, cut them all off, and they would have nothing to live on. It would be too much shame for him to bear, and his heart was not soft enough to allow a compromise. Arrabella would be an outcast, and her family along with her if they supported her, which of course they would. Elizabeth could not imagine abandoning her sister now, and for all her faults, Janet was a steadfast mother.

"What am I to do?" Arrabella said between gasping breaths. "Without a father, my baby will be nothing. I will be nothing."

"I'll take you north," was Janet's decisive answer. "You can have the babe up there and give it away. No one of consequence need know."

"But it's cold in the north."

Elizabeth felt sick. Give up her niece or nephew, her flesh and blood? Arrabella may just be indifferent enough to do it, but Elizabeth doubted she would be. She would be forever wondering how the child fared, what it looked like, did it want for anything, if it was loved.

"All is not lost," Janet soothed, patting Arrabella's hair. "Perhaps somebody else can be blamed for the murder. A vagabond, or one of the villagers."

"Mother!" Elizabeth cried.

"Greville is important," Janet told her. "He attends court. That should count for something."

"You're right!" Arrabella wiped her nose with the back of her hand. "It must have been a vagabond. Greville didn't kill anybody. I don't know why Edward thinks he did."

"It's not just Edward," Elizabeth said. "And you cannot go about blaming others without proof."

Arrabella shoved her away. "Lizzie, how *could* you do this to me? I'm your *sister*."

There was no winning the argument with either Arrabella or Janet, so she didn't try. "If he's ordered to stand trial, then there is something that can still be done to save your reputation and allow you to keep the baby."

Arrabella narrowed her swollen eyes. "There is?"

"Marry him before he goes to the gallows. That way the baby will have his name."

Arrabella nodded her head slowly, but it was Janet who spoke. "What a grand idea! If the baby is a boy, he'll become a baron before he's even born!"

"Mother, I don't think—"

"Yes!" Arrabella clasped her mother's hands. "Oh yes! I shall be baroness after all, and my baby will inherit the title. Of course, we'll miss Greville terribly," she added with a pointed look at Elizabeth. "I do love him, you know. I love him dearly. Of course we'll try to blame someone else, but if Greville cannot be saved, then this is a good idea. You're forgiven for your role in this sorry mess, Lizzie."

"Thank you." Elizabeth doubted her sister caught the sarcasm in her voice. She was too excited by the new plot to notice.

"It is a good idea," Janet agreed, tapping her cheek in thought. "Jeffrey won't cut you off if you're a baroness. He may even raise the annuity to help with the babe. Don't worry on that score."

"Greville's property will be forfeited to the crown though," Elizabeth said, thinking out loud. "And Jeffrey may not *want* to support the widow of a murderer."

"Help me dress." Arrabella ran back into her bedchamber. "I'll go to Greville now." It was as if she hadn't heard Elizabeth's reservations.

Janet went after her, no longer looking quite so droopy.

Elizabeth thought of stopping them, but decided there would be no point. Her sister wouldn't be swayed from the idea, and it was probably best to organize the wedding as soon as possible. She only hoped Greville would be amenable to moving it forward. A special license would have to be arranged too.

A knock sounded on the outer door, and she opened it. Edward stood there, his face a mask. Something was wrong.

"What is it?" she whispered, not wanting to alarm her mother or sister.

"Greville's gone."

She frowned. "Gone? How? You locked him in."

"One of the wall panels in his bedchamber was a door. It was open. Beyond was a passage that led through the walls of the house, underground, and outside. It must have once been used for priests to escape. I didn't know about it. Lynden was with me, and he didn't know about it either. Greville must have."

"He may not have gone far."

"Lynden is organizing his men to search, but…" He shook his head. "If Greville escaped immediately after I left him, he's had all night to get far away."

Elizabeth pressed a hand to her chest where a tight knot formed. "Good lord. What will become of her now?"

"Your sister?" He caught her hand and enveloped it in his own. "She'll be all right. Indeed, I think Greville was having second thoughts about the wedding anyway."

"He would have had to go through with it regardless of his heart's desire." Her gaze locked with his. He frowned and arched an eyebrow. "She's carrying his child."

Edward's jaw dropped at the same time that Jeffrey roared, "She's *what*?" Elizabeth hadn't seen or heard his approach. He came up to them, fists planted on his hips, his brows crashing together. He barged past Elizabeth. "Arrabella! Arrabella, come out this instant."

Elizabeth clutched at his arm. "Allow me to tell her about Greville going missing first. She's in a delicate state."

"God's blood, forget her delicate state. That is her own doing. If she'd not been such a flirt, she wouldn't be in this mess."

"Greville is as much to blame as her."

He wasn't listening. "Arrabella!"

Arrabella and Janet emerged from the adjoining room. She'd thrown a housecoat over her shift. "What is it?" she asked. "Is it Greville?" She glanced at Edward then back to Jeffrey.

"He's escaped," Jeffrey said. "The men are out—"

"Escaped!" Arrabella's screech was high enough to hurt Elizabeth's ears. "He's left me? He left me here?" Her tears started anew. "How could he? How could he do that to me? I love him. He loves me."

Edward's gaze shifted to Elizabeth. She shook her head slightly. Her sister didn't need to know about the change in her betrothed's feelings.

"He's afraid of the gallows, Bella," Jeffrey said without an ounce of sympathy.

Arrabella streaked across the room and grasped his arms. Jeffrey's eyes widened in alarm. Perhaps he thought she was going to attack him. She looked wild enough to do it too. "But he's not guilty!" she cried.

"He is. This proves it." He pried her fingers off one by one. "Stop this madness. There's no call for it."

Arrabella did indeed look mad. Her eyes were huge and darted about the room. Her fingers, freed from Jeffrey, scratched the backs of her hands over and over. "What will happen if he's caught?"

"Justice will be swift."

Arrabella made a choking sound, and scratched harder, drawing blood.

"So it's true," Jeffrey said, once more stamping his fists on his hips.

Janet put her arm around her daughter's shoulders and nodded. "You will be kind to her, won't you, Jeffrey?" Her voice was small, pleading. Elizabeth had never heard her mother plead for anything.

Jeffrey's mouth curled up in disgust. "My God. You expect me to take care of her and the whelp after she brings shame down on my head? On yours too, Aunt?"

"She's my daughter. The baby will be my grandchild. Perhaps we can find a way to—"

"She must get rid of it."

Elizabeth's heart dropped to her toes. She'd hoped Jeffrey would be kind to his favorite cousin, but it seemed his own vanity was too strong. He could not show his face at court again if it were known he supported a cousin who bore a bastard child.

"Her chances of a good marriage would be over," he went on. "She'll be ruined. If she bore that child, no gentleman would have her."

It was true. They all knew it. It didn't make Elizabeth want to accept it.

"I cannot afford to have it discovered," Jeffrey went on. "Not now that I have become known at court. I cannot be seen to support such a dishonorable girl. If you don't have that baby in secret and get rid of it, Bella, then I'll not be able to support you. Or you, Janet. Elizabeth too. You'll all be tainted, and I'll want nothing to do with any of you. Is that clear?"

Arrabella sobbed. She clawed her housecoat at her belly, pulling it away from her body as if she would tear it off. Janet tried to console her, but Arrabella thrashed at her, pushing her away. "I hate you!" she screamed. "I hate all of you!"

"Perhaps some more time is needed," Edward said quietly. "You might think differently later, Lynden."

Jeffrey wrinkled his nose. "I will not!"

"You," Arrabella growled. She pointed a shaking finger at Edward and bared her teeth. "This is your fault."

"Calm yourself, Bella," Elizabeth said. "You're not thinking clearly."

But Arrabella didn't seem to hear her. She stepped up to Edward. Elizabeth could feel him tensing, bracing himself.

"*You* scared Greville away," she snarled. "*You* accused him of the murder, *you* locked him up. Did you tell him how to escape too?"

"Why would I do that?" Edward's voice was cold steel.

"Because you want me all for yourself. You, the carpenter's son, want me. Ha! What a joke."

"You don't know what you're saying," Edward said.

Elizabeth took her sister by the shoulders, but Arrabella wrenched away. She didn't take her eyes off Edward.

"The only way you can have me is through trickery," she sneered. "By tricking all of us, and Greville too. You can't bear for anyone else to love me so you devised a plot to get rid of him. Did you murder those men, Edward? Did you?"

"Stop it, Bella!" Elizabeth snapped. "That's absurd."

"You *can't* have me. You won't have me." She spun round and marched off to the bedchamber. She slammed the door so hard the wall shuddered.

Elizabeth touched Edward's hand. His fingers curled around hers, reassuring. "Pay her no mind," she said. "She's upset."

His smile was grim. "What about you? Are you all right?"

"I will be." She had him now. No matter what happened, *she* would be happy.

Janet sidled up to Jeffrey and clasped his arm with both hands. She peered up at him through fluttering, damp lashes. He did not look at her, but stared at the closed bedchamber door. "You can rest easy, dearest nephew. I will take Bella north and see that the baby is given a good home." She smoothed her hands over his doublet sleeve and smiled crookedly through her tears. "Of course, we'll need some money to give the family who take in the babe."

Jeffrey blinked slowly as if startled from deep thoughts. He looked to Edward, then back at the door, then to Edward again. "I am not completely unfeeling," he said slowly. "I understand that mothers are loath to give up there babes. I have a solution that would mean she could keep it. It's not perfect." He sighed heavily. "Indeed, I do wish Greville could wed her. But we must consider other alternatives now, and I think this one is the best." Again his narrowed gaze slid to Edward's.

Elizabeth let go of Edward's hand. He glanced at her, frowned. He hadn't guessed what Jeffrey would propose, but she had. It sickened her.

"You shall wed her instead," Jeffrey announced.

Janet gave a little sob into her handkerchief.

Edward stared at Jeffrey. Then he laughed. "Don't be absurd."

"Why not?" Jeffrey said with a shrug. "You've wanted her for most of your life, now you can have her."

Edward's lips flattened. "I don't want her anymore."

Jeffrey waved his response away. "You will again. She's a sweet girl." He shot a glance at the door. "Most of the time. Come now, man, you must see that it's a good solution. You get your heart's desire, and she gets the protection of your name for herself and the baby."

"You forget, my name means very little. I am no gentleman."

"Aha, that's where you're wrong. You received a letter today, sent on by Lord Oxley. It's from the College of Heralds, asking for more money to secure your coat of arms."

Edward was going to purchase himself a coat of arms? Whatever for? Or should that be, *whoever* for?

For Arrabella.

Numb, Elizabeth turned to him in the hope he would deny it, or tell her it no longer mattered. But he didn't even look at her. His face was set hard. His flint-gray eyes focused on Jeffrey. "You read a letter meant for me." His voice was quiet, an unspoken threat running through it.

Jeffrey swallowed. "I, er, it came to my house." He stretched his neck above his high ruff. "I am master here. I need to know what happens within these walls."

"You do not read letters meant for me again. Understand?"

Jeffrey cleared his throat and tugged on the cuffs of his doublet. "As to my proposal—"

"I won't be party to it," Edward said.

Elizabeth breathed again. She hadn't noticed that she'd stopped.

"I know the girl doesn't particularly like you at the moment," Jeffrey conceded.

Janet snorted.

Jeffrey shot her a sharp glare. "But she'll come around when she realizes this is the only way she can keep her baby and not bring shame down on this family. I'll let you think upon it," he said to Edward. He looked pleased with himself for coming up with the solution to *his* problem. "The herald is clearly scheming for more money to feather his nest, but no matter. I'll pay him what he demands. After the wedding, I'll give you an extra annuity on top of what Arrabella already receives. It will be generous, Monk, never fear. There now, is that not a good way to end this sorry mess? Everybody is happy. You get Arrabella, she can keep the baby, and my money will make your lives comfortable."

"It's ridiculous," Edward said. "It's not what anybody wants."

"What my cousin *wants* is beside the point. She has no choice."

"But I do."

Jeffrey frowned and lifted his hands in question. "Why would you not wish to go through with it?" He spluttered a laugh. "Good lord, man, marrying her will raise you to great heights. Think of where you came from, and where such a fine marriage could take you!"

"Perhaps I don't want to be raised." It was not an outright denial. Nor did he tell them about his plans for Elizabeth.

Perhaps he never had any intention of making plans for a future with her. Perhaps he was considering Jeffrey's proposal.

Elizabeth's heart somersaulted once in her chest, then stopped dead. She held herself tight and willed it to restart. Of course she was overreacting. He would not be lured by the promise of fortune and status. That was the old Edward who wanted those things, along with Arrabella. This Edward wanted her, and nothing more.

Didn't he?

"Think on it," Jeffrey was telling him. "Think of what you will gain, and the baby she will keep. Think of her *family*, my dear fellow. This way the baby is safe, and their reputations are saved."

"Another man," Edward muttered, somewhat desperately. "What about another man who desires her, one who can be secured quickly. Were there any other gentlemen in London beside Greville who took an interest?"

"There are no others," Jeffrey said with a sad shake of his head. "She favored Greville from the beginning. No other gentlemen had a chance to speak to her."

"If there was another, do you not think we would ask him first?" Janet wailed. Her tears began again. "To be brought so low as this. My poor girl."

"Stop it," Elizabeth hissed. "All of you, stop this madness. Arrabella will not have Edward now that she thinks him responsible for Greville's disappearance, and you should not try to force Edward to take on another man's baby, or a wife who despises him. Everybody needs time to calm down and think clearly."

She glanced at Edward. He did not look at her, but at Janet. He offered her his handkerchief and she took it to wipe her cheeks.

"This is not *your* concern, Lizzie," Jeffrey said, bristling. "Kindly keep your meddling nose out of your sister's affairs."

"Perhaps if I meddled more she wouldn't be in this mess."

Jeffrey clicked his tongue. "Selfish girl. This is not about you. At least Bella *tried* to secure herself a good husband. *You* didn't flirt with any of the gentlemen at court, even though many of them couldn't take their eyes off you. Several asked me if you were available. They would have gladly made an offer if you hadn't been so prickly. Stupid, selfish girl. Always thinking of yourself and not your family."

Elizabeth threw up her hands. It was hopeless. There was no point it trying to argue with him. His reasoning was warped.

"If your father hadn't told me to give you your head in matters of the heart, I would have forced you to wed Lord Carrick," Jeffrey went on.

"Carrick! He must be forty at least!"

"He took a great interest in you, and he's a viscount. A viscount! But no, you didn't like him, and now you have nobody."

"That isn't true." She looked to Edward. Still he did not look back at her. Why wouldn't he acknowledge their night together?

"Indeed, you're fortunate that Arrabella is marrying Monk," Jeffrey said. "If she wasn't, it would be up to you to rescue the family's reputation."

"But my father wished—"

"He's dead. I am your master now. You do as I say, girl. By God, I would have you in Carrick's bed before the end of the week. Consider yourself fortunate that you're saved—"

Edward closed the gap between them in a flash. He stood very close to Jeffrey, towering over him. His fists opened and closed at his sides. A muscle pulsed in his jaw. "Enough! Do not speak to her that way again, Lynden, or I will thrash you."

Janet whimpered and shrank back. The color drained from Jeffrey's face. "H-how dare you! I'll throw you out of my house."

Edward gave a guttural laugh. "No, you won't."

Jeffrey swallowed heavily and tugged on his cuffs again. "I'll ignore your behavior this time. However, once you wed my cousin, you would do well to remember that your annuity is dependent upon my goodwill."

"I have my own money."

"Is it enough to satisfy Arrabella?"

Edward said nothing. He did not tell them he wouldn't wed Arrabella. He did not reassure Elizabeth that it was her whom he wanted.

The walls felt like they were closing in on her. She couldn't breathe, couldn't stand being in the room anymore. She picked up her skirts and fled.

* * *

EVERY PART of Edward ached to go after Elizabeth. But he did not. He could not reassure her or make any promises when he didn't know what would happen in the next hour, let alone the rest of their lives.

He wanted to be with her. Wanted to marry her more than anything. No, not more than anything. The thing he wanted most of all was her happiness. And how could she be happy if her family was ruined, her niece or nephew given away to strangers? Elizabeth would tell him her happiness depended on being with him, and he knew that would be how she felt *now*. But in years to come, when the blush of first love faded, she would come to see that their marriage had led to her family's downfall and the loss of the child. It wasn't in her nature to blame others, but he was certain she would blame herself.

He couldn't bear that.

There was no alternative. As a family of women with no means of their own, they were utterly dependent on their nearest male relation—Lynden. Without his support, the family would be turned out of their home and cut off from their friends. As much as Edward wanted to help, he couldn't afford to care for all of them plus a baby. Lynden, the piss-weak cur, would not change his mind. He was the sort of man who put pride above family, and never backed away once he'd made a decision. He was determined that Edward should wed Arrabella—and Edward was considering it.

Yet he couldn't face telling Elizabeth yet. There was a good chance Arrabella would refuse anyway. A very good chance.

He set about keeping himself busy by coordinating the search for Greville. Men rode through the fields and around the estate boundary. Others rode into the village. All reported no sign of Greville. He must have bypassed the village altogether. If he'd done that yet kept to the roads, he would have headed toward Larkham. Of course if he avoided the roads altogether, he could be anywhere.

"I'll ride out today," Edward told Lynden in his study.

"Very well." Lynden indicated Edward should sit. He did not. Lynden sighed and rubbed his temple. The lines radiating from his eyes and bracketing his mouth were deeper, his hair disheveled as if he'd tugged at it. He'd aged in the last few hours. Edward felt not an ounce of sympathy. "You do understand my position, don't you, Monk?"

"No. I don't see why you won't support the family and let Arrabella keep the baby. You can afford to."

"I don't expect a man in your position to understand what we peers must do. Your master, Oxley, would. He and I both have a responsibility to marry well, and ensure our lineage is in good standing when we pass the reins on."

"You're thinking of marrying?"

"Of course. All men in my position must wed and carry on the line. It's our duty. Oxley would tell you that."

"Yes, but Oxley is not a… Never mind. Are you telling me *your* marriage prospects are tied to Arrabella's behavior?"

"Precisely! So you do understand. I cannot support the girl. I would be shamed, ruined. No peer in good standing would want me to wed his daughter. It would be out of the question." He held up a folded sheet of parchment. The red seal of the College of Heralds had been broken in half, each piece dangling from the edges of the sheet. "Write to the herald, and tell him that I will pay what he wishes."

"I can pay it myself. There is one point you haven't considered, Lynden."

"Hmmm? What is it?"

"That Arrabella won't have me even with this."

Lynden leaned back in his chair and steepled his fingers. He didn't look so much the fop anymore, but more like the head of a household with great responsibility on his shoulders. Edward didn't envy him. "That girl is as fickle as the wind. She'll change her mind. You'll see. Now, to the matter of Greville. Will you ride out to find him?"

"Can't your men do it?"

"I need them here, and none of them are as competent as you. Please, Monk, do this for us. I cannot have a murderer wandering about the valley."

For once Edward agreed with him. "I'll set off now."

He left and was met on the stairs by Janet on her way up. She clutched the balustrade and hauled herself up to the step below him. "There you are." She pressed her hand to her chest and sucked in three deep breaths. "I've been looking for you." Another two breaths. "Bella will speak with you now."

He didn't move. Arrabella wanted to talk to him? Fickle indeed. A cold lump of ice settled in his stomach.

"I need to see Elizabeth first." Needed to explain to her. Needed to prepare her. Needed to hold her one last time.

Janet waved her hand. "She's gone for a walk. Go now. Go to Bella. You haven't got all day."

Indeed he did not. He had to find Greville.

"Where is Elizabeth walking?"

"I don't know. Talk to her later. Go to Arrabella now." She gave him a little shove. "She doesn't like to be kept waiting."

He found Arrabella sitting in the window embrasure of her bedchamber. She was dressed, her hair combed and pinned back. Her eyes were still bruised from crying, but not quite as much as earlier. She lifted a shaky hand and waved weakly at the chair arranged nearby. He remained standing.

"You wanted to see me," he said.

She gave a small nod as if it were an effort to make even the minutest movement. Her hands rested on her belly, the long fingers starkly pale against the crimson gown. He was reminded of a statue of the goddess Diana in Lord Whipple's garden—beautiful but lifeless.

"I'll do it," she said simply.

It took him a moment to grasp her meaning. Then it hit him with the force of a blow to the body. She had just agreed to marry him.

CHAPTER 17

*I*t seemed like a thousand years had passed since Edward wanted to hear Arrabella say those words. It was as if it had been another man who'd desired her, not him. He couldn't imagine ever *not* loving Elizabeth. Surely he had all along and his affection for Arrabella was nothing more than a strange dream.

His hands gripped the chair arms. He was going to have to tell Elizabeth. He was going to have to find the words somehow. How could he tell her he was going to marry her sister despite loving her? He always would love her. Always.

But he had a duty to perform too, and that duty was to ensure Elizabeth and her family were safe and cared for in the years to come. Marrying Arrabella was the only way to ensure that happened. One day Elizabeth would understand.

"Well?" Arrabella tipped her cheek to him. "Aren't you going to kiss me?"

"No." He must have said it too vehemently because she pouted. "Why did you change your mind? You were adamant Greville was innocent."

She turned back to the window and rested her head against the embrasure wall. "I was in a state of disbelief. I've had a chance to think it through, and I've come to realize there is no other option.

You're the only man who will wed me on short notice because you're the only one who cares enough." She gave him a thin, watery smile. "I know you're doing this for her, not me. I'm not so vain that I still think you're in love with me. I see how you look at my sister. When she's in the room, it's as if no one else exists for you."

It was true, he realized.

"It fades you know," she said.

"What does?"

"That hopeless love-sick feeling. It lasts a few months at best. I ought to know. I've been in love many times. As have you, once, remember? You loved me, although for quite a bit longer than mere months."

"I was not in love with you. That was infatuation. I know the difference now." Nor had she experienced true love if she thought it would fade in 'mere months.'

He expected her to press her point, but she did not. It was as if the essence that made up Arrabella had leaked away along with her tears. "If you say so." She nodded at the window. "Are you going to tell her, or am I?"

He peered past her. Elizabeth sat on the edge of the fountain in the garden, trailing her hand through the water. She was too far away for him to see her face. His heart constricted into a tight, fragile ball in his chest. It was still intact, but one squeeze would shatter it.

"I will," he said.

"I know you're doing this so that she doesn't have to wed some old goat of an earl."

He said nothing. It was the truth. Everything he did, he did for Elizabeth.

"You could refuse to marry me, you know," she went on. "Jeffrey may not consent to your marrying her, but you could live together, far away."

"I wouldn't do that to her. She won't want to be cut off from her family. Besides, what will happen to you and the baby? Elizabeth would not be happy if Jeffrey cut you off, nor would she be happy if you were forced to give away the child."

"Oh, I know that. I just wanted to make sure you knew it too." She smiled at him. He was surprised to see that it was genuine. It was perhaps the first proper smile she'd ever given him. All those years when he thought her smiles were real, and just for him, came rushing back to his memory.

He remembered desperately wanting this woman to be his wife. Wanting to father her children, care for her, have her in his bed. Now he was on the cusp of seeing those longed-for dreams fulfilled.

Nightmares more like. He couldn't look at Arrabella anymore. Her face reminded him of his youthful foolishness. A foolishness that had led him to this point and the loss of his one true love.

He turned to go.

"Thank you, Edward." Her voice was so soft he almost didn't hear it. "Thank you for taking care of us."

He paused. Such moments deserved a speech with profound sentiments, but he could think of nothing he wanted to say. "I'll try to be a good husband," was all he could manage.

He didn't stay to hear her response. He made his way out of her chambers, but had to pause on the landing and press his hand against the wall paneling for balance. Everything was going so fast. The world spun out of control and he was losing his grip.

Last night had been perfect. Today that perfection lay shattered at his feet, and he wasn't entirely sure how it had happened.

* * *

ELIZABETH COULD FEEL Edward's intense gaze on her long before she heard him approach. She looked up. His ashen face told her what she already knew. What she'd been dreading would happen.

He was going to marry her sister.

She didn't cry. She didn't shout at him or beat her fists on the stone edge of the fountain's pool. Her hand stilled in the cool water. A curious fish inspected her fingers then darted away in a flash of silver. She stared at a lily pad and wondered if the numbness would ever go away. Or was she destined to travel through life never feeling anything again?

Edward stopped beside her. She did not look up, but switched her focus from the water to his boots. They were dusty, the leather scuffed. They were the boots of an active man, not an idler like Jeffrey. Edward was nothing if not active. That was the problem. He'd actively set about becoming a gentleman for Arrabella, now he'd actively stepped into the vacant role of her betrothed.

He touched her shoulder then drew his hand back as if that simple touch stung. "Elizabeth." His voice sounded thick and heavy. He said nothing more.

"I know." She started trailing her fingers through the water again. "There's no need to say anything."

"There is." He sat beside her and suddenly cupped her face. Just as suddenly, he withdrew his hands. There would be no touching between them now. "But I don't know how to start."

Still she did not look at his face. Seeing his eyes would be her undoing, and she *needed* to nurture the numbness, not banish it. "Start by telling me where you will live."

He didn't response immediately. Perhaps he wasn't expecting the question, but it seemed the most reasonable one to her. She didn't want to see either Edward or Arrabella after their wedding.

"I live on Oxley's estate in the gatehouse. We'll go there. It's not as grand as what she's used to, but it's comfortable and warm in winter."

"She will have Oxley's mother for company, and his wife when he weds," she said. "That's good. Bella would be unbearable to live with if she had no company."

He said nothing. Perhaps, like her, he was thinking that Arrabella would be unbearable to live with regardless of the company. She would have laughed if it was happening to someone else, but the numbness didn't allow her to laugh, or to cry.

"Elizabeth. Look at me." He touched her chin.

She jerked away and shook her head.

He shifted so that his back was to the fountain and rested his elbows on his knees. He lowered his head. "This is happening." He spoke as if trying to convince himself that it wasn't a dream. "It's not what I wanted. But it's what must be, for everyone's sake."

"Everyone?" she echoed. She finally looked at him as he tilted his head to peer at her. "No. Not everyone. Not for my sake."

His thick lashes lowered. A deep line gouged his forehead and smaller ones fanned out from the corners of his eyes. "I know it doesn't seem like it now, but you will come to understand in time. I'm doing this for your family. For you."

"For me!" She shot to her feet. Water dripped from her hand onto the stones where she'd been sitting. The emptiness inside her filled up with a swell of anger, vanquishing the numbness. She welcomed the anger. It was better than being sad. Much better. "I know you think you're doing the honorable thing, but you're not, Edward. You're simply laying the foundations for a miserable future. For me, yes, but for yourself and Arrabella too."

"Elizabeth, please." He touched her hand, but she pulled away. He swallowed heavily. "You may be right about the future, as you're so often right about everything else. But at least you and your family will be safe."

"I see. You're martyring yourself. How noble of you." She hated hearing the sneer in her voice, but she couldn't help it. Her anger soured everything like old milk.

Edward winced as if she'd struck him. He stood and faced her. He lifted his hands to hold her, but dropped them again without touching. "Do you really want the alternative to befall your family, Elizabeth? The shame, the poverty, the loss of the baby?"

"I know what will happen."

"Then you understand why I'm doing it."

Of course she understood. She'd thought through all possible outcomes, and come up with the same answers he'd just given her. It was all very reasonable, very sensible.

Very wrong.

Her head might know why he was doing it, but her heart screamed in protest. It felt like it was being clawed to shreds.

"We could get through this," she whispered, unable to put any strength in her voice. "We could plead to Jeffrey's better nature after the baby was born. He couldn't turn away a little child, surely."

"He doesn't have a better nature."

Edward was right. After Jeffrey had unexpectedly found himself the baron of Lynden, the worst in him had come out. His vanity increased ten-fold. In London, he was embarrassingly syco-phantic and utterly without shame as he sought to inveigle himself into the good graces of the most prominent peers. He would not throw away all that he'd gained because of a foolish cousin and her bastard.

"If I don't wed Arrabella," he said, "you'll be forced to marry a man of Lynden's choosing."

"I don't care. The only man I would ever choose would be you anyway. If I can't have the man I love, it doesn't matter whom I wed."

His eyelashes fluttered closed. His chest rose as he sucked in air. "Please," he whispered. "No more talk of love. It's too…hard."

Was it because he didn't love Elizabeth enough? She had no doubt that he desired her, even cared for her, but as to love, she couldn't tell. Perhaps he did, in part, but not enough to fight for her. Or worse, a part of him still wanted Arrabella as his wife. It had been a long held desire, a habit. Habits were difficult to break, especially when that habit still occupied a corner of his heart.

"Besides, marriage isn't about love," he said. "It's about honor and duty, and the future."

"You think Arrabella will give you the future you want? The one you always dreamed of because she's more ambitious than me?"

"God no." He reached for her, but she backed away. She couldn't bear his touch. She was holding herself together by the thinnest thread. It would not take much for it to snap. His face twisted as if he was about to crack, but he drew in a deep breath and seemed to calm. "I care nothing for rising beyond what I am now."

"Then why did you request the College of Heralds grant you with a coat of arms? You've paid them a considerable sum to become a gentleman, haven't you?"

He flinched. "That was when I thought I wanted to marry her. I knew she'd require me to be a gentleman before she accepted me. Lynden still requires it. I have no tender feelings for Arrabella anymore, Elizabeth. You *must* believe it." He spoke with fierce urgency, as if he could will her to believe. "I'll wed her because I feel responsible. That's all."

She turned away. She couldn't look at him anymore. It was just too hard. "We're not your responsibility, we're Jeffrey's."

"You *are* my responsibility, Elizabeth. You always will be, whether we see each other or not after this. If taking care of you means that I must take care of your sister and her baby, then I'll do it. But know this." He spun her round to face him and their gazes connected. His eyes darkened to the color of stormy clouds. His fingers dug into her shoulders. They trembled. "I do it for you, Elizabeth. Always you. I cannot do anything else."

She wrenched free and ran. She hardly knew in which direction she headed. Tears streamed down her face. Her heart hammered against her ribs. She kept running until finally her heart felt like it would burst from her chest. She found herself among the orchard. A butterfly fluttered away, frightened by Elizabeth's sobs.

She plopped down on the ground under a tree and buried her face in her skirt.

* * *

EDWARD DID NOT RETURN to the house immediately. He sat on the fountain's edge and fisted his hands in his hair. Pain clawed at his scalp, but he didn't care. His entire person was in pain, but nothing more so than his heart. It lay broken and bleeding in his chest.

He'd hurt Elizabeth badly with his decision. He'd known it wouldn't be easy to tell her, but he could never have imagined how soul destroying it would be to see her tears. To see such a strong, vital woman brought so low was shattering. He only hoped that one day she would understand that he did it for her.

He wiped his damp eyes and pushed himself up. His limbs felt heavy as he trudged back to the house. He looked up and spotted Arrabella's face at her window. She pulled back out of sight.

He made his way to the stables and ordered Warren to prepare his horse. Then he went inside to gather supplies and tell Lynden that he was leaving to search for Greville. Perhaps, if he were lucky enough, he would find him and could take out his anger on the turd for destroying so many lives.

ELIZABETH DISCOVERED that Edward had left when she returned to the house at dinnertime. She excused herself from dining with her mother and Jeffrey, and kept to her room. She didn't want to see anyone, especially Arrabella. She cried again until there were no more tears to spend, then lay on the bed and slept.

She awoke mid-afternoon with a strong desire to do something useful. Lying in her room all day would only cause her thoughts to wander to Edward and her sorrow, and *that* would drive her mad. She would go for a ride. A long one, far away from the house.

She crept out of her room, only to be met by her sister curled up in a large chair in the outer chamber. She sprang to her feet upon seeing Elizabeth and blinked wearily.

"Go away." Elizabeth strode past her.

"Wait, Lizzie. I wish to speak to you."

"I *don't* wish to speak to you."

Arrabella grasped at Elizabeth's arm, but she shook her off. Arrabella gave a little sob. "I know you're angry, but—"

Elizabeth rounded on her. "You're mistaken. I am not angry. Of all the things I feel right now, that emotion isn't one of them."

Bella's face crumpled. Elizabeth turned away. She was so close to breaking again, and couldn't cope with her sister's distress on top of her own misery. "Please, Lizzie. Let me explain why I agreed to the arrangement. I must explain it to you. I must make you see."

"Why? So you feel better? To assuage your guilt? That is if you do feel guilty. It would require you to think about someone other than yourself, and I doubt you're capable of that."

She left, her sister's sobs ringing in her ears.

She ran down the stairs and found herself in the larger parlor. It was empty. Her sister's embroidery hoop sat on a chair near the window as if she'd only just set it down. Elizabeth passed through the room only to stop short when she saw two maids in the smaller chamber beyond. They hadn't seen her.

"Don't know where it's all got to," said one. She held a small pail in one hand and scattered herbs onto the rush matting with the other. "But I'll wager it's got somethin' to do with Tilly goin' missin'."

"Aye, it must've been her that took it," said the other, rubbing a cloth along the window sill. "Lucky she left b'fore the master hears of it, I say."

The first maid turned to address the other and spotted Elizabeth. She blushed and gave her a sheepish look. "Sorry, ma'm, we didn't see you there."

The second maid bit her lip and bobbed a curtsy.

"It's all right," Elizabeth said. "But may I ask, who is Tilly and what has she done?"

The first maid bit her lip too and lowered her gaze.

"I won't tell Lord Lynden," Elizabeth assured her. "In light of recent events, it's important that everyone's movements be accounted for, and if this Tilly is somehow involved, I need to know. If it's relevant, I will pass on the information as if it were my own. No names need be mentioned."

The second maid glanced at her friend. When the first continued to bite her lip, she stepped forward. "Tilly is one of the laundry maids, ma'am. She's missing."

"Missing? Has anyone gone to find out if she's returned home to the village?"

"Aye, ma'am, one of the grooms went this morning, but she ain't there."

Dread pierced Elizabeth's chest. "You mentioned that she did something wrong. What was it?"

"Some linen's gone missing, ma'am. We think she stole it."

"Stole it? Why would she do that?"

"Don't know, ma'am. Sell it, I s'pose."

"What is your name?"

"Martha, ma'am, and this here's Frances."

"Well, Martha and Frances, what do *you* think happened to her?"

The maids exchanged glances. "We think she's hiding," Martha said. "If the master found out she stole the linen, he'd beat her. She's prob'ly afraid and is waiting for it to be forgotten."

It did seem the most likely course for her to take. She could have left the valley altogether, but she'd be even more foolish to do that. Young maidens couldn't go wandering about the countryside, friendless and far from home.

"How do you know the linen is missing? Did another laundry maid notice when she counted it?"

"No, ma'am, I noticed it," Frances said, ducking her head. She was very young, perhaps no more than fifteen, and as shy as Elizabeth had been at her age.

"I went to tidy up Mr. Paxton's room after..." Frances shuddered. "After he died. No one wanted to touch it before that. There was no linen on the bed, and none in the bedchamber where them others slept neither. I asked the other maids, but no one had collected it. That's when we noticed Tilly weren't up yet. I went to fetch her, but she weren't in her bed."

"So you don't know for certain that Tilly took the linen?" Elizabeth asked.

"No, but it must have been her, ma'am. Otherwise, why would she hide?"

Why indeed.

Elizabeth thanked them and went up to Paxton's bedchamber in the upper corner of the house. It was a small room, and there was no trace of recent occupation. All his possessions had been in his pack, found with the body. She inspected the lumpy mattress. Wool poked out of a small hole in the middle. She lifted it to look underneath and dropped the mattress with a gasp of horror. The underside was covered in dried blood. She lifted it again. Definitely blood. Someone had flipped the mattress over to hide it.

She made her way to the bedchamber where the other men had slept. Both beds also bore bloodied mattresses that had been flipped over.

The men had been killed in their chambers.

Oh God, it made the crime so much worse. Elizabeth and her family had been in the house, Edward too. All the servants slept in chambers near the outbuildings, so at least they'd been safe, but what if one of the family had disturbed Greville as he went about killing these men in their beds as they slept?

She covered her mouth and leaned back against the door. She'd not liked Paxton, but to die in such a manner was horrific. And to think it was Greville! She'd not thought the man capable of such cold-bloodedness.

She wished Edward were there to talk to. They could discuss this development and consider the problem of the missing maid together. He would know what to do next. She felt lost and alone without him.

She slumped against the door and began to cry. She would never talk to him again, about this or anything. Her sobs quieted after a few minutes, and she gathered her wits and left. There didn't seem much point in going to see the place where the men were found, but she decided she would anyway. If nothing else, it got her away from the house and Arrabella.

Warren saddled a horse, and she rode out alone to the western field where Umberley had found the bodies. The shallow graves where they'd been hastily buried were easy to identify from the newly turned earth. There was not much blood at the site. Nicholas Coleclough and Edward had said wounds to the throat produced a lot of blood. The lack of it on the ground only confirmed that they hadn't been killed there, but back at the house. Greville *must* have lied when he claimed he saw them pass by him as he hid in the larder. If nothing else, finding the place where they'd died was confirmation that they'd accused the right man.

She searched the area and found more turned earth several feet away behind bushes. She used a stick and her own hands to push the dirt aside. It didn't take long to uncover the bloodied linen and…rope? What was the rope for?"

She pictured the scene in her mind. Greville had killed the men in their beds, wrapped them in the bed linen and carried them one by one down to the stables where he'd saddled their horses and *tied* them to the saddles so they didn't fall off. That explained the rope. He'd then led the horses here, untied them and buried the men before letting the horses wander off.

Good lord, he went to no small effort.

She shuddered. To think, her sister had been going to marry him and bring him into the family fold. There would be no such problem with her newest betrothed.

Elizabeth gave a wry twist of her mouth, only to be swamped by fresh tears.

She hastily dashed them away and rode back to the stables. She went in search of the maids again and found them both in the kitchen along with two others. They were laughing as Frances chased a clucking, flapping hen around the large central table. The laughter stopped when Elizabeth walked in.

"I have some more questions," she said, leaping out of the way as the hen and Frances barreled past.

"What questions?" the cook asked from where she stood by the steaming cauldron hanging over the fireplace, ladle in hand. She reminded Elizabeth of her mother, an enormous bosom hindering the sight of her feet, with apple-red cheeks and several chins. The only difference was the cook's missing teeth.

"She were asking after Tilly," Martha said. She continued chopping vegetables into small chunks on the table. "Go on then, ma'am. Ask away."

"Could Tilly have been the one to tell Lord Greville about the old priest's escape route through the house? Did she know about it?"

"She couldn't've known," Martha said. "Hardly any of us did."

"Only old Betty," Frances said, giving up her chase. The hen quieted upon sensing the immediate danger was over. "I asked around and seems she's the only one been here long enough to know."

"She works in the laundry on account of her bad eyes now."

"Could Betty have told Tilly about it?"

Martha shrugged. "S'pose, but she did say she'd forgotten about it until yesterday." She looked to the others for confirmation.

They all nodded, except for the cook, frowning in thought. "Tilly's ma used to work here. Her grandma too. Mayhap she heard about it through them."

It was a good theory. A very good theory. "Do you think she would have told Lord Greville about it?"

The maids returned to their tasks, not meeting her gaze.

"I see," Elizabeth said. "Tilly and Lord Greville were…keeping one another company."

Frances giggled. The cook hissed at her and the girl blushed fiercely.

"Tilly were his favorite girl, aye," said Martha. "Pretty thing, but there's no bigger fool than her hereabouts. I tell her to mind her own business when that handsome Lord Greville come, but she won't listen. All he had to do was wink at her, and she fell into his bed."

The man sank even lower in Elizabeth's opinion. If Arrabella wasn't carrying his child, Elizabeth would have said good riddance.

Martha chopped violently through a carrot, sending half of it skittering across the table surface. "If she and he were…together then it's likely she told him about the tunnel since he were in that room."

"Very likely," Elizabeth said. "If you hear anything from Tilly, or learn where she might be, please come see me immediately. Not Lord Lynden. Understand?"

"Aye, ma'am," Martha said. She bobbed a curtsy.

Elizabeth thanked them and left them to their tasks. She only hoped they were right and Tilly was indeed hiding from Jeffrey until the matter blew over. The alternative—that she'd been murdered because she knew too much—was too shocking to contemplate.

CHAPTER 18

The laborer at Coleclough Farm had been most helpful. If it weren't for him, Edward wouldn't have known he was heading in the right direction. He'd ridden to both Stoneleigh then on to Cole's place, asking everyone he came across whether they'd seen Greville pass through. Only the Coleclough Farm hand had, and only then because he'd gotten up earlier than usual to see to a birthing ewe.

It was doubly fortunate that Greville was on foot, not horseback. Finding him would have been impossible if he'd taken his horse. He would be long gone. But, inexplicably, he'd left it in the Sutton Hall stables.

Edward reached the village of Larkham just before sunset. It was smaller than Sutton Grange, not being a market town, with only one inn offering accommodation for travelers. He rode into the innyard, keeping a wary eye on his surrounds. Mere weeks ago he'd been embroiled in a mystery involving Larkham folk that had seen Cole almost lose his life at the hands of a mob of villagers. The situation could still be volatile.

He dismounted and handed the reins to the ostler. The heavy-set fellow greeted him with a nod and an arch of his ponderous brow.

"You're back," the ostler said, looking past Edward. "Alone."

The hairs on the back of Edward's neck stood up. "Aye."

The ostler considered this a moment as he rubbed the horse's nose. "That wise?"

"Why wouldn't it be?"

The ostler shrugged one bulky shoulder and glanced past Edward again. Edward resisted the urge to look around, but he kept alert to any sounds of movement. There were none. "Some in this village ain't forgotten what your friend done."

"My friend removed a canker from your community. You should be grateful."

"Aye, no argument from me." His lips parted in a smile, revealing crooked teeth. "I never liked the fellow. Just keep your wits about you, sir, is all. You staying long? Taproom's through there if you're looking for an ale and some supper."

"Thank you. Actually, I'm looking for a man who may have arrived on foot today. He's a fine fellow, not someone you'd expect to see wandering about without a horse. Has he been here?"

"Aye. It was strange seeing a gentleman come on foot. He looked out of sorts too. I expect he was in need of an ale or ten." He laughed. "You'll prob'ly find him in the taproom still."

Edward thanked him and headed to the door the ostler pointed out. Inside, the taproom was busy. Edward kept his hat low and looked around. There was no sign of Greville. He wove his way through patrons drinking and supping and approached a serving girl carrying four empty cups. He described Greville to her. Her cheeks flushed, and she bit her lip.

"So he is here," he said when she didn't answer.

She glanced toward the stairs. "He don't want no one to disturb him, sir. He asked me not to tell anyone who came looking for him. But I didn't, did I? You already knew."

He gave her a reassuring smile. "I already knew." He slipped a shilling into her palm. "I also looked into every guest chamber until I found him in the…?"

"Fourth one."

He thanked her and made his way up the stairs. He knocked on the fourth door. "Supper," he called out.

The door cracked open. Half of Greville's face appeared. "Fuck!" He went to slam the door shut, but Edward pushed his weight against it. Greville stumbled backward and fell onto the bed.

Edward marched in and shut the door with his boot. "Found you."

Greville held up his hands in surrender. He wasn't even going to fight? Pathetic. "Monk, I can explain. You've got it all wrong."

Edward grabbed Greville's shirt at his chest. His doublet and jerkin were neatly laid out on the bed, and his boots were set on the hearth. He looked clean and tidy, his hair combed as usual. There was no evidence he'd been walking half the night and all day, except for the blisters on his toes. The raw flesh looked sore. Edward kicked one and received a yowl in response.

"Got it wrong, have I?" Edward drawled. "You mean you didn't leave the house via a secret passage?"

"Er, well, that part is true."

Edward twisted his hand in the shirt. Greville mewled like a kitten. "But I didn't kill anyone," he added quickly. "I swear on the Holy Bible, I did not kill Paxton!"

"Then why run away?"

"It's complicated."

Edward let him go. He picked up a chair and set it in front of the door, then removed his sword from its scabbard. He sat and set the sword across his lap. "I have all night."

Greville glanced at the sword and gulped. He nodded quickly. "I left Sutton Hall because I saw it as an opportunity to get away from…people."

"Aye, in a casket after you were hung for the murders."

"No! I escaped, didn't I?"

"You didn't get very far. It was easy to track you here."

Greville scrubbed his face with his hands. "So I see. I didn't think anyone had seen me. Indeed, I didn't think you would look too hard. Lynden doesn't strike me as the sort of fellow who'd expend too much time or money searching for a peer who may not be guilty of murder. Surely he'd find it easier to blame a passing vagabond and leave it at that."

"Circumstances changed. And Lynden didn't send me."

Greville's swallow was audible. "I had to disappear, you see. Even though Paxton was gone, another would be sent in his place. I could never escape. Never."

"Until you paid Hicks the goldsmith the debt you owe him."

"Or until I died. I thought this way I could disappear for a year or two and then rejoin the world and court when all is forgotten."

"You think the goldsmith's memory is that short?"

"Well, no. I'd hoped to make enough money in that time to pay him back."

"How? You have no skills, no land, no means. How could you possibly pay him back?"

Greville shrugged. Edward didn't know if he truly hadn't thought it through, or whether he was protecting his Catholic family's roots. If Greville's brother was involved in plots, it would be easy enough to intercept his correspondence and blackmail the other plotters. It's what Edward would do if he wanted a lot of money quickly.

Once, it was what he would have done. He'd been desperate to better himself for Arrabella, if not in status, then in wealth. It had been the driving force in accepting a position in Hughe's Assassins Guild, although he would now gladly do it for a lot less financial reward. Money wasn't as important to him anymore. He had everything he needed for a comfortable life, and to wed and raise a family on. Not only that, but he no longer cared about becoming a gentleman. Indeed, he'd forgotten about the herald's commission until Lynden had shown him the herald's letter.

When had he stopped caring?

Around the time he'd fallen in love with Elizabeth.

Elizabeth. He hadn't thought of her since arriving in Greville's chamber. It had been the first time all day in which he'd *not* thought of her. The long ride had allowed his mind to wander, and it had always wandered to her and the wretched look in her eyes when he'd told her he planned on marrying Arrabella. It made him ache all over again for her, for them. For what may have been.

He closed his hand around the sword hilt. The man responsible for breaking Elizabeth's heart sat across from him. If he ran him through, would it ease the ache?

"You're a coward," he snarled at Greville. "You should pay your debts like a gentleman and own up to your mistakes."

Greville snorted. "You think being a gentleman means all the things it used to? Of course you do. You don't go to court. You don't see the false chivalry, staged for the queen and her ladies like a play. It's a rat pit in there where the most devious survive. Only a fool pays all his debts. A clever man avoids it for his entire life."

"You are not clever."

Greville sighed and hung his head. "Thank you for the reminder. There are other reasons I chose to run too."

"You're worried about stretching your pretty neck?"

Greville rubbed his hand across his throat above his ruff. "There is that, aye, but I did it for Arrabella too."

"I doubt she wished to be abandoned by her betrothed." He didn't tell Greville about the baby. It was her news to tell, not his.

"She will be better off without me." He raked his hands through his hair and down his face. "I'm a poor man. When she discovers that after the wedding, she'll be miserable. I should never have trapped a girl like her into marriage with me. She's much too vibrant to have an impoverished baron as a husband. She deserves someone who can shower her with gifts."

Then she was in for a rude shock once she wed Edward. Expensive jewels weren't something he could afford either. "She deserves a husband who loves her," he said.

"Ah. Well. That's the other thing." A bead of sweat trickled from Greville's brow down his cheek. "I don't love her."

Edward looked to the ceiling and huffed out a breath. "Do you mean to tell me you borrowed money to impress a lady who you've now decided you don't want to wed because you don't love her?"

Greville screwed up his face as if he were in pain. "It sounds absurd, but you know Arrabella. She was so easy to be with in the beginning, so compliant. She would have made a wonderful wife. But she changed soon after my arrival here. I don't know why, but I think what I saw in recent days is the true Arrabella. She's a viper, Monk, with a nasty streak through her. I couldn't bear to be saddled to her for the rest of my life!"

And now Edward would be. The irony made him laugh harshly. "You could have wedded her, bedded her and left her at home while you attended court. You wouldn't have to see her except to get children on her."

"Aye, but the truth of it is that she's not as wealthy as she let on. Her cousin is, and the annuity he provides for Arrabella and her family is a generous one, but…" He winced. "He told me the annuity would end once she wed me because I could afford to keep her. He thought I was well off, you see. It's how I wanted him to see me at first, so he'd think me worthy of her."

Edward would have laughed for real if it weren't so tragic, or if it wasn't left to him to clean up the mess. The little prick was a coward and a cur. He and Arrabella were so alike in all the worst ways, they would have made each other miserable. It would have been fitting to see them wed.

Greville flopped back on the bed, his hands covering his face. "Marrying Arrabella wouldn't have solved anything! I wouldn't be able to pay Hicks back without Lynden's annuity. I had to get out of the marriage, get away from her…from everyone! If I hadn't escaped, Lynden would have held me to the promise. He's not such a fool that he'd let me walk away from it. I had to do something drastic. I had to disappear."

He was right on that score.

Greville sat up again. He fixed Edward with the sort of stare a trapped deer gave the hunter. "Say something, Monk. Tell me you understand why I left."

"Don't look for forgiveness from me. I'm not your friend."

"But you must see why I did it." Greville's voice was high and thin. "To be free of Arrabella, allow her to wed another and to escape Hicks. It was the only way. That's why I let you think I killed Paxton."

"Running away solves nothing. You'll always be a sought man, not only by Hicks, but by the law."

"Over *Paxton*! Don't be ridiculous. Go back to Lynden, tell him you think a stranger did it, not me. Tell him I'm long gone. He'll stop looking for me if you advise it."

"And if I don't?"

"Good God, man! You'd allow an innocent to go to the gallows?"

Edward stood. He held his sword at his side, his fingers holding the hilt tightly. Too tight to wield it with any agility. "I have no sympathy for you. Besides, I think you're lying. I think you did do it."

"No! No, I didn't."

"Then who did?"

"I don't know. Best perhaps. He's the only one I can think of who may have had a reason to see Paxton dead."

"Aside from you."

Greville glanced at the sword and swallowed heavily. He nodded. "Put that away and let me explain."

"No. Explain anyway."

Even before Greville began, Edward's mind raced back to his conversations with Best. He liked the man on the whole, yet he'd been quick to suggest Greville was to blame for Paxton's murder. Too quick?

"I received a message in London from my brother John that his man Best would deliver a document to me. It never reached me before I left, but I knew Best would pursue me to Sutton Hall. I stayed overnight in the village, against my better judgment, but he didn't come before I headed up to the house. He sought me out there the next day and told me about the document that my brother wanted me to deliver to a friend in the north. I know this friend. He's got strong opinions. Catholic opinions."

"As has your brother."

Greville nodded, grim-faced. "I suspected the document contained a message that if it got into the wrong hands could prove fatal for anyone associated with it. Not least for me if I carried it. You must understand, I'm not particularly pious like John. Catholic, Protestant, I don't care overmuch. I wasn't going to put my neck on the line for something that means nothing to me."

Edward couldn't blame him for cowardice in this instance. It wouldn't be just his neck on the line, but his innards, limbs and other body parts too.

"So I refused to even look at it," Greville went on. "Best said he wasn't leaving until I did. Paxton already had the idea to use the document to blackmail the intended recipient, and my brother too."

"And you refused."

He nodded. "Paxton saw it as a way for me to pay back his master, and free me from Arrabella if I chose. He knew I was wavering, and was worried I wouldn't go through with the wedding after all. I hadn't told him about Lynden cutting off the annuity, nor did I want to. He would have removed one of my fingers then and there." He cradled his hand in his lap and the color drained from his face. "Even so, he must have seen the document as a more lucrative option."

"You think Paxton fought Best for the document, and Best killed him? Deliberately?"

"Aye. One death could be considered accidental, but not all three."

True enough. "What evidence do you have?"

"None, only that Best had other opportunities to give me the document and never did. Indeed, he never tried again after Paxton confronted him."

It wasn't making sense. Why hadn't Best tried to foist the document on Greville again? Or, if he'd given up, why not just leave? There was something else going on. Something more sinister.

"The thing is," Greville went on, "my brother isn't a fool. He's never gotten himself involved in plots before. He stays away from the troublemakers and keeps his faith to himself. Few know about it. He may be a greedy, lying prick, but he's no traitor. So why now? Why send his man all the way to find me to deliver a document to some nameless plotters? Not only is it out of character, but he would have known I'd refuse."

"Unless it was all a ruse." Edward sheathed his sword and paced the room.

"My brother isn't the only greedy man at Greville Hall. Best is too."

Edward stopped suddenly in front of Greville. "Tell me about him."

"He was born on the estate in my grandfather's time and has lived there all his life. He was devoted to my father and taught John and I to ride and hunt as boys. As we grew up, I went to court with Father and John remained behind. He resented it. He hated being the second son and told me he should have been the heir. He claimed he would have made a better landlord. Best agreed. He told me in no uncertain terms that I was lazy, hopeless. Of course it wasn't my fault the estate ended up the way it did!" he whined. "The rot set in during Father's time. It was too late to stop it after I inherited. The debts were enormous. I had to sell off much of the land just to keep a roof over our heads. But my brother resented the loss of every acre. Best too. I exiled myself to court just to get away from them."

"And escape your responsibilities."

Greville shot to his feet. "What do you know of it? You own nothing." He pointed a finger at Edward's chest. "People like you don't know what it's like for us noblemen."

Edward very deliberately and calmly pushed Greville's offending finger away. "I know you like to keep all your limbs in perfect working order, so kindly refrain from pointing at me, or you'll find it snapped off."

Greville sat again and tucked both hands under his thighs. "Fuck," he muttered. "I think my brother orchestrated all this as revenge."

"It's an extreme measure. Why not just have you killed? There are men who can be hired for such a task."

"I don't know. Perhaps Best's instructions were to kill me, then he was presented with a better option by blaming me for Paxton's death."

"Then your brother would get nothing. A convicted murderer's property and title are confiscated. His heirs cannot inherit."

"I know that, but I'm not sure Best does."

"Even if your brother assumed he would inherit, why would he want an impoverished estate?"

"An impoverished one with a title is better than nothing."

Edward only laughed. A few short days ago he would have agreed with that sentiment, but not anymore. Elizabeth was the only thing he wanted. He would do anything to have her as his bride. Anything. Including clear Greville's name and drag him back to his betrothed. He was finally seeing a way through the mire to a solution.

Greville certainly didn't look like a murderer. His shoulders drooped and misery clouded his eyes. He looked exhausted, beaten and utterly lost. Besides, the man was too lazy to kill three men and bury their bodies, and much too stupid to think of taking the packs and horses too. The murderer had gone to great pains to make it look like the men had left in the middle of the night then been set upon on the road. Greville was no forward thinker.

"You must think now, Greville," he told him. "Think about anything that will prove Best did it. Lynden won't dismiss you as the murderer unless we present him with facts about Best."

"No," Greville said on a pained whine. "There's nothing."

Edward started pacing again. "Let's go through the events of that night again. You returned to your chambers, but went down to the kitchen some time later. Do you know how late it was?"

"I'm not a time piece. A few hours after the house was all asleep." He shrugged.

"Then you saw Paxton and his men pass and hid in the larder."

"Actually, that never happened. I didn't see them."

Edward stopped. "Why did you make it up?"

"I wanted to protect Best. It never occurred to me that he'd actually done it at the time. I simply didn't want you thinking he had. Being the stranger in the area, suspicion would have immediately fallen upon him. He's my brother's man, Monk. My father's. He taught me to ride and shoot!" Greville looked as if he'd cry.

"Then why are you blaming him now?"

"Because telling the truth is the only way I can save myself. I don't *like* pointing the finger at Best. I hate it. I wish there was another."

But someone had to take the blame away from Greville himself. Loyalty only went so far it seemed. "Then why not tell me it was a lie when you were accused?"

Greville shrugged. "It never occurred to me. When you came to lock me in my chambers, I was drunk. I wasn't thinking straight. It wasn't until I arrived here that I began to think everything through and remembered the lie." He shrugged again. "There was no harm in it. It makes no difference anyway."

"It makes a lot of difference. It means the men could have been murdered in the house. In their beds."

"Perhaps, but that fact doesn't exonerate me."

"It does disprove the traveling vagabond theory."

"How does that help me? If anything, it makes it worse. I can't blame some nameless wanderer. Nor does it help the theory that Best did it."

He was right. Edward sat again on the chair and stretched out his legs. There was only one thing for it. "We have to find Best and take him back to Sutton Hall. The coroner might get some answers out of him." Or Edward would, one way or another.

"And me? Do I have to go back too?"

"Of course you do. You're getting married."

And Edward was going to rejoice all the way back until he could break the news to Elizabeth himself.

* * *

MARTHA BURST into Elizabeth's outer chamber without knocking first. "Miss Buckley! Miss Buckley, come quick!"

The maid's stricken face told a worrying tale. She wrung her hands in her apron. "What is it, Martha?"

"It's Miss Arrabella. She's fallen."

Oh God. Elizabeth raced after the maid, taking two stairs at a time, and followed her outside. They met one of the laborers in the courtyard carrying Arrabella in his arms. Her eyes were closed, her long lashes dark against marble white cheeks. She moaned softly.

"Bella," Elizabeth said. "Bella, can you hear me?"

Arrabella muttered something unintelligible and moaned again.

"Take her to her rooms," Elizabeth directed the laborer. "This way." She held her sister's hand as she was carried inside and up to her bedchamber. "Martha, have someone ride into the village to fetch the wise woman. Then collect cool cloths and clean water. Oh, and my mother."

Martha sobbed into her apron as she ran off to perform her errands. The laborer had already melted away as soon as he'd set Arrabella down. More maids entered, carrying the things Elizabeth had asked for. She pressed the damp cloth to her sister's temple.

"Bella? Bella, can you hear me?"

Arrabella stirred, shifting her head from side to side. She moaned again, louder, and gave a small sob. "Lizzie? Oh, Lizzie, is it gone?"

"Is what gone?"

"The baby, silly."

Elizabeth's stomach rolled and plunged. Oh God. She was going to be sick. She touched her sister's flat belly. *Please let it live.*

She dismissed the maids and thanked providence that Janet hadn't arrived yet. She could cope with only one madwoman at a time.

"How did you fall?" she asked.

"I was out riding."

"But you never ride."

"The groom saddled a big brute of a thing. Black as night, he was, with fierce yellow eyes." A small shiver wracked Arrabella. She placed her hand over Elizabeth's.

A bad feeling settled in Elizabeth's chest like a rock. The only black horse in the stables was indeed a big, powerful one. It would take a rider of great skill to control him. "Why in God's name did they let you ride him?"

"Don't blame the lad. It's not his fault. He didn't want me to take him, but I said I was a good rider. As good as you, Lizzie, that's what I told him." She smiled weakly.

Elizabeth tried to muster a smile in return, but couldn't. She switched her attention to her hand, linked with her sister's over Arrabella's waist. "Bella...did you *want* to fall off?"

Bella's nod was slight but unmistakable.

Elizabeth snatched her hand away. She tried to breathe, but it wasn't easy. Her chest felt too tight. "Dear God, Bella, that's madness!" And yet part of her could see her sister's reasoning. The baby changed so many things. It changed Arrabella's life and not in a good way now that Greville was gone.

Arrabella's face crumpled. "Stop it! Stop judging me. Can't you see? I'm doing this for you?"

"Me?"

She nodded. "I don't want to marry Edward. *You* do, and he wants you too, not me. This way, with no baby, I can free him. It works out perfectly."

Elizabeth stood and stared down at her sister. The horror on her face must have been plain to see because Arrabella flinched. Her face crumpled, and she began to cry. Elizabeth didn't care. "No. Do not put the blame for this on Edward or me. Understand? Do not kill that baby on our account. That is grossly unfair to lay the blame at anyone's door except Greville's."

"But you have a chance with Edward if there's no baby. I know it's what you want."

"What I want is for that baby to live and be loved!"

"Come now, Lizzie, don't be a fool." Her voice had turned harsh. Gone were the little moans, the tears, the pathetic eyes. "If this baby could be born under happier circumstances, then I'd gladly have it. But it's only bringing misery to everybody. How can I bring a child of misery into this world? It's cursed."

"Stop it." Elizabeth spun away from her and strode to the window. Tears pooled as she scanned the horizon for Edward. She didn't know why she wanted him back so desperately. Seeing him again would only make her unhappy.

Arrabella cried out in pain. Elizabeth spun round. Her sister was trying to sit up, but fell back to the pillows with a whimper.

Elizabeth ran to her. "Are you all right?"

"Everything hurts. My arm, my hip, my leg, my shoulder." She pulled aside the sleeve of her bodice and the shift underneath. A purple bruise bloomed large.

"What about...down there?" Elizabeth asked. "Are you bleeding?"

Arrabella shook her head. "All this for nothing." Her bitter words twisted Elizabeth's gut.

"Wait for the wise woman," she said. "She'll know for sure if you've lost it."

Arrabella caught her hand as Elizabeth rose. "And if I haven't?"

Elizabeth stared at her. Her stomach rolled again, but her heart felt numb. Empty. "We go on as before. You wed Edward."

"No. I don't want him. He's not the husband for me. I assure you, Lizzie, I am destined for greater things."

Not if that baby were born out of wedlock. "How?"

Arrabella pouted at her sister's sneer. "I don't know yet. All I do know is that I'm not going to marry Edward. You're welcome to him." She spat out the offer as if the very thought were distasteful.

"How magnanimous of you."

Arrabella's eyes narrowed. It was likely she didn't know what the word meant or understood the sarcasm.

None of it mattered anyway. Even if Arrabella wasn't forced to marry him, Elizabeth wasn't sure Edward was as prepared to give her up yet. He had, after all, gone to great lengths to obtain a coat of arms for her. He had also loved her for a very long time.

Janet announced her arrival with a flapping of her handkerchief and a high-pitched wail. "My princess! My dear girl!" Two maids carrying more water and cloths followed her in. They looked frightened out of their wits. No doubt they thought there'd been another death.

"I'm all right, Mother," Arrabella said with an exaggerated sigh. "Stop fussing."

Janet spotted the bruise on Arrabella's shoulder and let out another wail. She collapsed on the bed beside her daughter, almost sending the structure crashing to the ground under her weight. The mattress sagged and the posts groaned ominously.

"Lizzie, can you *please* do something about her," Arrabella cried. "She's crowding me."

"Bella?" came Jeffrey's shout from the outer chamber. He appeared at the bedchamber door without wearing either jerkin or doublet. It was tantamount to disarray in his book. "Dear child, what happened? Are you all right? And Aunt Janet too?" He leaned over Janet's form and peered into her face. Just then she sat up, knocking him in the nose. He cried out and reeled back, covering his face. Blood seeped through his fingers. Upon seeing it, he declared that he was going to faint.

A maid scurried to fetch a chair to slip underneath him, but wasn't quick enough. He missed and sat heavily on the floor.

Elizabeth blinked at the chaotic scene. She couldn't breathe, couldn't think.

She fled.

"Lizzie!" her mother called. "Lizzie, where are you going? You're needed in here. Lizzie, come back here at once!"

CHAPTER 19

The wise woman's arrival at Sutton Hall was a welcome
event. Not only because she had extensive midwifery
knowledge and a calming manner, but also because she brought
Tilly the maid with her.

"Her ma and pa are my neighbors," Widow Dawson said as she
climbed down from the front seat of the cart that had brought her.
Two girls hopped down from the rear. One looked to be about ten,
the other sixteen or so. The latter glanced around them, her teeth
nibbling her bottom lip. "I seen her come home two days ago, but
she never left again. I asked her ma, and she didn't answer me
proper. Then I heard that one of the maids from the big house had
gone missin', and I knew it were her. It's not goin' to do her no
good hidin', and she can't hide forever, so I told her to come up
with me today and explain."

The older girl, Tilly, flushed scarlet and dropped her chin to
her chest. She would have been quite pretty if it weren't for her
crooked teeth, but she did have a lush figure, something Greville
seemed to like. The cur. How could he have taken advantage of
this girl in the way he had? He deserved a flogging.

"Can we go inside now, Ma?" the younger girl asked. "I can't
wait to see them nice hangings again."

Widow Dawson tugged her daughter's plaits. "There'll be no idling, Bel, we've got work to do."

"I'm not sure a child should be present while you inspect my sister," Elizabeth said with an apologetic smile at Bel.

Bel screwed her nose up at her. "Ma needs me." With a *humph* of indignation, she marched off toward the house.

Widow Dawson chuckled. "Got a mind of her own, that girl. Ain't no leavin' her out of the sick room when there's work to be done."

"Very well, if you're sure she'll be all right."

"Aye, she'll be all right. Been helpin' me for an age it seems like."

"One of the maids will take you up to my sister's chambers." Elizabeth eyed Tilly who was looking nervously about. "Follow me to the kitchen, Tilly. No more running away, understand? You're fortunate that you returned today. I asked the house steward not to tell Lord Lynden until we knew the reason for your departure. He agreed to wait only until suppertime."

The maid nodded quickly and gulped. "Yes, ma'am. But…is that man gone?" Her gaze darted to the house then all around again. "Only I'm scared of him."

"He's gone. Come now," Elizabeth said, softer. "Let's go inside and you can tell me what happened. You're in no danger."

The party headed to the kitchen entrance. The cook and maids stopped clattering pans and chopping to stare at Tilly. One gave a squeal and hugged her.

"I was so worried!" she said. "I knew you wouldn't steal that linen. You didn't, did you?"

Tilly's eyes widened and she shook her head rapidly. "Stole some linen? No, not me. I ain't no thief. Please, miss," she implored Elizabeth. "You've got to believe me."

"I believe you. Frances, take Widow Dawson and Bel up to Arrabella's apartments." She waited for them to leave before directing Tilly to sit on a stool at the table. "So your disappearance had nothing to do with the missing linen?"

"No, ma'am! I ain't no thief, I swear!" She gulped back tears, but failed. They slid down her cheeks into her collar. She screwed her hands into fists and jabbed them into her eye sockets. "You be sure to tell his lordship that I stole nothin' from him. He'll beat me if he thinks I thieved from him. Please, ma'am, please."

Elizabeth drew the girl's hands away from her poor eyes. "I'll be sure he knows. But you need to tell us what happened. Why did you run away? Were you afraid Lord Greville would try to kill you too?"

She gasped. "Lord Greville? What's he got to do with it?"

Elizabeth cocked her head to the side and regarded the girl. She seemed genuinely puzzled. All the other maids drew in closer, as if they could sense an interesting story was about to unfold. "He killed Paxton and his men," Elizabeth said. "You helped him escape by showing him the priest's tunnel out of his room."

Tilly blinked. "No, Miss Buckley, I didn't! I swear to you I know nothin' about no tunnel. I was talkin' about that fellow Best what hid in the brewery. *He's* the murderer."

Gasps echoed around the kitchen. One of them was Elizabeth's. Best killed Paxton and his men? That couldn't be right. If the men had been murdered in their chambers and carried out in the sheets of linen, how could Greville have seen them walk past as he hid in the larder? He must have lied, but why lie if he didn't do it?

"Are you sure?" she asked Tilly. "Perhaps you only think it was Mr. Best."

"No, miss, it were him. I met him one day when I went to the brewery to fetch some ale. Gave me a fright, he did, when he popped out like that. But he was very nice to me." Her eyes became unfocused and a wistful smile played on her mouth. "So very nice, he was. I took him food. Only what no one wanted, mind. I never stole it, I swear!"

"Of course," Elizabeth said before any of the maids could make their thoughts on that known. It was unlikely that any uneaten food went to waste. Between the servants and the animals, nothing would be thrown out.

"We became…friends." She blushed again and lowered her gaze.

One of the maids snorted. "You was friends with that fellow *and* Lord Greville?" When Tilly's blush only deepened, she added, "God's wounds, Till, you shouldn't be surprised when the other girls call you Tumbling Tilly behind yer back."

"That's enough," Elizabeth chided. "So you and Mr. Best became friends, yet you think he killed those men. What made you change your mind about him?"

"I saw him early the next mornin' with blood on his shirt. He weren't wearing it, but packed it away with his things. I saw it pokin' out of his pack. He was annoyed that I'd seen it and got real mad with me. He said I was sneaking about, but I wasn't! I swear! Anyway, he calmed down some and told me the blood was his own. He cut himself. I offered to look at it, but he wouldn't show me. Then I said I'd clean his shirt and bring it back fresh. So he gave it to me, I cleaned it then took it back." She shrugged. "I believed him then, but later, I heard about them fellows being murdered. I went to find Mr. Monk, but he was nowhere about. Then I saw him with you, miss, talkin' to Mr. Best. But Mr. Best saw me. I could see in his eyes that he knew I was goin' to tell about the blood on his shirt. Real small and black his eyes got. Evil, they were. I grew scared again, miss. Real scared." She leaned forward, her hands grasping both of Elizabeth's. They shook. "He was goin' to kill me if I told you. I know he was! I left that day. Ran all the way to the Grange, I was that frightened. Oh, miss, he is far away from here, ain't he?"

"Yes, Tilly, he's gone. He won't trouble you." She studied the girl. She was indeed terrified, there was no doubt. Nor did she doubt her story about the blood. The only explanation for it was that he'd come into contact with the bodies, or committed the murder himself. He'd not mentioned it to Edward at the time, which implied guilt. Yet Greville's lie about seeing Paxton and his men leaving the house pointed to him being the murderer. Besides, he wouldn't escape if he were innocent.

She kept her hand linked with Tilly's. "Come with me to see Lord Lynden. You need to tell him everything you told me."

Tilly's eyes grew rounder. "If you think it's best, miss, I'll do it."

* * *

JEFFREY LOOKED up from his desk upon Elizabeth's and Tilly's entry into his study. "What news of Arrabella?" He did not mention the baby specifically. Only the family and now Widow Dawson knew Arrabella was with child. Not even the maids knew, and that was how it would remain until after the wedding.

The wedding. Now that Best was implicated in the murders, Greville could marry Arrabella. That's if Edward found him.

Elizabeth would not allow herself to hope yet. Besides, even if Edward was released from his obligation, would he be pleased about it? Or would he be reluctant to let Arrabella slip out of his grasp so soon after finally securing her?

"I don't know," Elizabeth said. "I haven't been to see her yet. Widow Dawson is with her now."

He nodded and sighed. "We'll pray for her and…" He glanced at Tilly. "And everyone."

Elizabeth pushed Tilly forward. "This is one of your maids," she said. There were so many at Sutton Hall, she wasn't entirely sure if he would recognize the girl. "Her name's Tilly. She's got something to tell you."

Tilly repeated the pertinent parts of her tale. Once finished, she bobbed a curtsy and hurriedly left upon Jeffrey's dismissal. He didn't admonish her for absconding once Elizabeth explained that she was frightened. Elizabeth sat in the chair opposite the desk and watched as he digested the news. He seemed elated at first, but his smiles didn't last as long as she expected.

"She can wed him," he muttered. "She'll be baroness after all, and the baby will be heir." He rested his elbows on the desk and pressed his interlocked fingers against his lips.

"As long as Edward brings him back," she said.

"Monk will bring Greville back. The issue is, Greville is still poor. I don't think Best lied about that."

"A poor baron is better than a man with no birthright, surely." *Forgive me, Edward.*

"Perhaps, perhaps not. Greville is poor *and* a Catholic."

There was that too. To be associated with a noble Catholic family could be dangerous for Arrabella and the baby, even if Greville kept his faith private. He would always be implicated in plots against the queen, always be one of the names high on the list of potential traitors. Worse, he would always be pursued by those dissident Catholics who needed a nobleman on their side. He could never escape them.

She watched Jeffrey as he battled with the decision. After he'd weighed everything, there was a chance he would see Edward as the better option and still try to force their union.

And if Edward did indeed want it, Arrabella's opinion wouldn't matter. Nor, of course, would Elizabeth's.

She left him to his thoughts and went to her sister's rooms. She found Bel packing away cloths in the bag Widow Dawson had carried in. The wise woman sat on the edge of the bed, a sympathetic frown on her brow as she looked down at the face of a weepy Arrabella.

"The baby," Elizabeth whispered. Her legs gave way and she sat on a chair. "Oh no."

"No, Lizzie, dear," Janet said. She tried to heave herself up from the chair by the bed, but gave up with a click of her tongue. "The baby's still inside."

"It's too soon to tell if it lives yet," Widow Dawson said. "But there's no blood or pain, and that's a good sign."

Arrabella let out a wail. Elizabeth understood now. Her sister still wanted to rid herself of the baby. At least Elizabeth could give her some good news about Greville's innocence. If only she could tell her he was coming back to marry her.

* * *

EDWARD KEPT an eye on his charge as they raised a hue and cry across the valley for Best. He needn't have worried. Greville didn't try to escape. He seemed keen to find Best too to prove his innocence once and for all. Or perhaps he was simply resigned to his fate. Maybe he'd decided that facing up to his obligations was better than running and hiding for years.

He might also think he could still get out of the wedding. That was another reason Edward wasn't going to tell him about Arrabella's state. It might scare Greville away and plunge him into hiding so deep that he couldn't be found.

They made their base at the Plough Inn and sent out enquiries —at no small expense—with the farmers, merchants, peddlers, and other travelers who wandered in and out of Sutton Grange. A response reached them from a laborer late in the afternoon that had Edward riding hard out of the village. The laborer came from a farm to the north. He claimed to have fed a man matching Best's description only a few hours earlier. The farm, being set between two fast-flowing streams, had only one road past it. It was on that road that Edward and Greville traveled at speed.

Best wasn't there. They rode past the farm twice, and still nothing. "He's left the road," Edward said. Damnation! It would be much harder to find him if he was crossing fields and meadows.

"Ah well," said Greville. "Let's give up and return to the Hall." He sat high in the saddle of the horse they'd hired from the Larkham inn. She was a jaunty gray mare, and he rode her well. He seemed to be aware of just how well. He held the reins loosely in one hand and rested his other on his hip. He took pains to nod to people he passed in the village high street and bow to the women. The prettier the woman, the lower he bowed and the more he preened. The man acted like a king. It was bloody sickening, and Edward was glad to leave the village behind.

"We'll ride up there and look around," Edward said, nodding at a nearby hill.

Greville pulled a face. "Why?"

"Because it's the highest spot hereabouts and will give us a view of the surrounds. We might spot Best."

"But there's too many trees! They'll be in the way."

"We'll climb one. See that tall yew? We should be able to see for miles from up there."

"You want *me* to climb? In these hose? They're silk!"

"And orange."

Greville looked down at his hose. "Is there something wrong with orange?"

"Do you really want to take fashion advice from me?"

Greville took in Edward's black breeches and black doublet, twisting his mouth with distaste. "Good point."

They rode up the hill. It wasn't steep, but the woods slowed them down. They finally reached the top and the gnarled old yew tree that Edward had seen from the base. It rose above the others like a fat giant surrounded by dwarfs. He began the ascent and wasn't surprised when Greville didn't follow. At least he didn't ride off.

Once at the top, Edward scanned the area. The hill wasn't so high that he could see the entire valley, just the surrounding tenant farms, most of which belonged to Lynden at Sutton Hall. Tracks cut through the patchwork of fields like scars and two streams snaked through the landscape, bypassing the nearest farmhouse. He spotted horses pulling plows, laborers working beneath the hot sun in their straw hats. All worked in groups on tasks that could be discerned even at a distance.

Except one. A figure walked alone through a meadow with what appeared to be a pack on his back.

Edward climbed back down the tree, jumping the last few feet. "Let's go," he said as he landed on the soft earth.

Greville had dismounted and sat on a fallen log. Anyone else would have lain down on the ground and dozed the few minutes away, but no doubt Greville hadn't wanted to dirty his orange silk hose. He flapped his hat in front of his face and dabbed sweat from the back of his neck with a handkerchief. "You found him?"

"It's difficult to tell. There's a man some distance away who may or may not be Best."

"Let's get this over with and get out of this infernal heat. I'm sweating in uncomfortable places."

They remounted and rode in the direction of the lone man. Edward spotted him first, walking through the long grass, a pack on his back.

"God's blood!" Greville declared. "You *did* find him."

Had he expected Edward to fail? Edward didn't ask, nor did he wait for Best to see them. He charged his horse forward.

At the sound of the hooves, Best turned. His eyes widened. He swore aloud. Then he dropped his pack, set his feet apart in a solid stance, and drew his sword.

Edward reined in his horse. So that's how it was going to be. A sword fight. Bloody fool. Hadn't he learned after the last time?

Edward dismounted and drew his sword too. He wouldn't use the unfair advantage being mounted gave him. "Put it down, Best," he said.

Best glanced at Greville, still mounted. He shook his head. "What do you want?" he asked Edward.

"I'm taking you back to Sutton Hall. You'll be a guest of Lord Lynden until you're bound over for trial at the next assizes."

"Guest?"

Edward shrugged. "In a chamber with a lock and no escape route. Indeed, it'll probably be the cellar alongside the bodies. On the bright side, it's cooler down there."

Best bared his teeth and flexed his fingers around the hilt. "You expect me to come back with you when you're going to hang me for those murders?"

"Peacefully? No, I don't expect that. I expect you to put up a small fight, lose, and bleed all the way back to the Hall. I hope you make it to your trial, but if you bleed out beforehand, it'll save everyone time and inconvenience."

"A small fight, eh?"

Edward feinted a strike. Best parried and stepped neatly aside. He scowled at Greville, still sitting astride his horse. "Are you just going to sit there?"

"What choice do I have?" Greville said.

"You could help me! Two is better than one."

"Not in this instance. I saw him fight Paxton."

"You pathetic little whelp! I raised you since you were a pup!"

"That may be, but you were always John's man. Even when we were children you favored him."

"That's because your father ignored him in favor of you, you fool! He *needed* me more. Come now, Greville. We're as good as family."

Greville snorted. His top lip curled up in a sneer. "You were born on one of our farms! You're no more family to John and me than you are to the queen."

Best's face dropped. Where before he'd seemed warily confident, he now resembled a man bereft. He even lowered his sword. "Is that how you see me? You and Ayleward?"

"Of course. You're just the hired man." Greville scoffed and turned away as if he couldn't bear to look at Best anymore.

Best's disappointment vanished. His eyes gleamed like two hard, polished stones. "So that's how you're going to play this now."

Not for the first time, Edward wondered if the two men had acted together. He wouldn't put it past them. He no longer trusted either man. But to what end? There was so much that didn't make sense. Like why did Best suggest Greville was the murderer? And why did Greville claim to see the men leave the house when he couldn't have? Had he truly been trying to protect Best?

He pointed the sword at Greville. "Dismount."

"Why?" Greville said, petulant.

"Because I told you to."

"I don't take orders from you."

Edward flicked the sword and sliced through the laces on Greville's boot. Greville gulped and dismounted.

"You," he said, turning to Best. "Tell me why you came to Sutton Hall."

"This here is the baron of Greville," Best said. "He owes you no explanation, and as his man, nor do I." The tilt of his chin was so high he was going to hurt his neck.

"Very well. Tell Lord Lynden. I don't mind either way."

"You have to capture me first." With a battle cry that would impress ancient warriors, Best lunged. He moved to the right, so Edward stepped to the left.

But Best changed direction fast and struck left. The tip of his sword cut through Edward's doublet sleeve, and scraped the flesh beneath his shirt. Bloody hell, he hadn't expected that. Best was a more capable swordsman than he'd been in the brewery.

Interesting.

But Edward had no time to ponder that further. The sting in his arm distracted him, and he had to keep his wits about him as Best attacked with quick, strong thrusts. There were no opportunities for Edward to get in strikes of his own, only defend. Each thrust forced him backward, away from Greville who took no part in the fight. Was he waiting to see who won before he picked a side? Or was he simply a coward?

Edward stepped in a hole and lost his balance. Best seized the opportunity and pressed forward, slashing at Edward. He fell onto one knee. The position wasn't a good one. He managed to duck a particularly violent slice of Best's sword before it cleaved his neck, but he was too unbalanced to do any more than lash wildly back.

Best sneered and lunged again. Edward dove out of the way as he parried, but Best kept coming after him. Blood soaked into Edward's sleeve, and the cut stung like the devil. If he didn't get onto his feet soon, he'd suffer more cuts. One of them might be fatal.

He settled his mind and recalled his training. Cole had taught him to fight with his fists, but Hughe had done most of the sword-fight training. The earl was a master swordsman.

Best knew he had the upper hand. Edward could see the battle excitement in his eyes, the slight curve of his lips in arrogant confidence. It would be his undoing.

He lunged again. Instead of parrying the blow, Edward rolled out of the way. He used the momentum to spring to his feet. Without so much as a pause, he thrust. The excitement vanished from Best's eyes. A few more feints and thrusts later, panic set in. Mistakes too. His strikes became sloppy and his parries hesitant.

It was easy to slip through Best's defenses. The strike that ended the fight entered his side, just below the ribs.

Best stumbled to the ground. He touched the wound. His hand came away bloody. He looked up at Edward with huge, round eyes. There was surprise in them, but admiration too. "I knew you were good, sir, but I've never met the likes of you in a fight."

Edward felt sick. Despite having assassinated two violent rapists and a man who'd beaten his child to death in the months since joining the Guild, he never liked taking a life. This time was no exception.

"End it," Best said, wheezing. He fought for each breath, but could only grasp shallow ones. The color slowly leeched out of his face. "End it, man, please. This is agony."

"Not yet," Edward said. Christ, he hated this. "I need answers."

Greville came up alongside him and peered down at his brother's man. "You fought well," he said, kindly. "Rest now."

Best coughed and spat out blood.

"Where is the document you wanted Greville to deliver?" Edward asked.

Best smiled. "There is no document. Neither Ayleward nor I have ever plotted against the realm. He's not like that, and you know it, boy."

"Ha! I told you." Greville poked Edward in the shoulder. "Best did this to implicate me thinking John could get my title after I was hung. Isn't that right, Best? Go on, admit everything to Monk here. Tell him I wasn't involved."

Best's hesitation was so long that Edward was afraid he'd died. His cloudy eyes stared at Greville, but it was unclear whether he could actually see him or not. "You used to be such a good boy," he said. "I liked you as a lad. Now..." He coughed again, sending blood spurting from his mouth.

Greville surged forward, but Edward put out his arm and blocked him. "Tell him you killed those men!" Greville cried. "Tell him it wasn't me! You have to tell him!"

Edward watched the two men staring at one another. An unspoken message seemed to pass between them, and finally, Best nodded.

"I killed them," he said. "Then I implicated Greville. That night, I helped him escape through the tunnel."

"You knew it was there?" Edward asked.

"Aye. I know all the old priest escapes in the big houses in this part of England." He smirked. "All good Catholics do."

"But why kill them and implicate Greville? His property would be forfeited to the crown. Ayleward wouldn't get any of it."

Best said nothing.

Greville snorted. "My brother wanted to get rid of me, so he could finally shine like one of the stars he liked to study. Or so he thought."

"It wasn't his idea," Best wheezed. "It was mine. I killed Paxton accidentally. I had to remove the others or they'd come after me. Afterward, I saw it as a way of removing Greville. You have always been my master's thorn. For years I watched as you tried to bring him down with your petty attempts to be better. You weren't. He outshone you in everything. Once Paxton and his men died, I realized I could blame Greville and get away with it."

"You almost did," Greville said heavily. He no longer struggled against Edward, but Edward did not let him go. If he looked troubled by Best's accusations, he didn't show it.

"Why did you come to the Hall in the first place if not to deliver a document?" Edward asked.

Best closed his eyes. His breaths were so shallow that his chest hardly rose at all. It was only when he licked his lips that Edward realized he still lived. "Ayleward wanted me to appeal to his brother to have the wedding at home. He wanted to see him on his wedding day." His eyes drifted open and he stared up, sightless. "Now, be a good fellow and end it."

Edward raised his sword over Best's throat. Greville turned away. Edward plunged his blade cleanly through, then knelt beside the body. He closed Best's eyes and said a silent prayer for the man's soul.

"We should get back to the Hall," he said, rising. "It's growing late."

Greville didn't respond. His head was bowed and his shoulders shook. Edward left him alone while he hefted Best's body onto his horse. He tied it to the saddle and mounted. A few moments later, Greville mounted too. His eyes were red and streaks tracked through the dust on his cheeks. He didn't once look at the body behind Edward, but straight ahead.

Edward looked forward too. Forward to seeing Elizabeth again and holding her in his arms.

CHAPTER 20

*E*lizabeth watched Edward and Greville return through her window, her emotions in turmoil. Relief chief among them, but hope too, and fear that Edward would not want to see her. Then finally horror as she realized what was draped over the back of his horse.

She did not wake her sister and ordered her mother to let Arrabella sleep. She then went to alert Jeffrey and they both went downstairs and out to the courtyard.

Her gaze flew immediately to Edward's. He was watching her with such intensity that she couldn't hold it and had to look away. She didn't know what it meant. His thoughts were locked behind a stern mask.

She listened as Greville and Edward answered Jeffrey's questions. It seemed Edward had found Greville then gone in search of Best after Greville declared his innocence. They'd found him, fought, and Best had died after admitted to killing Paxton and his men.

"You don't look surprised," Edward said to her.

"We suspected it was him. One of the maids told us she saw Best covered in blood, and he tried to stop her telling anyone. She went into hiding and only came out today."

"That's probably why Best hadn't gotten far from the Hall. He remained to look for her."

"He must have killed them in their beds and wrapped them in the bed linen. The mattresses are covered with blood, and I found the linen and rope near where the bodies were buried."

Edward's eyes shone with admiration. "You've been busy in my absence."

She turned away. She couldn't look at him anymore and let him see how heartbroken she'd been these last few days. "I didn't want to be idle."

"I'm innocent," Greville declared with a preening puff of his chest. "It was all Best's doing. He decided to blame me and free my brother from my shadow."

"That's an elaborate scheme," she said.

Edward agreed. "But the main thing is, Greville is back and free to marry Arrabella."

Elizabeth grabbed a hold of Jeffrey's arm for balance. She'd not thought she'd be so deliriously happy at the outcome, but she was. Oh, she was.

She looked to Edward again. He was still staring at her. He breathed deeply and blinked.

"Are you…is everything all right?" he asked softly. "You look a little pale all of a sudden."

"My sister had a riding accident," she told him. "She's all right," she added quickly. "Just some bruising." She'd expected to see some concern in Greville's eyes, but his demeanor didn't change. "She's asleep, but you may go to her, my lord."

"I'm filthy," Greville said, slapping dust off his sleeve. "I need to change."

"After that then."

"I'm starving. Tired too." He yawned.

Why was he stalling? Did he not want to see Arrabella? She glanced at Edward. Edward grabbed Greville's arm. His grip must have been tight because Greville yelped.

"Go to her," Edward said through his clenched jaw. "Now. Tell her you're looking forward to the wedding."

"Ah, yes, about that. It may not go ahead."

"What?" Jeffrey and Elizabeth blurted out.

Edward swore. "It bloody well will go ahead, or I'll kill you. Understand?"

Greville gulped. He held up his hands. "But she may call it off after I tell her how poor I am," he squeaked. "And that I don't love her."

Jeffrey stepped up to him. They were of a height, and at that moment, Jeffrey seemed more fearsome than even Edward. "You are going to marry her, you little turd. I don't care whether you two hate each other, or how poor you are. I'll give you money. But for God's sake, man, marry her. She's carrying your child."

Greville wiped his mouth with the back of his hand. He looked to Elizabeth and she nodded in confirmation. "A son! I'm going to have a son!"

"Or a daughter," she told him.

He waved her suggestion away. "I'm sure it's a son. Firstborns usually are."

She rolled her eyes and caught Edward smiling at her. He shook his head. She smiled back. "Now will you go to her, my lord?" she asked.

"Of course. Directly. Right after I change and eat something. Wouldn't want to interrupt her rest."

Elizabeth didn't argue. Arrabella did indeed need her rest, according to Widow Dawson. She watched as Greville sauntered off to the house, a swagger in his step.

Edward untied Best's body from his horse. He winced as he hefted it onto his shoulder. "Are you hurt?" she asked him. He was covered in an awful lot of blood.

"Just a scratch on my arm."

"Don't you get any of that blood in my house," Jeffrey ordered. "Take the body straight down to the cellar then get cleaned up. Come to my study immediately afterward."

"I wish to speak to Elizabeth first."

Her heart tripped. She didn't dare look at him. Didn't dare hope.

"There'll be time for that later. There are matters to discuss."

Edward headed into the house carrying Best's body. Jeffrey followed him and Elizabeth went up to her sister's bedchamber. Arrabella was awake and sitting up in her bed. Janet must have told her about Greville's return because her gaze swept past Elizabeth to the empty chamber beyond.

"Where is he? Where's my Greville?" She fairly bounced with enthusiasm.

"Cleaning up," Elizabeth said. "He'll be here soon."

Arrabella fell back against the pillows with a pout. "He should have come to see me straight away. I don't care how dirty he is."

"You would if you smelled him."

Arrabella wrinkled her nose and the pout vanished. "I do hope you told him not to be long. I'm so impatient to see him and tell him my news!" She rested her hand on her belly. It would seem she was happy to be carrying the babe now that she knew her future was secure.

Elizabeth sat on the bed as her sister prattled on about her plans. She didn't hear a word of it. She couldn't stop thinking about Edward, not with happiness that he was free, but with concern. How disappointed would he be that he'd lost Arrabella after being so close to possessing her? It might crush him. He might not be able to see beyond to a different future. A future with Elizabeth.

Greville arrived sooner than Elizabeth expected. She suspected Edward had a lot to do with it. He marched the baron in, one hand clamped on his shoulder as if forcing him. Both wore fresh clothes and had damp hair. Fortunately, Arrabella didn't seem to notice her betrothed's reluctance. She squealed with delight upon seeing him and opened her arms wide. Instead of accepting her embrace, Greville caught her hands in his own and drew them down to her belly.

"We're going to have a son!" he declared.

"Oh yes." She grinned. "It must be a boy. He's strong to have survived the fall."

He frowned. "You fell?"

"It was an accident."

"Arrabella, my sweet. You need to be more careful. You're holding precious cargo now. No more exercise of any kind. From now until the birth, you will be abed and do nothing but eat, sew and sleep."

"But I'll be so bored!"

He wagged his finger at her. "There is nothing more important than the health of my son. Nothing. We'll be married in here."

"I refuse to be married in a bedchamber. Mother, tell him."

Elizabeth sighed and glanced at Edward. He jerked his head toward the door. She rose and left her sister and mother arguing with Greville. It would seem the dramatic love affair had come to an abrupt end, and both had caught a glimpse of their long, unhappy future together.

Elizabeth stopped in the outer chamber. Edward shut the door to the bedchamber and leaned back against it. His gaze did not leave her face. "It would seem I've been released from my obligation."

She nodded because she couldn't trust her voice. No doubt it would betray her love for him, and her fear that he hadn't recovered from his love for Arrabella.

"Elizabeth," he murmured, stepping toward her.

She stepped back. She didn't know why. Instinct? Fear? She folded her arms against a sudden chill and turned away so he couldn't see the tears welling in her eyes. She only wanted to be held by him, and be wanted for herself, not because she was the closest replacement he could get to her sister.

"Elizabeth?" he said again, his voice a whisper. "Say something."

She cleared her throat of the lump clogging it. "I doubt Bella will thank you herself, so allow me to thank you for finding Greville and bringing him back for her."

He came up to her shoulder and stood very close, but did not touch. "I didn't do it for her. I didn't do it for you either. My reasons were entirely selfish."

Her curiosity got the better of her. She turned her face a little to see him. His dove-gray gaze stared back at her, full of dreamy tenderness. He touched a stray tendril of hair at her temple and tucked it behind her ear.

"I did it for me," he said thickly. "So that I could wed you."

"Me?" Her voice sounded distant, not her own. She barely heard it over the thump of her heartbeat.

He nodded. His knuckles swept down her cheek, incongruously gentle for such big hands. "I've thought of no one else since meeting you again. Five years ago, I was a fool. I didn't see you."

She wanted to tell him it was all right, that she'd been only a girl, but her voice failed her.

"But now I see you. Even when you're not with me, I see you. In my dreams, my waking ones and sleeping ones. You're all I think about. All I want." He gently turned her around to face him fully. She met his gaze with her own. Her heart swelled. Her body ached to press against his. "I thought I was in love before, but I know now that it was a pale imitation. What I feel for *you* is love, and I've never felt this way about another. Not even close to it." He took both her hands in his and held them to his lips. "I know I'm not the sort of man you would hope to one day marry, but I will protect you and our children with my life. I'll love you until the day I die." He wrung her hands as tears dripped down her cheeks. "Will you marry me, Elizabeth? Will you take this poor carpenter's son as your husband?"

She nodded eagerly because she couldn't speak a word. She threw her arms around his neck and pulled his face down to kiss him hard. She hoped that was answer enough.

It seemed it was because he wrapped his arms around her and held her tightly. His chest rose and fell deeply. His breaths came in shuddery gasps against her mouth. There was so much to say to one another, yet she didn't want the moment to end. It was blissful and sweet, tender yet urgent too. Emotions roiled inside her, swirling and bursting to get out. She kissed him back. Her lover. Her betrothed. Her heart's and soul's desire.

She broke the kiss so that she could cup his face in her hands and look at him. Just look. He gave her a wobbly smile and she returned it.

"I love you too, Edward."

He drew in one deep, shaky breath and let it out slowly. A smile played on his lips, but did not break free. "Are you sure you won't regret it? I am considerably older than you."

"Ten years is not considerable."

"I have no prospects beyond working for Hughe."

"I can think of no better employer than one of the most influential and wealthy earls in the country. Besides, you and he appear very close."

"Your family will expect you to marry a man more worthy of your status. You're not with child like Arrabella. There's no rush for you to wed. They'll want to choose a proper gentleman, not one who needs to bribe the herald.

She touched his cheek. "There is no one more worthy than you. If Jeffrey can't see it, then I'll walk away from my family forever. We'll be together no matter what."

"I don't want you to be cut off from them. Nor will I insult you by installing you as my mistress. It's marriage or nothing."

"Then we'll just have to make Jeffrey agree, because I go where you go. I will not be parted from you."

"In that case, I have something important to tell you. But not here."

"Does it involve what you do for Lord Oxley?"

He arched a brow. "You, my love, are far too clever for the likes of me."

He took her hand and led her out of the chamber, only to be stopped by the house steward. "Lord Lynden wishes to see you, Mr. Monk."

"Not now, I'm busy."

"He says it's important."

"We'll go," Elizabeth said to Edward. "We'll be as quick as we can."

* * *

"I FOUND this in Greville's pack." Jeffrey handed a leaf of parchment to Edward. "What do you make of it?"

Elizabeth looked at the document over Edward's shoulder. She was aware of Jeffrey scowling at her, but he did not scold her. Perhaps he suspected that Edward would do as he pleased and what pleased him was to let Elizabeth read it too. She closed her fingers around Edward's arm. The muscle tensed and he hissed out a breath as if in pain.

"You found this in *Greville's* pack?" Edward asked before she could enquire if he'd been hurt.

Jeffrey nodded. "Strange, don't you think? Especially after Best claimed he had no document for Greville. This could only have come from him."

Elizabeth read the letter over again. It seemed to be nothing more than an ordinary missive between friends, although there were some odd word choices. *Weather came early this year*, for example, instead of *rain* came early, or *summer* perhaps. And another sentence didn't finish at all.

"Do you think it's in code?" she asked.

"It's likely," Edward said.

"Can you decipher it?" Jeffrey asked.

"Perhaps, given time."

Jeffrey groaned and rubbed his hands over his face. "So he's a conspirator after all. God's blood, what are we to do? This document may very well prove to be treasonous."

"I would say there's a good chance that it is." Edward's lips flattened and he glared daggers at Jeffrey. "Whatever happens now, Lynden, I will not marry Arrabella. I'm marrying Elizabeth. She and I have made a promise to one another. It's legally binding and cannot be broken."

Jeffrey spluttered, sending spittle flying onto his desk. "It can be broken if I refuse! Were there witnesses?" Elizabeth was a valuable commodity, and with Arrabella making a poor match, Jeffrey wasn't prepared to give Elizabeth up to a nobody. She'd expected this argument, but it troubled her nevertheless.

"You will not refuse consent, Lynden," Edward said. "Not with Lord Oxley as a witness."

"Oxley! But he's not even here!"

Edward only grinned.

Jeffrey stopped spluttering. His face became drawn, his nostrils flared. "You and Oxley are friends," he muttered. "I'd almost forgotten."

"Oh yes," Elizabeth cut in. "Very good friends. Lord Oxley told me himself that Edward is his favorite."

Jeffrey sighed. He shifted in his chair and finally slapped his palms down on the desk. "Who am I to stand in the way of true love? I suppose your father did direct that you should be able to choose your own husband, but I doubt he would have thought you'd choose so unwisely."

"Father would definitely have approved of my choice, Cousin. He was a good judge of character."

"You can wed her, Monk, but first, we must be sure that Arrabella is settled."

"I know how to do that," Edward said. "Have your steward fetch Greville."

Greville arrived only a few minutes later, looking like a man who wished he was elsewhere. "Thank you for rescuing me," he said, flopping into a chair that had been set for him beside Edward's. "These Buckley ladies are exhausting, don't you think, Monk?" He laughed, but when no one laughed with him, it died. "What is it?"

Edward handed him the document. "This was found in your pack. You didn't hide it very well."

Greville didn't even glance at it. "It's only a letter from my brother to a friend. I decided to deliver it since Best can't."

"Best said there was no document. You never looked through his things after his death. When did he give it to you?"

Greville stood abruptly. "It's just a letter! There's nothing treasonous in it."

"We deciphered the code," Elizabeth said, taking a chance that he would fall for her lie.

"What? How?"

Edward winked at her. Jeffrey looked impressed, something she thought she'd never see directed at her.

"When did he give it to you?" Edward repeated.

Greville's body sagged. He'd given up. "That night you locked me in my chamber after the murders. He came through my bedchamber wall. Scared the wits out of me. I was already halfway drunk and seeing him emerge from the wall was not a spectacle I wish to see again. He forced that letter onto me, told me I had to escape through the tunnel and deliver it. He said if I didn't do as he said, I'd be hung for the murders."

"So that's why he came to Sutton Hall in the first place," Edward said. "I didn't think it had anything to do with offering well wishes for your wedding. If that were so, he would have come into the house and openly declared his presence instead of skulking in the brewery."

"And that was why Best helped you escape," Jeffrey said to Greville. "So you could deliver that. Why not deliver it himself?"

"Probably because my brother didn't want his man involved at all." Greville snorted. His mouth twisted into an ugly sneer. "Better to send *me* on the fool's errand than someone he actually cared about."

"He and Best were close?" Elizabeth asked.

"Like father and son." Greville sighed and ran a hand through his hair. "I do believe him when he said my brother had nothing to do with the murders. Indeed, I believe Best never intended for any of this to happen. He told me Paxton died during an argument.

Paxton wanted that document, and Best refused to give it to him. Perhaps they fought and Best won. He had to kill the others because they'd cause problems once they found out their master was dead. Afterward, he saw his opportunity to be rid of me too by blaming me. He must have hated me. I knew he thought me a fool and my brother a paragon, but I had no idea how much he resented me until now."

"Why did you lie about seeing them leave the house?" Elizabeth asked. It was something that had bothered her for some time.

"I suspected Best was the murderer, and I didn't want him implicated. If I told everyone I saw them leave then you might conclude that a vagabond did it. Seems I felt more sentimental about him than he did about me." He didn't sound angry anymore, simply sad. It was understandable. He'd been betrayed by someone he'd cared about, and it hurt.

"But in doing so you implicated yourself once the blood was discovered in their chambers."

"I didn't consider the blood."

Elizabeth suspected he didn't consider much at all. The man wasn't the brightest star in the sky.

"What happens now? Are you going to hand that document over to the authorities?"

"We have to," Jeffrey said. He snatched the document off Edward.

"But I'll be arrested for treason!" Greville screeched. "Do you know what happens to Catholics accused of treason?"

"It's only what they deserve."

"Have mercy, Lynden." Greville rounded the desk, a look of earnestness on his face. Jeffrey stood too and placed the parchment behind his back. Greville grasped his shoulders and shook them. "Please, have mercy. I am to become a father. Don't deny my son his birthright. Please, my lord, have mercy."

Edward took the letter back. Jeffrey protested but did not try to take it again. Edward threw it into the fireplace and opened the tinder box. He struck the flint and the spark lit the parchment. The edge singed then it caught alight. No one stopped him.

"That document never existed," Edward told them.

Greville let out a sob and hugged Edward. "Thank you, Monk."

Edward pushed him away. "I didn't do it for your worthless hide. I did it for the baby. He needs a father, Greville, and you had better be a good one, or I will make you more miserable than you've ever been. Understand? No more secret documents, no plotting of any kind. Tell your brother it ends now."

Greville nodded quickly. "I'll tell him. And I'll be a good father to that child." He was like an eager puppy trying to win the favor of his master. On a puppy it would have been adorable, but on a grown man, it was pathetic.

"Even if it's a girl," Elizabeth told him.

"Of course. But it's a boy. Arrabella is sure of it too."

Edward looped his arm around her waist. "It seems you and I are to be brothers-in-law, Greville, so I can keep an even closer eye on you."

Greville gawped at him. "But you're not even a gentleman! You approve of this union, Lynden? I'm shocked at your lack of standards for your dear cousin. Shocked!" So much for his gratitude.

"Shut up, Greville," Jeffrey growled.

Elizabeth laughed and hugged Edward tighter.

"That reminds me." Jeffrey flicked through a stack of documents on his desk and pulled out one with the seal broken. "Ah yes, the herald's letter. Write and inform him the money he requests will be available from my London agent. I'll give you an address. Congratulations, Mr. Monk. You'll be a gentleman in a matter of weeks."

Edward hesitated. Elizabeth could feel the ripple of muscle in his body as he tensed. His swallow was audible. "I don't need your money. I have enough of my own." He went to take the letter, but Elizabeth got it first.

She tore it in two and threw it into the fire where the embers of the other letter set it alight.

Jeffrey and Greville both gasped loudly. "What did you do that for?" Greville cried.

"Foolish girl," Jeffrey scolded her. "Luckily I memorized the amount needed to pay him. All is not lost, Monk, but I urge you to discipline your future wife. She's much too headstrong. It'll be the bane of your existence if you don't knock it out of her now. I'd do it myself, but she's no longer my responsibility."

Edward strolled up to him and bent down so he was level with Jeffrey. "The only reason I don't thump you for saying that is because I'm so happy to be marrying Elizabeth. Say it again, and I won't feel so sentimental."

Jeffrey tugged on his cuffs and didn't meet Edward's gaze. Wisely, he said nothing.

Greville was not so wise. "Good luck to you, Monk. It would seem you're going to need it more than me." He clapped Edward on the shoulder then strode out of the room. No one stopped him.

* * *

MUCH LATER, Edward stayed Elizabeth's hand as she unlaced his shirt in her bedchamber. She looked so lovely. The light from the candles danced in her eyes and gilded her hair. He still couldn't believe that such a remarkable woman was his. Finally, all his.

"What is it, my love?" she whispered.

"Are you sure you don't want me to pursue the grant of arms?"

"Very sure. It's not important to me. You are a gentleman in every sense of the word, and a far more worthier one than many who are born to it."

He'd not thought his heart could swell any further, but it did. It was so full it would surely overflow. "It might be important to our children one day."

"Our children will be raised to know that it's a person's character that matters."

He didn't pursue it. She was undressing him again and he couldn't think straight. He might still go ahead and pay the herald, if only for their children's sakes. He knew, without a doubt, that Elizabeth didn't care. And if it didn't matter to her, it didn't matter to him.

She tugged his shirt off over his head and gave a little cry. "Edward! You're injured." She inspected his arm. The cut wasn't deep, but it was long. "Why didn't you tell me?"

"I forgot."

"You forgot? You fool, it might fester if we don't put an ointment on it. How could you forget about it?"

"I was distracted by you."

She scowled at him, one hand on her hip. He kissed the end of her nose and smiled.

"Distracted by you agreeing to marry me," he went on.

She stopped scowling. Her face softened.

He kissed her cheek, so silky smooth against his lips. "It's been a momentous day."

Her lower lip wobbled.

"The most important day of my life." He kissed the wobbly lip. "The most amazing, wonderful day."

She gave a little sob. He kissed her throat below her ear. Her pulse throbbed.

"So you see," he murmured against her flesh as he moved down to her cleavage. "I've been much too overwhelmed to think of anything other than what you're going to look like the first time I make love to you as Mrs. Monk."

She sucked in a steadying breath. "That won't be for some weeks. The banns must be read, preparations made, guests invited."

He smiled against the swell of her breast, rising above the bodice. "There's no reason why we can't get some practice in first."

She wrapped her arms around him and trailed her fingernails lightly down his back. "No reason at all," she agreed.

Then she unlaced her bodice and removed it, and he could think of nothing else except how fortunate he was and how bright their future would be together.

EPILOGUE

Three weeks later.

*A*rrabella Buckley and Lord Greville were wed as soon as the last of the banns was read in church. It was a rollicking event according to everyone who attended, with dancing, music and an abundant feast put on by the bride's cousin. Everyone was filled with love on the happy day. Everyone, it would seem, except the newlyweds who either avoided one another or argued.

The couples that did display their love in what some, namely Lords Oxley and Lynden, thought was a sickening display, lounged on the steps leading down to the terraced garden as the sun set. Orlando Holt cradled his new baby, his lovely wife beside him. Another newlywed, Lucy Coleclough, sat on the lowest step, nestled in her husband's arms. Edward lay on a step too, his head in his betrothed's lap, enjoying the way her fingers stroked his hair. Music from the great hall filtered out to them, bold and lively, but not quite loud enough to drown out the laughter and occasional cheers for Lord and Lady Greville.

It was Lord Oxley himself who interrupted the peaceful scene. "There you all are! I've been looking everywhere. Why did no one invite me?" He pouted and thrust out his hip. His hips were particularly exaggerated tonight with the wide trunk hose of green and purple silk. "Ah, I see. You're all coupled up, and I'm a single."

"You seemed to be enjoying yourself," Edward said. "We didn't want to interrupt you."

"Interrupt away, please! Between Greville and Lynden, there is far too much arrogance for one room to take. I couldn't fit in, and Heaven knows if I can't be the most colorful person in a room, I don't want to be there."

Everyone laughed.

"So." He dropped a kiss on the baby's head then sat on the grass too. He stretched out one leg and rubbed it, something which he needed to do from time to time to alleviate the pain from an old injury. "Are the plans all in place for your wedding, Elizabeth?"

"Everything is set for three weeks hence," she said. "Will you return for it, Hughe?"

"Of course! I live hardly a day's ride away, so it's nothing for me to come. Besides, I wouldn't miss the wedding of my good friend for anything. You will make a happy couple, I'm sure." He sighed. "But next time, I'm going to employ real monks. They won't run off and get married on me."

"We are sorry to take away your best men," Susanna said, smiling.

"We'll loan them to you from time to time if necessary," Lucy offered.

"As long as it doesn't involve leaving the valley." Orlando watched in wonder as his baby wrapped his tiny fingers around his father's big one. "I cannot bear to be apart from my family."

His wife kissed his cheek and exchanged a smile with her husband.

Hughe blew out a breath. "Where will I find good men to replace you all?"

Elizabeth nudged Edward with her elbow. "You don't have to," he said. "I'm not leaving your employ. Indeed, you're gaining another guild member, with conditions placed on her employment."

Hughe's eyes narrowed. "*Her*?" He looked to Elizabeth.

She nodded. "Edward has told me what you do and I agree that it's important work. I hope I can be of help, although not in any, er, active role."

"She won't be killing anyone," Edward clarified.

"I understood that part," Hughe told him. "So what is it you can do, Elizabeth?"

"She's clever," Edward said. "She'll be good at solving knotty problems and organizing things."

"Anything I can do to help," she added.

"Then you're welcome to join us, but I refuse to put you in any danger."

"I wasn't suggesting you do," Edward ground out.

He'd refused the first time Elizabeth had told him she wanted to be involved. He'd refused the second, third and sixth time too. He gave in on the seventh request, because it was more of a demand than a request, and she'd said she would not involve herself in the more perilous work.

"Well then," Hughe said. "It's settled. When do you return home to the gatehouse?"

"As soon as we're wed," Elizabeth said.

"Ah, good. Then you'll be there to welcome the new member of my household."

"You're getting a ward?" Cole asked.

"Who would entrust *him* with a ward?" Orlando said.

"Good point. A new dog, perhaps?"

"I wish it were a new dog." Hughe sighed heavily. There was none of his usual theatrics in his manner. Indeed, he was quite melancholy. Edward grew worried.

"The Dowager Countess has a companion she's invited to live with her?" he suggested. "One who makes your mother look like a saint?"

"Worse," Hughe mumbled. "I'm getting myself a wife too."

LOOK OUT FOR

The Sinner
The fourth ASSASSINS GUILD novel.

Hughe, Lord Oxley, finally meets his match. Read his story in the next Assassins Guild book.

To be notified when C.J. has a new release, sign up to her newsletter. Send an email to cjarcher.writes@gmail.com

A MESSAGE FROM THE AUTHOR

I hope you enjoyed reading this book as much as I enjoyed writing it. As an independent author, getting the word out about my book is vital to its success, so if you liked this book please consider telling your friends and writing a review at the store where you purchased it. If you would like to be contacted when I release a new book, subscribe to my newsletter at http://cjarcher.com/contact-cj/newsletter/. You will only be contacted when I have a new book out.

ALSO BY C.J. ARCHER

SERIES WITH 2 OR MORE BOOKS

After The Rift

Glass and Steele

The Ministry of Curiosities Series

The Emily Chambers Spirit Medium Trilogy

The 1st Freak House Trilogy

The 2nd Freak House Trilogy

The 3rd Freak House Trilogy

The Assassins Guild Series

Lord Hawkesbury's Players Series

The Witchblade Chronicles

SINGLE TITLES NOT IN A SERIES

Courting His Countess

Surrender

Redemption

The Mercenary's Price

ABOUT THE AUTHOR

C.J. Archer has loved history and books for as long as she can remember and feels fortunate that she found a way to combine the two. She spent her early childhood in the dramatic beauty of outback Queensland, Australia, but now lives in suburban Melbourne with her husband, two children and a mischievous black & white cat named Coco.

Subscribe to C.J.'s newsletter through her website to be notified when she releases a new book, as well as get access to exclusive content and subscriber-only giveaways. Her website also contains up to date details on all her books: http://cjarcher.com She loves to hear from readers. You can contact her through email cj@cjarcher.com or follow her on social media to get the latest updates on her books.

facebook.com/CJArcherAuthorPage

twitter.com/cj_archer

instagram.com/authorcjarcher

pinterest.com/cjarcher

bookbub.com/authors/c-j-archer

Made in the USA
Columbia, SC
08 December 2019